Swedish Tango

Also by Alyson Richman

The Mask Carver's Son

Swedish Tango

Alyson Richman

WASHINGTON SQUARE PRESS
New York London Toronto Sydney

Washington Square Press
1230 Avenue of the Americas
New York, NY 10020

ISBN-13: 978-   0-7434-7642-3
ISBN-10:   0-7434-7642-5
ISBN-13: 978-   0-7434-7643-0 (Pbk)
ISBN-10:   0-7434-7643-3 (Pbk)

First Washington Square Press trade paperback edition September 2005

10 9 8 7 6 5 4 3 2 1

For information regarding special discounts for bulk purchases, please contact
Simon & Schuster Special Sales at 1-800-456-6798 or
business@simonandschuster.com

Till min svenska familj

Swedish Tango

Give sorrow words; the grief that does not speak
Whispers the o'er-fraught heart and bids it break.

—*Macbeth*

Prologue

Santiago, Chile
February 1974

She awakened to the sound of birds singing, the morning mist rising above the tall grasses from where she now lay. Her face imprinted with the shapes of crushed daisies, the small flowers folding underneath her fragile face.

A small ant scampered across her arm. A butterfly landed on her mass of matted, black curls before fluttering to an azalea bush. And beneath her, she inhaled the intense and heady smell of the soil.

Several seconds passed before Salomé de Ribeiro realized that she had not died and gone to paradise. She was not dreaming, she was not hallucinating. She was now free. The prison was now miles away from where she lay.

They had let her go in a park. A blindfolded, bruised shadow tumbling from a van. She had fallen to the ground with barely a thud, for there was far too little weight on her to cause much of a sound. A hundred tiny bones encapsulated in a delicate, purple skin. The earth had welcomed her, the wet ground sinking slightly beneath her falling form. She had drifted in and out of consciousness for several hours before waking to the sunrise. And now she heard the first sounds of life surrounding her. There was the tolling of the bell from the cathedral; there was the sound of the cars rushing down the streets below. Santiago was waking just as she was, and she savored the sounds and the smells of life.

She had grown so used to the sight of darkness that it took several minutes before she realized that, while her senses were alive, she was still seeing black.

She fumbled to remove the blindfold that had been tied tightly around her head. The morning sun was just coming up and Salomé squinted into the valley where the city's lights still twinkled in the haze.

Her fingers fell into the soil. Her knees, shaking and badly scraped, dragged underneath her tired frame. She tried to gather herself, ignoring her bruises and her broken bones, to wander in the early hours of dawn and find her way back home to her husband and children, who lay sleeping in their beds nearly ten miles away.

She walked through the iron gate, her last ounces of strength nearly exhausted. As her hand went to turn the handle of the front door, her body collapsed like a basket weakened by the rain; a whisper of an echo falling to the ground.

Octavio rushed to investigate the disturbance on the front porch, cautious that it might be someone who had come to harm either him or the children. When he opened the door and found his wife splayed out before him, he fell to his knees.

As he held her to his chest, he could feel the sharp wings of her shoulder blades, the narrow barrel of her rib cage. She was so delicate that he was afraid to move her, fearful she might tear. So, she lay in his arms, lavender and shriveled, a dying delphinium, dehydrated and torn.

Octavio had no time to wash and care for his wife before their children arrived at the front door and saw her. They barely recognized their mother. Her hair was wild and matted below her shoulders. Her dress was torn and her left breast was partially exposed from a long rip that extended across half the neckline.

She was a fraction of the size she had been before they had taken her. Never a large woman, she had been petite but curvaceous. Now, she appeared almost childlike. A tattered orphan whose complexion was marred by swatches of dirt and patches of bleeding bruises.

Octavio guided his wife into the kitchen and sat her down on one of the dining room chairs. She could see her children before her. She was unable to muster even the slightest sound. She wanted to tell them how much she had missed them, how she had dreamt of them every night since she had been away, but her voice faltered. She could not speak. She just remained in the chair, her fingers shaking in her lap and her eyes staring wide.

Salomé didn't want the children to be afraid of her. She could only imagine what a sight she must be to them. She couldn't remember the last time she had bathed, the last time a comb had been run through her hair. All she wanted to do was to sleep and be able to embrace those three small faces she had missed.

It was her eldest child, however, who had the courage to embrace her as she so desperately craved. Rafael did not hesitate. He walked right up to his mother and hugged her.

She did not wince as her eldest squeezed her, even though his embrace felt so powerful that, inside, she screamed. He pulled back her hair, ignoring the lice and the tangles, and kissed her cheek. "Welcome home, Mama," he whispered, and whirled around to make sure that his younger sisters would not be afraid and would also welcome her back.

First, the middle one came up to her, then the youngest. Each of them fighting hard to ignore her smell and to smile.

Salomé began to cry. Not because of her physical pain, for she had grown used to that. She cried because Octavio, their children, and their home appeared the same as when she had left. But she had returned so very different.

That was a deceptive impression, for they had indeed changed over the past two months. And even before that. From the moment the coup had begun, the Ribeiro-Herrera family's idyllic world had ceased to exist. The effects of the coup and the consequences of Octavio's actions were still unraveling before them.

As Salomé struggled to embrace her children, her own mother returned. Doña Olivia walked into the kitchen carrying two loaves of bread. Octavio had not asked her to do the errand, but she had risen early, as she often did. She had grown used to her inability to sleep and tried to at least make herself useful in her waking hours. But she had not anticipated seeing her child upon her return. Resting on a stool, her daughter, with a penitent Octavio kneeling at her side.

Doña Olivia dropped the loaves of bread and rushed to embrace her child. She took the towel from Octavio and pressed her daughter's palms to her own cheeks, weeping as she touched her daughter's face, cursing the monsters who were responsible for such a horrendous crime.

Over the next week, Salomé was cared for and waited upon by her mother as if she had been reborn an infant. Doña Olivia brushed her daughter's hair each morning and recombed it each evening, so that it finally returned to its original luster. She perfumed it with a spray made from diffused gardenia and bee balm, and curled the ends into tiny ringlets by twisting the strands tightly around her finger.

On the outside, Octavio's wife appeared like a wounded empress. Her regal bone structure was even more evident than before, for now her maternal roundness had vanished. Over the week, her almond skin resurfaced and the bruises were absorbed. But still she remained fragile. She refused to speak of the details of her kidnapping, and Octavio did not press her. He was just so grateful that she had been returned. He knew that they were already more fortunate than so many others. For, each of the two times Salomé was kidnapped, she was eventually returned. Should there be a third time, they might not be so lucky.

On the eighth night following her return, Octavio held his wife and told her that they would have to leave Chile. "It is not safe for us here any longer," he whispered to her while she lay in their large, canopied bed. "Sweden has accepted our application for political asylum."

Salomé heard him but did not answer. But, the next day, she rose from her bed and began packing. Octavio noticed, as he labeled the five boxes to be shipped to Sweden, that his wife had not packed their old Victrola. He thought that strange, but he did not question her. Although she might not want the old machine now, Octavio thought one day she might regret not having it. So he opened one of the half-filled boxes and packed it anyway, believing someday his wife would thank him for his foresight.

Part I

One

ᵕ🙟🙝ᵔ

Vesterås, Sweden
November 1998

More than twenty-three years had passed before Salomé could listen to music without being reminded of the terror it had once caused her. It seemed ironic, then, that on the afternoon that the letter arrived, her old Victrola was humming in the background, the needle skipping over Satie's lonely notes.

After carefully reading the words, she folded the letter neatly into thirds and placed it in her desk drawer. Her skin was cold and her body shivered.

She went over to the gramophone, rested her hand on the shiny black horn, and released the arm. The music ceased as the record slowed its spin. Salomé was soothed by the silence that followed, relieved that the only sounds the music masked were the icy gusts rattling a half-opened window.

Inside there was darkness and outside it was dusk. It was only 3 P.M., but night had already arrived in the Swedish sky.

Aside from the cold air that penetrated the apartment, Salomé's apartment appeared tropical. When her children visited, they knew that, no matter where their mother lived, she possessed a divine ability to re-create their Santiago childhood home. The rooms smelled of dried geranium leaves, eucalyptus, and wild mint, for she had hidden tiny sachets filled with these fragrant leaves throughout the house, and had covered the walls with old cinema posters of their father, from when he had been famous. She had created small collections from things she had found—things that people had disposed of thinking they were of no value. But she treasured them, those displaced things, and amongst the shelves lined with beach glass and dried lemons and pears, she gave them a home.

She had been the same way back in Chile. A collector. Their home in Santiago was enormous, many times the size of her present apartment, but still she had covered every open wall with a painting or drawing and every shelf with something she had found. She took the skins of hollowed-out avocados and strung them over her tiled stove. She filled jars with colored sand and kept a basket filled with seashells by the bathtub, scattering them into the water so the children could pretend, even in wintertime, that they were swimming in the sea.

They could not bring most of these items with them when they left. Time—and the Chilean authorities—had not been generous with them, leaving Salomé only a few days to pack their belongings. So when they closed the iron gate of the house for the last time, Salomé left it in very much the way she and her family had lived. Often, she wondered what the renters had done when they'd arrived. Whether they had slipped into her house, worn the clothes hanging in the closets, or used the soap that had been left in her grandmother's dish. She often pondered if the family who sent her a check each month ever thought about *her* family, all that had happened to them and why they had been forced to leave. Or whether they had purposefully chosen not to think of them and, instead, only to marvel at their great fortune to be able to live in such a big, beautiful house.

She had finally unpacked the Victrola a few months before, deciding it was time to go through some of the boxes she had left packed for so many years. She had screwed the black horn to the wooden base and replaced the worn diamond needle with one she found at a secondhand shop. The children, now grown, came over, as did her ex-husband, Octavio. And in her modest apartment, with the smell of eucalyptus fragrant around them, they all danced. They put Pablo Ziegler on, and Rafael danced the tango with one of his sisters, Blanca.

"Do you remember when we found that old thing?" Octavio asked his ex-wife, nestling a glass of wine in his hand. He wondered if now, with so many years having passed, his wife finally appreciated that he had packed the Victrola.

Salomé smiled as she allowed the music to embrace her. She tapped her foot over the wooden floorboards, the heel of her sandal twisting back and forth.

"It's wonderful to be able to listen again and have only good memories return," she said softly. And as she closed her eyes, Salomé remembered how she and Octavio had played the antique record player when they were first married. He had led her across the floor of their new home, thrusting open the French doors leading to the veranda, and the melody from the old machine had filled the rooms of the empty house and floated into the garden, overgrown with fruit trees and wild roses.

From that night on, she had begun to collect tango records. El Cantón, Piazzolla, and Calandrelli were all stacked by the Victrola's side. And how she adored them. She loved it when her husband would place the needle down and the record would begin to spin and the music would permeate the air. The children loved it too. They taught themselves to dance by watching their parents. They mimicked the wrapping of their hands, the entwining of their legs, and the swiveling of their heels. But, after Salomé's disappearance and her subsequent return, the music in their home had stopped. The Victrola remained where it had always been, but the records were no longer played.

There are some things that a woman knows she cannot tell even her family. It is part intuition and part self-preservation. Salomé had always believed that God had made women with wombs so that, after they had children, they had a place to store their secrets.

And indeed Salomé's secrets were not to be shared. Memories of a mother's kidnapping and torture were stories a child should never hear.

She never told them what was done to her back in Chile, although she knew that the children divided their lives into two halves: from the time before their mother was taken, and from the time when their family exile began. When everything changed.

Salomé believed she could limit her children's pain by never telling them what she had endured. So, she kept it all to herself, until it became too much, and she sought the expertise of a doctor. He was now deceased and her secrets were hers alone. Not even Octavio knew her story in its entirety.

But now, as Salomé sat alone in her apartment listening to Satie, she could not ignore the letter, postmarked in Great Britain, that had arrived in that afternoon's mail. The phrasing was blunt and to the point: "We are collecting the stories of the victims of Pinochet's regime," the letter from an international human rights group stated in cold black letters. "It is in the interest of history and for justice that the atrocities caused by General Pinochet be recorded and that he be held accountable in a court of law for the murder of thousands ..."

Salomé knew that, days before, a Spanish prosecutor had requested that England extradite General Augusto Pinochet, the man she held responsible for ruining her beloved country, nearly destroying her, and forcing her family to flee in the night to the shores of a cold, foreign country. Now, perhaps, he would be held responsible for his crimes against her and the rest of humanity.

But it seemed almost painfully too late. Now with nearly twenty-five years having passed, she was being asked to remember. And it was not that she feared her memory would fail her if she testified. Far worse. It was knowing the impact it might have on her children. She knotted her fists into her stomach to try to alleviate the sudden pain she was experiencing. "It's only nerves," she told herself. But those secrets she had kept buried for so many years were relentless. She could not ignore them, just as she could not turn a blind eye to the letter calling for her testimony. She would need to decide if she was finally going to unearth those memories she had kept tucked away since her therapy had ended. She knew she was strong enough to face the demons of her past, but she feared the pain it might cause her children and even her ex-husband.

Two

❦

Vesterås, Sweden
November 1998

He recognized it was her calling even before she uttered her first word. He could detect her breathing. She revealed herself by that first hesitant pause she always took before saying his name.

"Octavio," she said quietly. "I need to see you."

He had waited a long time to hear her say those words, and although they were murmured softly—barely audible to a less tuned ear—he heard them as if they were fireworks exploding over the wire.

"It's rather urgent," she added.

"I'll be there in a few minutes," he said.

He hung up the phone and went to change into fresh clothes. He combed back his graying curls, patted scented tonic onto his cheeks and neck, and smoothed out the creases in his trousers with his palms.

Every time he went to see her, he performed the same ritual. His memorized ablutions. It was as if he were in his student apartment once again and he was nervous with anticipation at the sight of her. He needed to look his best.

He fingered his trouser pocket, checking to see that the small silk pouch that Salomé had embroidered for him so many years before was still there. It remained his most treasured talisman. The stitches that had quilted his name were worn and loose, but it was still dear to him. A faded, tattered reminder of a love that, no matter what others might think, he, in his heart, knew had endured.

Pulling on his coat and adjusting his scarf around his collar, he turned off the light and locked the door to his house. Once outside, he buried his chin into his coat's collar and shuffled briskly to Salomé's apartment.

Salomé's voice had been urgent on the phone and he wondered what had motivated her to call him at such a late hour. In a few minutes he would be at her door and he would know the answer. He only hoped that, once there, his presence would bring her some comfort.

Every time he saw her, his heart seemed to break a little more. She would stand in the threshold, her thick hair still majestically black and cascading down her shoulders. Her tiny, curvaceous body, usually wrapped in a bright sheath of silk, still looking very much like that of the teenager he had fallen in love with long ago. Over the years, he had tried to mask his feelings. He had even practiced his greeting to her over and over in his tiny bathroom mirror, hoping to ensure that it didn't betray his longing. For some time now he had tried to be a friend to his former wife, to understand her more fully. But only recently had he been able to reconcile the two Salomés he had in his mind: the young girl he had courted through poetry and the grown woman who had suffered tremendously because of him. For the rest of his life, Octavio would agonize over whether he had made the right decision. For his high principles had placed his family in exile, caused his wife to be kidnapped and tortured; in the years that had passed, he had lost almost everything he had had before the coup. He could not deny that his wife and even his children had forever been changed by what had happened to them so many years ago in Chile. But, even if none of them had noticed, Octavio believed so had he.

Three

❧

$\mathcal{T}$he first time he saw her, she had walked outside the convent to pick up the fallen oranges. Her dark blue uniform grazing below her soft, smooth knees. Around her feet, the small yellow and orange fruit nestled, and the smell of the freshly cut grass and the perfume of ripe citrus lingered heavy in the air. She knelt down and pulled out her skirt to fashion a basket, filling the cloth with the fallen fruit.

She was truly a vision. Long black hair, slender arms, and skin the color of crushed almonds. She turned her head slightly to recover from the sun, and it was then that he first caught sight of her face. He saw past the slight wrinkling of her nose, and the slight squinting of her eyes, and saw her poetic brow, delicate nose, and full, ripe mouth. He imagined the weight of her thick, black hair, envisioned his hands undoing her combs, and the canopy of curls falling over his palms, and spilling onto his knees. She was so beautiful that he, almost a grown man, could have wept.

He attempted to whistle, but the sound he made was too weak to reach her ears. She was lost in her activity, for this was the happiest moment in her day.

What the mother superior considered a chore, she considered a luxury. The other girls' responsibilities were far more tedious: assisting the cooks in the kitchen, cleaning the bathrooms, or raking one of the church's several gardens. Salomé was only asked to gather oranges and bring them to the kitchen, where they would later be squeezed into juice.

Here, amongst the heavy green boughs and the yellow-dotted ground, she savored her time alone. Sometimes, when the fruit was particularly ripe, she would pierce the rind with her fingernail and place her lips over the hole, sucking the juice out, in one long swallow. Other times, she would cross her legs while the oranges lay heavy in her lap, and she would admire the flight of a butterfly or the silver-green fire in a wing of a praying mantis.

Little did she know that, from a balcony only twenty-five meters away, a university student stood alone with his mouth open and his heart pounding, absolutely consumed by love.

Every day, he anticipated her arrival as she emerged, like clockwork, from the stone convent walls at a quarter past nine. He began to groom himself for her. Hoping that one day she would look up and see him, a figure in the distance, standing on his balcony alone.

He wore wrinkled shirts to his classes, saving the pressed ones to wear for the few minutes each day while he watched her. He shaved before her arrival, combing his thick, black hair behind his ears and patting his cheeks with a perfume he hoped would reach her by air. Weeks went by, but she never took notice of him. And then, when he had nearly gone mad with wild desperation, he finally devised a way in which they could meet.

Each night, he pored through volumes of the world's greatest poets until his candle burned out and he could find no more light. When he discovered a particular verse that captured his own feelings of love and ardor, he copied it in his neatest hand onto tiny scrolls of parchment paper he had cut. Three weeks later, Octavio had transcribed more than two hundred poems.

In the middle of the night, with several dozen slips of paper in his pockets and a small knife in his hands, he went to the gates of the convent and stood where the orchard began. He climbed the trees and rustled the branches. He shook the boughs until the oranges fell to the ground. Then, with the moonlight above him, he carved out each fruit's navel, rolled up the love poems, and inserted them within.

The next morning, he rose, having slept less than an hour. He stood on the balcony and waited for her to arrive.

She came, wearing her simple blue uniform. A wicker basket dangled from her arm. He noticed how, when she sighed, her rib cage swelled underneath her cotton blouse, how her whole body bent in exhaustion at the sight of so many oranges.

She knelt down to examine the first fruit of the day and immediately smiled as she noticed the thin cigarlike roll of paper tucked neatly within. After searching to see if anyone was around, she withdrew the first poem:

> *Acogedora como un viejo camino*
> *Te pueblan ecos y voces nostálgicas*
> *Yo desperté y a veces emigran y huyen*
> *pájaros que dormían en tu alma.*
>
> *You gather things to you like an old road.*
> *You are peopled with echoes and nostalgic voices.*
> *I awoke and at times birds fled and migrated*
> *that had been sleeping in your soul.*

She recognized the poem from Neruda's *20 Poemas de amor y una Canción Desesperada,* "*Para mi corazón,*" and wondered who would have placed it in the orange. When she knelt down to pick up another piece of fruit, there again was another scroll of writing. When she unraveled it, therein was a love poem by Mistral.

She looked around again to see if anyone was there, thinking one of her classmates had played a trick on her. But she saw no one. As she looked straight ahead, she noticed the entire ground was littered with oranges. Each one with a thin roll of paper protruding from its center. Each one with its own magic wand.

From as far away as he stood, Octavio could hear her joyful laughter, and he leaned over the balcony to gain a better view.

For several weeks, Octavio continued to court Salomé through the poem-filled oranges. In between his studies, he transcribed so many poems that his wrists grew weary and the nib on his fountain pen bent from overuse. Still, he wrote to her until he had exhausted all of his volumes of poetry. But there were so many things he had not yet said. Realizing he could no longer rely on the cushion of another man's words, he held his head for many hours, struggling to form his desires into words. He listened to his heart and poured out its contents. He wrote of her black eyes and dark hair. He wrote of her majestic gait, her long, regal neck, and her slender arms. He imagined their first kiss and the warmth he might find in her embrace. If he had been musical, he would have composed a song for her, written an aria, and created a concerto in her honor. Had he brushes, he would have tried to re-create her image in a palette of rich, creamy paint. But, as he only had pen and paper, he continued to write.

One evening, when he rested on his arms, his eyes heavy with exhaustion and his pen nearly dry, he wrote to her for the last time. "In a star-filled sky, I wish to see you. I will bring oranges to lay down at your feet. Come to me, dearest to my heart. I shall wait for you and sing you poems of love." He carefully inserted the poem into the orange, then slipped in a second paper that specified a place where they could meet.

His heart soared with wild anticipation. He only hoped that she would come.

Four

❦

Las Vertientes, Chile
November 1964

$\mathcal{H}$olding one of her early-morning oranges tightly to her breast, Salomé Herrera lowered her chin, grazed her cheek over the fruit's cool pebbled skin, and wondered if it was really true, that this evening, in only a few hours' time, she would meet the man who had sworn her as his one and only love.

She had been dreaming since she was a little girl of her shining and amorous knight. She had always believed he would find her and take her away in his strong and protective arms. Her evocative name had contributed to nurturing a far more adventurous spirit than another girl might have had coming from a bourgeois background such as hers. Yet the circumstances of her conception had created an aura about her.

She had grown up hearing how her parents had named her in honor of the great heroine who had danced the dance of the seven veils. According to family legend, her mother had dressed as Salomé on the night of her daughter's conception. Doña Olivia, at the height of her beauty, had swathed herself in transparent veils of lilac and blue, her hair plaited high over her head with a single pearl strung over her bronzed forehead, as she attended with her husband a lavish costume party for the doctors of Santiago.

When their daughter was born nine months later, and she was brought to her parents wrapped in a crisp, white blanket, her brown forehead peeking out from beneath its many layers of starched cotton, her eyes sparkling and bright, both Doña Olivia and Don Fernando agreed without any discussion that the girl would be named Salomé.

Now seventeen years later, the young girl's heart was pounding. She closed her eyes and tried to envision her poetic admirer.

She imagined him tall and slender, smelling of sandalwood and spruce. She envisioned herself coming to him in a dress made from the silvery leaves of birch bark, her hair brushed loose, and her ankles wrapped in vines.

She told no one of her secret, trusting no one with the knowledge of her plan. She would wait until her classmates had all fallen asleep and the sisters had made their rounds, and then she would go to him. This man who wrote her poems and stuffed them within hollowed-out oranges. This man who claimed to love her from afar.

The prospect of this rendezvous thrilled rather than frightened Salomé. And thus she went through the motions of her afternoon, anxiously awaiting their meeting, wondering if he would be as beautiful as the words he wrote to her each day.

She went to bed with the other girls, washing her face and braiding her hair. She knelt by her bedside and said her prayers. Through the large convent windows, she could see the moon and she wondered, as she lay there swaddled in linen, if he had already begun his journey to her. To meet her under the constellations she had memorized by heart.

An hour later, upon hearing the constant sounds of sleep emanating from her classmates, and the last footsteps of the nuns in the rooms above, Salomé began to make her preparations.

She unbuttoned her nightgown and unbraided and fluffed her hair. Careful not to make a sound, she unrolled from underneath her pillow her favorite lavender dress, the one with a square neckline and Empire waist, the fabric light as a veil.

She bit her lips to give them color, moistened her lashes with fingers dipped in her bedside water, and smoothed back her curls. If she heard the slightest stirring, she froze her motion; even her breath she kept contained within. Only after she was absolutely certain that no one would hear her, did she make her way out of the bed.

She placed her bare feet on the floor (as sandals would make too much noise) and escaped out the window, gripping the trellis like a salamander, winding down into the garden across the cloister and past the orchard. Passing a handful of freshly fallen oranges, glowing like tiny lanterns in the warm, satin light of the moon.

He waited for her in a field a short distance away. He stood there alone, his features sharp as a sparrow's, his white suit offsetting his jet-black hair. He could not believe that she had actually come to him. She a vision, with her hair brushed loose and her lavender dress billowing behind.

He brought the oranges as he had promised and placed them on the grass in a mad attempt to align them with the stars.

He seemed almost too embarrassed to look at her. The curve of her body melting with the fluidity of the dress. Her skin beaded with pearls.

He wanted to fall to the ground and kiss her naked toes. Long and rounded at the tips, with fine, naturally pink nails neatly manicured around the edges. Her ankles were thin and tapered. The wet grass clung to her calves like seaweed. She, like a canvas, white and smooth.

He knelt on the ground and reached to kiss her hand. She smiled, her head filled with the frenzy of butterfly wings, as if they were fluttering inside her, pressing their edges against her skin.

He told her then and there, repeating it like one of his many poems, that he loved her. That he had watched her for an eternity, that he had loved her since the beginning of time.

She thought he looked far more nervous and vulnerable than she had expected. A boy of nineteen, no more than two years older than she. But he was so handsome. A tall, magnificent figure cut in white linen, whose terra-cotta hands were large and strong, whose movements were elegant and well-mannered, and whose face radiated the sublime light of pure adoration. He beamed, quite simply, with love.

The silver light flattered him, casting shadows over his smooth face. With two black eyes that appeared trimmed in sienna, she imagined they were two large cherries, warm and delicious, ripening in the night.

"You've come," he said as if to remind himself that she truly was there before him.

"How could I have resisted?"

He watched her carefully. He studied how, when she spoke, the top of her lip curled upward, how her brows furrowed when she waited for his reply.

"Promise me you'll visit every evening. I never want to know a night without you."

His intensity beguiled her.

"I promise."

Every evening thereafter, Salomé sneaked out of the cloister to meet Octavio under the stars, where he would ask permission to hold her, to stroke her hair and then her warmest areas below. She brought him small gifts made by hand, his favorite being a silk pouch she had embroidered with their names. "It is for you to store your poems," she whispered to him. And from that evening on, he carried it with him, no matter where he was, and when they were together, he would withdraw one or two poems and read them to her aloud.

He followed Salomé when she returned home for vacation, for one night apart from her was too difficult a burden to bear. He saved up his money for the train fare and kept the piece of paper on which she had scrolled her family's address close to his breast.

Her parents' home was not far from Santiago's center, and one week before, Salomé had carefully drawn her lover a map. "My bedroom is on the ground floor, my parents' in the room above," she said, her finger tracing in the sand. "But we must be careful not to be discovered by my parents," she forewarned him. "Octavio—you must promise to take care."

The following week, as she rested in her childhood bed, she turned off her bedroom light—the sign that she now waited for him. And so, with bated breath, Octavio went to her. He climbed past the bushes, pulled up the cuffs of his trousers, and tiptoed through the patch of grass.

He saw her silhouette before he saw her completely. The moonlight illuminating her in a soft haze of white. Her body veiled in crisp linen, her black hair swept loose. To him, she had never been more beautiful.

He climbed through the window and fell into her arms. He kissed her neck and her eyelids, her mouth, and her breasts. He wanted to devour her, his flower, his orange gatherer, his love. But she held him as if he were a child, in the basket of her arms. She drew him into her bed, quietly, softly; the only sound uttered from her were her small, delicate breaths.

In her childhood bed, she wrapped him in muslin sheets scented with verbena, encasing their steadfast embrace. And she held him as she had learned over the months, her gestures like a dance, her movements motivated by love. And he came to her with soft moans, her breast a pillow for his sleeping head.

Had she too been asleep, she would have not heard her father's footsteps descending the stairs.

"Salomé," he called to her.

Quickly, she pushed Octavio deep into the blankets below.

As a child, Salomé had always felt secure when her father came to check up on her in the middle of the night. She had always smiled when she saw her father, tall and slender peering out from the small window above her door, looking straight into her bed to make sure she was secure.

But in this moment she dreaded it.

She heard his footsteps come closer, saw the tuft of his gray hair bobbing close to the door. In the windowpane, she saw his eyes, darting into her bedroom and scouting out her bed.

"Good night, my darling," he whispered through the door. His head arched like a crane as she saw his gaze through the door's top window. "Just making sure you are all right."

"Yes, Papa," she said softly, pushing Octavio farther down into the tangled covers below.

She waited until she heard her father's footsteps winding to the second floor. Then she retrieved her crouching love. And with her shutters flung open, they held each other until morning came. He knew he had to leave before her parents awakened. So, regretfully, he kissed her on the forehead and promised to return the following night.

Upon her return to school, their love affair continued. Every evening, she stuffed her bed with her uniform and spare pillow, molding the material to create an effigy of her form, and stole away to be with him. Months later, when the orange trees were in bloom, the branches heavy with flowers, she told Octavio that she suspected that she was with child. He was not angry, as she had feared, but rather rejoiced at the news. Months before he had vowed to marry her, to gain permission for her hand. He did not fear the wrath of her father or her wizened grandfather. He swore that he would go to the ancient hacienda, where the family spent their summer, or to her home in Santiago. He would go anywhere and demand her for his wife.

Now, as she was pregnant with his child, they would have no other choice.

Her family, whatever they felt about him, would have to concede.

F i v e

*B*efore they told her parents, Salomé hid her pregnancy from view. She bound her stomach with torn pieces of silk and switched uniforms with a girl who was two sizes larger than she. She ate little to ensure that the child did not grow so fast and made sure that she came to her classes always prepared. However, dark circles began to appear underneath her eyes. Her breasts swelled and her feet began to retain water, making it difficult to squeeze into her shoes.

"We must tell my parents before the nuns do," Salomé insisted.

"I will tell them that we were already planning to wed," he replied.

He placed his hand on her stomach and wondered whom the child might resemble. Should it be a girl, he imagined her beautiful like her mother, with those long, marquise eyes and full, ripe mouth. They would call her Blanca, as she would be the symbol of their love. White and pure.

Should they be blessed with a son, he hoped he would be strong and truthful. That he would grow into a man who could shoulder responsibility, who, in times of struggle, could survive. They would call him Rafael, because Salomé thought the name magical and divine. "In ancient Hebrew," Salomé whispered to her betrothed, "it means 'God heals all.'"

*   *   *

Traveling to meet his future in-laws, Octavio tried to hide his nervousness. He realized that his background was inferior to that of the woman he loved. His father had worked in the same store since he was seventeen, and although he had been promoted several times, the family lived modestly and simply. Their house was far smaller than Salomé's. He had shared a bedroom with his two elder brothers and his parents had slept on the floor, in a tiny room adjacent to the kitchen. He was the child of working-class parents and had disappointed them greatly when, as the first child to attend university, he chose to major in literature rather than a more practical field such as medicine or law.

But then again, he had never been practical. He had buried his head in books since the time he'd learned to read; a perpetual daydreamer, he was absentminded of his chores and considered by his family not to be grounded in the real world.

Since the age of twelve he had known he could never have a life like his father's. A man who traveled to the same wooden storefront, selling hardware to the same people in the same small town, day after day, year after year. So the boy studied hard and earned himself a scholarship; his only way out. At school, he found not only poetry but now, even more importantly, love.

He did not want Salomé to think that he was intimidated by the prospect of meeting her father. Inside, however, he was trembling. Salomé's father would be the first doctor, aside from the man who had treated him as a child, that he had ever met. He knew that he had no title, no job, and no money of his own. But he had love. He naively believed that would be enough.

Her parents were far from pleased when Salomé returned home from school, three months pregnant, and Octavio in tow. The beautiful daughter they had sent off to a convent had returned home very much the bohemian. Her hair was long and wild, no longer in the tight braids she had maintained since she was a little girl. Her bosom was full and peeking out from her uniform blouse, and there was the small bulge of her burgeoning stomach. She was only eighteen.

"We're in love, Papa," she insisted. Her father stood before her, tall and slender as a baton. He gazed upon her with stony eyes, unable to fathom that his beloved daughter was carrying a child.

Don Fernando had always nurtured high hopes for his only daughter. He had always believed that his spirited and brilliant child would marry a man who matched her. Now he stood before his prized jewel, unable to fathom that she could be in love with this penniless, jobless student.

"I love your daughter, Dr. Herrera," Octavio said in a practiced voice that veiled his nervousness. "There is nothing I would like more in this world than to have her as my wife."

"How old are you, may I ask?"

"Twenty years, sir."

"Have you a job?"

"No, sir, I am a student of literature at the university in Concepción."

Don Fernando did not find the irony of what the young Octavio had just said the least bit amusing. "And how will you support a wife and child on a student's allowance?"

"We will manage, sir. I have always worked hard. I received one of the university's few scholarships—"

Don Fernando cut the young man off. "You think you can exist on such a pittance for long?"

Tiny beads of perspiration were beginning to form on Octavio's forehead. He wanted to reach for his handkerchief, but feared revealing the extent of his nervousness.

"Love must come before money," Octavio said with a strong voice. He desperately wanted Salomé to think him brave and not cowardly in front of her father. "I realize that your daughter and I come from different backgrounds, but I love her. I am devoted to her. I will dedicate my life to making her happy. I would hope that you would see that I am an intelligent person who has worked to better himself through education and has the sincerest of intentions—"

"What I see," Don Fernando interjected, his voice bordering on a boom, "is that you are a man who has defiled my daughter, filled her head with nonsensical poetic notions, and that you are a ridiculous student who has absolutely no idea how the world works!"

Doña Olivia was standing next to her husband, her face frozen with disbelief. How, she wondered, could her daughter have returned to them this way? She felt wounded that her daughter had not confided in her. She tried to hide her true feelings that, perhaps, her initial instinct had been right. They should never have sent her to a school so far away from home.

By speaking, Doña Olivia hoped to restore some sense of calm to the situation. "Don Octavio," she said quietly, "how are we to know that your love for our daughter is sincere?"

Octavio turned from the stern gaze of Salomé's parents and looked deeply into the eyes of his beloved.

"She is whom I rise for each morning, whom I think of when I hear songs of love. I have never known such sweetness before, never dreamt that I could find a creature that could captivate both my mind and my soul. Grant me permission to be her husband and I will cherish the title. I will protect her. I will always see that she is safe, that she is loved, and that her life is full of wonder and joy."

Doña Olivia was moved by the young boy who stood before her, but her husband was clearly not.

"I am a fifty-three-year-old man and I know that providing food and a roof over your family's head requires more than just love."

"Papa . . . ," Salomé interrupted.

"No, it's all right," Octavio reassured her, as he slipped his hand into hers. He was trying to appear strong, though clearly Don Fernando intimidated him. He had little to impress the old man with. He knew that after he completed his degree from the university, he would have limited career opportunities. He could be a teacher or perhaps a journalist, but neither would provide her with the childhood luxuries she had been accustomed to.

Yet, somehow, Octavio believed it would all work out. Perhaps because he had always been something of a dreamer. Perhaps it was his innate belief that life and love were intended to have a happy ending. So, he stood there and gazed into his future father-in-law's disapproving eyes and said with his most inspired voice, "Let us have an agreement, Dr. Herrera. Allow me to marry your daughter before her belly gets so big that a church wedding will not be possible and I will vow that, by the time the child is born, I will have a job that will ensure your daughter and grandchild of the life they deserve."

Don Fernando remained skeptical of the young man, but in the end, fearing the disgrace of an unmarried, pregnant daughter, he reluctantly agreed.

Six

❧

Mikkeli, Finland
January 1942

$\mathcal{T}$hey chose her because she was the youngest and she could not yet form complete sentences. A little blond girl incapable of asking for an explanation.

Still, it was difficult for them. The most difficult thing they would ever have to do.

Kaija, their first and only daughter, had been born in the snow. Beyond the dark forests and the frozen lakes, under a patch of blue-white sky.

The day of her birth had begun much like any other. Sirka had risen early, her round belly camouflaged by a long flannel dress and wool sweater, her pale blond hair swept into a loose bun. She had been mindful not to wake her husband, Toivo, who slept soundly, his red beard spilling majestically over the white sheets she had embroidered the month before they were wed.

In the adjacent room, their three sons divided themselves between two beds that Sirka had carefully arranged to ensure they would be close to the hearth. She had knitted woolen slippers for them from coarse, unbleached yarn and given them the blanket from her own, sparse bed.

Today, they planned to go skating. They would pile on their sweaters, slip into their worn boots made from reindeer skin, and allow their mother to rub their cheeks with cod-liver oil, as they prepared to go to the lake three kilometers away.

But for now, except for Sirka, the small house nestled in the dark forest did not yet stir. She stood for a moment and looked over her sons. In their slumber, they had returned to the way she remembered them as infants. Their mouths half-open, their cheeks flushed and smooth. Inside her womb, the child also slept peacefully. Sirka rested her hands on her belly and wondered to herself if maybe this time she would be blessed with a girl. Someone who might look like her, someone who would one day grow up and become her best friend.

Sirka had few memories of her own mother, who had died from pneumonia when Sirka was only five. The only thing she had to remember her mother by was a small wooden crucifix that hung from a thin, black string. She had worn it around her neck ever since her father had given it to her, never taking it off, even when she went to bathe. Even when Toivo unwrapped her from her nightgown and held her naked in his arms. Aside from her gold wedding band, Sirka considered it her most valuable possession. A gift from someone who had left her before she was old enough to form a memory. A gift from someone she hoped loved her from beyond a snowy grave.

She noticed that the wooden crucifix had become even smoother and more beautiful over the years. A soft rosewood, the color of mulled wine. When she was nervous or when she knelt down at night to pray, Sirka clutched it around her fingers, felt the neat angles of its simple, perfect shape, and sensed, for a brief fleeting moment, that she was being watched over, cared for, and was safe.

Her whole life, she had feared being alone. The mere thought of being left alone in their small wooden house was enough to terrify her, so she received the news of her pregnancy with great relief and delight. The youngest boy would be going to school next fall, and she was thankful that she would have the baby to keep her company.

She was not unaware that another child would be a strain on the family. But she had been shocked by the intensity of Toivo's response when she'd informed him that she was pregnant. It was the first time she had seen him cry.

He tried to assure her that he was crying tears of joy, but she knew better. She saw how his face had been transformed over the past months. He hadn't been the same since he had been sent home from the Russian front. He had left home a year and a half earlier a tall, strong man with broad shoulders and arms that resembled the thick tree trunks he had chopped since he was a small boy. But he returned a thin, frail man with sunken cheeks and a shattered foot.

The evening he first returned home, she stood in the doorway for what seemed like a long time, too shocked even to invite him in. He appeared ghostlike. The white clothes, the pallid skin. Even his eyes seemed lost in a sea of white. The frost had penetrated him to the bone.

She unwrapped his bandages herself that first evening. His white uniform was soiled with dried patches of blood, the tracings of dry earth and dirty snow; his red-raw fingers grasped a single crutch that supported his slender form. She took his fur-lined hat from him and laid it by the fire and placed his crutch in the corner. Silently, her fingers replacing words, she motioned to him to sit on one of their small wooden chairs, placing his swollen foot in between her thighs. She could feel the heat emanating from the flesh buried deep beneath the layers of cloth as she peeled the bandages off slowly, placing the strips of fabric in a pot of boiling water that rested on a stool beside her knees.

He winced as she got closer to the foot. His eyes darted between the face of the wife he had longed for months to gaze upon and his bloody, disfigured foot.

"You shouldn't look at it, Sirka," he whispered, his voice faint from the difficult journey.

"Hush, be still!" she chided in a voice that quavered despite an attempt to be strong.

"I don't want you to see this!" he said, wiggling his leg so that the foot slipped from her thighs.

But she grabbed his ankle, her strength surprising even herself.

"If you get an infection, you will die, Toivo! So stay still and let me clean the wound and then sterilize these bandages!"

He became quiet again. He had little energy left to argue with her, and he did not want to awaken the three sleeping boys.

"It's not so bad," she whispered to him, trying to force back the tears that were beginning to well in her eyes. The battered, oozing mass of his foot lay there, exposed in the orange glow of the fire, two toes curling against Sirka's white apron, the other three gone forever, replaced by gouges and ribbons of blue and purple, striating the flesh like the lines of an ancient stone.

"It will heal, Toivo," she said, her voice trembling as she placed his foot in a pot of warm, soapy water.

"Never. I'll be a cripple for the rest of my life."

"You can walk, Toivo, don't be ridiculous." And she paused, regaining her composure. "Thank God you're alive, Toivo. We must thank God for that!"

She raised his foot from the soaking water and kissed it gently.

"Shall I wake the boys? They will be so happy to see their father!" she said, her face blushing slightly. Although only five months had passed since he'd joined the army against the Russians, to Sirka it seemed like an eternity since she had last been with her husband. How nervous she seemed with him now! It was as if Toivo were someone from her past she had forced herself to forget, for the wait for his return had been nearly too much for her to bear.

Yet, now, she not only had to reacquaint herself with his presence, but also to deal with the reality that he would never be able to farm or fish as he once had. Their lives would be difficult, but she truly believed that God would watch over them and that somehow, no matter how difficult it might seem, they would manage.

Now, nearly a year after his return, she had become pregnant again. But this time, unlike with her other pregnancies, the news of the arriving baby seemed to paralyze Toivo. Nearly every day and every night she would see his face lined with worry. "How will we feed another mouth, Sirka?" he asked her one evening as they lay in their birchwood bed. "The five of us are already existing on scraps alone."

Sirka just stared at him. There was little she could say. She knew how little food they had. The tin canisters of flour and sugar had been empty for months. The boys had stopped fighting each morning over the pieces of flat bread she broke into tiny slivers, which had become so small that they had quietly realized it wasn't worth the quarrel.

Every morning, she performed the same ritual, dividing the scraps from the day before into small rations. In actuality, the parts were not even. She gave the boys a fraction more than Toivo because they were growing, and took for herself only the crumbs. Had it not been for the baby, she would have eaten nothing at all.

She tried to convince Toivo that they would all be all right. That God would watch over them. He did his best to smile and agree with her, but the lines in his face and the furrows on his tired forehead only betrayed his tension and despair.

The boys were beginning to stir, and through the crocheted curtains, she saw the sun beginning to weave through the branches. The Karelian birches were silver with snow.

It was a perfect day for skating. The sun would be out for a few hours, and Lake Saimaa was so beautiful when frozen. She enjoyed the summers, when Toivo would row her and the children into its center and they would sing old folk songs. But in her heart, Sirka preferred winter. Then, the lake stretched like a sheet of platinum, the tiny waves frozen underneath a thin glaze of ice.

How she loved the forest! She loved the sounds of the snow crushing underneath her footsteps. She loved the howl of the wind as it navigated its way through the drifts and the plateaus of frozen earth. So, even though Toivo urged her to stay at home that day, Sirka insisted that she join him and the boys. She was too far along in her pregnancy to skate, but she sat majestically on the small bench of the kick sleigh with a woolen blanket wrapped over her lap as the boys pushed her through the forest.

The boys laced their boots and thrust their small hands into their mittens. Toivo placed his one good foot in a skating boot, leaving the other to trail along in a shoe. "Hold my crutch," he called out to his pregnant wife, as he tossed her the wooden support over the ice. Sirka sat there watching the four of them slipping and sliding over the shimmering ice, their laughter slicing through the cold.

Yet, now, Sirka's back was beginning to ache. A low, deep pain that she brushed off as a mere muscle spasm. But the pain began to increase, and in the blue light of winter, her cheeks lost their flush, her pallor now like the snow.

She had planned not to say anything. When they returned home, she would boil herself a cup of water and sing to the baby inside her. Her breasts were heavy, and she was grateful that, once the child was born, she would be able to feed at least one of her children with her milk.

When Toivo returned with the boys, he saw that Sirka was not herself. Her eyes shone with pain and her forehead was wet and white. In a panic, he told the boys to be quiet and fumbled for his crutch.

"I will go look for help," he told his frightened wife, who begged him not to leave.

"The baby is coming," she said, and in the blue light of winter she looked like a small, terrified deer.

She felt too modest to inform him that her dress was now soaked underneath the blanket, and that she imagined icicles forming around her knees. She remembered that her other children were born only a few hours after her water had broken, and that this child seemed far more eager to be born.

The boys began to grow rowdy. In his despair, Toivo told them sternly to leave the two of them and to play a few meters beyond.

"I could go find a doctor," he said as he reached to hold his wife's hand. She smiled at him and told him that she'd rather give birth here in the cold than be left alone.

So he took the woolen blanket and draped it on the snow. And extended his one free arm to guide her from the sleigh to the ground. A little over an hour later, her legs covered by her husband's sheepskin coat, the drops of blood dotting the snow crimson, she gave birth to a beautiful, green-eyed daughter.

A daughter that, two years later, she would be forced to give away.

When Sirka held her daughter for the first time, she noticed that the child's hair was white, while the three boys had been born with red. She wrapped the child in her sweater. She examined the girl over in her entirety. She studied the child's limbs, the moon-shaped fingernails, and the half-closed eyelids, to make sure that she was properly formed, and sighed with a mixture of exhaustion and relief as she brought the child to her breast.

Even with the shortage of food, the little girl had not been a problem for the first two years of her life. Sirka nursed her, and Toivo often watched her suckle the child, trying to mask his own hunger and desire. She knew he secretly wished that she could feed the entire family at her breast. And sometimes, at night, he would reach underneath her gown and drink from her, before falling away disgusted and ashamed.

The little girl, however, was beginning to grow weary of her mother's milk, and Sirka saw how the child had already begun to steal scraps from the table.

But still, she was small for her age. Tiny, pale, and white. Her favorite thing was a small toy bear, whose ear she sucked on at night.

Sirka insisted, as all mothers do, that she loved all of her children equally. But, in her heart, she knew that she loved her daughter just a little bit more. She loved the boys too, but the three of them had grown so fast and wrestled themselves further away from her with each passing year. She saw how they had their father's hair, his unusually dark brown eyes, and his passion for the outdoors. But this little girl was hers completely.

She had the same blond hair and green eyes. When Sirka cradled her in her arms, she saw her own features in miniature. The cupid bow of her mouth, the straight line of her nose, and the roundness of her brow. She relished the child's sweetness, her curiosity, and the sheer joy she displayed from discovering the simple things around her.

So, when Toivo came home one evening with the newspaper in hand and a bouquet of winter violets, nothing could have prepared her for what he was about to ask.

He showed her the paper's headlines: "Swedish Government to Accept Thousands More Finnish Children in a Gesture to Its Scandinavian Brother As War Continues."

"The children who went there in the first wave were very happy," he whispered to his wife. "It won't be permanent, just until the war ends."

"No, Toivo. No—" she pleaded. "How could you even suggest

such a thing?" In the lamplight, her face revealed her despair, her brow quivering as she spoke. "She is our only daughter . . ."

"This is no life for our daughter. For anyone." He slid into one of the chairs and propped his leg on a low wooden stool. "We have no food now. The Russians are pushing farther west. Our soldiers are basically fighting on skis in our backyard! What kind of life is this? And nobody knows when it's going to end!"

"It will end, Toivo. Eventually." She began to cry.

"The women who are volunteering for the war effort in town, the *lottas*, are taking names of children to be sent on the SS *Arcturus* in the next few weeks." He paused. "I put Kaija's name on the list, Sirka," he said as he covered his brow with his hand.

She knew even before he said her daughter's name that she would be the one he would choose. For, not only was Kaija the only girl, she was also young enough to forget them. But, for Sirka, it would be far more difficult. No mother could erase the memory of any of her children. Particularly this little girl with the white hair who asked for nothing but the love of her mother, her milk, and the company of her small bear.

Sirka wept nightly and the violets beside her bed soon wilted and died. Outside their modest home, the snowdrifts piled high and the sun shone for fewer hours each day.

Three weeks later, Toivo arrived home with lowered lids and hunched shoulders. "One of the *lottas* will be coming to pick Kaija up for the transport," he said as gently as he could.

She heard him, his words veiled in a whisper. She turned from him so her back faced him and her eyes wandered to the window.

"The *Arcturus* leaves Friday," he said sadly. "We must leave her in God's hands now, Sirka." He embraced her. "God will watch over her while she's in Sweden, and we will know that at least there she will be safe."

That Friday, she packed a little bag for her only daughter. She washed her only dress, a little blue-checkered smock with a small white collar, in a bucket of melted snow and dried it by the fire. She folded two sweaters and a pair of woolen tights and placed a small prayer book on top of the small red suitcase. Inside the prayer book, she placed a letter.

Dear Kaija,

    Be a good girl and appreciate all that your new family does for you. Please never believe that your father and I have abandoned you. We love you and only want you to be safe. You have three brothers who will miss you too. Someday soon, when the war ends, you will be returned to us. We love you and you will always be in our thoughts and prayers.
    God will watch over you.

Love,
Your mother, Sirka

She wrapped the book in a small blanket and tucked it into the valise, along with the only photograph she had of herself. Her wedding portrait. A black-and-white photo of her and Toivo, with her in her mother's white dress and a crown of flowers in her hair.

Lastly, she removed her mother's wooden crucifix. She held it one last time in her palms, traced its straightness with her finger, and pressed the smooth center close to her lips. If only her daughter could retrieve her kiss, she thought to herself, as she placed it in the bag.

Toivo stood in the threshold of the bedroom watching his young wife. He came over to her and rested his large palm on her shoulder as she knelt to shut her daughter's little red bag. Through his palm, he could feel her shudder as his wife began to weep softly. And she begged her husband once more not to make her send Kaija away. He buried his face in her shoulder and pleaded for her not to ask him again. For all of this seemed far worse than death. Sending your child to a home, a country, you did not know. Where you knew they could never love her as you had loved her. For she was your own.

Overhead, the sirens blared and the red lights stretched over the snow with scarlet beams, as Toivo went to fetch young Kaija, who slept quietly in the kitchen. The young *lotta* stood in the doorway, her navy coat and hat appearing incongruous with the rustic surroundings.

Sirka buried her head in her pillow, unable to endure the pain of watching this stranger take her daughter away. But from her bedroom, she heard her little girl calling, *"Minun nalle karhun, minun nalle karhun,"* "My bear, my bear."

As Sirka rushed to the doorway to hand Kaija her little stuffed animal, she met the eyes of her daughter one last time. The little girl, sensing her mother's despair, began to wail.

And through her flannel gown, Sirka's milk began to run.

Seven

❧

Karelia, Finland
January 1942

$\mathcal{T}$hey had rounded the children up. Confiscated their suitcases and burned the clothes their mothers had packed for them for fear of lice. Kaija's dress and socks were thrown on the fire, but the photograph, letter, and crucifix were all repacked into the little red suitcase with far less care than Sirka had originally placed them.

Kaija's tiny body was stripped and examined by a medical doctor, who wrote notes on her physical condition and inserted them into her file. She was reclothed in a new outfit that was donated to the war-effort program and given a new woolen coat with a matching navy hat.

As with the hundreds of children who would be joining her on the SS *Arcturus* from Abo to Stockholm, an identification tag was placed around her neck detailing her name, hometown, and date of birth. She stood there completely bewildered, her green eyes stricken with fear and confusion, her blond curls damp underneath her woolen cap.

The children were encircled with a long white rope to ensure that they didn't separate from the group. Their small hands were encased in mittens, their feet in shiny new boots.

"Come now," one of the *lottas* spoke softly to tiny Kaija as they boarded the boat. "You'll be going to a wonderful new home."

In the dark cavern of the boat's belly, she understood nothing of what was going on. Her tiny bear pressed to her tearstained face. The other children crying as the boat rocked back and forth, the lights of the airplanes circling overhead, the sound of sirens, the crush of the boat's bow breaking through the ice.

In Stockholm, she was the last of the children to be chosen. A little blond girl in a bright blue dress, holding nothing but a small bear and a red, round valise. Pinned on her jacket was a piece of paper with the name *Kaija* inscribed in neat black letters.

The childless Swedish families who had arrived with the expectation that there would be a Finnish boy or girl there for them with bright eyes and a wide smile, each came and left with a toddler matching their wish. The throng of children who had arrived off the boat and stood with their names attached to their coats whittled down to one. One little girl by the name of Kaija.

She stood there alone. Her eyes betraying her confusion. She did not understand the bustle of the administrators and families around her or the strange language they spoke. Men searched for their fountain pens to sign the necessary papers so their wives could bring home the new children, who now dangled from their arms, as quickly as possible and make them their own.

Only one couple remained. Having arrived late, they had missed the selection. The husband was the first to remark about the sweet little girl who stood all alone, somewhat frightened, clutching her bear.

"There seems to be one child left, Astrid," the man hollered out to his wife, who was rushing only a few steps behind. "Aren't we lucky!"

The tall man, slender and modestly dressed in his Sunday finest, pushed through the departing crowd to the ropes that had been set up to corral the children. He had already taken off his hat and was wiping the perspiration from his brow when he knelt down to get a closer look at the little girl. "She certainly looks sweet," he called back to his wife, who was now close enough to see for herself.

"She looks sad and sickly, Hugo! We arrived too late!" Her annoyance at her husband was obvious and her voice cranky and stale.

"Look at her, Astrid," he said pointing to Kaija, "she's only frightened. She's all alone."

"I thought we agreed we wanted a boy."

"I never said that; any child will do."

"I wanted a boy. We can come back next week when the next boat arrives. Next time we'll be on time."

But her husband had already made eye contact with the little girl, and he felt that it would be cruel to abandon her.

"Come on, Astrid," he pleaded. "I think having a little girl around would do us a world of good."

The shiny blue car drove home, the handsome driver smiling triumphantly, the two female passengers lost in dissimilar sadnesses. The little girl in the blue dress holds her bear to her cheek, her two blond braids, like two woven ropes of straw, pushed back behind her ears. She no longer weeps, her tears having dried on the bear's paws hours before. Yet, now she is gripped with the most terrifying fear. She does not recognize the two faces who are taking her away. She does not know where she is going. She wonders where her mother is.

In the large rearview mirror, Kaija sees the handsome man who less than an hour before reached out to hold her small, pink hand, smiling at her. Beside him, his wife stares out the window, her small, veined hands rocking restlessly in her lap.

The lids of the woman's blue eyes are heavy and forlorn, her thin lips feathered with fine lines. A bullfinch cloaked in a brown coat, a pinched mouth that in profile resembles a tiny wooden beak. She looks distantly out the window, into the snow-swallowed birches. Her gaze cut in ice, her pupils cast in the blue-gray frost. She fumbles as she buttons her coat up to her chin, her fingers, stiff like icicles, pull at the loops.

And the little girl stares at the woman's head from behind, wishing that she could instead see the beautiful and familiar face of her mother. Hoping that when this long and winding car ride finally ends, her mother will be waiting for her with her arms outstretched and her scarf blowing around her pale white face.

She wants to *will* herself home. She tightens her thin arms around her small bear and recalls the sensation of her mother's embrace. How her mother's blond hair wove into her own. How she was gently kissed at night and how her mother's clothes smelled like fresh air and melted snow.

Yet, the scent of home has already begun to recede from her memory. Blue-spruce and white-fir branches crackling on the fire. Now, she is enveloped by the smell of fresh leather seats and thick walls of carpet. Years later, even when she is a grown woman of twenty, she will be struck by the poignancy of this smell. For, every time she steps inside a new automobile, she will always see herself as a girl of barely two years of age, sitting in the backseat of a 1942 Volvo, struggling because she is unable to articulate her feelings into words. Struggling because she is incapable of communicating her overwhelming sense of loss.

Eight

Karelia, Finland
January 1944

$\mathcal{S}$he had written to her daughter several times, carefully inscribing the envelopes with the address that the war agency had sent her in the mail a few days after her daughter had been transported to Stockholm.

Sirka realized that the child was too small to read or even to understand these letters. But she wrote them anyway, hoping the family in Sweden might reply to them even if they wrote to her in a language she couldn't comprehend. Yet, as many letters as Sirka wrote, she never received a response.

Still, for nearly two years, Sirka continued to write. The letters remained a one-way dialogue between her and her only daughter, the little green-eyed girl whom she still carried closely in her heart.

Ironically, life had been no easier for them since the little girl was taken. The family still remained hungry and the fighting continued. At Sunday services, when Toivo and the boys would travel to the church only a few kilometers away, the priest's list of boys who had perished in the fighting continued to lengthen. Now, as the fourth year of fighting ensued, with little chance of peace in sight, Sirka began to worry that, in a few years, her own sons might be drafted.

It sickened her to pass by the cemetery now: the rows of iron crosses for the lives already lost, the red flowers that grew from underneath the snow. All those young boys, their fathers—those husbands—it was too many to count.

Sirka continually reminded herself that, despite her hardship, at least her husband had returned from the front alive. Despite his wounds, she had to be grateful for that.

She had given up hoping that Toivo would return to his former self. Before the war, he had been larger than life. A robust man with a contagious laugh and a passion for the wilderness. Not to mention a passion for her. But he had returned not only with a physical wound, but with one far deeper in spirit. Incapable of fighting with his fellow soldiers, he sank deep into depression. He lost all of his physical strength, his muscles atrophying so that the flesh hung like wet linen on his bones. For hours, he would sit on the narrow wooden chair by the fire, his crutch propped against the corner, his fingers trembling at his sides.

As her husband was now incapable of fishing, Sirka and the three boys became responsible for obtaining what little food they could harvest during the cold, long winters. Three days a week, she would place birch woven shoes over her reindeer-skin-lined feet and tread through the snow. A basket slung over one shoulder and a fishing pole slid under her arm.

Her body had become more stocky over the past year, as she was required to do far more physical work than she had done when Toivo was in full health. Now, sometimes when she would go to fish on the lake, she would wear his old army parka and hat—the white ones that blended with the snow.

She had gone to the lake all by herself that afternoon, as the boys had yet to return from school. Dressed in white, her blond hair tucked underneath the fur-lined cap, she made her way into the wilderness. The Karelian birches were heavy with snow, their white trunks blending in with the drifts that had piled high. She sang softly to herself as she walked through the forest and raised her chin to gaze at the steely gray sky.

Walking carefully on the frozen lake, she treaded over the ice with footsteps as delicate as a deer's. She punctured the ice slightly to insert her tackle. She wiggled the line to lower her bait.

The enemy must have seen her sitting there, her back bowed

over the hole where the fishing line floated gently underneath. Yet, from the rear, she appeared very much a Finnish soldier dressed to fight.

They opened fire on her without hesitation. Five Russian bullets hitting her from behind. Only meters from where she had once given birth, her blood spilled once more. But this time, there was no blanket, no hand of her beloved, as her pale white face fell against the ice.

A band of Finnish soldiers found her three hours later. They had seen the body lying on the frozen lake, and in her pale white parka and cap, they had believed they had come across one of their own.

But, as they drew closer, they noticed her pale blond curls, delicate nose, and soft, pink mouth.

"She's a woman," one of the soldiers remarked, his voice echoing with regret. He knelt down and took hold of her small, ring finger. Her thin gold wedding band sparkled in the descending light.

They scooped her up like a fallen, white swan and carried her several kilometers to the church. There, the priest identified her as the wife of Toivo Laakso, a mother of three.

"Or was it four?" he pondered aloud, a thin white finger tapping against his bearded mouth.

"In times like these," he told the three soldiers, his pale blue eyes staring blankly, "it's difficult even for me to remember."

Nine

༄

Lima, Peru
September 1968

Samuel Rudin had his guilt that he took with him wherever he went. He had only a few memories of prewar France: the images of his mother scrambling to pack their suitcases and the piles of clothes that would not fit inside; the objets d'art his father told her to leave and forget, saying that, God willing, they would have new ones soon.

In his child's eye, he saw her in her black clothes that contrasted with white satin cuffs nipped with a single pearl button, and a collar trimmed in silk. He could conjure up the sound of her footsteps, softly treading over the oxblood carpets, her fingers threading one last time through the curtains that veiled Paris from view.

In his memory, she kneels and whispers to him and his two brothers not to be afraid. She holds him by his shoulders and buries her face in his small five-year-old chest. When she rises, she leaves an imprint of her powder on his jumper and quickly instructs him to change. The image of her tear-streaked face, the scent of gardenia faintly clinging to her neck, always made him cry even at the age of thirty-four.

He never knew exactly how his father had obtained the fake passports, but he knew that his aunts and uncles had not agreed with him and had refused to go. "They'll never come here," Tante Rosa had insisted. "Besides, our family has been French citizens for over one hundred years!"

"The German Jews said the same thing!" Samuel's father responded. His fist hit the dining-room table with a thud. "Shall we too wait until we are corralled up like animals, or worse?"

"We'll take our chances," Samuel's uncle said softly. "Peru is on the other side of the world to us. We will have nothing when we arrive. We don't speak the language, we will be treated like immigrants. Rosa and I will wait and see how things unfold." He paused, raised his glass of wine, and nodded to his wife and then to the rest of the family that huddled around the table. "If things get worse, we can always come later."

"You're a fool, Jacob," Samuel's father muttered into his wine, clearly annoyed by his brother's stubbornness. And Samuel's mother looked at Tante Rosa, her eyes speaking in octaves: *Come with us,* her brown irises pleaded. But Rosa just smiled and bowed her head, her pursed lips delicately saying to his mother, "I must do as my husband wishes."

Isaac Rudin and his wife, Justine, left France in November 1939, on a steamer bound for Peru with their three children, Samuel, André, and Théo. "We will have a new life, children," Samuel's father told them as they boarded the boat in Marseille. "Be good, children," he said as he patted each of them on the back. "The first few months will be difficult for all of us, but particularly for your mother. So, let us not give her any unnecessary trouble." He stroked his beard and watched as the tip of the French coast faded from view. Behind them, Justine lay wrapped in blankets, her long, lean legs stretched over the deck chair, her black calfskin pumps carefully shined and polished. Even with the wool blanket draped over her, Samuel recalled how elegant his mother appeared then. Her makeup was fastidiously applied—pale skin and a perfect red mouth. She had packed in only a few days, leaving so much behind. But, as the boat sailed farther from the shore, she was not thinking of her closets full of dresses, her ermine fur, or her twenty-four-person set of bone china that she had left untouched. She was thinking of her parents, of Rosa and her family. Those whom she couldn't pack neatly away. Those whom she had left behind.

The Rudins settled in a modest home not far from the gates of Miraflores in the bustling capital of Lima. Nearly every week, Justine wrote to her sister-in-law begging her to reconsider her decision and pleading with her to convince her husband that they must come.

At night, she slept poorly. Dreaming of her parents, of Rosa and the others. It was as if she could anticipate the horror that would befall them, yet she remained powerless some hundred thousand miles away.

She tried to convince Isaac that he must *act*, that he must be stronger with his brother, Jacob, and insist that he and the others come before it was too late.

"What can I do, Justine?" Isaac cried. His thin, wiry body looked like a violin that was having its strings plucked every time his wife insisted he wasn't doing enough.

"They all refused to come! And your parents . . . Justine, they insisted they were too old to make such a journey."

In the end, by the time Isaac's younger brother realized he had made a mistake in not joining his brother and his family, it was too late. Less than a year and half later, they received their last letter from Jacob. Not even the money Isaac had sent could buy them new passports and a ticket to Peru. The Nazi soldiers had already taken the neighbors, and perhaps, within hours, they too would be taken. The irony of the last line of Jacob's letter was even too much for Isaac to bear.

"I close this letter, dearest brother, with the admission of my foolishness. Isaac, I wished I had listened to you. In the end, dear brother, you were right."

For months after that, Justine and Isaac prayed for another letter to arrive. But nothing came.

"We need to begin mourning them," Justine whispered one night after it was clear that there would be no more letters, that the headlines of what was happening back in Europe were true.

The night they began their official period of grieving, she tore the children's clothes as tradition dictated and covered the mirrors with heavy black cloth. That evening, as she and Isaac traveled to the small Sephardic synagogue to say the kaddish, Justine's eyes were red from crying. Her willowy frame appeared haggard and concave. From underneath her black crepe dress, Samuel could see the trembling of his mother's limbs, the high relief of her collarbone, the two round knobs so pronounced that her pearls seemed to hang like a rope strung across two pegs.

His father appeared defeated. His suit hung like wasted wool, as if it lacked the necessary form to fill its lines and seams. The old man's face appeared frozen. As if he could not contain his disbelief that he was mourning for a family that he could not bury. Without a proper burial, without going through the rituals of death—the interment of the coffin, the throwing of dirt on the grave—it was tempting to believe that he could maintain the fantasy that his brother and his brother's family were still alive and safe.

Both Justine's and Isaac's guilt consumed them. It fed off their bones; it harvested the light from their eyes. They were no longer capable of having a conversation between them. They could not even enjoy their food.

"This has no taste," Isaac would say as he pushed his plate away from him. "I have too much work to do to eat." He would then leave his wife and three sons and retreat to his office, where he would not do a single shred of paperwork. He would simply stare at the ceiling for hours.

Samuel's mother, however, would remain at the dining-room table while her three boys ate their dinner. Her attendance was not derived from any sense of maternal duty, but could rather be attributed to the catatonic state she had slipped into after the arrival of Jacob's last letter. Like her husband, she hardly touched the food on her plate, and she remained silent as the servants entered the dining room serving and clearing the dishes with care. On the few occasions she did speak, Samuel recalled that it was always about how they should be grateful, that their cousins and other relatives were far less fortunate than they. His two brothers would always grumble as their mother spoke. As young boys, they were far more eager to shovel the food into their bellies and be out of the house where they could meet friends and be where things were far less strained. Samuel, however, rarely left the table until his mother stood up from her seat. He thought if he was good enough—if he waited patiently enough—that one day the mother he had had back in France would return.

That day never came. With each passing month Samuel's mother seemed to retreat further from him and the rest of the family. The chic woman who had sat on the boat dreaming of the faces of her loved ones had been replaced by a ghost who spoke little and cared even less for her appearance. Fine lines channeled through her once porcelain skin. And the smile he had known as a child vanished and was replaced by a permanent expression of strain.

Unlike her husband, who was able to mask his grief, she appeared to be ravished by hers. It was as if she would have preferred to die rather than to live with her guilt at her good fortune of having survived. And even though she never spoke of it aloud, her face betrayed her. The flesh of the eyelids ebbed downward, her mouth was tense, her lips permanently pursed. Every day, from the moment she rose until the time she lay down in her bed, she wondered why it had been her destiny to marry the wiser brother.

Silently, she cursed her brother-in-law for his foolishness. But she was far more severe on herself. She truly believed that somehow—no matter how difficult it might have been—she should have done more.

Her light-boned hands became even thinner. She wrung them so much that the skin became cracked and raw, the veins so pronounced you could chart them, her once pink nails now a mottled blue.

Her thick, black hair became gray before her fortieth birthday, and she wore it like a widow, coiled in a bun, stuck with stickpins at the back of her small, sparrowlike head.

She no longer cooked, leaving the meals to be prepared by the maid. She no longer ate more than a nibble, as if she were tempting fate to see if she could survive.

"Mama," Samuel would call to her, and try to crawl into her lap. But she would look at him and instead see her late nephew, Tovi, the boys having shared the same week of birth. And she would reference everything with "If Rosa were here," her sister-in-law's memory, like a shadow, hanging over her in the heavy, humid air.

Unlike most families, Justine considered her husband's family her own. Rosa had welcomed her like a sister, and their friendship was genuine. Rosa was the first one she had told when Justine suspected she was with child. Before her mother, before Isaac. And Rosa held her and told her that she too believed she was pregnant. "They'll be the same age," she said, and her black eyes were now wet from her tears. "Let's tell the men separately and let them have the joy of discovering on their own that the children will be born in the same month, perhaps even the same day!" They both reveled in their sisterly conspiracy and went into the kitchen to prepare their afternoon tea.

The boys were born within a week of each other, and Justine had loved Tovi as if he were her own son. After the children's births, their circumcisions having been completed, the two women confessed that they felt as though they had each given birth to twins, their hearts so full with love for the other's child.

After Jacob had refused to leave with them, Justine had begged Rosa to try to change his mind. "We will all be together," she tried to assure her. "Together, the journey will be less hard, the transition not as difficult." Rosa was shaking her head and repeating, "I cannot influence this decision, it is not mine to make." Rosa wrapped her sister-in-law in her shawl and held her close. "I promise we will come if things get worse. You understand, I must trust my husband."

They bade each other farewell in the early hours of the day they were to leave. Justine knelt down and kissed her nephew and rubbed his cheeks one last time. "Write us," she said to Rosa, and tried to muffle her breaking voice. "We will see each other soon." From a few meters beyond, Isaac beckoned Justine to hurry, insisting that they could not be late. As she approached the car, she turned once more, catching sight of her sister-in-law one last time. Rosa's tiny fingers waving good-bye, her face tightening as it tried to force back her fear. Years later, Justine was forever haunted by that last glimpse of her sister-in-law's face. Often, she replayed it in her mind, imagining herself running back to the three of them, dragging them into the car and insisting that they leave Paris. If only, she thought to herself again and again, so much that even her dreams gave her no rest. If only she and Isaac had done more.

Justine knew that Isaac had no satisfaction in that his intuition had been correct. But still it was as if she had to punish both herself and Isaac for their and their family's survival.

"We left them there, Isaac. Rosa, Tovi, Jacob, my mama, my papa . . . all of them. We should have insisted they come."

He was quiet. His gray face bearded white.

"Don't speak to me of what we should have done," he said solemnly. "I see how you look at me every day, as if I am to blame."

"No," she begged, and began to weep. "It's only . . ."

Isaac looked at his wife sprawled out on the bed, her face buried in the pillow. Her long black hair spreading on the linen, like the feathers of a large black bird.

"I'm sorry, Justine," he said, his own voice cracking, for it was nearly impossible for him to communicate his grief. He reached out to stroke his wife's back. "You mustn't blame yourself." He felt his throat beginning to constrict. He was struggling in dealing with his own emotions, let alone those of his wife.

So, he rose to his feet and began to walk out the door. But as he reached the threshold, he placed his palm on the sideboard and said softy, "It was I who should have been stronger. It is I who am to blame."

In his last year in medical school in America, Samuel learned that his mother had passed away. She had lasted longer than anyone had expected, as she had spent the past twenty years of her life living wedded more to her regrets than to her equally tormented husband.

Inspired particularly by his mother's anguish, Samuel had begun publishing papers on "survivor's guilt" in the months before and had decided that was what he wanted to focus on during his psychiatry residency.

Years later, when he received an offer to run a mental health clinic in Göteborg, Sweden, for survivors of torture and war, he wondered if he could meet the challenges of the job. He spoke five languages and had written extensively on the subject. But what did he really know? He hadn't even been able to help his own mother, and she had never been physically tortured, nor had she directly witnessed the atrocities of war.

But he would always remember her face; that sight of her after his parents had returned from reciting the kaddish for the family they had loved and lost, his mother's face resembling that of one of those classical sculptures in a museum—a face that is still beautiful despite the crack running down its side. Even at the age of seven, he had wished he could rub out those lines of sorrow. How he had wished, so many times, that he could place his hands on her tired eyes and rub back in the radiance he remembered from when he was a young child before the war. There was so much sorrow in his own family life that all he wanted to do was help those who had suffered.

Perhaps, he thought, if he had the ability to help just one person, then all of his studies and papers would not have been in vain, and his childhood failure to save his mother could finally be redeemed.

Ten

❧

Santiago, Chile
February 1966

Octavio Ribeiro had never expected to be famous. It came, as most things do, by surprise. But he welcomed the opportunity, not because he had any desire to be an actor, but because he thought it would afford him the means to support his beloved Salomé and their unborn child as well as gain the respect of his disapproving in-laws.

He was sitting in a café when it all began. Nearly two months had passed since Octavio had spoken with Dr. Herrera, and he had yet to find a job. He was trying to finish his final papers for his pending graduation while drinking a coffee and picking at a slice of lemon loaf, when he noticed a man staring up at him.

The man was dressed in a pale yellow suit and his head was cloaked by a stiff, white fedora. He was sipping a glass of sherry with one finger gently tapping against the rim.

Octavio tried to resume his writing, but still, the man continued to stare.

After several minutes, Octavio stood up and approached the man.

"Is there a problem?" Octavio asked, clearly bewildered. His thick black curls were hanging over his forehead and his large brown eyes were framed by two furrowed brows.

The man extended his hand and smiled. His white teeth

gleamed like a row of glazed white tile and his impeccably manicured hand now dangled in the air.

"I am Juan Francisco de Bourbon." His evenly brown hand
remained unshaken and he used the opportunity to make a self-
referring gesture.

"May I ask you a question, señor?" he asked Octavio politely.

Octavio nodded his head.

"Do you go to the movies often?"

Octavio stared back at him, his wide eyes betraying his bewilderment. "When I have the money," he answered.

Juan Francisco looked at Octavio with great intensity. "Young
man, may I tell you frankly, I have been staring at you for nearly an
hour, and now as I look at your features even more closely, I am confident without a doubt that you have one of those rare faces that are
destined for the screen."

"What the devil are you talking about?" Octavio replied curtly.
He was naturally suspicious of such kinds of flattery from another
man. Now, as he stood there dumbfounded by the conversation he
was having, he was beginning to be annoyed at himself for leaving
his writing. His coffee would soon be cold and his paper still half-
done.

"I'm sorry I haven't the time for a conversation. I am trying to
work and you were distracting me."

"Please accept my apology," Juan Francisco said, his teeth flash-
ing white. "It was just that you've intrigued me and it is my business
to find faces such as yours."

He reached into his jacket pocket, the inside lined in mustard-
colored satin, and withdrew his card.

Octavio gazed upon his fastidiously manicured fingernails as
they pushed the small, professionally typed business card in his
direction.

Juan Francisco de Bourbon
Artistic Manager
4 59 3765

"I have no background in acting," Octavio told him. "I am a student of literature and poetry, not of cinema or the stage."

"It's your face I am interested in," the man said flatly. "Your high cheekbones, your large eyes . . . your face has all the angles we look for in the film business."

"My girlfriend is far more beautiful," Octavio insisted.

"We have too many girls who want to be actresses. The studios want me to find actors who can match the beauty of the female leads." The man grinned again at Octavio. "You, I believe, have star-quality assets. With a little more polish, we could probably make you the Cary Grant of Chile."

Octavio shook his head. What this man was telling him seemed ridiculous and rather far-fetched. After all, he had never considered himself handsome, believing that his mind was his most valuable possession.

"Take my card and think about it, son," Juan Francisco told him in a well-practiced voice that almost seemed paternal. "Call me if you're interested." He leaned over to Octavio, swallowing his last sip of sherry. "I assure you, the money is well worth seeing if you have any talent."

Octavio visited Salomé that evening. Her belly was beginning to show, and in a few weeks she would have increasing difficulty in disguising her pregnancy.

"Have you any luck finding a job, darling?" she asked him as he sat beside her, his hand resting between her small fingers. He could tell that she was becoming nervous about their situation and the promise he had made some months earlier to her father.

"None of the local schools have responded to my applications," he replied quietly, his eyes fixating on her swelling abdomen.

"Something will open up," she said, trying to sound hopeful.

"I had a strange thing happen to me this afternoon, though. A man approached me and gave me his card." Octavio reached into his trouser pocket and fumbled to retrieve Juan Francisco's card.

He handed it to Salomé.

"What's this?" she asked, obviously perplexed. "Artistic manager? I don't understand."

"He thinks I should take a screen test."

"Screen test!" Salomé couldn't contain her laughter. "He thinks you should make movies?"

Salomé's reaction only increased Octavio's embarrassment. "I know it sounds ridiculous. I know I have no experience, nor really any great interest in the movies, but he said the money would be well worth my time."

"But what about your books, your poetry . . . your teaching?" she asked gently. "Would you want to give that up?"

Octavio didn't reply. He was feeling the weight of responsibility mounting on his shoulders.

"Perhaps I will be able to return to that, but now I must think about your condition and the promise I made to your father. We will need to get married shortly or it will become uncomfortable for everyone."

Salomé clasped Octavio's hand over her lap. She giggled once again to herself. "To think, I thought I was going to marry a poor, starving poet and now my future husband might become a screen star!"

Octavio shook his head. "Star? No, perhaps just a small role or two so we can make ends meet. And who knows even how this screen test will go . . . I doubt I have any talent for such things."

The next week, Octavio met Juan Francisco at one of the major film studios in Santiago. Amidst the chaos of the set, he was ushered to an area where three girls were waiting with scripts in hand.

"First, we'll put some makeup on you and take some shots of you alone. Then we'll have you read with some of the girls," Juan Francisco informed him while making small gestures with his hand. As he smiled at Octavio, the brim of his straw hat cast shadows over his already dark complexion.

"Don't forget to read slowly and to make the best of those eyes of yours!" he whispered to his young protégé as Octavio made his way into the makeup chair.

Octavio nodded. He was nervous. His stomach was in knots. If it wasn't for the pressure of having to prove himself to Don Fernando and Doña Olivia, he would never have gotten his nerve up to go through with it.

Luckily, Salomé had practiced with him in the days leading up to his audition. They had taken a copy of Cyrano de Bergerac out of the library and he had rehearsed the lines until they came to him.

"You're a natural at this!" Salomé said in between her girlish giggles. "Who would have known that you had such talent! It's a shame you wrote me those poems and didn't recite them aloud!"

"I will recite them aloud for you anytime you wish, my darling."

She smiled up at him, her complexion radiant from her pregnancy and her unflappable affection for him.

"When I see the camera, I will pretend it is your face," he said poetically. "I will gaze into the lens and pretend it is your eyes I see, your mouth trembling for a kiss, and then I will never suffer from stage fright."

He went over to her and knelt by her side. She ran her fingers through his thick black curls and whispered her unyielding love for him into his small velvet ears.

Now, nearly seven days later, Octavio stood in front of the camera. He held his script between his trembling hands and saw the monstrous camera being wheeled in his direction.

"Start from paragraph one!" the director shouted out to him.

Octavio began tentatively. Yet, somehow even before he uttered his second stanza of lines, his nervousness vanished. His limbs stopped shaking. It was as if he were in the garden alone with his beloved Salomé.

His voice became strong and his lips formed each word perfectly. His eyes were sincere, and through the camera's lens, the planes of his face seemed to both reflect and radiate light. He appeared sensual, lithe, and full of grace. Gestures came to him without his thinking, as if he were moved by a spirit not his own. The character of the lovesick hero seemed made for him. His eyes captured the depth and despair for which the director had been searching, but had yet to find.

Octavio mesmerized the entire set. When the director yelled "Cut," every person on the soundstage remained quiet.

The rest was history. From that moment on, Octavio Ribeiro was billed as Chile's Cary Grant. The nation's new leading man. Their next rising star.

The young man who had once stood alone in the orange grove waiting for his love to join him, now stood alone on a movie set with an airbrushed sunset in the background. Microphones dangled from the ceiling and a camera zoomed in on his expressive face, as Octavio recited the lines he had memorized only minutes before.

Eleven

Santiago, Chile
March 1966

$\mathcal{T}$wo weeks after he signed his first contract with the studio, Octavio and Salomé married in a small ceremony in the chapel of her grandfather's hacienda. Salomé wore a high-waisted gown with a square neckline, a lace mantilla cascading down her shoulders, a garland of lemon blossoms in her dark, black hair.

Before they were wed, they exchanged gifts. He had given her a book filled with the pictures of the Fayum, the ancient Egyptians who painted their eyes with thick, black lines of kohl. He had nicknamed her "my Fayum" because of her long almond eyes, the dark brown irises, and thick black lashes. When she gazed upon him, she looked quite simply like an Egyptian princess. The night before their marriage, she had given him a book of poems by the Roman poet Catullus and promised to perfect her Latin so that she could translate the poems for him when they lay in each other's arms.

He swore they would live a life of love, the child in her belly there to remind them of their eternal vows. They would live simply and poetically. Their union never to be broken, their eternal bond forever sealed.

He had not wanted his job to change what they already had. He did not want to change himself. But somehow he feared that the wheels of his destiny were already in motion and there was little he could do to slow it down.

The studio had signed him to a three-movie contract, and all of his roles would be the same—that of the romantic hero, driven to capture the heart of the woman he was cast to love.

With the money from his first film, *Buenos Dias Soledad,* Octavio purchased a huge house for his pregnant wife on the outskirts of Santiago that the previous owners, two spinster sisters named Maria and Magda, had painted red. On the day they finalized the sale, the elder sister, Maria, approached the young couple and begged them never to repaint the house, for the sisters had painted it vermilion as a symbol of their unrequited loves. Octavio agreed, hoping to give the two now wizened women some peace in their old age. And even though the house had faded in color over the years, so that it was more a faded pink than a vibrant red, Octavio upheld his promise and even affectionately renamed the house La Casa Rosa.

Uninterested in taming things that were meant to grow wild, Salomé was far less diligent in maintaining the sisters' garden. The lush and intricately planned yard that the spinsters had cultivated over the years had fallen upon two owners who had no patience for weeding or planting new bulbs. While it had once bloomed different flowers each season, peonies in the summer, dahlias in the fall, the garden soon grew like an enchanted forest with untamed vines wrapping over the fence and fruit trees overloaded with unpicked bounties.

Living in such bohemian and lush surroundings, Salomé found her creative energies heightened during the last months of her pregnancy. She painted one of the upstairs bedrooms yellow, using the saffron threads she used to tint her paella as her inspiration. She crocheted white curtains with outlines of elephants and giraffes into the intricately woven pattern.

Doña Olivia brought the cradle in which she had rocked her own daughter, and Salomé painted it with lemon leaves and lemon fruit, inspired by her own garden, which was now fragrant with the scent of verbena and rose.

At night, when Octavio returned home exhausted from the studio, his eyes dark with fatigue and his jaw tired from rehearsing his lines, he still had time to hold Salomé in his arms and stroke her full belly underneath her long, white nightgown.

He would bring her head between his two brown hands and kiss her delicately on the mouth.

"My precious Fayum," he would whisper to her. "Tell me our love will be forever."

"Our love will be forever, my darling," she would whisper back to him. She would turn her brown eyes up to his, her delicate lashes fluttering in the moonlit room.

And then he would sigh. His naked chest rising and falling in small undulations. "One day this house will be filled with children and you and I will grow old together."

"Yes," she would say. Salomé knew these were her husband's nightly musings. The affirmations he needed to maintain his hectic schedule of filming and rehearsing.

Octavio hated talking about his daily activities. His hours were spent meeting various publicists, managers, and impatient producers. It embarrassed him. And Salomé sensed his tension. She herself was dreading the completion of his first film, for she knew that once the studio began its promotion, she and her husband would have even less time to themselves.

They each agreed to make the most of their weekends when he was not busy with work at the studio. Octavio suggested that they scatter some vegetable seeds in the garden in the hope that they might have a small harvest to coincide with the birth of their first child. He mixed a sack of tomato and squash seeds and carried his pregnant wife through their already blossoming backyard—encouraging her to throw the seeds into the air.

"You're ridiculous, Octavio," she giggled as he walked over the vines of wild strawberries and petunias. He was holding her tightly in his arms and pressing his nose into her thick mane of hair.

"You smell better than all the roses in our garden," he said.

"Octavio," she giggled again, as she withdrew another fistful of seeds. "Do you think they'll grow?"

"Of course they'll grow, my little Fayum."

He stood still for a moment before letting Salomé down. He placed her on her feet so that she now stood in the middle of the garden. Behind her the branches of the large fig and avocado trees framed her delicate face. "This is fertile ground here," he said as he tapped her belly with the back of his hand and smiled.

"I want to sit here and watch the sunset with you," she whispered as she placed the burlap sack of vegetable seeds by her toes.

That evening Octavio smoothed out a large blanket in the middle of their garden. He took Salomé in his arms and brought her close to his chest. And as the sky turned pink and gold, the sun sliding into the Andes, he told her again and again how much he loved her.

They fell asleep to the sound of the crickets. And when they awakened, they were struck by the glimmer of the stars, the fireflies circling above, and the light of each other's eyes, radiant in the night.

Twelve

❧

Santiago, Chile
July 1966

*U*nable to get away from the set in time, Octavio missed the birth of his first child. Doña Olivia and Don Fernando accompanied their daughter to La Clinica Santa Maria in Santiago and waited nervously in the waiting room as the hours passed and Salomé went through the pains of labor.

Before traveling by car to the clinic, Doña Olivia had telephoned her son-in-law to tell him that the baby was on the way. The studio assistant told her that Octavio was in the middle of a shoot and that he would get there as soon as the last scene was completed to the director's satisfaction.

Octavio didn't arrive, however, until the following morning; wearing his clothes from the previous day, unshaven and weary, he came to Salomé's bedside, carrying a bouquet of pink and white peonies.

"I'm sorry, Fayum . . . I couldn't get away."

Salomé nodded, trying hard to fight back her tears. Unable to look at Octavio, she gazed down at their infant son, who was now nursing at her breast. "I named him Rafael," she whispered as she nursed the tiny boy.

"God heals all," Octavio said, acknowledging that he remembered the significance of the name's meaning. "He's beautiful."

Octavio reached down to caress the child's forehead. "Just like his mother . . ."

"Please, don't . . . Octavio," Salomé whispered. She knew if she spoke any more, she wouldn't be able to restrain herself. Her eyes were still red from exhaustion and she knew if she told Octavio how truly disappointed she was, she would be unable to stop her tears.

She wanted to tell him that she couldn't remember the last time they had held hands, that those nights they had fallen asleep in the garden, under the canopy of stars, seemed like ages ago. She wondered if he had even noticed that their garden now had patches of tomatoes and squash. They had appeared only weeks before, but she had been unable to pick them herself because of bed rest. She imagined now that the vegetables were spoiling on their vines.

She wanted to ask him where his priorities were now. She wanted to chastise him for not getting away from his silly movie and coming to her side, as he had always promised. But she had known for quite some time that their child's birth was coinciding with the final scenes of the movie and that her husband could not control his schedule, let alone the direction of his life, at this moment.

It was just that she missed him and the way things had been only a year before. She had dreamt that when their child was born, he would be only steps outside the delivery room.

Now, as their life was changing so quickly, she was yearning for something to be constant between them.

"My love is constant," he had told her time and time again as she voiced her concern and her desire for her poet to return.

"Can't we at least get away for a weekend before the baby comes?" she had asked him more than once.

"This will only be for a short time, Fayum," he had said, trying to comfort her. "After the film wraps, we'll get away . . . just the two of us."

But she knew that those were naive words. Octavio was committed to at least two more movies after *Buenos Dias Soledad*. And she would have their baby by then. No longer would it be "just the two of us."

"We will plant an orange grove," he promised her as he drifted off to sleep. "I will write more poems when I have more free time," he whispered.

She never said aloud that she knew that it would never happen. That she could already anticipate the responsibilities of motherhood and foresee how he would respond to the responsibilities of fatherhood.

Somehow the pressures of life had caught up with these two people who had always believed they were destined for an uncomplicated life grounded simply on love.

But whereas Salomé could see the decisions that Octavio was making would affect their relationship, her husband seemed to still maintain his idealism that, one day, all would return to the way things were when they had first courted. She thought him naive, but well-intentioned. She only hoped he would not wake up one day and regret he had taken a path on which there were consequences he was ill-prepared to bear.

Thirteen

❧

*S*amuel Rudin hadn't been prepared for the Scandinavian winter. He missed the Peruvian sun. He missed the mountains. He hated rising in the morning and seeing darkness. Nearly every night, as he lay in his bed, his eyes closed shut and his fists clenched to his sides, he shivered himself to sleep. In his mind, he counted down the days until midsummer.

His apartment, a modest place cloistered in the old town, along the south side of the Göta River, was lonely and sparse. And when he returned there from seeing his patients, political refugees who had come to Sweden hoping for a better life, he would boil himself a cup of hot water, stir in a spoonful of Nescafé, and slouch into his sofa. Often, he would find his mind wandering back to his few memories of Paris, the long boat ride to Peru, the deterioration of his mother's mental health, and the depression that hung over his family like a wide bolt of mourning cloth. He saw his life like the pieces of a jigsaw puzzle, certain events disjointed from the main configuration. He frequently did not know what to do with the memories whose edges were not smooth and neat, the ones that didn't fit snugly into the picture he wanted to have in his head.

He had gone through psychoanalysis in school, where the roles were reversed and he was forced to be the patient. At first, he could not detach himself from the doctor within. He could hear himself answering the questions in a way that would reveal little of himself, as he was afraid that he might say something that might flag him as a poor candidate for the psychiatry residency. But after a few sessions his analyst told him that it was in his best interest to be honest with himself. "Every student believes he can outsmart his shrink," he told Samuel through a thick Baltimore accent. "But believe me, if you are truly interested in psychiatry, you will reach down and reflect on your own life and the reasons behind all of your choices. In the end, it will make you a better doctor, I assure you."

At first, it was hard for Samuel to talk about his childhood. There were events that he had pushed out of his memory, such as the time when he was nine and had returned home hungry from school. Having been unable to find one of the maids, he went in search of his mother only to find her slicing small lacerations into her wrists.

The family villa in Miraflores was not particularly large. Its grandest feature was the spiral stairwell that began in the modest vestibule and wrapped to the second-floor landing, where the family bedchambers were hidden behind heavy teak doors. Down the long corridor to the left was Samuel's parents' room; he had walked there quietly, thinking that perhaps his mother, who often slept during the afternoon, was asleep.

He remembered that he found the door ajar, that he pushed it open quietly, careful not to disturb his mother's slumber. But he did not find her in her tall, canopied bed as he imagined, but rather at her dressing stand. Her robe carelessly off one shoulder, her back bent like an archer's bow over a pair of frail, shaking hands.

In his memory, he sees her in profile. She, in front of her rosewood vanity, the three-paneled mirror reflecting her in a kaleidoscope of angles. Her black hair, now lined with silver, piled behind a pink scarf that is wrapped tightly around her small, delicate head.

He realizes now, as he withdraws into his memory, that he has always believed that his mother was the most beautiful creature. That he could accept her mental deterioration far more easily than the waning of her physical charms. She would always be that beautiful Frenchwoman in his mind, with perfect lipstick—the one with the black velvet suit and the white satin cuffs. Not the one dependent on sleeping pills, not the one who now wore oversize house-coats. The one of Paris, long ago.

But now, the memory of his standing at the threshold and see-ing his mother's spine twisting beneath the satin robe like the brittle branch of an ancient oak tree, her perfume bottles scattered over the tabletop and the drawers in disarray, returned.

"What did you see?" the therapist asks Samuel.

"I didn't see anything until she turned around and looked at me. Her face was all streaked with running makeup, her breast only barely covered by the quilted collar of her robe. In one hand, I saw Father's razor blade. In the other, I saw a small river of blood run-ning from her wrist.

"I don't believe she was trying to kill herself, I think she was only trying to release her pain."

Samuel winced. "I remember that when the doctor came, he bandaged Mother up and sedated her. I overheard him speaking with Father, telling him that the family was lucky this time, that she was trying to signal for help."

"And did she receive help?"

Samuel was quiet for a few moments. The vinyl sofa was begin-ning to feel sticky beneath him. The therapy was exhausting him.

"No." He paused and let out a deep sigh. "Father believed that this kind of 'help' was better kept between the family and the ser-vants. He was afraid of the stigma it might bring upon the family."

The doctor wiggled his pencil in the air. "How does your father feel about your decision to go into psychiatric medicine?"

"He's indifferent, I suppose."

"Indifferent?"

"Well, our relationship has been strained since my mother passed away. Since I didn't join my two brothers in the family busi-ness back in Peru, I think he feels there is little he can talk to me about.

"I don't want to make textiles and worry about whether a ship-ment is going to arrive on time or production costs are on sched-ule," Samuel said as he readjusted himself on the couch. "I find that tedious and boring. I want to help people. It's as simple as that."

"Simple?" his analyst questioned him, trying to evoke some self-reflection in this young psychiatry resident. "I think the reason that you are interested in helping people, especially considering your family background, is anything but simple."

Those days of sitting on the analyst's couch were over, and finally Samuel found himself where he'd always wanted to be—with a practice that was devoted to helping victims of war. Most of his patients had come to Sweden from volatile political climates such as in Algeria and Czechoslovakia. Some of the older ones were Polish Jews who had spent the past twenty-five years speaking to no one, not even their children, of their time in the camps. Somewhere deep inside, he hoped he might meet a French Jew—someone who might know what had happened to his maternal grandparents and his uncle's family, as if this knowledge would somehow appease something deep within him. Something that he knew had quietly destroyed his mother.

But Samuel had no such luck. The immigrant community was small, and most of his patients were more recent survivors from countries he had never even visited.

He realized that one never gets used to hearing stories of torture. Yet, the strength of the human spirit continued to amaze him. He learned to trust his intuition and to guide his patients back into memories that had often been shut for years.

Just by looking at the face of a new patient, Samuel could often gauge the extent of his or her torture. Ironically, the women who looked the most placid, the most vacant, were usually his most troubled victims. They were the ones who held everything deep within, speaking not one word of their vicious torture, the rapes, they had kept secret for years. If he had stuck them with a needle, they wouldn't have uttered a sound. That was how deep the pain was for them.

In a white-walled room, with a few small paintings of innocuous landscapes that were meant to calm, he sat and spoke with them. He spoke five languages, French, Spanish, English, German, and his Swedish, which, though not perfect, was getting better. Mostly, he was there to listen. But he was also there to steer them through their memories, so they could get on with their lives and learn to reconcile the atrocities of their past.

At first, he was skeptical about the position. He spoke limited

Swedish and knew little of the customs or the land. But upon his arrival, and after his first few days on the job, Samuel realized that his foreignness was an advantage. When an immigrant walked into the room and saw that the doctor too was an outsider, he or she relaxed.

There was absolutely no way Samuel, a very Sephardic-looking Jew, could be mistaken for a Swede. He had inherited his parents' dark looks. His skin was olive, his hair black, and his thin, narrow face had a natural intensity to it.

In Peru, he blended in with the local coloring, although the natives' features were far more Indian than typical Spanish. In Sweden, he felt like a shadow walking the streets, his curly hair bobbing in an ocean of blond. His prominent brow, his wide, dark eyes, and small, curved nose often making him feel self-conscious. The few weeks he had spent in Stockholm had been an entirely different experience for him. There, he discovered students from almost every country congregating in the streets, the cafés, the energy escalating, and the leftist philosophies floating through the air.

But in Göteborg, it was quiet. The cafés were filled with couples drinking tea and eating small cakes, the bars filled with businessmen and their sons. Samuel rarely went out after work, instead choosing to return home and drink his Nescafé in solitude.

One Sunny afternoon, Samuel found himself noticing a beautiful young woman not far from the city park. He had brought with him one of his medical journals and a brown bag of seed to feed the birds. She was sitting quietly by herself, a slender girl wrapped in a blue velvet scarf.

Samuel sat down next to her. The bone-gray pigeons at his feet poked around his heavy brown shoes, the birdseed having clustered around the bench.

"You should have thrown the seeds farther," she said as she turned to him.

Samuel stammered at the sight of the girl's bright green eyes. *"Du har rätt...,"* he tried to muster in his broken Swedish. "You are right, I should have."

She giggled as she rearranged her scarf, bringing it down closer to her chin and revealing her white hair, her face red from the wind.

He noticed that she had a sketchbook nestled on her other side and he inquired if she was an artist.

"I'm a graduate student," she said shyly. "I'm majoring in fine arts."

He leaned over and tried to stretch his neck in the direction of her sketchpad, hoping that she would open it and show him what she was working on.

He could see her hands twitching in her lap, each finger gloved in soft wool.

"I often come here to draw. I sometimes stumble across an interesting face or an unusual posture that I couldn't get with a model in class." She pointed to a small child sitting a few feet from his mother, who was reclining in a folding chair. "I could never find a child playing so naturally unless I sat here."

She took a stub of charcoal out from her pencil case and sketched the outline of the crouching boy. In a few abbreviated lines she had captured the arc of his back, the extension of his hand as he grasped a few blades of grass.

"Perhaps I could buy you a cup of coffee after you're finished sketching?" Samuel asked.

She agreed on the condition that afterward he would allow her to draw his portrait.

Over coffee, she withdrew her sketchpad and showed him its contents.

Samuel studied each page carefully. There were sketches executed entirely in vine charcoal, and there were detailed, labor-intensive drawings that were done in pencil. But his favorite was her self-portrait.

It was undoubtedly her. He could see the face as clearly as she was there sitting across from him. She had re-created the shape of her face perfectly, the high cheekbones, the sharp, intense eyes. But what he found particularly intriguing was how she had portrayed herself. She had clearly given herself the physical attributes of a woman, but she had contrasted those qualities with accessories that seemed meant for a child. For one thing, the coat she drew herself in was the kind a young girl might wear: the small notched collar, the four round buttons—two in each row—and the flared bottom. And instead of her clutching a handbag or a purse, she had drawn herself with a small, old-fashioned suitcase. One that was too small for an adult. And over the pencil shading, she had colored the suitcase completely in red.

Samuel touched the corner of the drawing and looked back at the slender woman sitting across from him.

"This one is my favorite," he said as he tapped his finger against the page.

She seemed to stiffen as he spoke of the drawing, as if by speaking of the portrait he was touching something inside her that she didn't want to be disturbed.

After several seconds of silence between them, she took the pad from him and closed it. "You have a sensitive eye; no one has ever commented on that drawing before. Not even my adviser."

"I'm drawn to things that have stories behind them."

She fidgeted. Trying to change the subject to something less personal, she took out her pencil case and placed it on the table.

"You promised that if I had coffee with you, you'd sit for me."

"Well, I have every intention of keeping my promise. Just tell me what I'm supposed to do." Samuel paused. "And, of course, you'll need to tell me your name."

"I'm Kaija Sorenson." She extended her hand to him.

"I'm honored to meet you, Kaija. I'm Samuel Rudin."

She smiled at him sweetly. "Well, Samuel, I need you to stay perfectly still."

Samuel laughed. "You might find a better model in that child over there." He turned and pointed to a young baby sleeping in a carriage near the entrance to the café.

"No, I intend to draw you," she said as she withdrew her pencil from her small aluminum case.

She traced him in outline at first. Choosing to portray him in profile, his chin slightly bowed.

Nearly half an hour later, she folded her arms against her chest and shook her head. "It's not right." She tore the page from her pad and crumpled it into a ball. "I'll need to start over again."

Samuel stretched his back for a second. "This modeling isn't easy work, you know. You'll have to promise me that you'll join me for dinner before I sit for another session."

Kaija giggled. "Very well. But this time, let's try it with you sitting directly across from me."

Samuel readjusted his chair.

"Yes, exactly, this way I can see your features more clearly."

In this position Samuel could stare at Kaija without difficulty. "I could get used to this," he flirted.

She looked up from above the edge of her sketchbook and smiled. And he imagined her as a young girl in that notch-collared coat, the tiny leather suitcase resting against her knees, and wondered what sort of stories this beautiful young woman might have packed tightly within.

Fourteen

❦

Göteborg, Sweden
April 1969

𝓕inally, Samuel had someone to share his free moments with. His first winter in Sweden was beginning to give way to spring and he rejoiced at the sight of the budding tulips. Since their initial meeting in the park, Kaija and he had begun to spend nearly all their free time with each other.

Before meeting her, Samuel hadn't realized how lonely he had been. Now, with her, he felt like a man reborn. He planned decadent evenings to counterbalance his difficult workdays. He made reservations at expensive restaurants that he would never have thought of eating at before. He took her stargazing and he made love to her on his balcony, not caring if the neighbors saw them or were awakened by the noise.

When he was alone, he longed for her. When he was with her, he could think of nothing else but ways to postpone her departure. He imagined himself nestled beside her, holding her birdlike face close to his (did she remind him of a tiny swallow?), her thin fingers buried in his dark curls.

They would arrange to meet several times during the week, but even that seemed too little for him. Often, he ordered extra courses at the restaurant because Kaija was so thin and frail that he wanted to make sure that she always had enough to eat the next day.

He loved to look at her, and during brief moments when her

eyes were downward and averted to the rim of her soup bowl or to a pedestrian on the street, he was unable to control the intensity of his gaze.

He had never seen a woman as luminous as she. It gave her a fragile appearance, making her appear far younger than she was. A small gazellelike creature with delicate bones and haunting eyes.

Some things, however, Samuel knew he had to get used to. From the first time he saw the tiny wooden crucifix around her neck, he was overcome by waves of nausea. Such religious symbols had an almost innate capacity to unnerve him. Only after they became more intimate with each other did he reach over and handle it from underneath her blouse, the wooden angles smooth and neat in his hand.

"It was from my mother," she told him, and he thought it strange that she was now whispering to him.

She fingered the crucifix in her thin, pale fingers before slipping it back into her blouse.

"It is one of the only things I have from my Finnish family. A crucifix and a prayer book. I never take the necklace off, even though I'm not religious at all."

He noticed that the leather cord from which it dangled seemed cracked and worn. It wasn't a particularly attractive piece of jewelry, he thought, trying to be objective without his own religious bias. The crucifix was heavy and masculine, almost peasantlike. Nevertheless, he felt that her sentimentality toward it was sweet and endearing.

"I'm what they call a Finnish war child," she said in a tiny, flat voice. They had been sitting in the park for some time now, and in the moonlight, she seemed even more waiflike than usual. Her thin, blond hair was pulled back in a loose bun, and her green eyes were wide with concentration.

"It's a dreadful name, isn't it? But that's what they call us, a footnote in the history books: 'Over seventy thousand of Finland's children were sent to Sweden during the war for safety and the prospect of a better childhood,' " Kaija mimicked. But her face suddenly became serious again. "You know, nearly all of the children were returned to their original families when the war ended, but not me."

He clutched her mitten-clad hand close to his.

"I suppose I did return once, but it was only temporary. Not a 'real' return." She sighed and pressed her nose into his shoulder. Clouds of steam circled from her mouth.

"That is a long story, best saved for another night." She looked up at him and managed a faint smile.

He nodded to her gently and extended his hand.

"Let's go home," she said.

She rose from the bench and Samuel was once again struck by how tiny Kaija was in contrast to him. Her small head measured to his shoulder. He slipped his large hand into hers and pointed out the beauty of the city's lights.

"I've never really cared much for the city life," she whispered as she clutched tightly to his arm. "I suppose I prefer the forest and the lakes. . . ." Her voice began to trail. "Especially in winter when they're encrusted in a shell of ice."

Fifteen

⤜❈⤛

Santiago, Chile
November 1966

Neither Octavio or Salomé could ever have anticipated the success of *Buenos Dias Soledad.*

"Never before have we seen an actor that brings such sensuality, such psychological intensity, to his character," the critics in *El Mercurio* raved. "We are blessed to have a face that can reveal the Chilean soul!" boasted the reviewers on the radio.

Overnight there were fan clubs established in his honor, billboards splashed with his image, and invitations to one event after another.

The radio advertisers begged him to make commercials; women stood outside the gates of his set waiting for his car to pull up and threw themselves in the path of the limousine. Nearly a week after the film's debut, the studios offered him another contract for six more films at a salary that he could never ever in his wildest dreams have thought possible.

"What should I do?" he asked his wife, who was busy with their infant son. Rafael had begun teething early, and even though she now had the assistance of a housekeeper, she was teetering on the edge of exhaustion.

"I can't answer that for you, Octavio. I've always believed that we are each responsible for ourselves in this life. You must decide what path you want to create for yourself."

"I have you and the child to think about, Salomé. This life is not limited to just me."

"After the royalties from this film are divided, after you finish wrapping the other two films in your contract, we should have enough money to last for several years."

"I'm not sure about that," Octavio said, scratching his head. He was easily overwhelmed by the topic of money. He had no idea how much money was necessary to keep his family living in the means he himself had never had as a child.

"I'm sure my success will just be temporary. Perhaps I have just two or three years before I am replaced."

Octavio was trying to be realistic. He was trying to convince himself that this roller-coaster life couldn't last. He hoped that eventually the decision would be made for him—that his career would eventually reach a point where there were no more movies to be made and he could return to a life of poetry without feeling guilty.

Now, however, he just wanted to make sure his family had financial security. He needed to feel that he was indisputably a "good provider" and that Salomé's father would utter his name with respect, not with the contempt that he knew he had spoken of him when they had first met.

And so Octavio did sign the second contract. He got up every morning and kissed his wife on the cheek, only to come home late every night, weary and exhausted. He tried to keep a low profile in his newfound fame, doing only the interviews that the studios demanded and attending only the premieres of the movies that he was part of. But sometimes he could not avoid commitments and several days would pass before he'd be able to return to the Casa Rosa.

Six months after *Buenos Dias Soledad* opened, his second film, *Escapando de un Sueño* premiered. Again, the reviews were spectacular and the attendance in the theaters unprecedented.

Still, Octavio remained unsatisfied by his success. He hated saying lines that he didn't believe in. He detested rehearsing the same scene over and over only because one of his colleagues had forgotten to memorize his or her lines.

Some days, when he was reduced to sitting around in his studio chair, he would fantasize about his life as it had been when he was a student. He was barely twenty-two now, yet his existence as it had been when he was inscribing poems by candlelight seemed like ages ago.

His nights with Salomé remained the highlight of his day. In between scenes he would always try to squeeze in a brief telephone conversation with his wife, because Octavio was well aware that by nine o'clock, when he usually arrived home, she would be so tired from taking care of their infant son.

Still, she would allow him to hold her to his chest and to stroke her long black hair. If Rafael was sleeping soundly, sometimes he would take the Victrola upstairs, turn the volume down low, and extend his hand to her sweetly so that they could dance a tango or two in the privacy of their bedroom.

Salomé knew that the endless hours her husband spent on the set were wearing him down. And she had grown used to his reluctance to speak of it. But she also felt that it had been his choice to sign the extended contract.

Still, she hated seeing him so tired and unhappy.

Octavio tried to make the best of the characters he was assigned to play. The movies he starred in mimicked the psychological dramas being imported from France and Italy. "They're second-rate scripts," Octavio complained. "The European writers aren't concerned with this ridiculous romantic melodrama!" he grumbled to Salomé over his morning coffee and *churro*.

The females he was cast against were caricatures. Written as one-dimensional characters whose only purpose was to show off the prowess and emotional fortitude of the leading man, whom Octavio was invariably cast as. Their physical appearance was uninteresting to him. Their black hair was never as lustrous nor as thick as Salomé's. Their eyes were flat and devoid of the depth that he had recognized in his wife's from atop a balcony twenty-five meters away.

The plots were silly and inane to Octavio. He had just received the script for his third film, *Siempre Carmen*, in which he was to play the object of an older woman's affection.

He knew that he was blocking off his wife from his daily life. He knew that even after her exhausting day with their infant son, she still tried to make a few hours available so she could dote on him.

But he had been unable to open up and tell her how he truly felt about the direction his life was heading. He thought such complaining might appear unmanly. Hadn't men suffered for generations in jobs that were far less glamorous than his? And hadn't they toiled for wages that were far less lucrative? He knew, in one way, he should be grateful because now Salomé and Rafael would want for nothing. In a few months' time, as his contract began paying out his royalties, there would be little that he could not give his family. Even if he wasn't intellectually satisfied, he had to find some contentment in the fact that no one, not even Dr. Herrera, could say that he hadn't provided them with the best life possible.

Sixteen

❦

Santiago, Chile
January 1970

*A*s Octavio's career became more demanding, and Salomé became pregnant with her second, then her third child, she would often seek the comforts of her family's hacienda during the summer. The house, situated just outside Talca, had been owned by the family for centuries, and Salomé loved to go there and breathe the fresh air and spend time with her mother.

The train from Santiago to Talca was not a long journey, but Salomé always prepared small sandwiches and tea cakes for Rafael and his younger sisters, Blanca and Isabelle. They sat with their noses pressed to the glass, their childlike wonder reflected in the brass railings of the train's passenger compartment.

Their grandmother would wait for them at the platform. Her unusual, natural blond hair twisted like a *churro,* her face shaded by the brim of her broad straw hat. Rafael was old enough to run to her, to bury his cheek into her side, and smell the scent of marzipan that always clung sweetly in the basin of her palms.

The Herrera family had maintained the same carriage for over a hundred years, and Salomé could not help but smile at the joy on Rafael's face when he saw it waiting there at the station for them. She had been the same way when she was a child.

The carriage had been cared for over the years like a family jewel. The forest green exterior sparkled, the black canvas top had been polished and tightened to perfection. But it was the inside that Rafael adored the most.

The interior of the carriage was the color of crushed marigolds. Thick, yellow leather upholstery that smelled of polish and the hide's natural oils. When the driver hoisted Rafael's tiny body deep inside, his heart soared. Here, he felt like a king. His father would be joining the family in a week's time, so he was the man of the family for the brief time until the carriage reached the hacienda. His grandmother, mother, and two small sisters surrounded him and busied themselves with their female chatter. But he, with the damask ceiling above his head, and the narrow window close to his face, was steeped in wonder.

The roads leading to the estate were narrow and unpaved. Country roads where the dirt kicked up from beneath the carriage's wheels like clouds of brown steam. The women's heads bobbed back and forth, their shoulders sliding into one another, their knees rocking to each side. But Rafael adored it. He could feel each rock crushing underneath the carriage's wheels, he could hear the rhythm of the horse's footsteps, he could see the mountains and the shore beyond.

The hacienda was by far the grandest home he had ever seen, and he secretly wished his grandparents lived there year-round. His great-grandfather Don Isadore was the only one, aside from the servants, who maintained a full-time residence there.

Don Isadore, like his son-in-law, Salomé's father, had also been a doctor. Now ninety-two years old, he was an intimidating figure to the young children. Although he spent the majority of his day laboring over his experiments, cultivating strange, hybrid fruit trees in the garden, he did so while dressed in formal attire. Rafael had no memory of his great-grandfather in anything but a dark black suit, starched white shirt, and one of his many intricate, brocaded vests. Tall and slender as a cat's tail, he maintained an ample head of smooth white hair and full mustache. He seldom spoke, preferring to stare and to nod, as if those gestures were words themselves, interpreted by those who knew him well enough after all these years.

His wife, Salomé's grandmother, had died before Salomé was born. But the house, originally made of stucco and mud walls, still retained a trace of her former presence.

The entrance to the house was marked by tall iron gates, the decorating finials the shape of small, delicate birds. And inside the house, the expansive wooden floor ebbed and flowed like a large chestnut-colored river, the occasional board popping up or bowing like a small, undulating wave. Each room was designed with its own entranceway, usually an arch shaped out of white plaster. Only the room that had been Don Isadore's wife's remained different, for that one had a circular door.

Inside, it remained exactly as the former mistress of the house had left it, with Chinese wallpaper completely covered with images of a thousand birds. In delicate black ink, colored by hand in a palette of pastel hues, every variety of bird imaginable was rendered. Tall, elegant cranes posed on one slender foot, hummingbirds with straight, narrow beaks and rosebud breasts nestled in pale green blades of grass, and dusty brown sparrows all fluttered over washes of delicate blue sky.

The birdcages scattered over the rococo furniture, however, were now empty. The iron baskets with peaked domes and filigreed borders were but a sad reminder of the birds that had once sung to the woman the doctor had loved.

She had been called *pequeña canaria*—"little canary"—by those close to her, as her sitting room was an aviary completely designed by her own hand. She had waited nearly two years for the Chinese wallpaper to arrive, and at night, as she lay down to sleep in her elaborately carved four-poster bed, she would close her eyes and dream of seeing it unrolled for the first time.

She imagined each bird expertly painted. The feathers so real they seemed to rustle off the paper. She envisioned the reams of paper on their voyage across the sea, the rolls carefully packed in silk tissue, boxed in split-bamboo crates. She slept on pale lemon sheets, her hair raven against the dyed cotton. And when she slumbered, the birds from their cages serenaded her with their tiny chirpings, a melody that, until her untimely death, she associated with love.

Rafael had always been fearful of the little canary woman's former bedchamber. He seldom went in there, although he loved to explore the hacienda's other rooms. The heavy brown furniture was sturdy to play on, and he created fortresses in which he could spend hours in endless amusement. But his great-grandmother's room was too foreboding. When he was four years old, his great-aunt came to spend a week at the hacienda. Never married, she reveled in her role as cranky spinster. She dressed only in black woolen clothes, even at the height of summer, her pale, lined face staring down at him from a stiff, satin collar.

At night, she would come into his room and tell him stories. Not stories like his mother or father would tell (his favorite being the one of the uncollected fortune his paternal grandfather had left in Spain). The elderly woman's stories were far more terrifying. Worse yet, she seemed to take great delight in hearing the young Rafael squeal with fear.

She told him how her veins were filled with floating needles from the pins she had swallowed over her years of sewing. She pulled her black crepe sleeve up to her elbow and revealed a stretch of white arm, ribboned with blue veins.

"The needles float through here," she said, pointing to the crosshatch of veins and tiny vessels. In the moonlight that streamed in through his bedroom window, her skin looked so white that it too seemed almost blue.

But her story that frightened him most was of how Don Isadore's late wife had died.

"She was attacked by that which she loved most," his great-aunt whispered into his ear. "Her birds."

Rafael's eyes were now wild with fright, his linen drawn tightly to his chin.

"Your great-grandfather was jealous of those birds, envious of how she spent her days caring for them, feeding them from her palm. One night, after she had rejected his advances of love, he decided to play a cruel joke on her. He waited until she was deep in slumber, then, stealthily as a thief, went to the porcelain container where she kept her specially milled seed and generously sprinkled it all over her hair, her body, and her sheets. Then, he went to the cages, where the birds now slept, opened their doors, and let them fly to her bed.

"Hunger came over them and they knew not whom they were feeding from. As the birds got tangled in her hair and their beaks pecked at her breasts, she awakened suddenly, screaming with fright.

"She died of a heart attack right before your great-grandfather's eyes."

Rafael was shaking. "Can what you say be true?" he asked, fear now beading him with sweat.

"Yes, absolutely," she lied convincingly, her yellow teeth gleaming like a row of corn. "Your great-grandfather was a sneaky little devil. I *should* know. He *is* my brother."

"But what did he do?" Rafael cried. "Why is he not in jail?"

"Ah . . . that is why he is so clever. He swept up all the remaining birdseed and closed the door. When the servants arrived the next morning, they discovered the birds nestled at the mistress's head and fingertips. Her body cold as ice." The old woman looked straight into Rafael's terrified eyes. "They buried her the next day, and Don Isadore ordered the birds to be poisoned and the circular door of her bedchamber forever shut."

Rafael was now upright in his bed. "I hate him!" he shouted. "I will never kiss him hello again!"

"Don't hate him," she whispered to him before standing up from her chair to bid him good night. "It's bad for the soul."

In the moonlight, Rafael's eyes were shining like two round, polished shards of coal.

"And do not fear, dear one," she whispered as she slipped out the door, "*pequeña canaria* has been known to visit him at night. Half woman, half bird, she hovers over his canopy and sings to him in eerie chirps, those haunting, beautiful songs of love."

Even before hearing this ghostly tale, Rafael had been fearful of Don Isadore. Aside from his formal attire and wizened face, he was far too eccentric for the young boy to understand. He spent his days in the orchard where he cultivated strange fruits, creating hybrids the world had never even dreamt of. He tied a sapling of a cherry tree with that of an orange tree and produced fruit similar to a blood orange, the flesh a gleaming red.

He would leave for the orchard before the others had even touched their breakfast, his pocket watch dangling from an intricately patterned vest. With white hair and blue eyes, black coat and sterling-tipped cane, he walked through the fields, nodding to the servants as he went to the place where he would remain for the day completely undisturbed.

He would return at dinnertime, where his daughter, now a

woman in her mid sixties, a grandmother herself, sat at the seat she had once sat in as a child, her own daughter and three grandchildren in the seats surrounding the long Gothic table. The husbands had chosen to remain in the city until August, when they would take two weeks' leave. They too dreaded being in the company of the eerie doctor.

The strangest thing he did, however, that which neither Salomé nor her mother had an answer for, was the ritual Don Isadore performed after every formal meal, a ritual that, according to her and her mother, he had always performed: after every dinner, he summoned his snake.

At the sound of the patriarch's cane hitting the wooden floor, the snake would slide from a tiny hole in the mud wall and slither to his feet. The doctor's pale blue eyes would brighten, and his face would seem to fold into itself as he laughed.

For Rafael, there was nothing more terrifying. He would pull his knees close to his chest, his toes gripping his seat, and close his eyes tightly shut. Salomé and her mother just shook their heads, knowing there was little they could do or say.

The snake would slither around each seat eating the scraps that had fallen to the floor. Then, once it had returned to where Don Isadore sat, he would tap his cane and the snake would quietly retreat into its hole, deep into the wall of the cavernous house.

Still, Rafael loved the hacienda. He loved the animals, the pigs and the hens, the horses and the cows. He loved that there were so many rooms to play in, and that the driver would take him into town in the carriage whenever he had the whim. At the hacienda, his mother allowed him to be spoiled by his grandmother, who cherished him as if he were her own son.

In her room, Doña Olivia secretly kept her own little treasures. Sculpted marzipan, cans of whipped Chantilly cream, peppermint sticks ribboned with green and red. Her furniture was equipped with many drawers that could only be opened by the tiny keys that she kept on a long satin cord underneath her blouse. At nighttime, she would tell Rafael to come to her room, and well into the night, she would feed him sweets taken from tiny wooden compartments.

He learned to appreciate the finest confectionery, turning his nose up at the dime-store variety his classmates often carried with their lunch. He learned from his grandmother that sweets are an art form. To be both colorful and textured, whose flavor was not to be overpowered by sugar, whose packaging was almost as important as taste. The finest candy shops always wrapped their sweets in expensive wrappers, tied them with pretty satin strings, and Rafael could recognize their signature flourishes at a glance. He became his grandmother's protégé and the child she missed the most during the times the family spent apart.

Never would either of them believe that in a few years they would be forced to separate and that Rafael would never be able to spend another summer in his beloved hacienda. Still, Doña Olivia always kept the keys under her blouse and her rosewood chest stocked with marzipan and candies, hoping that one day her daughter's family might return.

S e v e n t e e n

༖

Santiago, Chile
February 1970

$\mathcal{N}$early four years had passed since Octavio's film debut, and in that time he had become a household name in Chile. Now he had money, fame, a wife and three children, and having fulfilled his contract with the studio only a few months before, he had been taking some well-deserved vacation to think about his next career move. Never would he have imagined, however, that, on the one day he was relaxing in the house, his hair uncombed and his face unshaven, Pablo Neruda would arrive unannounced at his front door.

Octavio had been toiling in the garden alone when he heard the bell ring, and as the maid, Consuela, had gone out to the market to fetch the ingredients for that evening's meal and Salomé was busy dressing one of the girls, he brushed off his trousers and went to see who it was.

He opened the large green door and his mouth fell open. Standing on the front porch of the Casa Rosa was the great poet himself, a long black cape shrouding his massive form, a fedora casting a slight shadow over his heavy-hooded eyes.

"Señor Ribeiro?" Neruda asked as he touched slightly the rim of his hat. "I hope I have not come at a time that is inconvenient for you. My name is—"

"Señor Neruda, you need no introduction," Octavio stammered, only because he was temporarily caught off guard by the surprise nature of the bard's visit. "I do not know what possible honor I can attribute your visit to, but please, please come in."

Octavio extended his arm and motioned the poet to enter the family's cluttered vestibule. "I must apologize for my manners. Our maid is out at the moment, but I should know better—can I take your cloak for you?"

Neruda bent his shoulders slightly and untied the silk cords of his cape and handed it to Octavio. The smooth black fabric draped softly in Octavio's hands, and he felt the need to caress the edges, as if to reaffirm to himself that indeed the nation's most beloved figure stood there before him. That his idol had called upon him quite unexpectedly, speaking to him within the very walls of his own house.

"This is quite a home you have here, Señor Ribeiro," observed Neruda as he followed Octavio through the corridors stapled with colorful posters from his movies, past the shelves lined with Salomé's myriad menageries. "Reminds me a little of the one I kept with Matilde when we were living off the coast of Italy."

Octavio smiled, amused that Neruda was drawing a parallel between them. "I'm sure your home was far more orderly than ours. You must excuse the mess. Salomé and I have three small children, and the house and garden seem to run wild, much like them."

"No, no, it's delightful," Neruda said, waving his hand.

Octavio was completely awestruck. He knew that Salomé would be beside herself when she discovered Neruda standing here in their home. She was a devoted fan of Neruda's, ever since that day when Octavio had first copied one of Neruda's poems and slipped it into one of her fallen oranges' navels. Octavio decided it would be best to walk Neruda through the kitchen and into the garden, and to go up and tell her himself so she had time to primp. Once Neruda was in the garden, Octavio would motion for him to sit on one of the old wrought-iron chairs that had belonged to the two spinster sisters, Maria and Magda. Octavio had always imagined them sitting there together, sipping tea and admiring their roses, their backs to their treasured red house and their eyes lost in the greenery they had cultivated with their four delicate hands.

"Is this all right, Señor Neruda?" Octavio asked, as he pulled out one of the chairs. "I will tell my wife that you are here, but she will not believe me. What a surprise! I still do not know what luck has befallen me. This is too incredible for words."

A subtle smile came over Neruda's lips and he tipped his head slightly and lifted his palm.

"Perhaps it is better if you and I speak privately before you call the madame. As much as I would have liked this to be a purely social call, I have, sadly, come in the guise of business." The old poet silenced himself for a moment. "Perhaps *business* is the wrong word. *Politics* is more accurate. I have come on behalf of the Social Democratic Party, on behalf of my compatriot Salvador Allende."

"Allende?" Octavio was shocked. He pulled over a chair and sat down abruptly. "What interest would you all have in me? I'm a movie actor," he said, revealing his own embarrassment. "I have never even voted."

Neruda's thin smile returned and his thick eyelids ebbed over his watery pupils. He nodded as Octavio spoke.

"I am sorry to hear that you have never voted, as you must realize that I have devoted much of my life not only to my poetry but also to fight for every Chilean's right to partake in fair, democratic elections. But I am not here to lecture you, Señor Ribeiro. I am here to beseech your help."

Octavio was stunned. "My help?"

"Yes, you have something of which most men would be envious. You probably are completely oblivious to it, but anyone who watches your films—and I happen to be a secret admirer, I might add—is fully captivated by you."

"I'm not sure I am following you, Señor Neruda. Captivated?"

"You are a master of eloquence and fluidity. Your inflection is melodious. When you speak, people listen. When you gaze into the camera, neither men nor women can resist staring back at you. It is the root of your success, comrade! You are a genius on the screen."

Octavio was in complete shock. The former literature student was now sitting in his garden with the nation's most revered poet, whose poems he had used to court Salomé years ago. The hero of his youth was complimenting Octavio on *his* craft! If people, even in passing, had told him that they had heard Neruda was a fan of his films, he would not have believed them. But, here, Neruda was not only telling him that he had seen Octavio on the screen, but also that he marveled at his talents.

"But what does Allende have to do with all of this?"

"Ah, yes, that is the root of my visit. Allende."

"I am not sure what he would need from a man in my position," Octavio mused, "but ask me whatever is on your mind. In many ways—my wife would be very embarrassed if I told you why—I owe you more than I can ever say. If I can help, I will."

Neruda smiled and relaxed back into his chair. "Well, I am not sure if you are aware, Señor Ribeiro, but there will be presidential elections this year and Allende will be running for the fourth time."

"Yes, we have heard rumors about that."

"Well, it is no longer a rumor, but a fact. Allende will run, and hopefully, this time, he will win. I believe in the man, I always have. Honest, decent men such as he are rare in this world. In the political arena, they are even more of an endangered species. However, we all know that Allende is not a politician by formal training. He has had a distinguished career as both a doctor and a lawyer, and thus, sometimes, certain intricacies that might come naturally to a more glib, overpolished politician evade him. You see, Señor Ribeiro, Allende has always been more concerned with the future of our nation and the plight of the worker than about himself and his own image."

"Yes . . ."

"And, well, I believe that this election might be the last one he will run in. Therefore it is necessary that the party take all the necessary arrangements to ensure his success."

"Yes . . ."

"Well, to speak quite frankly, a few of us closest to Salvador believe that television will play a major role in this year's elections. For the first time in our history, the political speeches of each candidate will be nationally broadcast. It is not my intention to imply that Don Salvador is not an eloquent speaker. Some of the speeches he made in the city center or on top of the tower on Santa Lucía Hill are deeply embedded in my mind. They are the passionate songs of a man with conviction. But on television a man must be more subdued, his gesticulations less wild. His elocution carefully manicured. Little problems such as a slight stuttering of speech or a nervous tic in the eye must be kept at bay." Neruda smiled. "We hope we have learned something from the Kennedy-Nixon debates. My American friends tell me that Señor Nixon's wolfish appearance in a television debate cost him the election ten years ago. If only it had happened the second time as well, but that is another story.

"In any event, that is why I have come to you, Señor Ribeiro, for assistance. I believe you are the best, and the party needs you to coach their most cherished candidate just a little. Perhaps only eight to ten sessions at the most."

Octavio was dumbfounded. He could not believe his ears.

"You want me to help Dr. Allende with his speeches?"

"With his *delivery* of his speeches, Señor Ribeiro. You, more than anyone, must know how the camera can be unkind to a man who is not used to the lens. Otherwise, if everyone had your talents, you'd be out of a job!"

Octavio ran his fingers through his hair. "It certainly is an intriguing offer, and I am overwhelmingly flattered that you have come to me, Señor Neruda." He still could not believe that someone as intelligent and as worldly as Pablo Neruda would have seen any of his films. He had always thought his work embarrassingly melodramatic.

Octavio was just about to ask Neruda a question when he suddenly heard Salomé's voice calling him from upstairs. He did not answer at first because he had not yet thought of a suitable explanation for why the great poet was now sitting on their slightly rusty iron chairs in their garden. But, before he knew it, Salomé was calling for him again.

"Octavio! Octavio!" she hollered. Then, suddenly the upstairs window flung open. He looked up above and saw her cascade of long black hair hanging over the side and her small, round face peering down at him and his guest.

"Who in heaven's name do you have down there with you?"

"Pablo Neruda, my love."

"Very funny. Who is it?"

"Pablo Neruda, my love."

Neruda looked up at her and waved.

Octavio would never forget that look of shock on Salomé's face when she came running down in her housecoat, her hair full and her face without makeup, and found the cherished poet sitting there beside him. It was an utterly priceless memory for him.

"Oh my God!" she squealed as she covered her mouth and a deep blush swept over her face. "It can't be! It just cannot be!"

"It is indeed, madame," Neruda said as he stood up, took off his hat, and bowed slightly at the knees. "So pleased to make your acquaintance, dearest lady," said Neruda with a genteel formality and innate sparkle that echoed an earlier time. "I see that a movie star such as Señor Ribeiro has a starlet of his own at home."

Salomé could not help but smile back at Neruda, and Octavio could tell immediately that his wife was smitten with the old poet's charms. "You must excuse me, Señor Neruda," Salomé begged, "I had no idea that you were arriving. My husband told me nothing of your visit." She gave a quick fierce look at her husband, to signal to him that he would be receiving her wrath later that evening.

"He knew nothing of my visit," Neruda said as he smiled at Octavio, fully amused by the situation.

She turned to go upstairs but changed her direction midway. "Oh, heavens, I see Octavio has not offered you a drink! May I bring you a glass of sherry or iced tea?"

"If it is of no trouble, a pisco sour would be delightful! Thank you."

"One for me too, darling?"

However, Octavio could already see the back of his beloved wife's head shaking as she went to prepare the drinks in the kitchen. He would have to have some great explanation this evening. Otherwise, he would be relegated to sleeping in the hammock for sure, with only the hermaphrodite tree as his companion.

Neruda, Salomé, and Octavio spent the hour sitting in the garden, as the girls and Rafael tumbled in and out of the house. Salomé changed into her favorite dress and tied back her hair in an artfully arranged bun. Neruda remained silent on the subject of his spontaneous visit, never mentioning Allende in Salomé's company. When she tried to inquire why he had arrived, he brushed her questions off lightly, saying only that he was a longtime fan of Octavio's films and had been in the neighborhood.

He said little else except for the normal pleasantries that typify small talk. But the garden enthralled him. So taken by the garden was he that when he stood up to announce his departure, he asked if he might have a quick tour of it.

"It would be my pleasure to take you on a tour, but you must mind your step, as it is a jungle in there, I assure you."

"I adore jungles, madam."

He held on to Salomé's arm to steady himself and marveled at the lushness and wildness of the place.

"Smells like jasmine and hollyhock. Wisteria and sterling roses . . ."

"You have quite a nose, Señor Neruda," Salomé admired.

Octavio watched them from the wrought-iron chair, holding his glass of pisco sour in one hand. He still could not believe that the man whose poems he had transcribed to court his beloved wife was now in their backyard. He saw the old man reach out and pick one of the roses and tuck it beside Salomé's ear.

The two of them were completely giddy when Neruda left. Salomé did not scold Octavio for not giving her proper notice to change her clothes and apply some lipstick. He, in turn, did not tell her what Neruda had asked of him.

That night, they made love as if they were teenagers again. He rummaged to find the silk pouch she had embroidered for him, the one that still contained his carefully written poems. Later, as Salomé lay on the bed, her legs peeking out from the lace trim of her nightgown, Octavio pulled each rolled paper from the silken pouch and read each stanza to her aloud. She listened to him, her eyelids closed and her mind far away, for she was lost in the sound of her husband's voice. Lost, as she imagined herself as that seventeen-year-old girl again, lying in the orchard with a thousand oranges falling from a star-studded sky.

Eighteen

Santiago, Chile
February 1970

$\mathcal{T}$he following evening, as Octavio and Salomé stretched out in their bed and gazed at the ceiling fan circling in the air above, Octavio remembered that he had yet to tell his beloved wife of the conversation he had had with Neruda the day before.

"Salomé, darling," he began as he reached out to stroke her leg, "Neruda has asked me to assist with the Allende campaign."

"What? You?" She began to giggle at the absurdity. "You can't be serious?"

"I am."

She sat up and looked straight at him, her nightgown falling languidly over one shoulder. "Why you? You are not a political man. You didn't even vote in the last election. You're an actor!"

He could smell her hand cream on her upturned palms, and suddenly he regretted that he had chosen this time to tell her. He would much rather be making love to her than having to explain the details of his and Neruda's conversation.

In his heart, he knew his wife was right. He had never shown the slightest interest in politics. Now that he was finally enjoying some well-deserved time off from acting, he preferred to spend his hours looking at his poetry books or spending time with the children, playing a tango record on the old Victrola to their delight. But he had to admit, he was flattered that the great Neruda had come to him.

"I'm not exactly sure why the party feels I'm the most qualified. I only memorize scripts, I don't write them." He reached out to massage the back of her calves. "Yet, I must admit, I am intrigued."

"Intrigued, Octavio?"

"Yes, my little Fayum, I'm intrigued. Neruda believes that television will play an important role in this year's election, and he thinks I would be the perfect person to help Allende prepare for his debut. After all, the man has practiced as a doctor and a lawyer, but probably has little experience in matters of presentation. He has always made his political speeches on the streets of Santiago, never before in front of the camera."

Salomé placed her pot of cream on the nightstand and turned to Octavio. Her thick, black hair was full around her shoulders. "Well, I know little about Allende, though I've heard that he is well intentioned. And of course I trust Neruda. Just promise me that you'll be careful. You and I both know how volatile the political situation can be here . . ."

"Of course," he said as reached over to kiss her. "Still, we must remember the way we were as teenagers . . . remember how adventurous and pure of heart we were then." His voice was full of nostalgia. "Salomé, imagine, only a few years ago I was quoting Neruda in hopes of seducing you, and now he comes to me for assistance."

"Yes, Octavio." Her eyes were now serious despite Octavio's mischievous grin. "Just be cautious. I just wouldn't want anything to jeopardize our happiness." She extended her palm and stroked his cheek gently. "You must remember it is not only the two of us now. We have a family to consider."

He turned to kiss her once more. "Don't worry." He sucked on her small, delicate mouth. "Haven't I always looked out for us?" She smiled back at him as he rolled on top of her and turned off the light.

The following week, Octavio received a handwritten letter from Neruda requesting that he meet Allende and some of his aides at a café not far from the central station.

Octavio arrived and noticed the middle-aged doctor immediately, recognizing him by his ivory-colored suit and thick, black glasses. He was far more elegant in person than Octavio had imagined. Neruda was at his side.

"Thank you for coming, Señor Ribeiro," Neruda said, greeting him like an old friend. The old poet stood up to shake Octavio's hand. He tossed his cape over his left shoulder. "Let me introduce you to the good doctor."

Allende rose from his chair and extended his hand. "Thank you, Señor Ribeiro, for coming to see me at such short notice. I realize how busy a man in your position must be."

The doctor seemed taller in person than in the pictures Octavio had seen in the papers. He had a strong, physical build and a face that reminded Octavio of a professor he had had when he was at the university. Behind the thick, black eyeglasses, soft, draping eyelids, and heavy, full mustache, Allende evoked a sensitivity and sincerity that Octavio immediately warmed to. How refreshing, Octavio thought to himself, that Chile had a political candidate who was completely devoid of pomposity.

"It is a pleasure to meet you, Señor Ribeiro," Allende said quietly. "I am an avid fan of your films."

"The honor is mine, Doctor," Octavio replied as he took his seat in the chair, the chair that Neruda had withdrawn for him.

"I hope my friend the poet has not inconvenienced you by asking you here today to meet with me."

"No, no. Not at all. It is my pleasure."

"I see," Allende said as a smile passed over his lips. "Are you a supporter of the party?"

Octavio readjusted himself in his chair, withdrew a handkerchief, and patted his brow. "No, sir, I am not."

"I see." Allende smiled.

"I've actually never voted."

Allende and his aides let out a few short laughs.

"I see you're a true artist, one with little interest in the activities that plague the common man."

"No, I'm just lazy."

"One of the great pleasures of life," mused Neruda.

"Well, I hope your lack of interest in politics won't dissuade you from thinking about taking the job. As my comrade Don Pablo probably mentioned, I'm a bit nervous in front of the camera. I don't want any of my nervous habits to get the best of me. When I don't have a crowd in front of me, I can get stiff and my oratory skills tend to weaken. I don't want that to affect my campaign.

"What I need," Allende continued, "is for someone to direct the camera, someone I trust, who will ensure that I am filmed in the most flattering light." He paused again as if he wanted to clarify his expectations a bit more. "I assure you it is not out of vanity. I only want the people to listen to me, not to be distracted by my eye or my occasional hesitations of speech."

"Yes, of course." Octavio nodded. "I suppose I could give you a few pointers that might put your mind at ease."

"That is exactly what I need, Señor Ribeiro. And who knows, by the end of all of this, I might just make a socialist out of you!"

"Yes, you just might, Doctor. Stranger things have happened. And I just might make a legend out of you."

That evening, Octavio told Salomé in detail what had transpired between him and Allende that afternoon.

"The man is terrified that the camera might affect his campaign. He just wants a few pointers so he can make a good impression on the television. With the right lighting and camera direction, with a few sessions on speech delivery, he'll be fine."

"He sounds a bit vain," Salomé observed.

"You think?" Octavio seemed hurt at his wife's suggestion. "No, I don't think so," he answered after pondering for a few seconds what his wife had just said. "I believe his concern was not based on vanity, as he had little interest in appearing handsome. But, rather, he wanted to ensure that his words were heard clearly and without distraction."

"What exactly are you going to teach him? You've never coached anyone like this before."

"I will teach him the pointers of the trade. How to speak clearly, how to look directly into the camera when making promises. How to level his chin and maintain the intensity of his gaze." Octavio paused. "I have it all worked out. It won't be that complicated."

"But you said he had certain tics?"

"Yes, his right eye twitches when he is under excessive strain, and sometimes, when he is nervous, he has a slight stutter. But I told

Allende that, if he trusted me and allowed me to coach him, I thought we could overcome any of those problems by teaching him some simple breathing techniques."

Salomé listened to what her husband had just told her. "Do you really think one's TV appearance is that influential? Do you really think voters will be swayed if one candidate is more awkward than the other? I would never be persuaded by one candidate just because his speech patterns are better than the other."

"Darling, these things can work on a subconscious level. People are always more keen toward an attractive and well-polished candidate. Allende has lost three elections in the past. I cannot change his physical appearance, and anyway, he has a distinguished air about him. But I can help him with the delivery of his speeches. I will not be writing for him; whatever he promises will be his own words! And why shouldn't people hear his words clearly?" Octavio paused and laid his palms on Salomé's crossed knees.

"If Neruda is the man whose poems had the capacity to lead your heart toward me, we should trust him and his support of the best presidential candidate. And"—he looked Salomé straight in the eyes—"I think we should do whatever we can to help him win."

Salomé was silent. She was surprised that her husband was suddenly so passionate in his support for Allende. This was a man who had spent his youth copying love poems, not political slogans. It was becoming a bit overwhelming for her. The two girls had given her and the maid trouble all day, and Rafael had been complaining that he missed the hacienda. She was too exhausted to discuss the matter further.

"You're probably right," she acquiesced as she went to turn the overhead light off. "It sounds as though he is a good man who needs your help." She slid over to his side of the bed and pressed her cheek close to his. She wanted to share his enthusiasm, but something in her heart told her otherwise. Still, she whispered into his ear, "He'll be lucky to have you as a teacher, my love. Just remember your promise to be careful."

Nineteen

❧

*W*ith his new "coaching" role underneath his wings, Octavio seemed to be refueled with a new zest for his life and career. Finally, he was able to be engaged in a project that he found intellectually stimulating. Never could he have imagined that Pablo Neruda would come to him and ask him to help one of the country's presidential candidates. He felt reborn.

At night he would stay up and read all the articles he could find on Allende. He clipped out copies of the speeches Allende had made in the past and read the critiques of his platforms from the various national newspapers. Little by little, he was able to piece together the vision of a man he felt was not only brilliant but deeply compassionate as well.

"This socialism that he speaks of would afford the children who are less fortunate than ours to have a better life," Octavio told Salomé as the two of them sat in the garden watching Rafael and his two little sisters, Blanca and Isabelle, play under the shade of the avocado tree.

"He wants every child to be able to go to school, have free milk, better health care . . . who can find fault with a man who has come from such privilege as he has and still has sympathy and feeling for those with less means."

Salomé nodded her head. "I agree with you, Octavio, but there are people in our country who will not want such a drastic political change. It requires a complete overhaul in our nation's thinking. Not to mention Chile's economy."

"Oh, my wife, ever the bourgeois," Octavio chided. "You have to remember that I didn't come from such privilege."

"I'm serious, Octavio. Things aren't that simple! Nothing is black-and-white with politics."

Octavio bit the tip of his pencil. "Well, it might not be simple, but Chile will still have to change its ways in order to progress. We can't maintain the mentality of a gray elephant where the rich stay rich and the poor remain impoverished."

"Octavio," Salomé said with a slight hint of caution in her voice. "Just because you are helping Dr. Allende doesn't mean you have to become the spokesperson for the socialist party. Try and keep some distance."

"I cannot help a man that I don't understand. The more I read, the more I understand and sympathize with his platform. He has a vision and I admire him for it."

"Admire and undertake as your own are two separate things. We both have seen how quickly politics can change in Chile. How many presidents can you count who were in and out of office since you yourself were a little boy?" She looked at him sternly. "Too many, I bet, to count!"

"You don't understand, Salomé." And for the first time in their marriage, Octavio seemed to almost patronize his wife. "I am going to be part of a fundamental change in our country's politics, and I am excited about it!" He paused and looked out past the garden, past where the children were quietly playing and into the hills. "I haven't been this excited in years about anything. Finally, I'm getting to use my acting skills *and* my brain. I just might be able to use my talents and influence to do some good in this world, not just sell cinema tickets that make the studios even richer than they already are."

Salomé shook her head. "I understand completely, Octavio. Believe me, I understand all you've sacrificed for us over the past five years. I just don't want anything to jeopardize our happiness. Is that so wrong of me?" She couldn't help being cautious about her husband's burgeoning political involvement. She had grown up overhearing her father and grandfather discussing politics during her childhood summers at the hacienda. She knew that few governments enjoyed a long life in Chile.

Salomé shook her head.

"Nothing can change what we already have," he told her gently as he got up from his chair and ran his fingers through her long hair.

Had the cameras been rolling at this moment, Octavio might have realized that the words he was uttering were spoken without reflection and that, if he were a character in a script, he couldn't have sounded any more naive.

Twenty

❦

Göteborg, Sweden
April 1970

*A*ll her life, Kaija had imagined herself on her wedding day looking as her mother did in the portrait Kaija had carried since she was small. As a child, she had stood in her bedroom in Sweden with a cluster of violets and sweet peas between her hands, and blossoms in her hair, and tried to imagine that day when she would look into that faded black-and-white photograph and recognize herself in the image of her long-lost mother. For, in her mind, her mother never aged. She would always remain that slender, silent woman in the photograph whose delicate features seemed to be cut from a wedge of freshly fallen snow.

Now her wedding day to Samuel had arrived, and Kaija began to prepare herself for the ceremony. As her adopted parents were no longer living, she had asked Samuel for a small civil ceremony, because there was no one to give her away.

True, she did not miss having Astrid's company. The old woman had never been kind to her and would never have risen to the occasion of her adopted daughter's wedding. As far as love was concerned, Astrid had gone through all the books Kaija had had as a child, ripping out all of the pages that were devoted to love. Anything to do with sex was also naturally eradicated from the house. It was as if her own self-loathing had prevented her from ever seeing anything good in the world. And love became the enemy in her own self-waged war.

However, had Kaija's adopted father been alive today, he would have embraced her and held her to his chest before walking her down the aisle. She knew he was smiling down at her from above.

After some nervous pacing, Kaija decided to put on some light opera on the old phonograph, hoping that would calm her nerves. Rummaging through her records, she decided on Mozart's *Die Zauberflöte* and placed the player's needle down carefully. The music floated through the apartment as she washed her long blond hair, dried it, then braided it down the center, finally coiling it into a loose bun. "It would be silly to put flowers in my hair," she thought to herself, then chastised herself for being so sentimental. "After all, the ceremony is only at the town hall . . ." But for all these years, she had imagined herself looking as her mother did in that treasured portrait. Her solid stature. Her long, white dress, and the string of violets and stephanotis in her upswept chignon. Now, as she studied her own face in the mirror, she could see nothing of the woman she so desperately wished she had known and loved.

She would never know that her mother too had lost her own mother at such a young age. That the crucifix had been worn by the women in their family for countless years. But what Kaija did know was that the same necklace that had once touched her own mother's skin now rested against hers. And that, in some small way, brought her comfort.

Kaija went over to her nightstand and retrieved her mother's photograph, as an aria from the opera crescendoed in the background. The black-and-white tones had faded to a soft gray, the sun having absorbed much of the pigment over the years. Kaija looked at it intently.

"I must be joyous today," she instructed herself. "I am marrying the man I love."

Nevertheless, sadness weighed upon her. It was not that she lacked excitement for her marriage—indeed, she loved and cherished Samuel and desperately wanted to be his bride. She finally had someone to love her, to cherish her as if she were completely his own. It was only that she missed the female companionship that she imagined accompanied most brides. She wished she could have had someone to share these premarital moments with.

Yet, now, she was alone, with no one around even to help her get dressed. No one to braid her hair or massage her shoulders. And, more importantly, no one to share a last-minute giggle or calm the prewedding nerves. A girlfriend would have been the next best alternative. But Samuel and she had been inseparable since her first semester, and Kaija had made few friends since she had moved to Göteborg.

As she finished her makeup and dabbed a bit of perfume behind her ears, she wished she had chosen a dress to wear. The suit she had selected the week before seemed painfully plain on the hanger on the closet door. Kaija wondered why she had chosen it in the first place, as it seemed so unremarkable now.

The woman in the shop had told her that the silk was imported from France and that the short hem and notched collar were the latest trend. She also recommended a matching white pillbox hat and soft kidskin gloves.

Kaija unwrapped her purchases from the perfumed tissue paper, slipped into the suit, and pinned the hat on her head with bobby pins. She wiggled her slender fingers into the gloves and readjusted her skirt.

After several careful steps, Kaija took a long, studied look at herself in the mirror. She barely recognized herself. She thought she looked like an ambassador's wife, not a bride to be. Her crucifix was hidden behind a smattering of tightly closed buttons, and her braided chignon was covered by the pillbox hat. Even her tiny hands were hidden beneath a casing of leather.

"I cannot possibly go like this," she thought to herself, her fingers trembling as the clock was already striking half past ten. She was supposed to meet Samuel in less than an hour.

She picked up the photograph of her mother one last time, studying it even more intensely than she had only minutes before.

Her mother was radiant. She looked as a bride should, innocent and youthful.

The contrast with how she felt she looked so depressed Kaija that she decided to remove her pillbox hat and slip off her kidskin gloves. She unbuttoned her suit jacket and slid out of her skirt. Within seconds, she was standing in the center of her bedroom with nothing on but her undergarments, walking toward a closet that had almost nothing to offer her: a couple pairs of trousers, two pleated skirts, and one winter dress and one for summer. The summer dress she had bought the previous year. Made out of linen, it was not white, but rather a pale pink. A dusty rose color with an eyelet hem.

She pulled it out and into the sunlight. "It's almost white," she mused as she slipped into it and zipped up the back. It felt so much more comfortable to her than the constricting suit. "This will have to do," Kaija murmured to herself as she ran to the mirror and twirled around, the skirt billowing up like a bell. Finally, she felt like a giddy bride.

Samuel didn't even realize that his bride wore pink instead of white. To him, she was already the very image of purity and beauty. When he saw her for the first time that morning walking up the steps of the town hall, he was overcome with emotion. He couldn't believe that this exquisite creature had agreed to be with him for life.

She had sprinkled wildflowers in her hair, plucking them from the landlady's garden as she walked down the path to meet her anxious groom. And she had placed her crucifix around her neck so that it nestled softly between the cleavage of her small, rounded breasts.

Samuel barely noticed the crucifix anymore, as he had grown to accept it as though it were an extension of Kaija's body. Something that grew out from her, rooted in her heart and woven into her skin. He dared not envision what would happen to her if he asked her to remove it.

That morning, before they were pronounced man and wife, Samuel vowed to cherish Kaija always. He kissed her lightly on the lips and placed his arms around her waist.

She beamed because she could now build a future with the man she loved. They would make a family of their own together, as they were united in their desire to have what had eluded each of them for years.

"I want a big family," he teased her as they exited the gilded town hall, and she lovingly squeezed his arm.

"We will make our own family now, my love," Samuel said as he escorted Kaija into the waiting car. "A dozen little children . . ." And with that, he winked playfully at his radiant bride.

Twenty-One

❦

Santiago, Chile
April 1970

Octavio arrived at Allende's house on Guardia Vieja Street, a quiet residence filled with the scent of ripening fig and apple trees. He paid the taxi, walked through the gate, past the unfenced garden, and up to the porch. He straightened his tie, tapped the dirt off his shoes, ran his fingers through his hair, and readjusted his curls.

Nearly seconds after he rang the doorbell, Octavio was formally greeted by Allende's wife, Hortensia Bussi, a dark and attractive woman with small, delicate features.

"You must be Don Octavio," she said graciously, and motioned for him to step into the vestibule.

"Yes, and you must be Doña Hortensia."

She smiled back at him. "Yes, but please call me Tencha," she said as she extended her hand to him.

"Come this way." She ushered him through the dimly lit corridor, past Allende's study, the intimate parlor, and through two French doors that opened up onto a sunny terrace that overlooked a blooming garden of dahlias and sterling roses. There, Allende was sitting on one of the chaise longues with his hat pulled slightly over his brow.

"Salvador," Tencha called out to him, "Don Octavio has arrived."

The sun cast shadows over Allende's face. He now held his hat in his hand and was sitting upright, smoothing his trouser pleats with his left palm.

"Good afternoon, Don Octavio, so good of you to come. Can we offer you something to drink? A whiskey, some pisco, or perhaps a little boldo tea?"

"Yes, maybe some tea. If it is not inconvenient . . ."

"No, no, my good friend." Allende went to pat Octavio on the back. "A little tea sounds good before we sit down for some work. You must excuse my little nap. I have been working such late hours that I must have fallen asleep in my chair!"

"It happens to us all, Doctor," Octavio said as he sat down. "I've done it myself on many an occasion."

"Yes. Yes." Allende cleared his throat. "Well, how would you like to go about this little tutorial?"

"Well, I think it is best that we begin working on the presentation of your speeches. Have you any that you have recently prepared?"

"Yes, I do. They are in my study."

"Let's take a look at those. I'll have you read from them, and you pretend that I am the cameraman standing there in front of you."

"I've always done better in front of crowds. I feed off their energy. It gets my adrenaline going."

"Yes, I understand." Octavio's voice was warm and compassionate. "That is one of the differences between the stage and the screen. In a studio it is only you, your fellow actors, and the crew. In the theater, you have the thrill of the crowds. The interaction between the audience and the performer is invigorating."

"Exactly!"

"But now you must forget about those impassioned speeches that you used to give on top of Santa Lucía Hill, in Tierra del Fuego, deep within the copper mines, or in the freezing cellars of the meatpacking plants. I cannot teach you what you already know. However, television is an entirely different arena."

"Yes, I know."

"So I will teach you how to master it. I will instruct you how to hold your head, where to rest your hands, and when to raise your palms. When you make your political promises, you should gaze directly into the lens, and when you comment on the decline of our children's health and educational system, I will encourage you to bow your head ever so slightly." Octavio paused. "Dr. Allende, I will teach you to manipulate the camera to your advantage."

*   *   *

So, that afternoon, after Tencha had brought out the steaming cups of boldo tea, the two men practiced until evening fell upon the house on Guardia Vieja Street.

Octavio arranged the chairs so that Allende sat facing him, the speech he had drafted only hours before resting neatly on a garden stool in front of him.

"Men and women of Chile," he began, "I have dedicated my life to serving the people—"

"Slower, my friend," Octavio interrupted. "And when you are speaking, stare at my finger." He lifted his forefinger and positioned it so that it centered Allende's gaze.

"I have been inside the mines and seen the conditions in which our nation's people work for pitiful wages, for foreign companies whose only interest is to fatten their own wallets . . ."

"Good!"

"I have seen the small child whose limbs are twisted and whose growth is stunted because his family could not afford the proper nourishment that no child should be deprived of . . ."

"Yes, now take off your glasses and shake your head slightly to emphasize the shame of this!"

"But I won't be able to see . . ."

"You'll put them on as soon as you finish the sentence. I will have the cameraman focus on your eyes at that point. Dr. Allende, you are probably the only sincere politician alive. Let the viewers see that in your gaze. It is what attracted me into accepting this job, and I am confident it will have the same effect on the voters."

"I must confess, Don Octavio, that I am beginning to think this 'staging' of my speeches is bordering on insincere."

"You shouldn't think of it as that way."

"Perhaps the public should see me just as I am. An occasional hesitation of speech can't completely obliterate a past dedicated to community service?"

Octavio was silent for a moment. "I agree with you on a certain level. My wife actually shares a philosophy similar to yours. But, as Neruda pointed out, the Kennedy-Nixon debates showed that the public is partial to not only the more eloquent candidate but, also, to the more photogenic one. Neruda tells me that Nixon looked absolutely dreadful on camera, which probably cost him the election."

"Yes, yes, I know that, but . . ."

"If you trust me, I will make sure that you look your best and that your words are heard, without any distractions. There is nothing insincere about that. After all, they will be your speeches, crafted from your heart and carved from your mind."

Allende smiled. "All right then, let's get back to work."

For several hours each week, Octavio continued to visit the Allende household in private. There, the doctor relinquished his role as aspiring Chilean presidential candidate and became a student of elocution and mannerisms that would transfer elegantly onto film. He listened as Octavio read the speeches that Allende had prepared the night before, studying the inflection that Octavio placed on certain words and mimicking his hands when he wished to emphasize certain points. After several sessions, Allende began to learn the art that Octavio had become famous for. It was as if one were seducing with one's words, with one's gaze. "Imagine you are staring into a beautiful woman's eyes, like the way you did to your wife, Tencha, the first night after you were wed."

And, indeed, Allende understood the language in which Octavio spoke. He could envision all the images the actor urged him to think of when he was speaking. He heard Octavio's voice whispering in his head even when he slept, so that, even in his dreams, he was speaking in a mellifluous voice and holding his head straight and his spine erect. If he had searched the world over, he would never have found a better teacher than Octavio.

For weeks, they practiced maintaining eye contact and perfected the art of the pregnant pause. He assured Allende that, when his eye began to blink, if he paid it no attention and continued to speak eloquently, then people too would ignore it and concentrate on his words.

As the doctor triumphantly grew more confident in front of the camera, the stutter eventually ceased. And in the weeks that followed, he seemed more zealous than ever before.

It was inevitable that, by hearing Allende's speeches each day, Octavio became a passionate and learned listener of Allende's ideas. Sometimes, as he made his way back to his dusty pink house,

Octavio would recite some of the lines from Allende's latest speech and gesticulate on the street as if he were on a podium himself. The doctor's words inspired him. It brought out the performer in him. But these were not empty words from a script. They were passionate, well-intentioned words, ones with vision and the capacity to change the very fiber of Chile. Where men were treated equal regardless of class, and where industries were owned by the people, rather than by the rich multinationals. The more time Octavio spent with Allende, the more he came to agree and support him politically. He was no longer aiding him because it flattered him as an actor, but because he truly believed that Allende was the best candidate for Chile.

As time passed, Octavio grew to have enormous respect for Allende, not only as his candidate of choice, but also as a man, a husband, and a father. To each of his responsibilities, he seemed deeply devoted. Octavio was touched by the way Allende consulted with both Tencha and their daughter, Tati, about his campaign. He was mesmerized by the doctor as Allende recounted his meetings with Che Guevara and Fidel Castro.

When Allende offered to pay him for his services, Octavio refused. "When I do things, I do them for the passion or the purpose," he told the doctor. "I don't need the money."

"I want to compensate you somehow," Allende said firmly. "You deserve something for your efforts. What can I give you?"

"If you are elected, and only if my instruction has paid off, you can send my wife and me on an exotic trip for a few months."

"Very well," he replied, content with Octavio's reply. "Tell your wife in a few weeks' time she'll be off on an adventure."

By the time Allende's camera debut approached, he had benefited from nearly four months of intensive training.

"You will make sure the camera takes me from the appropriate angles."

"Yes, of course, Doctor, I will make sure. I will take care of it."

The two men had grown close to each other over the past few months. So much so that Allende embraced him before he went on air. "No matter the outcome of this election, I will always be grateful to you, Octavio. I will always be indebted."

Octavio laughed. "Go out there in the name of Chile and make me proud."

Allende sat down at the desk that had been prepared for him by the television studio. The television camera loomed in the foreground, and as he stared into the large black lens, he remembered what Octavio had told him.

"Keep your chin up high and your eyes focused on the center of the lens. Pretend it is the eyes of your wife on your wedding day." Allende remembered how he and Tencha had gone to the courthouse that afternoon so many years before. It had been a private day between them. No pomp or circumstance. No flowers in her hair. But he had looked into her dark eyes and promised himself to her. He had sworn his undying devotion to her, just as he was willing now to do to the people of Chile.

Allende folded his hands and cocked his chin, steadied his gaze, and began his speech in perfect, polished prose.

From behind the camera, Octavio stood beaming. His pupil was doing well. "Yes, yes," he whispered to himself. "Keep that chin up. Yes, now take off the glasses, stare directly into the camera." He pushed the cameraman, instructing him to zoom in on Allende's eyes.

Allende was doing everything perfectly. He paused at the right moments and looked squarely into the center of the lens when he made his promises. He came across as sincere and honorable, the two traits that were indeed truly his.

From behind the camera, Octavio was smiling with pride.

"You don't need me anymore," Octavio told him that night as he bade Allende farewell. "You were flawless."

Allende beamed.

"The rest is up to you and your campaign managers. You've been a wonderful student. You have both my vote and my best wishes for good luck."

"Thank you, my friend," Allende said as he embraced Octavio. "I will always be grateful."

Octavio nodded and smiled. "You know how to reach me if you need me. I will look forward with great anticipation to having the privilege of listening to your inaugural speech come September."

"Thank you again, comrade. I take it this year you will vote?"

"Indeed, I will! Viva Allende!" Octavio said with a wink as he packed up his satchel and waved toward the man he now considered his friend. That evening he went home smiling, eager to get back to his wife and children, who were waiting patiently for his return.

Twenty-Two

༈

Vesterås, Sweden
August 1970

*W*hen Kaija announced that she was with child, Samuel held her so tightly that she had to scold him, for fear he was crushing the unborn baby. She knew she was acting a bit ridiculously, but she was fearful. She just didn't want anything to go wrong.

Since discovering she was pregnant, Kaija couldn't believe how protective she felt toward this little thing growing inside her. It was as if, instantly, from the moment of conception, her maternal instincts had been awakened. It all happened like an explosion: a wondrous and miraculous thing. For the first time in her life, she felt magical.

Samuel noticed the change in his wife almost immediately. Her radiance intensified, her pale white skin ripened to a warm, golden hue. He always believed she could never have been more beautiful than the day he first laid eyes on her. Yet, now, he saw her as a woman transformed. Her delicate, birdlike features were replaced by a soft, gentle roundness. Her cheeks were constantly rosy, like the pale petals of a peony. Every night as they lay down in their bed, the crisp cotton swaddled over their naked limbs, Samuel would place his palm on Kaija's stomach and imagine the day he could feel the child's first movements. He would count down the months to the child's birth on his fingertips and tell Kaija how he longed for the day that he could place his ear to her navel and marvel at the sound of their child's precious heartbeat.

Only a few months before, they had moved from their small apartment in Göteborg to a large, four-bedroom house in Västerås. They had come upon the house almost by accident, having taken the car down a road they had mistaken for another. Yet there, amidst a canopy of apple trees and blue hydrangea, they found a house that seemed to claim them. The house could have been taken right out of one of Kaija's dreams.

"There is a For Sale sign!" Kaija said with great excitement. "Samuel, doesn't it look absolutely perfect!"

He had smiled over at her, pushing his hand past the car's stick shift and folding his fingers into hers. "Yes, Kaija, it does. There is a phone number on the sign. Why don't we drive to the center of town and ask if they might show us the house this afternoon?"

"Can't we just ring the bell, Samuel? I'm sure they would be excited at the prospect of a potential buyer arriving at their door."

"I'm not so sure, Kaija . . ."

"Please, Samuel," she pleaded. "I'll make the necessary apologies. You don't have to say a word!"

Against his better judgment, he had pulled into the small gravel driveway. People had never arrived unannounced at his parents' home back in Peru. It would have been considered rude and improper. But even after they were married, Kaija had maintained her childlike innocence, and he thought it sweet how excited she was. "We will offer to come back if it is a bad time, Kaija. Promise me that."

"Of course, Samuel. Of course." She jumped out of the car and smoothed back her blond ponytail. From behind, she looked no more than fifteen years of age.

In the end, everything could not have worked out better. The older couple who lived in the flower-filled home were overjoyed to have a young couple ring their bell. They welcomed Samuel and Kaija in and offered them tea and warm biscuits. Afterward, they spent nearly two hours showing them the house and reminiscing on how they had raised four children within its walls.

"We're getting too old to care for a house with so many rooms," the wife had lamented to Kaija, "but a lovely girl like you with a doctor for a husband, well . . . it would be just perfect for the two of you."

Kaija smiled and pressed her cheek into Samuel's shoulder. The tweed of his blazer scratched her delicate skin, but she was so happy at this moment she barely noticed.

"Do you have any children yet?" the elderly husband asked. "There are four bedrooms. You saw the big backyard, and the town has two school systems. So many children in this area.

"I can't believe how Vesterås is growing. So many artists and writers. Many immigrants relocated by the government. Still, I believe it will be good for the area. Some new blood in these parts."

Samuel smiled, nodding his head in agreement. "Yes, I know about the government's plans. That is exactly why Kaija and I are looking for a home around here. I have been thinking of setting up an office in the center of town, as my practice is dependent on the immigrant community."

"Well then," the older woman said, smiling, "this house will be perfect for you."

They bought the house within a matter of weeks and began to make preparations for the move a month later. Kaija packed all of their things in brown cardboard cartons and wrapped everything in generous clouds of crumpled, white tissue paper. They made love on the floor of their empty apartment with great fervor, each of them hungry for the other, each of them anxious to create a child that was symbolic of their love. They knocked down a tower of sealed boxes as they rolled in their passionate embrace, and afterward, as they held each other tightly to their chests, they giggled with nervous anticipation of the new life they were hoping to create.

Both of them knew that the new home would afford them ample room for their burgeoning family. So that evening, after they had been in the house barely two weeks and Kaija announced that she was pregnant, Samuel lifted her into the air and carried her upstairs, spinning her around each room, chiding, "Take your pick! Take your pick! What other woman has the choice of so many rooms for a future nursery!" He kissed her. "Finally, my love, you'll have everything you ever wanted!"

As Kaija's belly grew, so did Samuel's practice. Nearly seventy-five political refugees moved into Vesterås that year, and nearly twenty-five somehow got word of Samuel Rudin's success with his patients.

He took a small office on Skolgatan Street and bought a new desk, some wooden bookshelves, and a leather chesterfield couch for his patients to recline on. He walked home every evening, through the village square and to the grassy street where his pregnant wife waited for him. Even after a difficult day of work and seeing several new clients, he was always smiling. After all, things were beginning to fall into place. He was helping people who desperately needed his guidance. He had a loving, devoted wife, and even Sweden itself had warmed to him. Life, for Samuel Rudin, finally was good.

Twenty-Three

Vesterås, Sweden
April 1971

$\mathcal{W}$hen Kaija held her newborn daughter in her arms, she was overcome with emotion. Here, sleeping sweetly at her breast, was this tiny child that she and Samuel had created together. She was theirs completely. She looked at the infant's tiny head, which was covered in light blond fuzz, marveled at the delicate eyelids, which shielded two blue-green irises, and sighed with satisfaction. In all her life, she could not recall a child more beautiful than hers, nor could she believe that she, Kaija Sorenson-Rudin, could have the capacity to love anyone as deeply as she did the child that now lay sleeping in her arms. And it was these new and intense feelings that awakened her unanswered questions of her past. For as Kaija looked at her daughter with the blond hair and thimble-size nose, she could not help but see herself as that newborn infant. In her heart, she knew that she had once resembled her, sweet, pink, and round. That she too must have had the rosy skin, the thin, delicate eyelids, the hazy hue of newborn eyes.

She wanted nothing more than to love this child and to protect her. Even when Kaija slept, she wanted to watch over her, wishing that she could keep one eye open, just to ensure the child was safely beside her. She could not imagine a day without her.

And Kaija wondered whether this was how all mothers felt after they'd given birth. As though their child were born from the muscle in their heart and the cells of their body. That they were connected even after the umbilical cord was cut and the milk no longer flowed from their breasts. And if so, what had she done wrong so many years earlier? What could she have possibly done by the age of two that her mother could have had the heart to give her away?

There are so many things a simple wooden crucifix and prayer book cannot fulfill or replace. The objects cannot speak, and thus they lack the power to appease the ache of unanswered questions. And Kaija was still filled with that ache. Like a partially healed wound that is still sensitive to the sting of salt, she remained vulnerable to her past. Her childhood continued to be a taboo subject that Kaija preferred to relegate to the far corners of her mind, rather than release it to the present. Consequently, she spoke of it rarely. Keeping it buried inside, tightly tied and laced down in the depths of her memory. Only recalling it when it crept up on her uninvited. Like an unwanted web of ivy, chasing her every time she thought she had cut it down.

It was one of the two great misfortunes of her life that Kaija had absolutely no memory of her mother. She could not recall the sound of her mother's voice or the sensation of her touch. She had no idea if her love for drawing was inherited from either of her parents, or if her fear of abandonment was related to her adoption. What she did know was that every time she gazed at the faded wedding portrait of her parents, she felt cheated. She wished those old sepia-toned images could speak to her. She wished, as she was now a mother herself, that she could ask her own mother, "Why?" She wished she could hear from her mother that it had caused her terrible pain to give her up. She thought that might bring her some sense of comfort.

After Sabine's birth, Kaija began framing pictures of Samuel and their daughter and scattering them around the house. "Finally," she said to herself, "I have a family of my own."

She tried to think of her mother less, although it was nearly impossible for her to do. Seeing her own daughter growing before her, the privilege of seeing her discover the world around her, brought such joy to her that she wanted to pity her mother for not being able to see that in her. Yet, other days, it was enough to infuriate her and make her blood-boiling mad. So the woman in the photograph vacillated between saint and sinner, with increasing frequency, depending on Kaija's mood.

Her feelings for her father were far more distant and abstract to her. She had nothing of his, nothing that he had ever touched, nothing that she could now say had been his own. In the photograph, he didn't look a day older than nineteen. His face full and his eyes sparkling with both pride and promise. His body tall and strong.

She rarely let herself think of the man she'd met briefly after the war. Those three months in Finland were all but erased in her mind. She had become an expert in blocking those memories that were filled with anguish and despair.

But her memories of her first arrival in Sweden were still vivid to her.

Her first memory of the house she was brought to was the smell of bread baking. That wonderful, intoxicating perfume of rising yeast, butter, and flour was completely foreign to her. She remembered how the gentle man with the soft, sweet voice had told her to call him Papa, and how he had handed her a large slice of warm bread with honey spread over the top.

It was he, not his wife, who helped Kaija unpack her tiny, red suitcase. He folded her dress and spare pair of socks in the drawer. He withdrew the crucifix and placed it on a nail beside her bed.

What she had not seen, however, was the sight of her adopted father as he opened the prayer book and discovered the letter inside. As it was written in Finnish, he could not read the letter at all.

However, he knew by the careful penmanship, the deliberate and precise folding of the paper, that it was important and should be taken care of. He feared that it might get soiled by the small child if she came across it while she played, so he put it away in his desk drawer, promising himself that he would give it to her when she was old enough to understand.

Every evening after he returned from the office, Hugo Sorenson opened his top drawer, withdrew his fountain pen, and attended to his correspondence; and each time he saw the folded letter that had arrived tucked in the prayer book of his adopted daughter. But one evening, he was shocked to discover that the letter was no longer there.

At first, he thought it was only buried under a spare folder or a strip of stamps. But, upon closer inspection, he discovered that it could not be found. Panic struck him. Guilt that he had lost something so precious, that which could never be replaced.

He asked his wife, "Have you seen a folded letter written in Finnish, Astrid?"

"No."

"Are you sure? I've misplaced something important."

He thought she was acting strange, secretive. She avoided his gaze, her eyes firmly focused on the kettle of boiling water.

"Are you sure, Astrid?" he asked her one more time, hoping that she would confess that she had found it and inadvertently left it in another part of the house.

"No. I haven't any idea what you are talking about."

He went back to his office and scoured through all his files and drawers. Kaija had already gone to sleep. Perhaps she had discovered it. The next morning, he asked her if she had been rummaging in his desk.

"No, Papa," she said sweetly. "I would never do that."

He believed her. He didn't want to let her know what he had lost. She would never forgive him. So, for many weeks, he searched for the lost letter, never giving up hope that it might one day magically reappear. But it never did.

He thought about it constantly, wondering if he should tell Kaija as she grew older about what he had lost. But he hesitated. He didn't want to do anything that might cause the precious little girl any pain.

A few months after the letter went missing, Hugo Sorenson found himself agonizing over the welfare of his adopted daughter yet again. He had never known such fear, such deep despair, when the letter arrived from the government agency announcing that all of the Finnish children adopted during the war were being reclaimed. He feared he would lose her forever.

"How can this be?" he asked Astrid, his face now white with

grief. "She has been with us nearly five years. We are the only parents she knows."

"Let me see the letter, Hugo." She took it from his hand and stared at it, revealing that she too was baffled.

"We have raised her," she said, sounding indignant, almost insulted by the letter. "Now they tell us we must return her? How can that be?" She shook her head before placing the letter down by the kerosene lamp. Hugo looked at his wife with surprise. After all, it was the first time he could remember that Astrid had come to the child's defense. She had always been distant with Kaija, but now, he had to admit, she truly seemed concerned.

"Perhaps we can fight it," he offered weakly. "Perhaps they will make exceptions," he stammered. "Kaija was only two when she arrived!"

While the Swedish newspapers commended the families who had cared for the Finnish war children over the years, the consensus was that, now that the war was over, the children should be returned.

The man Kaija called Papa packed her bags for her. He bought her a new suitcase, as the red one she had arrived with was far too small to pack all the things she now possessed. He folded her six cotton dresses, the velvet one she wore on the eve of Santa Lucía, the three wool sweaters, the eight pairs of small cotton socks, and the tiny black patent-leather shoes that were still shiny and new. He laid out a yellow-checked dress with a white collar for her journey home and fluffed the wool coat they had bought her the last winter, the pale blue one with gold buttons that offset her warm blond hair.

He wondered what of his he could send along with her, that which in later years she could look back upon and remember them by. She was now old enough that she wore her mother's crucifix, yet young enough that she still clutched her old tattered bear.

"We should give her something by which we can be remembered," he lamented to Astrid.

"If she doesn't remember us after all we've done, then good riddance," Astrid said, but he saw that her eyes were filled with tears. He seldom understood his wife. Her words were so often cruel, but he had to believe that her heart held some form of compassion. After all, he had fallen in love with her. It was only after they had tried unsuccessfully to have children of their own that her moods had begun to blacken.

He often wondered if it was insensitive of him to insist that they adopt a child. He had originally thought it would be good for them, and for her especially. But it seemed that, with Kaija, it had been more difficult for his wife when the child had first arrived.

He thought things had been better for them over the past year. That she had warmed to the little girl, and that she was beginning to forget that the child was not truly her own. But then this had happened. The letter had arrived and they had no power to fight what was far larger than they were.

"She was never really ours," she said one night, but he heard the muffled tears in her voice.

She refused to help him get the child ready for her journey home. She wouldn't pack her clothes or organize her things, so he had been left to do it alone. He took a day off from the office and went into the little girl's room, where she had slept for the past five years, where she had played with her friends, and where she had slipped from being a stranger to daughter in a matter of days. He had loved her from the moment he had seen her standing there at the arrival center, with her kneesocks and tiny red valise. "We have a daughter now," he had whispered that evening to his wife, as the tiny, frail toddler slept quietly nearby, in her new, wooden bed.

She had not answered him. But he could see her in the moon-light, stroking her flat stomach, crying to herself, apologizing aloud. "As for Kaija," she said through her weeping, "she is not 'ours,' so how can we come to love her as our own?"

More than five years had now passed and Hugo had long given up trying to understand his wife. In his mind, Kaija had become their daughter. He could not understand how his wife could turn her emotions off so easily, how she could allow him to prepare for the child's departure alone.

But he did it anyway. He packed her things and told her as best he could where she would be going. He was surprised that she seemed to have memories of Finland. "Papa, I remember it was cold there," she said, and tried to smile, as she clutched her bear. "Not warm like it is here, with the smell of bread."

"You'll see your other mama and papa," he said, trying to fight back his tears.

She looked at him with those bright green eyes and he felt his words choking in his throat.

"You might have other brothers and sisters with whom you can play. You'll have the lakes and the forest that you love."

"Will I have bread and honey?" she said softly.

"Of course you will, *älskling*. Of course you will."

The night before she was to leave, he had yet to think of something he could send back with her. Something that, in the years that followed, she could hold and remember. Something like her crucifix that would travel with her and help her recall.

He rose early that morning, before anyone else awakened, and went to the kitchen. He could not send anything made of glass or ceramic, because it could break. He sat down on the stool and held his temples. His head ached.

On the table rested the honey jar and the little silver spoon that he had used to feed her with when she'd arrived. Astrid and he used it almost exclusively for honey now, but it was one of the first things Kaija had claimed as her own.

He reached for it and held it in his palm. The curled handle was smooth except for the faint engraving of a cluster of rose tendrils. Had it been Astrid's when she was small, or had it been his mother's? He couldn't remember.

The delicate bowl of the spoon had a soft patina; the slight arch of the handle seemed to retain the little girl's grip. He smiled as he remembered all of the times he had caught Kaija with it in her tiny pink mouth, the spoon mischievously protruding from her lips. He would send that, he thought to himself. He went to the cupboard and withdrew some scrap pieces of wrapping tissue and carefully rolled it between them.

He went to Kaija's room, where she still lay sleeping, her open mouth like a small lion's, her unlatched suitcase carefully placed on the floor beside her wooden bed.

He laid the spoon amidst the piles of clothes, the wedding portrait, and the prayer book that he had packed the day before and stood there watching her. He prayed that his memory would last him and that he would be able to remember everything she had ever done, committing to his mind all he had ever shared with her. He was so afraid that there might be some small detail of this child he might forget.

He knew he should try to mask the jealousy that was beginning to creep into him. After all, her parents had a right to reclaim the child they had brought into this world and only sent away so that she would be safe. But secretly he had to believe—because he had to harbor some hope—that she might someday return.

Little Kaija's return to Finland at the tender age of seven and a half was not the sort of reunion a child dreams about. No mother met her at the threshold with outstretched arms and tears that welcomed her and promised to never again let her go.

She journeyed first by boat from Stockholm to Helsinki, then by train to Mikkeli, arriving at a station that was bleak and whose rooftop was covered with charcoal-laced snow. Outside, the chimneys of the factories were blowing soot into the low, dark clouds overhead. In her pale blue coat, Kaija was the only bit of color in the landscape of ashen gray. Like a Chinese ink painting, a splash of pigment against a black-and-white sky.

The mayor of the town was there to greet her. She stepped onto the platform, to a group of unrecognizable faces, just a small gathering of people wrapped in woolen scarves and coats that were worn and thin.

"Kaija?" a voice asked softly and with hesitation. "Is it you?" She could not understand him, her father, as he stepped past the mayor and knelt by the little girl. He only remembered her by her blond hair and green eyes and her now threadbare bear.

She stood there and looked at him shyly. She did not remember him at all, and he didn't look anything like the photograph she had treasured and looked at every night by her bedside. His red hair was now gray, his face gaunt. His flesh hung like melted icing from a whipped-cream cake, and his blue eyes were lifeless as old flannel.

He motioned to two tall, gangly boys to come and greet her, and they too seemed foreign to her, their gaze distant and remote.

"These are your brothers, Kaija," he said to her, and although she could not understand Finnish, she understood who they were.

"Mama?" she asked, looking fervidly into the crowds.

But the man who was now once again her papa just shook his head, his eyes brimming with tears.

She later learned, as they passed the old Karelian church with the frosty, spiraling cupolas, that her mother and third brother were buried there. Two snowcapped crosses that overlooked Lake Saimaa. Sirka's only daughter's return was, sadly, three years too late.

Yet, her father tried his best to make his daughter comfortable. He gave her the bed that he and her mother had once slept in, their worn wedding blanket encasing the old, lumpy mattress with delicate blue flowers. The perfume of stale violets clinging faintly to its edges.

Toivo and the two other boys slept in the kitchen where they had slept since infants. However, now as the brothers had grown bigger, their shoulders pressed into each other and they argued about having to share a bed with their father.

The boys grumbled about the food too. The war had ended, but the shortage of food in the household had not. An extra mouth to feed did not go unnoticed, as the boys openly complained that they were still hungry after Toivo tried to evenly distribute the flat bread, the pieces of cheese, and the porridge gruel.

They looked at their sister, how she arrived softly rounded with baby fat, her pretty starched dresses, and blue wool coat, and their resentment was as raw as their hunger. And, although Kaija could not understand the exact words that her brothers exchanged in sharp tongues with their father, she could sense their resentment. It was incapable of being disguised.

So at night, she slept alone in the cold, large bed that had belonged to the mother she would never know. She longed for her old bed, the familiar embrace of her Swedish papa, and the delicious smell of baking bread and the full jar of honey. There was no place for the spoon her other papa had sent along with her. She would keep it wrapped in tissue paper, only withdrawing it at times to place in the stitched mouth of her bear, whose belly was as aching and empty as hers.

Her first few weeks in Finland seemed like an eternity for her. Every night, Kaija went to bed crying, and her tattered bear, now a wilted lump of matted fur and floppy limbs, brought her little comfort.

She dreamt of her adoptive father. His distinct smell of sandalwood and the faint perfume of his shaving foam. Every night since she was two years old, he had come into her room and kissed her on her forehead. She recalled, as her stomach now made loud noises from hunger, how he would bring her two sandwiches with honey and jam before bedtime. One for her, and one for her bear, and he would sit with her until she had devoured both of them and washed them down with a full glass of milk.

This man who was her birth father, she felt no affection for him at all. While in Sweden, she had hardly contemplated his existence. He remained simply an expressionless man whose eyes stared blankly at her from the wedding portrait beside her bed. It was the image of her mother that had fascinated her. The regal woman with the gossamer veil and the laurel of flowers in her hair. She had spent her five years as an adopted child wondering what kind of woman her mother was, wishing that she possessed tangible memories of her. If she could have had her own way, she would have chosen her Finnish mother and her Swedish father as her parents. Intuitively, she felt if that union had existed, she would have received the most love.

Now, in this cold house with barely enough food among them, Kaija understood little of what was happening around her. She could not understand what her birth father or her brothers said to her. Their Finnish tongues formed sounds that were foreign to her ears.

Some days, while her brothers busied themselves with the wood chopping and clearing the snow off the roof, Kaija would make her way to the railroad ties that lay only a few hundred meters from their house. There, under the canopy of silver birches and fragrant pines, she would walk on the side of the tracks, hoping to follow them. Hoping, since she remembered arriving on these tracks only weeks before, that she would be able to retrace them back to where they had started. Back to her home in Sweden.

The tracks were laid next to the river, a frozen, shimmering sheet of ice that, when melted, emptied into Lake Saimaa. Little Kaija in her pale blue coat stepped lightly beside the thick wooden planks, singing a Swedish psalm, her footprints embedded in the snow.

Her brothers had found her one evening when she had traveled too far. They had come looking for her with gas lights, their faces lined in frowns. Her father following them only a few steps behind.

"Where were you going?" they asked her in Finnish, and although she was not sure exactly what they were asking, she replied quietly in Swedish, *"Jag vill åka hem."* "I want to go home."

They scooped her up like a ragamuffin doll. Her frozen limbs sticking out from her woolen sleeves like sapling twigs broken off from the stem.

"She will be trouble," one brother said to the other. "Wild and spoiled girl," the eldest muttered to himself. Their father remained four steps behind. Silent, his back bent over his wooden crutches. His graying red beard covered in patches of frost.

"She hasn't just lost her mother, as you boys did," Toivo reminded his sons, as they carried his little girl home, tears welling in her eyes.

"She also lost us a long time ago." He shook his head sadly. "She was trying to find her way home."

They returned her three months later to Sweden, thin and fragile like porcelain. Hugo picked her up at the boat, his heart beating anew since he'd received word of her return.

Her father had been kind, and as difficult as it was for him to let her go again, he knew he couldn't provide the best life for Kaija. When Hugo took the letter to be translated, he couldn't believe that his prayers had been answered, that her father was asking if she might return to Sweden.

He never judged the man, though his wife did. He knew how difficult it was to feed a family, and with Kaija's mother gone, he could understand Toivo's insecurity in raising the girl alone. Hugo was just so grateful that, with his consent and the necessary forms completed, she could be returned to him. That finally, she would be theirs alone.

On his deathbed eighteen years later, he held her hand and confessed that which he had kept secret for so many years.

"There was a letter that was sent over with you when you first arrived, Kaija, and I lost it."

"That's all right, Papa," she said with tears brimming in her eyes. "Nothing is important now but your getting your strength back."

"I am beyond that, my darling," he said softly. "But please, listen. You must know what I am saying." She was kneeling at his bedside, her tiny hands enveloped by his.

"When you first came to your mother and me, you came with almost nothing." He paused and tried to gather himself.

"Yes, Papa, I know."

"No, no, you don't. When you arrived, I was the one who unpacked your suitcase. In there, I found a wedding portrait of your birth parents, a crucifix, and a prayer book."

"But I still have all those things." She clutched her crucifix to show him that she had kept it all these years.

"Kaija, dear, there was a letter written in the prayer book and I took it out for safekeeping because you were so young at the time. I placed it in my desk drawer and always promised I would give it to you when you grew old enough to understand."

"Do you know what it said, Papa?"

"No, and that makes my guilt even more terrible. When you left to return to Finland after the war, I thought you would find your mother there waiting for you, and the letter wouldn't be as important to you. . . . I had no idea she had already died."

Kaija remained silent.

"When you were returned to Astrid and me, and you cried in my arms and told me how you would never return to Finland because your real mama was dead and your brothers didn't want you, I so desperately wanted to give you the letter right then and there. I knew the letter was from your mother, by the penmanship, the careful, delicate strokes of a woman's hand. I knew it said how much she would always love you. Because I know how much I love you."

Kaija was crying now. Her face red and her lips trembling.

"You never found it, Papa?"

"No, and I am so very, very sorry." She could feel his fingers tighten against hers and she held them close to her lips.

"They loved you, sweet Kaija. How could they not have?" His eyes were now gray with death, his white hair swept behind him, his pillowcase imprinted with the tracings of his tiny head, a fleeting fossil in a weave of cloth.

"I know it has been hard for you here sometimes. But Astrid loved you too. One day, you will give birth to a child of your own and you'll have compassion for a woman who is unable to bear children."

Kaija nodded. She knelt down and pressed his brown-spotted fingers close to her cheek. "You have been the most loving father I could ever have hoped for. You cared for me, fed me . . ." Her voice was breaking and her face flooded with tears. "I have never doubted your love. The letter is unimportant."

"It was the only one . . . ," he whispered.

Neither the old man nor Kaija had any idea of the other letters that Sirka had sent Kaija during her first years in Sweden. The ones that been destroyed by a woman too angry to love. That would remain hidden forever, like so many small, silent tragedies of war.

Twenty-Four

Santiago, Chile
June 1973

*A*llende had been in office over two years before Octavio accepted his offer of a full paid vacation. Salomé and he had finally agreed to take a three-month journey. They had always wanted to visit the mountains of Peru and see their friends who had moved to Argentina. "We will live like Gypsies for three months," Octavio whispered into his wife's ear, as he caught one of her loose black curls and twirled it around his finger. "Your mother and father can sleep in our room and make sure that Consuela doesn't become complacent while the mistress of the house is away," he teased.

It had been a difficult year for Chile, and Octavio was looking forward to spending some time alone with his beloved wife. He was anxious to spend a few months away from Santiago, where he would not have to hear the picketing on the streets, be inconvenienced by the striking taxi and bus drivers, or become enraged by the continuing lockouts orchestrated by the industrialists. He was convinced that the maladies, like the constant food shortages, that plagued the country were not due to Allende's incompetency, but to higher forces that wanted the president to fail.

But Octavio believed that the opposition would itself soon grow weary from its efforts and would finally see that the president was not going to resign.

"We should take that vacation that Allende promised us," Octavio suggested playfully to Salomé.

At night, he tried to tempt her with different itineraries where they could go. He held her to his chest and played with her curls with his forefinger.

"Remember our honeymoon, how we went to Argentina and danced the tango every night?"

Salomé was smiling to herself. Like a Cheshire cat, smug and round. "I remember how we arrived in Buenos Aires and the little hotel you had booked had lost our reservation and had no rooms to spare!"

"Yes, but remember how I took charge and found us the most memorable room in town!"

"You bribed a sixty-five-year-old madam to let us sleep in one of the rooms in her bordello!" Salomé was now twisting and giggling in Octavio's arms. "Never in my life had I seen a room like that—red crimson walls, swags of drapery, and satin sheets on the bed!"

"Whatever do you mean?" he teased. "It was the perfect place for two newlyweds! I told the madam we would do our best to blend in with the activities in which the other guests were engaging."

"You were incorrigible, Octavio!"

"You didn't seem to mind, Fayum." He squeezed her tightly and kissed her.

"I was pregnant, darling. Remember?"

Octavio smiled at his wife mischievously. "Why don't we go back? It can be a second honeymoon of sorts. We can spend a few weeks in the city and travel north into the countryside, maybe even explore some parts of Bolivia. Wouldn't it be wonderful to just have some time to ourselves?"

"And the children? How could we leave them? It wouldn't be right."

"We have your mother, we have Consuela. Why wouldn't it be right?" Octavio asked, his hand gently caressing Salomé's thigh. "Allende has given me this gift. We would be foolish to refuse a three-month, all-expenses-paid vacation. When would we have another opportunity like this come our way?" After much convincing, Salomé eventually acquiesced. She worried about the political unrest that had become almost a daily occurrence in Santiago, but

Octavio promised her all would be fine when they returned. "The time away would do us some good."

Octavio would later be proved wrong. The opposition would not weaken. They would not give up until Allende was out of office or worse.

It was ironic and almost lucky that Salomé and Octavio began to travel back from their sojourn in Argentina and the foothills of Bolivia on September 6, 1973. As a result, their chauffeur-driven car arrived on the Chilean border on the morning of September 11, only hours before the coup.

Rafael and his sisters had been sent home early from school, the teachers having sensed trouble. By noon, soldiers had positioned themselves at every street corner, and the little Fiat that was driving Salomé and Octavio back from their journey, its rooftop strapped with presents and souvenirs, was being stopped by guards every few kilometers.

"What has happened?" Salomé whispered to Octavio, her face pale with fear. "We should never have left the children. We should never have taken this trip!"

Octavio tried to hush her. He too was frightened, but he tried to mask his emotions and to assuage his wife's doubts. "I'm sure everything is fine," he said before urging the driver to get them home as quickly as possible.

They reached the city limits just an hour before the streets entering the capital were officially closed off. The small, crowded car wound its way through the streets of Santiago's suburbs until it finally reached the driveway of the pale pink house.

Inside, Rafael and his sisters huddled beside their grandparents, who listened to the radio for news, while the children whispered among themselves that they wished that their parents would come home soon.

Octavio and Salomé hurried to the front door and were greeted first by the maid. "Señor Ribeiro," she said. "Thank heavens you have returned!"

They entered the large salon and their children immediately rushed to their side, Salomé's mother clasping her hands together with thankfulness and relief.

But in less than an hour's time, the family reunion would become a faint memory. Other distractions, far more momentous, would occur. There would be no sound of the tango ringing from the old Victrola, only the thunder of helicopters circling above, the sound of explosives echoing down the street from the rooftop of the nearby hospital, and from the soldiers firing down below. Yet, moments later, the Ribeiro-Herrera family would hear something far more terrifying from the transistor radio.

"La Moneda has been bombed!" cried Doña Olivia, her eyes wild and her voice shaking with fear. "Those animals are bombing the palace, with President Allende inside!"

From the voice box of the old radio, they heard the sounds of the bombs exploding Suddenly, emerging from the orchestra of chaos, came the voice of Allende addressing the people.

"I refuse to leave the office to which I've been elected by the people of Chile." With the sounds of the bombs now growing more intense, the connection over the radio could barely be heard.

"To be sure, Radio Magallanes will soon be silenced, and my voice will no longer reach you. It doesn't matter, you will continue to hear me. I will always be next to you, and at least in your memory, I will be a worthy man who was loyal to his country. The people must defend themselves . . . Workers of my country, I have faith in Chile and its destiny. Others will take on the struggle and surpass this gray and bitter day that the forces of treason claim to have won. Know that sooner than later the great avenues will open to free men who will pass down on them on their way to constructing a better society.

"Long live Chile, long live the people, long live the workers! These are my last words, spoken in the knowledge that the sacrifice is not in vain . . . and that at least there will be a moral punishment of the thieves, cowards, and traitors."

Upon that, the radio transmission went dead. The gas attack on the palace began, and the bombing continued.

Salomé turned away. The pain of listening to Allende's last words was unbearable. Doña Olivia and Don Fernando were shaking their heads, their mouths covered by their hands.

However, as pained as Octavio was, he was overcome by a strange sense of pride. He imagined Allende standing by the microphone, the bombs exploding beside him, the chandeliers breaking in pieces over his head, glass shattering beneath his feet, and fire burning the palace's velvet curtains. Yet, through it all, Allende's voice had never been more eloquent. He was shining in his darkest hour with grace and with conviction. During those moments of peril, he had not stuttered, his voice had not wavered. Octavio, looking beyond the transistor radio into the depths of his own wild garden, was now far away. He had temporarily transported himself to Allende's private chamber in the presidential palace. He saw Allende with his chin held high and his eyes firmly rooted ahead. He saw him standing there before him with his thick, black glasses and English tweed jacket, his hair elegantly combed back. He had remained stalwart: unwilling to board the helicopters that had been offered to take him safely into exile. He would remain the leader of the country who had voted him into office, masterful and determined, even to the very end.

Silence had enveloped the room, and at that moment Octavio realized the gravity of his pupil's fate. Only then, under the hush of his wife and children, did he understand that it was all over, that something terrible had happened to his beloved country. And although Octavio had no idea of the awful circumstances that would soon afflict his family, he felt himself sicken inside. Under the swirl of his wife's whimpers, his mother-in-law's wails, and his children's confusion, Octavio began to cry, for it was not the ending he had imagined for this great man. Had it been a script, he would have demanded a rewrite. He would have made it so that Allende walked out of the palace badly wounded but with his life, his pride, and his political vision still intact.

But Octavio had not yet come to understand that life had a way of thumbing its nose at happy endings. That's why people had always loved his movies. He made them believe that love and beauty could triumph over sadness and evil. Yet even Chile's most beloved cinematic treasure could not anticipate the horror and the trials of his next starring role.

Twenty-Five

❧

Santiago, Chile
November 1973

Octavio slipped into a deep depression after Allende's tragic death. The drama of the president's last moments seemed to give Octavio even more cause to deify the nation's slain leader.

"I will never support this Pinochet!" Octavio complained to all of his colleagues and friends. "The man's a butcher! What sort of man cuts down a leader who has been elected into office by democratic elections! A coward! A traitor!" There weren't enough words in Octavio's vocabulary to describe the bilious hatred he had for the general who, in his mind, had murdered his friend.

"You should be careful what you say, Octavio," Salomé warned. "And to whom you say it."

But he refused to listen to her. "I will not hide my feelings. I am not a coward!"

She had broken into tears on more than one occasion because her husband seemed so full of anger since the coup. Santiago itself was frozen in a stupefied fear. The new general had made promises to restore the nation's faltering economy, and to rebuild the presidential palace, which was now a pile of broken glass and ashen walls, but still he maintained a police state. Salomé had enough stress reassuring her children and her parents that all would soon return to the way things once were. But it was a poor charade she felt forced to play.

She knew this coup was different from the ones Chile had experienced in the past. Coups had been a part of Chilean life for decades. But, for the most part, they had always been short-lived. The president was forced out by the military, ushered into exile, and eventually, the general in charge would step down and let new elections take place.

Everyone in Chile was expecting Augusto Pinochet to be no different. But they were wrong. Nearly six months had passed and the general had yet to step down and allow democratic elections to install a new president. He had designated himself Chile's new leader, and it appeared he was there to stay.

The streets were lined with men in machine guns, and the palace remained a testament to the violence of Allende's defeat and death. Octavio seemed like a complete stranger to Salomé. Perhaps even more foreign to her than her city under siege. He wouldn't listen to reason. He spoke of forming his own political party to defy Pinochet and his henchmen; he told the writers at a studio that they should consider doing a film on the tragic and heroic life of Allende, in which he could star in the leading role.

"Your outspokenness about the coup is going to get you in trouble," Salomé again warned him.

"Don't be ridiculous," he chastised her. His voice was becoming increasingly patronizing toward her. On occasion, he sometimes even sounded cruel.

"You should be thinking about your family!" she cried.

"Haven't I always thought about our family!" he hollered out at her one night. "Can you actually sit here and tell me I haven't sacrificed for my family . . . always provided for them! Haven't you one of the largest, loveliest houses in this city!"

"Octavio . . ." And even through her tears, her eyes were ablaze.

"Stop looking at me like that, Salomé!" he shouted. "You know I would never do anything to jeopardize our family. Think about all I've done to get this far. I came from nothing! Unlike you!"

"What do you mean unlike me?" Salomé was fuming. "You begrudge me now because of where I come from?"

Octavio remained silent.

"I married you because I loved you, Octavio!"

She could tell he regretted what he had said to her just minutes before. But still he didn't offer an apology.

"I'm going to bed now," she said flatly. "I will not have you play out these scenes with me where you are the misunderstood hero."

Salomé did not sleep that night. She could feel her husband slip under the sheets hours later, his breathing irregular and his body twisting in frustration from their argument that remained unresolved. Salomé turned from Octavio and pulled the covers tightly to her chin.

Three weeks later when Octavio came home from work, his face lined in anger, Salomé couldn't say she was surprised to learn that the studio had fired him. That he found himself suddenly unemployed was a shock to him, but she had known that his comments against the new regime would get him into trouble. Once again, he had been naive and lacking in foresight. She shook her head to herself as she took his coat from him and told Consuela to prepare some tea.

"They'll see," he said as he thrust his fingers into his hair. He was pulling at the curls so violently that she feared he was going to make his scalp bleed.

"You could make things better, Octavio, if you went back and apologized for your behavior over the past months. They'll probably ask you to make a public retraction of your previous remarks, but it wouldn't be so terrible."

"Are you out of your mind, Salomé?" He looked up at her and she could see that he was beyond reason. "I would never be such a hypocrite. Let them fire me! See if I care!"

"I see," she said quietly. "Place your pride over your family then."

"What!" he cried. His face was now red. "What do I need to apologize for? We have enough money to live quietly for the rest of our lives."

"You? You, who always said you had to keep working to make sure there was enough money . . . always saying that it could easily run out one day and you had to keep working to make sure you had saved enough. . . . Now there is enough?" She began to cry. "You wouldn't stop working so that you could spend more than a few months with me and the children. But now to fuel your vendetta against Pinochet, you're willing to give up everything? I don't understand you at all!" Tears were running down Salomé's face.

"I took time off in between my sixth and seventh movies," he said quietly.

"Before Neruda came into our house, yes," she said, shaking her head. "I wish he had never, ever stepped into this house of ours."

"How can you say that, darling?" Octavio's voice had finally become soft again.

"We wouldn't be fighting like this if he hadn't."

"We might never have fallen in love without his poems." Octavio took his wife's hand. "We can't live our lives by censoring it with 'What if we hadn't done this or that?'"

She didn't want to spend another sleepless night with him, neither of them talking to the other. So she allowed him to hug her tightly. She allowed him to reach into her blouse and caress her breasts and kiss her neck. When he carried her upstairs and laid her on their bed and made love to her with long strokes of his hand and his pelvis, she locked her ankles around his brown back and didn't protest.

But their fight had left something unresolved in her and she was full of apprehension. When he fell asleep next to her, melting like warm chocolate against her side, she got up and went downstairs to drink the pot of tea that Consuela had made hours before, not even noticing that it was ice-cold.

Twenty-Six

Santiago, Chile
December 1973

*E*very day since he had been let go at the studio, Octavio left the house at the same hour he had done since Salomé and he were married. She knew he was too restless to stay at home and read his novels or work on his writing. He was incensed that he had been dismissed because of his political involvement and couldn't sit in the garden alone with his thoughts.

So Octavio ate his *churro* and drank his cup of coffee and set out to speak with friends about the different work he could do, the theater, television. However, they all said the same thing: they could not help him. Only one of his friends was honest enough to speak plainly: "You must change your opinion of Pinochet. You must openly accept him. We all have, even though we think he's a sneaky bastard. You cannot continue on this personal crusade, nothing good will come of it. You will only continue to remain blacklisted and you will never find work again."

"Blacklisted?" Octavio was completely shocked. He had never heard of such a thing. "They've blacklisted me?"

"Of course they have, you imbecile! You think you can make statements about the general being a murderer and the country being an embarrassment and not be reported? That those declarations have no consequences?"

"Who would report me? What sort of coward, what kind of spy?

I ask." Octavio was now fuming. " I have never said these things except when I was in the company of friends and colleagues!"

"The walls talk, Octavio. You must realize things have changed."

"I understand people have changed. But I have not. I will not."

"We all have changed. How can we not when the world around us has? I suggest you think about your wife and family."

"My wife and family," Octavio replied curtly, in the same tone he had used with his wife and his in-laws. "I assure you, my wife and family will be just fine."

He left his friend and returned home visibly annoyed. He was tired of everyone's inaction. "Why aren't people banding together and demanding that the general step down and allow democratic elections?" he asked Salomé when he sat down for dinner.

"People are afraid." Her voice now was terse and impatient. She was tired of having the same conversation with him.

"Afraid of what?"

"There is talk that people are disappearing in the city."

"You shouldn't believe such hearsay," he said, shaking his head. "You sound ridiculous saying such nonsense."

"It's not nonsense, Octavio. Why should anyone take risks . . . especially when every street corner has a soldier with a machine gun strapped against his chest."

"It's all for effect," Octavio said confidently. "Pinochet's trying to make all of Santiago look like the backdrop of a movie set, for chrissakes!" He pushed his plate to the side. Half his food remained uneaten. "The man is trying to make people fear him through cheap tricks. If the people of Chile stood up to him, I bet he would skulk away like the sewer rat that he really is."

"Do you think you should be the one to call his bluff, Octavio?" She could feel her blood boiling underneath her skin.

"I think any intelligent person should point out the injustice of this man's claim to legitimate office."

"I can't believe you! You are acting like a fool, Octavio!"

"A fool?" He hit their dining-room table with his fist. The empty glasses and plates from where the children had eaten hours before rattled against the wooden surface. Salomé knew that the maid had been afraid to interrupt them and clear them away.

"You have no understanding of politics!" he shouted.

"Perhaps I don't, but I have a deep understanding of family!"

"And I don't?" He was raising his voice once more.

"Go and wage your war, Octavio! See if I care!"

"You don't understand what I am saying . . . Salomé."

"I think I do. You think because I got pregnant and didn't go to university that I don't understand? That I can't possibly understand what is going on here?" Salomé's eyes were now wide with anger. "Octavio, I agree with you that the general murdered Allende. I agree with you that there should be democratic elections in Chile. But you cannot take this battle on yourself."

"But if I don't, who will, Salomé? Who will?" He was screaming at her now. "Tell me, Salomé. Tell me how will I live with myself if I know I stood by and did nothing. That I was silent."

"I can't tell you how to do that, Octavio!"

"I would rather be dead than live my life under such cowardice."

"You would rather be dead?" she screamed. "You would rather be dead and leave me a widow with three children, Octavio?" She was shrieking now and her entire face and throat were red except for the three blue veins that were pulsating in her neck.

"How selfish are you? How selfish are you, Octavio, that you'd rather risk your life for a cause than protect us from being on the government's hit list?"

Octavio said nothing to her. Outside the kitchen window, the sun was beginning to set, casting his face in deep orange light.

"Salomé . . ." This time Octavio's voice was softer than before. "You married a man who always prided himself on his principles. Do you want me to become a man who casts a blind eye to injustice?"

"I want you to be a man who places his family above all else." Her voice was now hoarse. "I want you to open your eyes and realize that we're no longer standing in an orange field. Chile has changed and you must realize that you lack the power to take on a general."

Salomé untied her apron strings, folded the material on one of the chairs, and began walking upstairs to their bedroom.

"Fayum," he called to her. But she had already reached the second tier of stairs. Octavio's voice became lost in the many rooms of the Casa Rosa. And Salomé, unfortunately, did not hear him.

Twenty-Seven

Santiago, Chile
January 1974

$\mathcal{S}$he had been dreaming of lilies the morning they first took her. The heat of the summer clung heavily to Salomé and she attributed her reverie to the fact that the water lilies would shortly be closing their petals and drifting off to sea.

They took her when the children were at school and while Octavio was out looking for work. They arrived in a black van, pulling up slowly to the middle of the driveway, parking by the flower beds that were in full bloom, the hydrangea turning blue in the summer light.

She had been alone that afternoon. Consuela was at the market and Salomé had spent the morning reading a novel, dreaming about lilies and wondering when she and the children would next go to the sea.

They had rung the doorbell and asked to speak with her, and she had asked politely what they were inquiring about.

"We need to ask you a few questions downtown, madame. It will only be a short drive."

She had hesitated at first, for the men had dressed with such measured efforts to appear inconspicuous that Salomé was immediately suspicious of them.

"I am leery to leave the house with no one here," she said gently.

"My children will be returning home soon and my maid has left for the day."

"It will only be an hour or so, madame," said one of the men, extending his hand.

Salomé looked around apprehensively, past the black van and into the tree-lined street. Neither Octavio nor Consuela could be seen approaching the house. She could see by the intensity of the men's eyes that had she refused to go with them, they would have taken her anyway.

"All right, but I hope this won't take a long time."

Walking over the gravel, Salomé sensed that something was wrong, that she wouldn't be returning for dinner. She tried to walk as slowly as she could in the hope that by some slight chance Octavio would return home early and stop these men from taking her in.

But Octavio never did arrive, and Salomé found herself not being escorted into the van, but rather shoved into it. The door slid closed behind her and another man was waiting for her once she was in.

Within seconds, she was slapped, beaten with a windmill of fists, blindfolded, and her hands tied behind her.

"Let me out of here!" she screamed.

"Shut your mouth, you communist *puta,*" one of the men barked at her, while another man tightened a gag around her mouth. And that was the first time Salomé tasted her own blood. Thin and bitter, it slid to the back of her throat like kerosene.

They had neglected to tie her blindfold tightly. They did not know that she could see her captors clearly out of one eye, and that she could make out a few images through the darkened van windows.

Santiago flew past her. She saw the city hospital, the faint lines of the parliamentary building, a few gated mansions, a schoolyard full of children at play. But then, there was more darkness. She could feel her cheek swelling. She could feel the sensation of a bruise forming under her left eye, the heat, the throbbing. For a split second, she was struck by the irony of her injuries, that the bruises would not be red like fire but, rather, blue like the sea.

The ride became bumpier as they traveled out of the main avenues of the city and onto the dirt roads of the farthermost suburbs. From beneath her blindfold, Salomé could now only make out the occasional tree and gathering of horses.

"Hurry it up, you ass!" one of the men hollered to the driver, butting his rifle against the front car seat. "It's already half past two!"

The men were arguing with each other in rough tones, swearing in foul language, and occasionally kicking Salomé with one of their heavy-bottomed shoes. Yet, minutes later, as the van pulled up to a gate heavily armed with guards and was waved in by a soldier no older than seventeen, they became quiet again.

From where she was lying, Salomé could see only a few details of the place she was being taken. She saw a dark, black gate, the faint traces of a flower garden now overrun by the trenches of a jeep, and a tower, a villa made of stone.

"Get out of the car, you traitor bitch!" one of the men yelled at her, reaching for her hair as if it were a web of weeds. She was dragged from the van and pulled through the courtyard and into the dark house.

Once inside, Salomé could no longer see clearly. The lights inside the villa's interior were kept low and the hallways were cavernous. The sound of her captors' footsteps against the cold floor was like the tapping of a cane, the sound of her own feet like the shuffling of a bag of rice.

"Get in there!" one of the men said as he shoved her into a room. "And we don't want to hear any more screaming out of you!"

She fell into the cell like a tiny, maimed bird. Sliding to the ground and crumpling like a sack of feathers.

Suddenly, through the walls, as if a stereo system had been piped into each room, she heard Mozart's music floating in the air.

The first time she heard it, it brought her comfort. The sound of the melody— the soft, fluid notes. At that time, she was not located in the prison section of the villa but, rather, in the interrogation holding cells. The place before the tortures began, a place that was impervious to the cries from a few hundred meters beyond.

The first time, she let it wash over her and soothe her. Take her to a place that was far from this nightmare. She prayed that the music would not stop until she was safely back in her beloved home.

When they came to question her, they took her to a windowless room with whitewashed walls and no music. They sat her down in front of a cheap, wooden table and pulled down her blindfold so she could see clearly the man who was questioning her. A forty-five-year-old soldier who smelled of *humitas* and week-old sweat, one of the ugliest men she had ever seen, with a crooked nose and chipped teeth.

"We know your husband was a strong supporter of Allende," he barked. He had a thick manila folder in front of him, filled with photos and scribbled notes. "We know he was essential in helping him reach the presidency."

"I don't know where you came up with that," Salomé denied.

"We have it right here," the soldier said as he tapped at the folder.

"My husband is not a political man. He is an actor. Check his voting record, he is not interested in such matters."

"Are you denying his involvement?"

"I am denying nor admitting nothing." Salomé paused, stifling her urge to cry. "I want to go home."

"You'll go home after you've answered our questions. Did you or your husband donate to Salvador Allende's campaign?"

"Donate? Donate what?"

"Donate money, what do you think I'm talking about?"

"No, we did not."

"Is it not true that your husband socialized with Allende?"

"My husband is an actor and a poet, I already told you that. Whatever reason he saw the former president was out of a mutual appreciation for the arts."

"For the arts?"

"Yes, they spoke of poetry together. Is that a national crime?"

The man was now staring at Salomé like a wolf. His hands folded, his chin like the blade of an ax, precariously next to hers.

"I want you to tell me the truth!" He banged his fist on the table; the manila folder, with its reams of white paper, slid to the ground.

"I have told you the truth."

"The new regime will not tolerate traitors. I want you to go home and tell your husband that. I want you to tell him that we will be watching him. If he knows what is good for him, he will support General Pinochet, who saved this country from communist bastards like Allende." He slammed down his folder.

"Get her the hell out of here!"

She was blindfolded again, the knots behind her arms retied tighter, before being led to the van and driven back to the main roads of Santiago. It was nearly nightfall when they threw her out of the van. She tumbled onto the sidewalk, not far from Independencía Avenue where Allende himself had once rallied his supporters. But Salomé could barely remember that time now. To her, it seemed like decades ago.

Twenty-Eight

❦

Vesterås, Sweden
January 1975

*A*s the political wars in Latin America brought an influx of refugees to Sweden, Samuel became increasingly busy with patients. Often, he returned home exhausted, overwhelmed by all those who needed his care.

Kaija watched over Sabine during every waking hour, hovering over her as if she were afraid she would awake and the child would be gone.

As Sabine's fourth birthday approached, Samuel began to suggest to Kaija that perhaps they should start trying to have another child. "I don't want Sabine to grow up as an only child. It would be so lonely, and I can think of nothing better than having a dozen little children who resemble you, Kaija."

"I want a son. For you, darling, so that I may look into his eyes every day and look at you." She was playing with the buttons of his shirt. "I hope our next child will have your black curls." As their bodies slipped deeper into the sheets, she giggled to him, "So you really want a big family, darling."

"More than anything," he whispered, entering her, holding her for several minutes until she let him come into her completely.

"We can name the next one after you," she whispered. And he closed his eyes and let himself be warmed by her. Reveling in the fusion between them and the thought of conceiving another child in love.

*   *   *

Samuel wasn't prone to fantasy. It wasn't his nature to let his mind wander to things that were not concrete, not firm and tangible. He needed to see something and hold it to know it was there before him. But having a son was something he could imagine. As he lay next to Kaija, her slender body turned ever so sweetly into his, her delicate curves like the lines of a viola, he was filled with love and contentment.

The thought of a large family made him smile. He wondered if his mother was gazing down upon him, happy that her child would replenish the family she had lost.

The following month Kaija missed her period and she confided in Samuel that she believed she was expecting. "I'll go to the doctor next week so we can know for sure."

That evening, as she fed and played with little Sabine, both Samuel and she exchanged knowing looks that perhaps they would soon have another addition to their home.

She postponed seeing the doctor immediately as she was confident that she was pregnant. She was often flushed and her skin felt constantly warm. She didn't mind the occasional discomfort, which she attributed to her early pregnancy.

"You should confirm your suspicion with the doctor," Samuel reminded her after a week had passed.

"It's only a silly test," she thought to herself, "after all, I know my body by heart." But eventually, she agreed to go.

The following week, when the doctor came back to the examining room and told her that she was not with child, she could not believe her ears.

"That cannot be," Kaija insisted. "I have missed my period. The only other time I have ever skipped a month was when I was pregnant with Sabine!"

"You are not pregnant, Kaija," the doctor said softly with a practiced, paternal kindness. "The test was negative."

Kaija, dressed only in a paper-thin examining robe, seemed to physically deflate after hearing the disappointing news.

"But how are you feeling otherwise, Kaija? You experienced no other symptoms except a missed period, right?"

"Well, I've been rather exhausted lately," she said with a deep sigh. "And I've also been a bit warmer than usual."

"Warmer?"

"Yes, it's as though I'm hot all the time . . . when everyone else seems to be unaffected by the temperature. But maybe it's just because I was getting myself excited to be pregnant again."

"Yes, maybe." The doctor's eyes darted over her chart once more. He scribbled some notes on the margin. "I'd like to do a few more tests before you leave."

"Why?" Her face appeared puzzled.

"I just want to test your thyroid and hormone levels."

She shook her head.

"I'll send the nurse in to do the blood work," he said kindly. "I'll call you in a few days when the results come back. Don't worry," he said paternally, "and get some rest."

Kaija did not mention to Samuel that she had visited the doctor that afternoon. She decided that she would tell him that she was not pregnant after she received the results of her tests. It would be easier to tell him everything at once, she thought to herself. The doctor had not led her to believe he was testing her for anything serious, so she did not give it too much thought. Her mind was more focused on her not being pregnant and that she and Samuel would have to try again.

She revisited her doctor the following Wednesday.

"I received your test results, Kaija, and it seems that one of your hormonal levels is sharply elevated."

Kaija's face fell. "What does that mean? Do I have something serious?"

"Serious? Well, if you mean *fatal,* then the answer is no. But the results might explain why you believed you were pregnant." He glanced down at his notes once more. "You mentioned the last time you were here, Kaija, that you were suffering from fatigue, an intolerance of heat, and an absence of menstruation, correct?"

"Yes," she said hesitantly.

"Well, these symptoms are indicative of premature ovarian failure."

"What?" Her eyes were now wide open and her face drained of color.

"It basically means that you are going through early menopause."

"Menopause? But I'm barely thirty-five years old!"

"While there are several theories as to the etiology, no one really knows what causes this premature failure. There does seem to be a hereditary component." He paused. "Do you know when your mother went through menopause?"

Kaija was silent. Her eyes fixated on a chart on the wall. A cross section of a woman's uterus with a hundred arrows pointing to various things every woman was supposed to have. She suddenly felt empty.

"My mother? No, I don't. I have no idea. I was adopted."

"I see," he said kindly. "But, Kaija, this is not all bad. You have one child already. You should consider yourself lucky. Some women I see will never be able to conceive at all."

Kaija was fighting back her urge to cry. This was all too awful for words. Only days before, she believed she was with child, and now she was being told that she would never be able to have more children.

"This can't be. This just can't be," she said over and over. "I am a young woman."

The doctor rose and clicked his pen. He gave her chart one last glance and pushed back his spectacles.

"I *am* sorry about this, but there isn't much we can do. I'm going to write out a prescription for some estrogen replacement and recommend that you take some calcium supplements. You should pick them up with the nurse on your way out."

Kaija nodded.

Alone in the cold, white-walled room of the clinic, with the lone poster, the only color in the room, Kaija began to cry. She wept into her palms, whimpering until her face was pink and her features swollen.

She didn't know how she could return home and face Samuel. He would be there when she returned, as he had taken off the day to look after Sabine. He would ask her if she had good news and she would need to tell him that her suspicions had been wrong.

But how could she tell him that they would have no other children between them ever again? It would crush him. They had always spoken of a large family and now she would be failing him.

She left the clinic without picking up her prescription. The cold air on her face felt refreshing, and she wondered if it would wash away the evidence of her tears.

She was wrong about that. Samuel knew her better than anyone, yet still not better than herself. She would learn that soon enough.

"What is it, darling?"

She began to cry in his arms.

"No baby? Is that all? Well, we'll try again. Again and again if necessary."

And that made her cry even more.

That evening, Samuel held his wife, trying to comfort her in his arms. "You should hold your tears for a real tragedy, Kaija. I assure you everything is going to be fine."

Kaija wanted to scream at him, "No, everything is not going to be fine! You don't know that! You think that! You think you can placate everyone with your gentle words and your knowing eyes, but you can't! You can't this time!" But she couldn't even manage a single word, let alone all the anger that was inside her. Every word she tried to manage just got stuck in her throat.

"We'll try again soon, Kaija," he murmured time and time again in her ear. Each time she cried deeper and grew more despondent, until finally she fell asleep. Like a small child, curled up in his lap.

Twenty-nine

Vesterås, Sweden
January 1975

$\mathcal{T}$he first few weeks that followed Kaija's visit to the doctor were the most difficult for her. She hated feeling that she was keeping something from Samuel. Every night, when she lay down beside him, she felt strange, as if she were bringing a third person to bed with them. She detested herself for keeping her condition a secret, but her fear of disappointing Samuel ran even deeper. So she contained it deeply within her, a small ball of fire that ate away at her once placid disposition, leaving her a bundle of raw, aching nerves.

The doctor had not bothered to inform her of the symptoms that accompany an early menopause. The flashes, the bouts of heat that radiated through her body like steaming needles. Some mornings, she would rise and find her face unrecognizable. Her skin, once porcelain white, frequently developed spotty, red patches. One morning, dipping her hands into a sink of cold water, splashing furiously to bring down the heat, she collapsed on the cold tile floor.

From two doors beyond, she heard Sabine beginning to call for her.

"Mama! Mama!" she cried. "Mama!"

She rose from the tile, like a weary mermaid from the sea, wrapping her robe tightly around her waist and drying her face with a soft, cotton towel. Walking through the hallway, she could see the snow falling through one of the large windows below.

"What is it, *älskling?*" she asked as she scooped the child up into her arms, burying her face in the child's smooth, ivory skin.

She inhaled Sabine's natural fragrance. It reminded her of milk and orange flowers, so sweet and delicious, like the summer air after a rain.

The child felt heavy in her arms. She could barely lift her anymore. Her round, chubby limbs and cherubic smile warmed Kaija's heart, but the mere thought that the girl would soon be too old to coddle saddened her deeply, and her emotions got the best of her. Kaija began to cry.

"There will be no more children," Kaija thought to herself as the tears fell over her red and splotchy cheeks. She wondered how Samuel would feel as the years passed and the large house they had bought for themselves echoed in its emptiness. The rooms they had always imagined filling with the beds of several children and their bookshelves and toys were now half-filled with only Sabine's belongings. She wondered if he would grow to resent her or, even worse, wish that he had never married her. Instead, secretly wishing he had chosen another woman, someone whose womb had the capacity to bear more than one.

She had tried to mask her despondency, to get these ridiculous notions out of her head. She thought if she cooked more and spent more time with Sabine in the outdoors, her sprits might lift and she would forget about her diagnosis. However, somehow Kaija's thoughts always returned to her fate. It was ironic, she thought one afternoon when Sabine was napping and she sat at the kitchen table with a mug of tea, how her adopted father had told her to have compassion for a woman whose womb is barren. She had never liked her adopted mother, and even in her memories, with the knowledge of her pitiful state, she never warmed to her. But now, wasn't she very much like the woman she had, for so many years, despised? Hadn't her moods begun to blacken and her face become more weary? Hadn't she been less pleasant to Samuel lately?

She wondered if Samuel or the child had noticed the change within her. She would need to try harder, she said to herself. She needed to maintain her spirits for the sake of Sabine and Samuel. She would not repeat the mistakes of either of the women who had raised her. No matter what, she would keep her grief tucked neatly within her and would not, at any cost, contaminate those whom she loved.

Thirty

Vesterås, Sweden
January 1975

She arrived at his office on Skolgatan Street nervous and full of doubt that this doctor—this so-called war-torture specialist—could possibly help her. Dr. Rudin's office was on the other side of the town, on a small cobblestone street not far from the village church. A place that was so nondescript she would never have found it unless someone had told her it was there.

One of the social workers overseeing the Ribeiro-Herrera family's transition to Swedish life had recommended Salomé see Dr. Samuel Rudin. And then, by coincidence, Salomé met an Argentinean man at the market who also mentioned his name. "He saved my life," the Argentine said to her frankly. "I couldn't make peace with what happened to me over there. But this doctor helped."

Salomé had resisted at first. The thought of seeing a psychiatrist seemed ridiculous to her. "The nightmares will subside eventually," she said to herself. "It has been less than a year. The memories will eventually fade."

But the reverse occurred. With each passing week, the nightmares seemed to intensify. Salomé would awaken at night, her brow beaded with perspiration, her nightgown wet against her breast. She could no longer listen to the radio since hearing *The Magic Flute* playing on the local airwaves.

The mere overture had been enough to terrify her and cause

tremors throughout her body. Upon hearing those seemingly light, airy notes, everything came flooding back to her. She could not control herself. She smashed the radio to the ground. She held her hands over her ears, yet the music inside her head just wouldn't stop.

Halfway up the stairway to the front door, she thought about turning back. "If I go home, nothing will have changed," she thought, reconsidering her decision to abandon her appointment. So, as tempting as it was for her to return home and not follow through with her first therapy session, Salomé Herrera gathered all her strength and pushed open the heavy, brown door.

She was so tired. It had been over ten months since they had arrived in Sweden, and she still felt nothing. She had gone through the motions of packing, emigrating, relocating to a new apartment, and unpacking the few things they had brought from Chile, and still she felt nothing.

The only time she felt anything was when her husband went to touch her and her skin felt on fire. The guards had made sure that everything that had once brought her happiness or comfort now either disgusted or terrified her. The only thing that remained unspoiled was the affection she had for her children. When her husband touched her, she couldn't help but remember what they had done to her. When she heard music, she couldn't help but remember what they had done to her. They had blasphemed two things that had once been beautiful and unblemished in her life. But instead of being angry or being depressed, she was left with an overwhelming sense of nothingness. As if they had returned her hollow, carved her out from the inside, scooped out all her joy, her confidence, her sensuality, and spit it on the cement with the shit and the urine without the slightest bit of remorse.

So the physical scars—the small lacerations on her skin, the small raised bumps on her breasts and her abdomen—were but superficial in comparison to the internal ones. She was empty and she was tired of feeling that way. And the only things that ever seemed capable of filling this emptiness were her nightmares.

"I cannot stand the sound of music," Salomé told Samuel bluntly in Spanish. She was struggling to mask her apprehension and, at the same time, settle comfortably on the long, black couch. "That is why I'm here."

"The sound of music?" he asked her softly, picking up his writing pad and a pen. "And why is that?" The tape recorder that documented Samuel's sessions with his patients hummed quietly in the corner.

"Have you ever heard the sound of a woman screaming because she is having electrical wires placed in her genitalia, while a recording is playing of some Teutonic soprano singing the 'Queen of the Night Aria'?" She paused and looked up to the ceiling. The exposed rafters were made of heavy, brown wood, and Salomé suddenly felt incredibly small. "Have you ever heard such a horrific duet? A harmony of cries and screams, pitched against an orchestra of fairy notes, a whitewash of strings and woodwinds?"

Samuel was silent for a moment, his pen twisting in the air like the propeller of a miniature plane. "No, I have not." He paused. "Tell me, what does it sound like?"

"What do you mean, 'What does it sound like?' " Salomé's face was now buried in her palms. "It is the sound of hell! And it never ends. I can still hear it in my head, the sound of the screaming, the pleading, the begging for mercy—all that merging with the same notes, over and over again.

"You have no idea," she said, shaking her head, the black curls falling over her eyes. "They piped in the recordings to each of our cells, but the main interrogation room bordered next to mine. I heard far more than most of the other inmates. Every night, I closed my eyes and tried to imagine the faces of my children in front of me. I tried to imagine other sounds, like the music of Calandrelli, how I once danced the tango in my husband's arms."

"And did this help?"

Salomé fidgeted against the leather upholstery. "I suppose it did at first. But I was there for several weeks. By the end, I could no longer remember any music. The sound of 'Papageno' had pecked out the sane channels of my mind and replaced it with madness. Since we've arrived in Sweden, I've been unable to listen to music of any kind. They have taken that away from me." She paused. She looked at her palms. The skin where she had grasped the bars to her prison cell had healed. Over the past several months, new layers of skin had replaced the small ridge of tiny calluses. But, underneath her dress, in her most intimate areas, Salomé knew there were scars that were never going to heal.

"They have taken almost everything else as well."

"Were your children and husband abducted?" Samuel asked.

"No," she said flatly. "They only took me."

"I have had patients who have lost their spouses, their children," he said gently. He let his words fall softly and Salomé winced.

Salomé was silent for a moment. "I suppose you've heard a thousand stories and you probably grade them in your head on the varying degrees of horror."

"No, Salomé, I don't do that."

"A woman who knows her children have been tortured is a thousand times worse off than I," she said quietly.

"No, Salomé, what happened to you was horrible and you need to accept that it was terrible and it was wrong."

"Well, that's pretty undisputable."

"But you also need to accept that you can't change the past and that you have to learn to live with your memories."

Salomé shook her head. "Doctor, I would rather I learned how to forget them."

"You can't forget them. You may be able to temporarily push them out of your consciousness, but eventually they will resurface." Samuel paused. "Trauma and the repercussions of that trauma can lie dormant in a body for years. Eventually, however, it needs to come out. Eventually, every person who has been a victim of brutality will have to reconcile themselves to their past."

Salomé fidgeted. "You're going to be the only person who knows my story. I am not going to share it with my husband, my friends, or even write it down for my own sake. Only here will I tell it."

Samuel nodded. "We'll take this slowly, Salomé. One session at a time." He looked gently at his patient, seeing through her determined expression of stoicism, noticing that she was actually fighting back her urge to cry.

Thirty-One

❧

Vesterås, Sweden
February 1975

$\mathcal{D}$octor Rudin, I had only been detained six hours, but it seemed I had been away a lifetime. By the time I arrived home, it was nightfall and Octavio and the children were frantic and near tears.

"My face was bruised and my clothes streaked with car grease and tar. But I still had my wits about me."

Samuel smiled slightly, nodding his head and writing on his pad.

"I knew that I would alarm the children if I just announced that I had been abducted by the secret police, so I told them I had been in a small bicycle accident and that I just need to wash up and take a bath. I ordered Consuela to hurry them to bed so that I could be alone with Octavio."

"He must have been worried, not knowing where you had gone."

"Yes, he was, and he realized immediately that I had not been in an accident, that something far more terrible had taken place. 'Salomé?' he asked softly, so that neither the children nor the maid could hear him. 'Was it the DINA?'

" 'Yes,' I told him, and I began to cry. I had been terrified for so many hours that only then did I feel safe enough to weep. 'What have they done to my precious Fayum?' he whispered as he held me. Through his shirt, I could hear his heart pounding, his skin reddening with anger at those who had abducted me.

" 'You cannot do anything. You cannot strike back at them,' I told him. 'This is not the old Chile. We are no longer free. Pinochet has made it a police state. We cannot trust anyone but ourselves and our family. Not even the neighbors. Who knows what they've already said about us.'

" 'But what did they want from you? Whoever could have said anything about you, my darling?'

" 'It was not me,' I told him, and I began to cry because never in my life had I been so afraid. So completely terrified. 'It's you they want.'

" 'Me?'

" 'They know about your meetings with Allende. They know you coached him.'

" 'How could they know that, Salomé? We told no one. How could they know that information?' I could see the fear in his eyes.

" 'I don't know, Octavio. Maybe someone at the studio saw you with Neruda. Maybe someone remembered seeing you at the café with Allende and his campaign managers. After all, you have a very recognizable face. But that is why I am saying that we can trust no one. Maybe one of Allende's assistants told them in an interrogation like mine. Someone has betrayed us and the police are using me to get to you.'

" 'Cowards!' he said, and I had to tell him again to whisper. 'They take a man's wife to get to him,' and he began to cry because he saw me standing there in front of him bruised and shaken, the victim of an injustice that he was powerless, at this point, to correct.

" 'What can I do, Salomé, to make them leave us alone? What did they want?'

" 'They want a man in your position to openly support Pinochet. A man with your appeal would be a perfect face for a poster or television commercial. If you support him, they believe it will be a gesture of good faith,' I said hesitantly.

"Octavio pulled out one of the kitchen chairs and sat down, cupping his face in his palms.

" 'How can I do that, my love?' he said, now looking up at me. 'How can I support someone who is capable of such brutality? Who can do what they did to you and to Allende. How can I do that?'

"I remember that I just looked at him blankly. My bruises were beginning to deepen and I needed to get some ice. I was so shocked by his response. I couldn't believe that he was still saying the same things even after I had been kidnapped!"

"I can imagine," Samuel said, nodding his head. "What did you say to him after that?"

"I think I said something to the effect of, 'You can do what you want, Octavio,' but really I was angry. I was truly furious. I couldn't believe that he wouldn't take the necessary steps to protect us and make sure this never happened again. I mean, wouldn't you think that a man would want to protect his family at any cost . . . even if that meant sacrificing his pride?"

"Yes, I would. Unless he felt that he could control the situation."

"There was no way anyone could control what was happening in Chile. Everyone was at risk!"

"You didn't tell him that you felt that way, Salomé?" Samuel asked her.

"No. I didn't."

"Why not?"

"I suppose I was in a state of disbelief. I thought it was his conscience, that he'd have to live with himself. I couldn't force him to make the decision I wanted him to."

Samuel scribbled in his pad and then looked up. "Then what happened?"

"He called after me. I went into the kitchen. I did not answer him. I didn't want to be near him. I slept in the spare bedroom that night and did not rise until the next morning. I didn't even get up to say good-bye to him when he left the house early that next morning."

Thirty-Two

Vesterås, Sweden
February 1975

$\mathcal{T}$ hree weeks after my first abduction, my husband and I were invited to a formal ball at a large villa to celebrate Chile's de facto leader, General Pinochet. The star-studded event was planned to be nationally televised, to show the people of Chile all the famous faces that supported the new regime. Naturally, my husband refused to go.

"I don't blame my husband for his decision. Neither of us, looking back on it, thought that this would be the deciding factor in determining our family's fate. Anyway, I was still weary from my abduction and I didn't want to attend the event either. I truly thought they would come and ask him to make an appearance with the general once the palace was restored. I thought it would be a personal invitation with no more than two to three other guests, and at that point, I would have insisted that he go. A party? Who would have known?"

"Do you think your husband would have gone if he had known what the consequences to you would be by not going?" Samuel asked.

"I have to believe that, though I guess I'll never know."

"So you believe he would have gone?"

"I know my husband loved me. That he still does." She paused and seemed to spend several minutes reflecting on the doctor's question.

"By the same token, supporting a dictator who had, in his mind, murdered his friend, a president elected by the people of Chile, would violate his conscience."

"Yes . . ."

"I tell you, we decided as a couple not to go to this ball. I wanted to spend time with the children and work on restoring my relationship with Octavio. I remember that he wrote back on the response card in front of me that, 'regretfully,' we could not attend.

"I tried to pretend life was normal for us now. But every night, I dreamt of being abducted. Some nights, as I lay dreaming, I could swear I was inhaling the scent of those soldiers, and I would awaken covered in a cold sweat.

"Octavio stopped publicly denouncing Pinochet, and I believed we would be left alone." Salomé paused. "Obviously, Dr. Rudin, I was very wrong."

Thirty-Three

✧

Santiago, Chile
January 1974

Salomé went to the market a week after her first abduction, hoping to calm her nerves by busying herself with errands. The perfume of the local *nisperos* and ripening melons filled the air, and Salomé felt her senses awaken. She had felt so numbed over the past few days, incapable of eating very much, and was despondent with Octavio. But now, with the colors and bustle surrounding her, she felt grateful and incredibly alive.

She inhaled the scent of crisp, green coriander and bushels of sharp garlic. She gazed at the pyramids of deep red tomatoes and small-clefted apricots. She filled her basket with bunches of grapes and peaches, bought two salamis, and bargained with the fishmonger for two kilos of *machas*. She decided that she would bake those for dinner that evening with a sprinkling of Parmesan cheese.

In the sunlight, her pale green sheath looked dazzling, as though she were dressed in a silk that had been dyed in the juice of limes. Her black hair was thick and full around her shoulders, her lean brown legs tapered and strong.

She had covered her bruised face with powder and a little bit of camouflage cream. At first glance, it was barely noticeable. But, upon closer inspection, one might glimpse a patch of blue beneath her cheekbone. As though a tiny plum had been trapped underneath a canvas of delicate skin. Occasionally, she lifted her hand when she spoke to a merchant, hoping to distract him from looking at her face too closely. She would pretend to smooth her eyebrow or brush off a fly, or sometimes she would just dip her head ever so slightly so that her hair would fall over her cheek.

She had not expected to meet anyone, as it was nearly three o'clock and the market was busiest before noon. However, as she turned to inspect some *gamberas*, she heard a strangely familiar voice calling her from behind.

"Salomé? Is that you?"

She turned around and saw a vaguely familiar face staring back at her.

"It's me, Manuel. Manuel Chon-Vargas!"

"Manuel?" Salomé grasped her free hand to her breast. "I can not believe it is you!" She put down her basket and embraced him.

"It has been too long," he lamented.

"How are you? I haven't seen you since those summers when we were children, and your parents visited mine at the hacienda. How are your sisters, your mother and father?"

"They are all well, thank you. And yours?"

"Fine, fine. You have a wife now, don't you?"

"She is well, though we have fallen on some difficult times, but that is a long story." He paused. "And what about you? I heard you're married to the famous actor Octavio Ribeiro."

Salomé blushed. "Well, I don't know about *famous*, but we have three children, a son and two daughters."

"God has been good to you." He gently brushed his hand against her cheek.

She could sense that he'd noticed her bruise, though he said nothing to her about it. She quickly asked him something to distract him from it.

"You should give me your telephone number and we should get together. It would be lovely for our spouses to have the opportunity to meet."

His smile seemed to grow tense. "That would indeed be wonderful, though Adelaida has been rather poor company lately, I'm afraid. Ever since our villa was confiscated, she has not been herself."

"Confiscated?" Salomé whispered with great disbelief. "What in heaven's name happened?"

"I can't really go into detail," he said in hushed tones. "But a band of soldiers came one evening and told us at gunpoint that we would have to leave."

"And you left?"

"At gunpoint, Salomé, one has little choice." He bowed his head. "You can imagine how awful this has been for my wife. The Villa Grimaldi was her ancestral home."

Salomé nodded her head. "Yes, I can only imagine how terrible this must be for you and your family." She wondered if she should tell him of her own ordeal, but decided against it. Perhaps he already suspected. It was well-known that Octavio had been voicing anti-Pinochet remarks in the weeks before her abduction. The national papers had even slandered him.

"The worst part of it all," Manuel continued, his fingers shaking over his mouth, "is that I believe the secret police are now using the villa as some sort of detention center to interrogate and torture people whom they consider enemies of the state."

Salomé's eyes widened. Immediately, she thought of the place she had been taken only a week before.

"But isn't it near the city? Could they do that in a place where people are so close by?" she asked coyly, hoping to gather information that would confirm her suspicion that she had, indeed, been taken to the same place.

"Unfortunately, it would be the perfect place for such a thing. It's located only a few kilometers away from the main city in a rural section of Santiago, not far from the mountains—no neighbors except for a few migrants in their temporary tents along the roads." He sighed. "We had always believed it would be a perfect place to raise children. You know, it used to be an old vineyard back in the forties. But only the terra-cotta jugs lining the entranceway are left from those days." He chuckled slightly, but the laughter was heavy with nostalgia and regret.

"It must have been lovely," Salomé said sympathetically.

"Oh, it was! There was even a tower to play in," he said regretfully, "and ancient gates to climb." He shook his head again.

Manuel now seemed completely lost in a dream as he stood there with his head bowed in front of her. As if he needed to recall that which had been taken from him.

"It was a beautiful place, Salomé. When my mother-in-law was alive, the garden was in bloom with round, powder-pink peonies, African violets, and cinnamon trees whose branches swept low and perfumed the air. And the kitchen . . . what a sight that was! Three stoves, a vaulted ceiling covered in cerulean blue tiles imported from the south of Spain. Copper pots reflecting the midday sun." He paused. "There was this beautiful cherimoya tree that grew outside the terrace. When we ate breakfast, we could see it framed in the pane of the center window. Those soldiers are such beasts, who knows what they are doing there. Certainly not observing beauty."

"Yes. Yes. It is such a shame."

Salomé had been listening to his vivid descriptions with great intensity. She would never forget that name: Villa Grimaldi. That must have been where she had been taken. She remembered seeing a gate and a tower, and the distance from Santiago seemed to be the same as well. She had seen the mountains from underneath her blindfold, as well as the *poblaciónes callampas*—the makeshift houses of the hobos along the way.

"I am sorry to have heaped all of this on you, Salomé. Adelaida and I are living off of Recoleta Street. You are right, it would be wonderful to have the chance to catch up with you and meet the famed Octavio Ribeiro."

"Yes," she told him again. "It would. Let's do it soon."

He kissed her good-bye, and they agreed to call each other in the next couple of weeks.

Salomé returned home and did not mention her encounter with Manuel in the market to Octavio. She thought it would only excite Octavio about another injustice of the new regime. However, she thought of it often when she was alone.

She never believed she would need the information for herself and, instead, tucked it away neatly in her mind in case a friend or relative was kidnapped as she had been.

But two weeks later there was another knock at her door. Octavio was sleeping in the garden, a newspaper spread over his face.

Salomé opened the door to find three men with machine guns staring at her.

"Salomé Herrera? We have come for you." They reached out to pull her by the arm.

"What do you want with me?" she pleaded. "I have nothing you need. You have asked me all the questions before."

"You are needed again," the shorter man said sternly.

Stricken with fear, Salomé knew she had to get word to Octavio, to tell him where they were probably taking her. Thinking quickly, Salomé looked back behind her and saw seven-year-old Rafael standing there with his eyes transfixed.

"At least, let me say good-bye to my son."

The senior soldier nodded.

She knelt down and whispered in Rafael's ear, speaking as slowly and clearly as she could: "Tell your father I have been taken. Tell him these words, if you can remember no others." The little boy nodded. She whispered in his ear something he would never forget: "Villa Grimaldi."

Part II

Thirty-Four

Santiago, Chile
January 1974

*S*econds after the dark van sped from the driveway, Rafael rushed through the house to find his father. He discovered him on the patio, his chest rising and falling with sleep.

"Papa," the little boy uttered to him, flicking the daily paper that covered Octavio's eyes. "Mama's gone."

"Where has she gone, Rafaelito?" he asked as he drowsily read-justed himself in his chair.

"Three men . . . they . . . they took her."

"What?" Octavio cried, nearly leaping from his chair. "What men?"

"The men who came to our door."

"When, Rafael? When did they come?"

"Just now, Papa."

Octavio ran through the garden and into the house. Rafael followed him, crying out, "Villa Grimaldi, Papa! Villa Grimaldi!"

But Octavio was not listening to the boy now. He was searching the house, hoping that his son was mistaken and that Salomé was busying herself in one of its many rooms.

"This can't be!" Octavio cried, his fist clutched to his mouth. "Why would they take her again?" He was in shock. His face was red, his black hair wild and high. They had taken her while he lay napping.

"Papa," Rafael softly said again. He stood next to his father. His trousers were rolled above his knees and his red T-shirt was soiled from his having spent the afternoon playing in the garden. "Mama told me to tell you something . . ." He paused and scrunched his face in concentration. "Villa Grimaldi."

"What?"

"Yes, Papa. She whispered it to me right before she left."

"But what does that mean? Are you sure, Rafael?"

"Yes, I'm sure. She told me not to forget."

Rafael stood in front of him, his voice shaking, as he clearly saw that the words that his mother had last spoken to him caused his father great concern and worry.

"Papa, what is it?" he asked as his boyish eyebrows wiggled like two soft caterpillars. "Will Mommy be all right?"

Octavio tried to mask his fear for his young son, but the shock of awakening to find his wife abducted was too much for even an accomplished actor to hide.

"Go and get your father a glass of water," he ordered his son.

As the boy ran back into the house, Octavio raised his fists to his face. "Bastards!" he cried, his eyes pink with anger. He was sitting on the edge of the lounge chair, his back curved with despair, when Rafael returned. Holding a glass of water in his trembling hand, he overheard his father mumbling to himself, his head bowed to his knees, "I was the one they should have taken. They should have taken me!"

Octavio prayed each of the first few nights after Salomé was abducted, hoping that she might be returned. He lay in their canopied bed and extended his arm to the side where his wife always slept. The empty space brought tears to his eyes.

"What have I done to my family?" he said aloud, knotting his knuckles into his temples. The reality of his wife's kidnapping weighed so heavily on him that his once smooth skin disappeared, replaced by a furrowed forehead and twisted brows. He felt as though he had failed in his role as father and protector. He had let everyone down.

The children had been asking for their mother for days, but he had no answers for them. Salomé's parents too had come in search of their daughter, and he could not lie to them either.

"They've taken her," he told them, his voice nearly collapsing from his despair. "They came to the house and seized her while I was asleep in the garden."

"You were asleep?" his father in-law asked with disbelief.

"Yes."

"He was asleep in the garden! Did you hear that, Olivia? Our son-in-law was asleep in the garden while our daughter was abducted by the military police!"

Doña Olivia shook her head. She withdrew a linen kerchief and dabbed her eyes.

"Octavio," she said gently. "What can we do?"

"Do! Do!" Don Fernando roared. "They have already taken her! Olivia, you have heard stories like this! The city is full of them. Parents whose children have disappeared. They vanish without a trace. They're impossible to find." The old man was yelling now, and the children began to approach from their activities in the garden. He lowered his voice. "The military are experts at making people disappear."

"I will find her," Octavio said quietly. "Salomé left me a clue."

"A clue?" Fernando asked incredulously. He was looking at his son-in-law with the same disdain he had when he'd first laid eyes on him some ten years before.

"Yes. She whispered in Rafael's ear, just before she was taken, the words Villa Grimaldi."

"Why would she have said that?"

"I'm not sure. But it obviously meant something. She explicitly told Rafael to tell me."

"I think that's the ancestral home of the Grimaldi family. Fernando, didn't the Chon-Vargas boy marry into that family?"

"Yes." Dr. Herrera nodded. "I think the villa is located a few kilometers outside the main city."

"But why have they taken Salomé there?" Doña Olivia's silk sleeves rustled as she fidgeted in her seat. "What has she done to deserve this?"

"She has done nothing, Doña Olivia," Octavio replied, his head bowed to his chest.

"They took the wrong person," he said after a long pause. "Salomé has done absolutely nothing to deserve this."

Thirty-Five

❧

Vesterås, Sweden
February 1975

$\mathcal{I}$ was bound and gagged, slapped and beaten, before being thrown into a cell that was no larger than three meters by two meters. It was nothing more than a concrete bunker that smelled of human waste and had no windows. I lay there for hours, my wrists handcuffed behind me, doubting that I would ever be returned. You must believe me when I tell you I thought that I was going to die in that prison, amongst the sound of screams and the drone of the incessant music that attempted to mask the wails. I have never known such a hell as I did there.

"Two hours passed before I was taken to the interrogation room. The guards came and pulled me out by both arms, dragging me through a long, narrow corridor that was illuminated by gas lights. I must have passed two dozen filthy cells that mirrored my own. The people inside barely seemed human. White eyes peered out from dirt-smeared faces. Some were covered with dried blood.

" 'Keep moving!' one of the guards yelled, as he shoved me forward. I remember that as I tried to regain my balance, I was kicked in the small of my back. This guard, I can still remember his face. He was a young boy. No more than sixteen years old. Kicking me as if I were nothing more than a sack of bones. 'You Marxist cunt!' he called me, time and time again."

Samuel shuddered. Although he had heard stories similar to

Salomé's before, listening to such a young, beautiful woman, a mother of three, recount such brutality was particularly disturbing to him.

"I don't even think I can bring myself to remember the brutality I endured during the first few days I was there. They did such horrible things," Salomé said, then paused. "Things no one should have to go through. And we women, what they did to us was so awful, so shameful . . . if Octavio had any idea, he would have never been able to look at me in the same way."

In the low light of Dr. Samuel Rudin's office, Salomé's face looked as though it had been stolen from a Velázquez portrait. Her regal features tightened as she tried to fight back her tears, and her long, black hair fell over her shoulders.

"During my first interrogation, I was slapped, punched in the face, breasts, and abdomen.

"I was told over and over again by the interrogator that I was a socialist whore, a communist bitch. Repeat after me, he screamed, 'I am nothing more than a fucking communist bitch!'

"I said nothing.

"Repeat after me, you fucking *puta:* 'I am a fucking communist bitch!'

"I started to cry. He hit me with the butt of his rifle and kicked me in the stomach with his boots."

Salomé stopped, lowered her eyes, and rubbed her temples.

"I don't know if can continue, Doctor."

"Take your time, Salomé. We're not in a hurry here."

Salomé inhaled deeply. The words eventually came to her. Haltingly at first, but then they seemed to spew forth.

"The interrogator unbuckled his belt and forced me on my back with the heel of his boot. Then he spread his legs over my neck, held me up to him by my throat, and then forced himself into my mouth.

"They told me that they would kill my husband and my children if I did not cooperate. They told me that I had to repent for my husband's sins or they would kill my children!"

She was now sobbing uncontrollably. Samuel reached for a box of tissues and handed them to her. In the light, her face was now red, her features swollen and lined with tears.

"Up until that moment, I had never known any other man

besides my husband. Can you imagine such a thing? Can you imagine?"

"No . . ." Samuel folded his hands in his lap and looked at his patient with great compassion. "I am so sorry."

Salomé blotted her eyes. She was surprised by the way the words were pouring out of her. It was the first time she had ever spoken of what had been done to her, and she felt as if a floodgate had been opened.

"When I refused to admit to conspiring against the government, my face was repeatedly forced into a bucket of urine and human feces. When I insisted that I had never committed a crime against the state, they called me a fucking liar over and over again. I was raped. I was given strong electric shocks. I don't even think I remember half of what I went through. The mind works so strangely . . . I think I'd go insane if I remembered everything they did to me."

Her nose was now running and she reached for a tissue.

"I suppose I came here hoping that, in a few sessions, I would be cured of my nightmares, that I would be able to embrace my husband as I had before. That I would be able to listen to music and feel joy, not terror, and not be paralyzed with fear and dread."

"You really thought that in a few fifty-minute sessions we would be able to tackle all that, Salomé?" He looked at her sympathetically, smiling slightly as he shook his head.

She smiled back at him, her eyes peering up from the crumpled tissue. "I know I am being unrealistic, but I feel like I am living a lie. Every day, I am forced to pretend that I am the same woman I was before this all happened to me. I must smile to my children and tuck them in at night, promising them that what they see in their nightmares are only figments of their imagination. Yet, I have actually lived my nightmares. No one can tell me they were only a dream."

"Yes, what you are saying is true," Samuel agreed. "But, Salomé, I understand that you would not want to share these feelings with your children, but surely you can unburden yourself somewhat to Octavio?"

"No, I cannot!" She continued to cry into her tissue. "I cannot share anything with him because I am afraid to!" She was shaking her head now. "If I begin to tell him how I feel, I'm sure I will say things I will regret."

"Like what?"

"I don't know."

Silence filled the room and Samuel continued to stare at his patient.

"I think you do know."

Salomé continued to say nothing.

"Do you blame him, Salomé, for what happened to you?"

"No."

"Not at all?"

"No."

"Then why are you afraid of what you might say to him?"

"I just am!" She paused. "Maybe I'm afraid he'll reject me if he knows how I was used in that prison. Maybe I'm afraid he won't be able to love me in the same way . . ."

"But, you've already said that *you* can't embrace him. Aren't you the one who has been doing the rejecting?"

"Yes, but . . ."

"But what?"

"Maybe because I'd rather be the one who is doing the rejecting than be the one who is refused."

"I don't think it's that simple, Salomé."

"All I know is that it is an awful thing to feel that your husband might look upon you differently. I mean, this is the man I have loved since I was seventeen! He is the father of my children, for God's sake! How could I live with myself, knowing that every time he holds me, he envisions another man raping me?"

"How do you know he would think that?"

"I don't know. But I believe that if he knew what happened to me, he couldn't help but think that way."

"So you don't want to tell him what was done to you—but, clearly, you are angry with him. Explain this to me: Are you angry with him for what was done to you, or are you upset that he doesn't understand what you are going through?"

"I have already told you, I'm not angry with my husband for what happened to me."

"All right then, tell me what you are angry with him about."

Salomé pushed her black hair behind her ears and straightened her back. She was becoming increasingly irritated.

"I'm sorry if these questions are annoying you, Salomé. It's just that I find it hard to believe that the entire time you were lying there in your filthy, cramped cell, after enduring endless brutality—the electric shocks, the rapes—all of that, you never once blamed your husband?"

"No."

Samuel lowered his voice even further, approaching his next question with tremendous caution.

"You never once said to yourself, 'Why is this happening to me? What have I done to deserve this? Why do I have to suffer for the actions of my husband?' "

"No! No! No!" Her eyes were closed now, and her hands covered her ears. Her whole body was shaking underneath her.

"Salomé?"

After a few minutes of silence, Salomé finally answered.

"Yes," she whispered.

"Yes, Salomé?"

"Perhaps I did. Sometimes."

"Sometimes what?"

"Sometimes I did think that." Her voice was now barely audible.

Silence again permeated the room. Samuel watched his patient carefully. Salome's face collapsed, and once again, she began to cry.

"I *was* angry at him."

"Of course you were."

"I suppose I was angry at him even before I was abducted. I was angry that he didn't stop and think about how his actions might affect us as a family."

"I think you have a right to be angry, Salomé."

"Do I? Sometimes I think I am responsible for what he did. There can be no other explanation for why he refused to listen to me."

"I'm not following you . . ." Samuel looked perplexed.

"Well, up until Octavio was approached by Neruda, he had made great sacrifices so he could provide the children and me with the best life possible. I know he felt intimidated by my background, and I know he played the role of movie star begrudgingly. In an ideal world, he would have been a poet or at least a schoolteacher. My husband had great expectations that he would bring beauty and knowledge into the world. He hated the vacuous life of a movie star. He was typecast as the same character over and over again: 'the romantic lead' . . . 'the man with the soulful eyes' . . ."

Samuel nodded. "Go on."

"Well, helping Allende was a role he cherished. Finally, he was approached by someone with intellect and vision. He thought it was a chance to use his talents to achieve something of greater meaning." Salomé cleared her throat. "Octavio believed in Allende," she stressed. "He was flattered that they thought he could help their campaign."

"But by doing this, he put his family in jeopardy."

"Yes, but I'm sure he didn't do it on purpose. He just didn't fully foresee the consequences."

"That sounds rather naive."

"Yes. My husband is naive. I suppose that's his most tragic flaw," she said, before pausing. "I fell in love with his idealism. It's ironic that the very trait that I cherished in him is the one that I now resent."

"You were eighteen when you married. You've experienced far more in those ten years since you were wed than most people do in a lifetime, Salomé."

"I know that, but still it's difficult to feel one has matured and developed but one's partner hasn't."

"Do you really believe Octavio hasn't changed? I find it hard to believe that a man who experiences the terror of having his wife abducted from his very home cannot be changed from that experience."

Salomé was silent for a moment. "Perhaps I can't see how he's changed. Perhaps I am so focused on how I have suffered . . . how I've lost part of myself, that now I can no longer see my husband clearly."

"Perhaps you can't." Samuel raised an eyebrow at his patient. He looked up from his notepad and was struck by how pale Salomé appeared. She suddenly seemed so unsure of herself, her face revealing her conflict of emotions.

"You need to understand that these feelings you are having—the anger, the resentment, the constant questioning of your current situation—these are all natural."

"Yes, I know. But it's difficult to admit that I have these feelings."

"Of course it is. But you cannot censor yourself. By denying certain emotions, you are doing harm to yourself and to those you love."

"I don't want to be angry or resentful toward him. I want to forgive him."

"Of course you do, but it is not only you who needs to get counseling. Has Octavio considered seeing someone? I can only imagine the guilt he must have."

"He refuses to see anyone."

"That concerns me, Salomé. He should see a counselor. Even without the trauma of your abduction, I would think he would have trouble adjusting to a foreign country and culture."

"You're right," Salomé agreed quietly. "And it has been especially difficult for him, considering that, at least before the coup, he enjoyed a position of fame and respect in Chile. Here, he has no identity other than a newly arrived immigrant."

Samuel nodded. "I know that feeling."

"And he has yet to find a job."

Samuel nodded sympathetically. "You both need to be speaking to someone right now. Each of you has your own pressures . . . your own pain and guilt. If you are unable to discuss these things between yourselves, at least try and have some professional guidance."

"I know, I know." Salomé shook her head. "I will try and speak to him about it again."

"All right then." Samuel folded his hands. He paused and pressed the stop button on his tape recorder, which was documenting their session. "Let's stop here for now. You must be tired from such a difficult session. But you did well, Salomé. It takes real strength to force yourself to relive such painful memories and admit the feelings you have about them."

"I just hope it's worth it in the end." She sounded weary and exhausted from their session.

"It will be, Salomé," Samuel said softly, trying consciously not to gaze too intently at his patient sitting demurely on the leather sofa.

She gathered herself from the couch, smoothing the material of her skirt over her knees as she stood up and shook out her hair with a toss of her head. Samuel was struck by Salomé's beauty.

"I hope to see you next week, then."

"Yes, of course, Doctor."

"Good. We'll continue where we left off." Samuel stood up to show Salomé to the door. "Until next week, then. I look forward to it."

He stumbled over his last words a bit. He thought, "It's quite all right to look forward to seeing a patient again." There was nothing wrong with that. After all, he was helping her on her road to recovery. And saving her marriage as well.

Now all he had to do was see about attending to his own relationship. Lately, his wife had not seemed like herself at all, and he was beginning to realize that perhaps he and Kaija had issues between them that they needed to address.

So, in the blue-gray winter, crushing the frost underneath his heels, Samuel Rudin hurried home to the family he knew would be waiting for him.

Thirty-Six

Vesterås, Sweden
February 1975

*T*hat evening, Samuel arrived home to find Sabine playing alone in the living room. He crouched down and hugged his little girl. "Where's your mama, *älskling?*" he asked the child.

"Sleeping." Sabine pointed with one of her small, pink fingers to the rooms above. "She's in her room."

Samuel was surprised by the state of the house. The lights were turned off in the kitchen, and when he flicked on the switch, he found the sink full of dirty dishes and a burnt pot on the stove.

"How odd," he thought to himself as he glanced over the room. Usually, Kaija maintained a fastidious household. This seemed rather out of character for his wife, though she certainly hadn't been acting like herself for the past few weeks.

Upstairs, he found Kaija asleep in the bedroom, one leg draped from underneath the covers, the other curled beneath a twisted sheet. Her cotton nightgown revealed the outline of her thin body.

Samuel sat down on the edge of the bed, untied his shoes, and loosened his collar.

He wasn't sure if he should wake her. It was already half past six, and little Sabine would be getting hungry soon. But Kaija really seemed to need this rest.

From the look of her swollen eyelids, he suspected that she had been crying.

He couldn't help but remember how his mother had been when she first began to spiral into depression. She too began with a proclivity for afternoon naps, a growing disinterest in her physical appearance, and a lack of energy to maintain the household. Seeing his wife lying in their bed, her face slightly swollen from sleep, echoed memories of his mother long ago. He was unnerved. For the first time, he saw troubling similarities between the two women who had dominated the different stages of his life.

He wondered if he had, on some subconscious level, married Kaija because he was attracted to her fragility and her vulnerability. Had he married a woman whose problems he thought he could solve simply by exchanging wedding vows and giving birth to children of their own just to compensate for his failure to save his own family?

If he were honest with himself, he would have sat himself down on his own couch and said, "Samuel, you suffer from helping syndrome. You're attracted to what's broken. You want to glue back what's fractured." Sometimes Samuel had to remind himself to take a step back and look at his own past and his own family. Like his patients, he had scars of his own, and he too struggled to live with them.

That evening, Kaija awakened from her nap and went downstairs to find Samuel clearing the dishes from the spaghetti meal he had made for himself and their daughter. She could not hide her embarrassment.

"I'm sorry, Samuel," she apologized. "I only thought I would sleep for a few minutes or so . . . I never meant to sleep this long." She was now rubbing her eyes. The long, terry-cloth sash from her robe dangled at her sides.

"That's quite all right, Kaija. I managed everything all right, I think."

Sabine was smiling at her father, her face covered in red sauce.

"Let me have that washcloth over there, Samuel," Kaija asked softly. "I need to wipe her cheeks."

"No, no, I'll do it," he said as he went to the drawer to get a fresh cloth.

"No, Samuel, give it to me." She started walking over to the table.

"Don't be ridiculous, I can do it. Go back upstairs and rest, sweetheart."

"I don't need to rest, Samuel!" Kaija said sternly. "I can take care of my child! I don't need you to patronize me like I'm incapable of doing the littlest thing."

"Of course I know that, Kaija . . ." Samuel seemed stunned that his wife could suddenly be this angry with him for something he thought so minuscule. "I'm just trying to be helpful."

"Well, you're not!" She went over and snatched the washcloth from his hand and wiped off Sabine's hands and fingers. "I think I am still capable of doing that, don't you think?"

"Yes, Kaija. But there is no need for hostility." Samuel placed his hand on the table. "I was only trying to give you the space I thought you needed."

"Space? Space?" Her voice was shrill, surprising both the little girl and Samuel.

Sabine began to cry.

At the sound of her daughter's wails, Kaija suddenly stopped midsentence. "I'm sorry, Samuel," she said as she went to Sabine and picked her up in her arms. "I don't know what's come over me."

Samuel nodded. He untied the apron that had covered his trousers and folded it over the sink.

"I understand," he said in his calm, practiced voice. "I understand how you feel, but it will do neither of us any good to yell at me."

"I'm sorry. It's just that I've been so exhausted . . ."

"I know," he said, trying to sound as compassionate as he could. But, clearly, he was losing his patience. "Kaija, I want you to know that, if there is anything—I mean *anything*—that you'd like to discuss with me, I am always here for you."

She tried to smile at him, her eyes crinkling at the edges like two paper fans.

"People tell me I'm a great listener," he said with a slight grin. "Some are even foolish enough to pay me to listen to their problems."

Kaija managed a small laugh. "I know, Samuel. It's just a phase I'm going through. It will pass."

Samuel, indeed, hoped that it would pass, but he remained

skeptical. Both his professional and personal instincts told him that something was clearly bothering his wife. But, she remained secretive, refusing to tell him exactly what was wrong.

Looking at his wife now, the fluorescent light of the kitchen intensifying the blue-white of her skin, the image of his mother returned to him once more. All Kaija needed was a housecoat and a kerchief tied around her head, and she would be the mirror image of his mother after the war. This time, he was old enough to help guide the woman in his life. Yet, somehow, he was still helpless to do anything. Once again, he remained on the outside looking in.

Later that evening, as the two of them sat in the living room, Samuel with the newspaper spread over his lap and Kaija with a magazine, the silence between them deafening, Samuel tried once more to broach the subject of his wife's recent depression.

"Kaija, are you sure there's nothing wrong?" He paused and placed the paper to the side. His voice, soft and tender, was the same voice he used with all of his patients. "This is becoming increasingly difficult for me. You're pushing me away and I feel utterly helpless. Perfect strangers open up to me every day, yet my own wife refuses to do so."

Kaija's eyes remained fixed on the pages of her magazine. There was nothing for her to focus on except the glossy image of a young woman in a bathing suit holding a platter of artfully arranged watermelon wedges, but she preferred to look at that than the beseeching eyes of her husband. Why, she wondered, couldn't he just stop it already? She attributed her increasing frustration to Samuel's constantly pushing her to explain herself. Couldn't he just leave her alone and let her deal with her problems on her own?

She didn't want to burden him with all the facts now—all the medical jargon about her condition. She knew that, as soon as she told him, he would jump up from his chair and head for his office. He'd pull down his medical encyclopedia and try to find the reason for her condition; he would want to explore every possible treatment. But the doctor had been clear. There was no cure. She, a young woman of thirty-five, could no longer conceive.

Kaija waited for several seconds before responding to Samuel. She could sense that he was desperate to have an argument, a loud and passionate discussion that would clear the tension between them. Yet, Kaija remained unwilling.

"I am fine," she replied tersely. "Please, Samuel, enough of this incessant inquiring on my behalf." She bit the small middle portion of her lower lip. "No more of this. I will *tell* you when I need you to assist me with my mental health. In the meantime, don't you have some work to do? Perhaps some files of a patient, someone who really needs your assistance?"

"I suppose I do," he responded quietly. He stood up and folded the newspaper, returning it to the place on the coffee table where he had found it nearly an hour before.

"Don't wait up for me," he whispered to his wife as he made his way upstairs. "I'll probably be a while."

Kaija made no indication that she was listening.

He entered his office and took out from his briefcase the folders of the various patients he had seen that afternoon. Salomé's was on top.

He opened up the manila file, turned on his desk light, and sat down in his heavy, wooden chair. Recently, Samuel had found himself thinking of Salomé more and more frequently. Sometimes, he would be caught by surprise as his mind lingered on a particular memory of her during one of their sessions. He smiled as he recalled the delicate movements of her hands—how they turned ever so slightly to punctuate her sentences.

He bit the bottom of his pen and pondered the majestic length of her neck, the curve of her collarbone, which seemed to be carved out in high relief from her fragile frame. Initially, it was her frankness that he had found so attractive. However, in the weeks that had passed between them, he had noticed a change. It was as if the frightened, vulnerable woman who had first arrived at his office was transforming herself into a stronger, more passionate woman. Undeniably, the combination of her courage and fire had intensified his attraction to her.

Salomé claimed she had initially come to him to recover from her inability to listen to music. But Samuel had realized, almost immediately, that she needed no prescription or intensive psycho-analysis. She only needed to be guided slightly, someone to ask her the right questions. Someone with whom she could discuss her anger and her resentment. Someone to whom she could reveal her story completely. He really was only there to listen.

With all his years of experience, Samuel had learned that the power of listening was entwined with the capacity to heal. And Salomé Herrera would be healed of her terror. He was confident of that. The only person that he was worried about, who might slip further away from him, was his wife.

He heard his wife's footsteps treading quietly into their bedroom. He saw her going into their daughter's room once more to make sure that the child slept undisturbed. There was so much goodness in his wife. He had loved her since that first moment she'd asked him if she could draw him in the park. He didn't want to think of his patient Salomé as he had been recently. It was wrong. It was against his professional and personal ethics. He desperately wanted to have eyes only for Kaija.

But Kaija was not herself. And he was at a loss to help her. Nor did she seem to want his help. Samuel closed Salomé's folder and tried to shake his new patient from his mind.

He turned off his desk light and sat down in his leather chair, falling asleep at his desk with his manila folders stacked before him. And, as it had been when he'd first entered the room, Salomé Herrera's file remained neatly on top.

Thirty-Seven

❧

Villa Grimaldi
January 1974

*T*he first time they applied the electrical wires to Salomé, they did not strip off her clothing. Instead, they applied the nodes only to her hands and mouth, shooting currents of fire through her delicate veins. She shrieked and hollered, writhing in the chair to which she was strapped. Begging them to have mercy on her. Pleading for them to stop.

The second, third, and fourth times, they took her to the interrogation room, ripped her clothes off, tied her to a metal table, and inserted clamps on her breasts and the folds of her genitalia. They turned the electrical currents on and poured water over her body to intensify the pain.

Her skin was burned purple in places that had once been delicate, white, and smooth. The flesh on her wrists, where the shackles had held her, now revealed a sliver of her bone.

Nearly every day, she was dragged from her cell and brought upstairs to one of the rooms where she was raped or tortured.

She had never known how sound itself could be a torture. When she lay in her cell and heard music piping in through the speaker, she knew that not far away another person was being beaten or electrocuted. She knew it because she had been that person. Her bruises and scabs were like a palimpsest where her torturer had marked her. She could trace his journey on her body like a blind man reading braille. For the scars were raised and the welts irregular, and even if she tried, she could not forget the history of how they had first arrived.

They had burned her from the electrocutions. They had played the music over and over as they clamped her with the metal clothespins. They had taunted her with the sound of dripping water, telling her that if she didn't confess, the water would be thrown on her and the pain of the electricity would only intensify.

She didn't know what she could confess. She knew she had never done anything against the new regime.

"I am a wife and mother," she said over and over. "I have never said anything against the general or his army. I am innocent," she said through tears and cries of pain.

The men who tortured her didn't know who she was. They didn't even know why she was there. They only knew that she had to be in the Villa Grimaldi for some grave offense against the government. So they did their job and relished doing it. They tortured an innocent woman into confessing to a crime she had not committed.

They filled a large Coke bottle with water, and one of the men drizzled a little on Salomé's forehead. She was handcuffed to a large metal surgical table, and as she writhed with great futility to free herself, more water was poured on her chest and her pelvis. Her dress was soaking wet when the younger guard told his superior officer, "The bitch is ready." Without hesitation, the other soldier flicked the little red switch and turned on the electrical shock machine.

Weeks later, after her limbs were swollen from the beatings and the electric shocks, and her body distended from lack of water and food, she sat crouched on the floor of her cell staring up at the cement ceiling like a wounded, mangled bird.

"What's the matter with you?" one of the guards asked.

"Are you talking to me?" she whispered. Her voice was hoarse from having screamed and cried for hours at a time.

"Yes, I'm talking to you. Why are staring at the ceiling?"

Salomé looked at the guard. He was young, carefully shaven. He couldn't have been more than twenty-two years old. "He's not a career soldier," she thought to herself. She could tell those men right away. They were the most brutal of the guards, the ones who thrived on violence and sought it out like starving wolves, hungry for blood.

The very fact that this soldier had asked her why she was staring at the ceiling differentiated him from the others. His was the first question posed to her as if, indeed, she were a person.

Her eyes scanned his carefully pressed uniform, his fastidiously combed hair, and neatly filed nails. His youth and the lack of badges on his breast pocket indicated that he must be a new recruit. "He's probably from a modest family, Allende's socialism didn't serve him well, and now he's siding with the ruling class in the hope of being a part of them."

Salomé's mind raced.

She would not reveal to the guard who her husband was, as Octavio's vocal support of Allende and refusal to support the new regime was well-documented in the press. Instead, she decided to curry the favor of this young soldier by convincing him she was a woman of great means who would never have embraced social-ism . . . someone who should be protected and whose imprisonment had been a terrible mistake. And that if he looked out for her, he would be rewarded in the end. Luckily, she remembered the infor-mation about the villa that Chon-Vargas had given her that day in the market.

"You know," she said to him as she dragged herself closer to the bars, "I was just thinking, it's amazing how much they've changed this place. Who would have known this was once one of the most beautiful villas in Santiago?"

"Villa? How would you know what this place used to look like?"

"Oh, I remember," she said, her eyes shining up at him. "I remember a lot. You know, I used to come here often when I was a little girl." Salomé knew that if she told him something that he could verify about the villa, something that no other prisoner would have known, it would give her story credibility. So, she created a story from the information that Chon-Vargas had given her that day in the market, reinforcing it with the images she had seen through her blindfold.

"Why would *you* be here now then? I thought we only had *comu-*

nistas here." He raised his eyebrows and leaned against the bars of her cell.

"Oh, me? I'm no communist. I come from a *familia gentil.*" She attempted to smile through her bruises, pushing back her hair with a slight, sensual gesture of her hand. But, the gesture was futile. Her fingers only became entangled in a web of matted knots.

"Yes," she continued, "when I was a little girl, we would summer here at the Villa Grimaldi. Just the name of it! To say it when I was small conjured up beautiful images of summer—gardens full of magnolia and bougainvillea. You know, the land here used to be an old vineyard. But, if I remember correctly, the family stopped that about fifty years ago. Can you still see those old terra-cotta jugs lining the outside?" Salomé coaxed, knowing full well what she said was true, as Chon-Vargas had told her that himself.

"Actually," the guard said, pondering Salomé's vivid description, "you're right. I've seen some remains of clay pots, but now they're just a bunch of broken terra-cotta shards in the entranceway."

"You see!" she piped up eagerly. "And what about the tower! Or the black gate . . . and the beautiful kitchen with the tiles from Spain?"

She had succeeded in gaining the guard's attention. From her descriptions, he could tell that she had been here before under far different circumstances.

"You mean the blue ones?"

"Yes, magnificent, cerulean blue tiles . . . And the windows . . . do they still overlook the cherimoya tree?"

"Yes, that tree's still there . . ." His voice betrayed that Salomé had captured his attention. "You can see it from the window." He paused. "Except the windows in the kitchen are now black with soot and streaked from the rain."

"Such a shame."

"Damn right. They should have used this place as a recreation center for us guards rather than a prison. Why waste a nice place like this on those damn communists? Allende ran this country into the ground! Before the coup, I hadn't been able to find a job in over a year . . ."

Salomé shuddered. She knew if Octavio were in her position, he would have defended his sainted Allende to the end. He would have tried to persuade the guard of his naïveté, and to see that the American multinationals had sabotaged all that the former president had tried to do.

Days passed before Salomé discovered the name of the guard whom she had convinced she was wrongfully imprisoned.

"Miguel!" a soldier called out to him one evening when he was posted nearby her cell. "The major wants us to bring him a prisoner, so take the bitch from cell sixty-eight to the interrogation room right away."

"Cell sixty-eight?" Miguel replied, realizing that cell was Salomé's. "I think you should lay off her a bit. She's looking kind of bad . . ."

"What the hell are you talking about, asshole? Of course she's looking bad!" the voice in the dark shouted. "She deserves it, the fucking communist!"

"I doubt that," Miguel retorted, his tone bordering on disrespectful.

"What?" His superior was incredulous.

"Doubtful. That's what I said. Look, the lady in sixty-eight knows she's in the Villa Grimaldi. She's some rich broad who used to come here every summer as a girl. If she dies, it'll be on our heads, not fucking Pinochet's, and you can bet your ass that someone's out there looking for her right now!"

Miguel had apparently managed to arouse his anonymous commander's concerns of self-preservation. "Fine! Just get some other whore then . . . I don't care which one you get. Hopefully, for your sake, the major won't either."

"Yes, sir. Just give me a second!"

She heard a cell unlock a few meters ahead of hers and then slam shut. The force of the closing door echoed into Salomé's cell. She nearly felt guilty for subjecting another prisoner to the terror that was meant for her. But she was too weary now for such a luxurious emotion. She only wanted to sleep. She wanted to hear nothing at all.

She imagined herself in her bedroom at home, serenaded by the sounds of the garden and the stirrings of her children. It was like a distant dream now, one that became increasingly difficult to recall, as the incessant wailing and tireless music never stopped.

* * *

Days passed, and her interrogation sessions became less frequent. When Miguel was on duty, he made sure that she received a bowl of *poroto* beans without worms. He would also bring her water if she asked.

"Tell me," he asked one evening, "did they have fancy parties here?"

"Well, of course, I was just a little girl . . . but I do remember that there were some nights, after we children were put to bed, when a band would arrive and the entire garden was illuminated by torchlight. The people would approach in horse-drawn carriages . . ." She paused and cleared her throat. "I remember, I used to peer out of the window with my little brother and see the ladies stepping out of the coaches with billowing white dresses, their throats wrapped in strings of pearls."

"I can't imagine that happening here. Outside now, there's nothing but mud."

"Back then, they had such tall trees. The big cherimoya, the cinnamon . . . an almond blossom. There were bushes of roses and honeysuckle. There were rows of African violets and parrot tulips the color of gold."

"What a shame. Why'd they turn such a beautiful place into such a shithole? They didn't have to bulldoze the gardens and pour cement into the reflecting pool. At least the soldiers could have enjoyed it on our off-shifts." He paused and shook his head.

Salomé remained quiet.

"I always wanted to go to a party like that. Dress up in a white suit, white shirt, and ask all the ladies to dance. But, lucky me, I have to watch over all these fucking Reds day in and day out." He tapped his rifle against one of the cement walls between the cells. "You know, most of these people deserve what they're getting. They're not like you and me. They're no-class pigs, nothing but bloodsucking anarchists."

Salomé nodded. She was spooning the last remnants of her bowl of *poroto* beans into her mouth.

"I bet your family's looking for you. They're going to be surprised when they see you, looking the way that you do."

"I must look dreadful." She tried to smile through the bars of her cell.

"I'm sure all your friends and family are pulling some strings for you now. I'm sure you won't be in here much longer."

"I hope so, Miguel," she whispered as she finished her bowl of *poroto*.

"Ah, so you know my name now, do you?" he said, taking the empty bowl as she pushed it through the steel bars. "You better remember it!" He laughed. "Tell your fancy friends that at least someone in this hellhole was kind to you."

"I will remember. I have a feeling I will remember everything." And the deep, penetrating sadness in her voice made even the young soldier shiver.

Thirty-Eight

Vesterås, Sweden
February 1975

*I*n a way, the stories from my family's past saved me," Salomé said, her voice tinged with nostalgia. Samuel remained transfixed, gazing into the eyes of his patient.

The afternoon sun bathed the small, carefully furnished room with warm yellow light so that in profile, both Salomé and Samuel were radiant. Their olive skins glowed like ripening pears.

"Well, Dr. Rudin," Salomé said as she readjusted herself on the couch, "the coup was staged to restore the power of the middle class and upper classes of Chile. It was a backlash against the socialism that Allende had tried to implement to help the working poor."

"Yes, I realize that."

"Well, the army was clearly on the side of the wealthy and the middle class . . . the bourgeoisie, if you will. So, I used the stories of my childhood and the information that Chon-Vargas had given to me to convince one of the guards, Miguel, that I was a rich woman who supported the coup, and that my incarceration was a mistake.

"Night after night, I told Miguel the stories of my childhood, ones that had no connection to my being the wife of Octavio Ribeiro."

"Stories?" Samuel prodded her.

"Well, stories like the legend of my grandmother—the *pequeña canaria*, who was pecked to death by the birds she was said to love more than her husband. And the story of my family's hacienda in Talca, where the rooms were vast and sprawling, the windows overlooked miles and miles of land and sky."

"And so you were successful in convincing this guard that you were from a bourgeois family . . . that you were a wealthy woman who was taken by mistake?"

"Yes. In a way, I was telling the truth. At least a half-truth. *I was from such a family.* I told stories of my grandfather. How he walked around in a brocade vest with a gold pocket watch, through the orchard of hybrid fruit that he cultivated in his spare time. How he struck his cane at dinnertime to summon his pet snake. All of that was true! It was only the part about my famous actor husband and his critical remarks about the Pinochet regime that I left out." Salomé took a deep breath. Her cheeks were flushed now.

"And," she added, "never in his life had a boy like Miguel, an aspiring bourgeois, heard such stories like the ones I told. I believe he soon became addicted to them so that, every day, he somehow managed to get a shift where he guarded my corridor."

"You were very lucky, Salomé, to have someone looking out for you like that."

"Yes, I was." She paused and looked down at her hands. "I know I was."

"And so the beatings stopped?"

"No." She paused. "They never stopped. They only lessened. Miguel obviously could not be on duty every day, every night. But when he was there, I was safer, and he always managed to make sure that I wasn't taken to the tower. Unfortunately, there were times when he was placed in other areas of the prison, and I was again taken to the interrogation room.

"Still, even with Miguel's presence and his protection, I became increasingly depressed. I never thought I would see my children, my parents, or my husband again."

"Of course."

"But," Salomé said with a long sigh, "somehow I managed to endure." She paused for a moment, as if remembering something else she wanted to say. "You know the strangest part? They had doctors that would come in to visit some of the prisoners. They would take our blood pressure, our pulse . . . things like that.

"They were just there to report back to our interrogators how much more abuse we could take! Did they care if I had blood accumulating in my elbows from the stretching on the 'grille,' or if my thorax was so swollen I couldn't breathe?"

Samuel was silent.

"Let me tell you, these men were not doctors! I came from a family of doctors—*my* father and *my* grandfather—men who had a sense of vocation! Men who wanted to help people, save lives, and cure diseases."

"Yes."

"These bastards were of another breed! They only wanted to see how much more torture we could possibly endure. They clicked their pens and glanced at our bloody faces and bruised limbs without a conscience. They didn't want to help us. They only wanted to *maintain* us."

Samuel shook his head.

"I tried to trick them, though. I would hold my breath for as long as I could before they monitored my heartbeat, so that its rhythm seemed irregular. I would also immobilize one of my arms for hours at a time, so that the swelling there intensified and I appeared far more fragile than the other prisoners."

"You were wise enough to use everything you had. That is 'survival.' You had strength, and in that regard, I think you were quite fortunate compared to some of the others." Samuel paused and looked directly into his patient's eyes. "You must remember, Salomé, you were able to survive and come back to your family and loved ones."

"Yes, Dr. Rudin, I realize all that." She paused for a moment before continuing. "I recognize I was one of the lucky ones. I had a guard who tried his best to limit my beatings. I even had some medical knowledge that allowed me to fake the intensity of my injuries so I appeared weaker than perhaps I really was." Salomé hesitated, her eyes falling to her lap. "And by some great miracle, I was released from that godforsaken place."

"Yes."

"But . . . I still feel like I am a prisoner. I still suffer every time I read in the newspaper a reference to my country. I am still horrified when I hear the sound of dripping water, because I associate it with the electric shocks. And I still cannot enjoy the simple pleasure of music. I have been robbed of any peace."

"I understand, Salomé."

"And I guess I can finally say it, Dr. Rudin, without feeling guilty about it." She paused and took a deep breath.

Samuel waited a few more seconds for his patient to speak.

"I guess you can say, I'm so goddamn angry."

"Of course you are, Salomé. What was done to you was wrong and unjust."

"There's more. I'm angry at my husband."

"Of course, you are angry at him. Have you thought any more about why you're furious with him?"

"It's as I said before, he put his needs before those of our family. He became consumed by his role of 'political activist, champion of Allende, avenger of his fallen friend . . .' "

"I don't know if that is really it, Salomé. I've met many German colleagues who have expressed to me great regret that their parents never spoke out against the Nazis. One has to wonder if millions of lives would have been spared if more people had spoken out against what they saw as an injustice.

"Now we think of those people who hid people or helped gain illegal passports at that time as heroes . . . but they did this at great risk to their families."

Salomé was silent.

"I think you're more upset with the fact that he didn't seem to *realize* what was at stake." Samuel shifted in his seat. "Think about what you said in one of our other sessions." He glanced down at his notepad and turned the pages back to quote something Salomé had said to him weeks before. " 'I fell in love with his idealism. It's ironic that the very trait that I cherished most in him is the one I now resent.' "

"Yes, that's true." Salomé nodded her head.

"I think that's the key here to why you're so angry at your husband. Even more than because of the choices he made."

Salomé looked at her therapist, her face revealing her puzzlement.

"Tell me, do you still consider yourself idealistic?"

"No, not at all."

"You've lost your idealism completely then?"

"I have seen great evil. I don't think after seeing that I could ever look at the world in the same way."

"So the young woman who was seduced by oranges long ago by her poet-courtier is dead then?"

"I suppose she is."

"You don't think she could ever return?"

"I think that would be impossible."

"And your husband, you don't think he has seen the evil you have? You mean to tell me that you don't believe he has the capacity to imagine how cruel and barbaric humankind can be?"

"No. I don't think he has any idea."

Samuel's head tilted slightly. "Don't you think he envisioned the worst when you were abducted? Don't you think it crossed his mind the terrible things that could have been done to you? . . . . And what about when you were returned . . . don't you think he wondered how those bruises and burn marks got there?"

"I think he chose to focus on the fact that I was returned, rather than concentrate on the more troubling aspects such as my scars."

"He's never mentioned them?"

"No. He cannot bring himself to ask and I choose not to bring it up."

"Perhaps you should, Salomé."

"What good would it do to dwell on my torture? I want to forget it."

"Do you think you can just forget such a thing? I'm afraid it's part of your history now. The reason you're here is so that you can find a way to live with that history."

Salomé turned her head away from her doctor. She was beginning to find it tiresome lying on this leather couch and discussing the same feelings over and over. She wondered why it couldn't be enough that she admitted that she was angry at Octavio. She wanted to be done with this exhausting inquisition.

"In a way, you're no different than your husband if you choose to maintain the silence between the two of you. You both are avoiding confrontation."

Salomé let out a deep sigh. She could not disguise her frustration. "Doctor, I am just so tired of talking. I'm just so exhausted by having my husband constantly ask how I feel. Shouldn't it be obvious? I was abducted, I was interrogated, I was tortured. How the hell does he think I feel? I feel awful!"

"Perhaps he still doesn't know how to approach such a delicate subject, Salomé. Men aren't equipped to deal with things that are as emotional and traumatic as the issues we're discussing here. He's probably having a hard time with it."

Salomé shook her head. "The problem with my husband is that he lives his life as though it were a screenplay. He expects a happy ending but doesn't want to work towards one."

"That is a problem." Samuel nodded his head. "I agree with you."

Salomé cupped her palms over her face. "I love my husband, I will always love him. But the very fact that he maintains this rosy vision of the world makes it difficult for me to live with him. It's not that I want him to lose his idealism completely. . . . If he were as jaded as I've become, then what kind of couple would we be?" Salomé took a deep breath. She could feel her skin flush underneath her blouse. "Life has its difficult and ugly moments, and I wish my husband could finally accept that."

Samuel nodded. "I think it's good that you're acknowledging these feelings."

"Is it? Now how am I going to go home and lie next to a man whom I know I'm angry with? I mean, he wasn't even able to save me. I had to rescue myself. He failed at even that."

"You cannot blame him for that," Samuel said objectively. "It was an impossible situation."

"I suppose you're right." She smoothed out her skirt. "I just don't want to go home now and deal with all of this. The children have been struggling in school. Rafael has been looking after his sisters because I've been too exhausted to be a proper mother. And Octavio seems to be sinking deeper into depression."

"You need to concentrate on *your* healing."

"I know . . . I've been trying . . ."

"Well, try and keep your chin up, Salomé. You're tackling some heavy things in our sessions, and you should be proud of yourself."

She shook her head. "Sometimes I feel worse when I leave than I did when I got here."

"I know," Samuel said compassionately. "But we're moving forward."

"Yes," Salomé said as she stood up to leave. She knew the doctor had let her speak a few minutes over her allotted fifty-minute session, so she tried to compose herself as quickly as she could. "I guess I'll see you next week then."

As she left, Samuel watched her exit elegantly through the door.

Thirty-Nine

·ᡣᡝᠥ·

Santiago, Chile
January 1974

Octavio could no longer sleep. His mind raced. His heart beat wildly in his chest. He did not know where to begin. Octavio was crippled by a moral dilemma. His actions and his commitment to his principles had gotten him and his family into this terrible situation. He had always prided himself on his conviction, his steadfast morals. Had he supported a regime that had executed the nation's president and ruled as a military dictatorship, he would have been a hypocrite. And just hearing that word made Octavio cringe.

Yet now, these convictions directly jeopardized his family's safety. His wife had been kidnapped and was possibly being tortured, all because of his stubborn refusal to go against his beliefs. It was too much for him to bear.

As each hour passed and Salomé still did not surface, Octavio's anxiety worsened. He contemplated calling up a newspaper and publicly renouncing all the criticisms he had previously launched at the new regime. He thought about writing to one of the army's generals and arranging a secret meeting in which he would say that he had rethought his views and now believed that Pinochet was a just and rightful leader. "How wrong I've been," he contemplated saying. "Just give me back my wife and I'll be a diligent and steadfast servant of the state."

But, eventually, Octavio reconsidered. What use would that be?

The generals would know he was lying, and he and his family would still remain under suspicion. No, he would not renounce his statements, but he would also not exacerbate the situation by making any more remarks criticizing the new regime.

"Tomorrow, I will drive until I find this Villa Grimaldi," he told himself. He would rescue his wife. He would find a way to make their lives good again.

The next morning, after his mother-in-law had told him where she suspected the Villa Grimaldi was, Octavio Ribeiro set out in his small orange Lancia to find his wife.

He gulped down a cup of coffee, kissed his children on their foreheads, and told the maid he was unsure of his exact return. "I am not sure how long I will be gone," he said. "But I will not stop until I have found their mother."

He still was in disbelief. He couldn't believe that in Chile a woman could be abducted from her family and held for a crime she had not committed.

Octavio's life had become a real-life drama, but one that he had to believe would have a happy ending. He had to maintain the hope that she was still alive and that he could save her. Without that as inspiration he wouldn't be able to play this role that he hadn't asked for—the role of rescuer and penitent husband. If he couldn't get her back, how could he live with having been responsible for her abduction? He hadn't listened to her, he knew that now. She had foreseen the trouble before he had.

He drove through the winding streets of Santiago. Past the rows of houses with their neatly manicured lawns and blossoming gardens, and past the schools with the busloads of arriving children. "How could things seem so deceptively normal?" Octavio thought to himself. If he had not known Allende personally, and had he not had his wife abducted from their house in broad daylight, perhaps he too would have thought that life in Chile had returned to normal.

He didn't know what he would do when he got there. He had no idea what the place looked like or how he'd get in. But he couldn't focus on all that now. He just had to get there, and then he would decide how to proceed.

His mother-in-law had thought the villa lay north, in the dusty outskirts of the city, in an area called Peñalolen. She had told him that if he drove fifteen kilometers north and turned onto one of the side roads, he would eventually come across it. At least that was what she recalled.

He stuffed a map into his leather satchel and threw in a change of clothes as well. He didn't know what he'd need for his journey. He only knew that he had to get moving and begin the search. Otherwise, he would go mad just waiting for a miracle to happen and Salomé to be returned.

Hours passed and he seemed to be driving with no sign of the villa that Doña Olivia had described. "There was a tower," she remembered. "If only I could call the family and find out the exact address." But they had agreed against doing that, as they wanted to keep news of Salomé's abduction within the family. "We can trust no one," Fernando agreed with Octavio. "No one can know of this, or we risk something more happening to the family."

He asked farmers on the way there. He asked a few women sitting by a bus stop. "Somewhere up there," they all said, and pointed. Almost everyone had heard of the place, yet no one knew the exact address.

Finally, having stopped for a small sandwich at a roadside café, Octavio found someone who gave him detailed directions. "Three more kilometers, and you'll find it. But it's all lined with carabineros," the old man told him.

Octavio nodded in thanks and left a few coins to pay for the elder gentleman's drink.

Now that Octavio knew where the villa was, he realized that he had to come up with a strategy. If what the man was saying was true, he should keep his distance, for fear of being noticed by the police. If they suspected him of spying on their headquarters, they would surely arrest him on the spot.

Driving a few meters ahead, he opted to pull alongside the shoulder of the road to think more carefully. He thought of all the things that one would do if this were a script in a movie: He might kidnap a soldier, steal his uniform, and enter the premises in disguise. He might camouflage his car in some bushes and wait until a jeep pulled down the road, then jump on the back as it drove past, thus being driven in undetected.

But, no, none of these was a plausible plan. He knew they could only be clichés hammered out in poorly scripted films.

Large military trucks continued to drive past his parked car, one after another. Green army jeeps with billowing canvas hoods sped over the road kicking up dirt. And suddenly, Octavio realized that what the man in the café had said was true. It would be nearly impossible for him to gain entry. He would only draw attention to himself. His face now burned from the afternoon heat.

"What am I going to do?" he said. His frustration was nearly choking him. Tears began to well in his eyes.

He pounded the sides of the steering wheel with his two fists. "Jesus Christ! What the hell am I going to do!"

Suddenly, he wished he had never ever copied those damn Pablo Neruda poems, and he cursed himself for being influenced by that poet who had introduced him to Allende. How he wished he could do it all over again. But, it was too late, the damage had been done. Frustrated and beside himself, Octavio turned on the ignition and began his way home.

Forty

⟜❦⟝

Santiago, Chile
February 1974

$\mathscr{A}$s the days passed, Octavio continued to rise every morning at half past seven, drink his coffee, kiss his children on the forehead, and make his way into the city to try to find someone who could help him get his wife out of the Villa Grimaldi.

It had been over three weeks since Salomé had been abducted, and Octavio, realizing he would be denied entry into the heavily guarded Villa Grimaldi, racked his brain trying to think of an alternative way to secure her release.

He called all of the friends he had made in the movie industry, from the highest-paid director to the lowest-paid extra. He asked if they had any connections with the military.

"I need to find my wife," he begged them, forsaking any of his previous stubbornness and pride.

"We warned you, Octavio," one said apologetically. "We told you to stop making those statements in public. . . . And now look where you've gotten yourself! There's nothing we can do. We also have families we must look out for."

Octavio slammed down the phone and cursed the dangling receiver. He kicked the glass door of the phone booth and shoved his fists into his pockets, swearing to himself like a madman.

When he returned home late at night, he hoped that the children would already have been put to bed by either Consuela or his mother-in-law. So he wouldn't be confronted by their faces begging to know if he had found their mother yet. He couldn't wrestle with one more night of that: returning home without their mother, without any answers or ideas about how to rescue her.

At night, his despondency only intensified. He would lie alone in their connubial bed, her empty side streaked with shadows from the moon. He couldn't bear the thought of how she must be suffering. Where did she sleep now? Was it in a cement cell, or in a barracks with several other prisoners?

He couldn't believe that they could have killed his beloved Salomé because of his stubborn refusal to support their bloody regime. Could they? He heard whispers amongst the people that there were mass graves in the countryside—big, open craters dug by soldiers, filled with bodies whose injuries rendered them unrecognizable. Could they have possibly done that to his wife?

He no longer slept. He lay in bed, stiff as mortar, beads of sweat dotting his brow. His hands fell to his sides like slabs of wax. His eyes were a cloudy haze.

It had now been twenty-three days since he had last laid his eyes upon Salomé. He rose in the morning as usual, kissed the children good-bye, and made his way out into the city. But, this time, he had no more appointments to attend to. He had exhausted all of his contacts. No one else would take his calls.

He drove until he had nearly depleted all the gas in the tank, until he thought he would collapse from the exhaustion and terror that his wife's abduction had caused him. Frustrated and confused, Octavio found himself not driving to the gates of the Villa Grimaldi but, instead, to the main cathedral in Santiago. With no other place to go, Octavio Ribeiro found himself drawn to a building he had neither entered nor contemplated entering for many years.

Octavio had not been in a church since his youngest daughter's baptism. Even then, he hadn't wanted to go, but his in-laws had insisted on the ceremony. He believed in the Church, the holy trinity, and the teachings of the sacrament. But he never felt comfortable sitting in the carved wooden pews, facing the gilded altarpiece and staring up at the dramatic re-creation of Christ nailed to the cross. It felt unnatural to him. Octavio believed God was far more likely to be found in his garden, among the wild roses and in the shade of the cinnamon and avocado trees, than in a temple made of stained glass and stone. God was in his wife and children.

Since his wife's abduction, though, he had begun praying silently to himself. Occasionally, when he lay alone in bed at night, he discovered himself muttering aloud. Now, as he drove along the streets of Santiago, he found himself trying to remember the words he used to mouth as a child:

Hail, Mary, full of grace . . .

Blessed art thou amongst all women . . .

The words now escaped him.

Hail, Mary, full of grace . . .

The Lord . . . The Lord is with you.

Blessed art thou amongst all women . . .

He started again, this time not thinking, only trying to remember the words as though they were lines he had memorized from a movie long ago.

"Blessed art thou," he repeated, "*amongst all women and blessed is the fruit of thy womb Jesus. Amen.*"

Was there more? He couldn't remember now. "*Holy Mary, mother of God, pray for us sinners now and at the hour of our death. Amen.* Was that it?" Perhaps he should have sent the children to Sunday school, he muttered to himself. How could he have forgotten these incantations, he railed as he ran his fingers through his hair and tugged at his curls.

"What's another one?" his mind raced. After all, he rationalized, he needed as much help as he could. "None of this could possibly hurt, right?"

"*Our Father, who art in heaven, hallowed be thy name. Thy kingdom come, thy will be done, on earth and in heaven. Give us this day our daily bread and forgive us our trespasses as we forgive those who trespass against us. And lead us not into temptation but deliver us from evil.*"

Was God listening to him?

He realized that all these prayers were rambling acts of desperation, rather than the utterances of a true believer. Yet, he also knew that he would do anything now. Try anything. All he wanted was to get his wife back.

* * *

He had been driving for what seemed like hours. Finally, he saw the tall spire of the cathedral and parked in the lot nearby.

He entered with trepidation. The church had a strange, yet familiar scent that he hadn't smelled in years. Was it incense or just the cold staleness of stone? He didn't know, but somehow, it instantly soothed him. As he stepped lightly down the aisle, he could hear the sound of prayer-book pages being shuffled and the unifying voice of the priest leading the congregation in their closing psalms.

He stood for quite a while before sitting down in a pew. Each row seemed nearly filled to capacity; mostly men and women older than Octavio, pensioners who had come for the midday mass.

"O holy men and women, we come together on this day and all others to help serve and propagate the name and honor of our Lord," the priest boomed into the microphone as the congregation readjusted themselves into their seats.

"My sermon today is inspired by the story of Jesus Christ, our Holy Father. It is in his example that we should strive to pattern our lives. For it was with his own blood that he showed us what selflessness means, what the true notion of sacrifice is." The priest was shaking his finger now at the carved crucifix above him, its image of the bloodied Christ gazing down at the congregation through painted-glass eyes. "We must extend ourselves to our families, to our neighbors, so that this country and our world are filled with love, not hate. We must look into the eyes of every man and woman and help those who are less fortunate than we are. We must force ourselves every day to be better people."

The priest paused and raised his arms. His red sleeves hung like the flags of a matador.

"Every day on earth there is darkness. Every day there is evil and sadness. Now, it seems, more than ever. There is despondency and there is despair. Let us all try to bring a little more light into the world. Let us all try to open our hearts and let truth and beneficence reign supreme."

As the congregation chanted "Amen" in unison, the priest prepared for communion.

Octavio sat there in the cold church, stunned. The vaulted ceiling and stained glass intensified his epiphany. Having given this sermon, wasn't this priest the perfect person to ask for help? This man would have no excuse, no reason to deny Octavio's plea for assistance. He had just preached that one must help others in need. That each individual should seize the opportunity to ensure that good always triumphs over evil. Surely, the priest would help him. So, as Octavio sat in the pew recalling the sermon, he began to rehearse his approach.

He waited until the sacrament was given and the congregation had filed out of the tall oak doors of the church. Then, as the priest began to retreat to his private quarters, Octavio stood up and rushed toward him.

"Father Cisneros!" he called out, having gleaned the priest's name from the program. In the hallowed walls of the cathedral, his voice echoed and caught the priest off guard.

"Yes?" he said quietly as he turned to face Octavio.

"I must speak with you. It's urgent."

"I am sorry, my son, but could you please come back in about two hours? I will be occupied until four o'clock with the confessional."

"No, I can't come back then."

"And why is that?"

"I have an important matter to discuss with you!"

The priest looked at Octavio quizzically as he had never seen his face in his congregation before.

"Father, you must see me now." Octavio was panting. "It is a matter of life and death!"

The priest raised his eyebrows and looked directly into Octavio's eyes. He was startled by the man's intensity. Incapable of turning the young man away, he nodded his head. "All right then . . . I suppose I can be a few minutes late. Please, join me in my office." He raised his hand and beckoned Octavio to follow him.

Octavio followed the priest into a narrow entranceway that led to a passageway of intricately carved walls. They passed an inner sanctuary, a private chapel with a tiny mosaic dome, and through a hallway that was lined with portraits of various cardinals, bishops in crimson robes, and gilded crosses.

"Please come inside, my son."

Octavio turned and walked into a small, wood-paneled office.

The priest began to take off his vestments. His outer white robe with the red sleeves and crimson middle. Underneath, he wore the black uniform with clerical white collar.

"Sit down."

Octavio did so, folding his perspiring palms in his lap.

"Now," the priest said, glancing quickly at his watch, "how can I assist you in this matter of 'life and death?' "

"Well," Octavio stammered. "My wife . . . the mother of my three children . . . has been abducted."

"Abducted?"

"Yes, she has been kidnapped by the military police."

The priest shook his head. He had been approached like this twice before, but he had encouraged the family members to go to the police. He had told them he was powerless to help.

Although each time it pained him to send the grieving relative away, the simple truth was that he did so because he was too cowardly to help. In the past month, he had heard of at least three priests who were reported missing, presumably at the hands of the government's henchmen.

The alleged brutality of the new regime disgusted him, but he had never been one to place himself in a potentially dangerous situation. As a visiting U.N. cleric from Columbia he had looked forward to coming to Chile because it meant a promotion to his career. One day he hoped to be a bishop, and he certainly didn't want to draw unnecessary attention to himself in the meantime by interfering with affairs of another state.

The priest said as delicately as he could, folding his pink hands on his desk blotter, "This all sounds just awful . . . but I am afraid there is not much I can do. I am only a priest, a foreigner at that." He sighed and reclined into the backboard of his armchair. "I really am sorry," he said as he raised his palms to the ceiling.

"What do you mean there is nothing personally that you can do? I just listened to your sermon, and there, in the church, you just beseeched at least a hundred men and women to help their neighbors. You told your congregation that, as the children of God, we should all join efforts to resist evil in this world!"

"Yes, of course I said that. But, there is nothing *I* can do to help you."

Octavio shook his head. "There used to be a time when if a man came to his church and asked for help, it would be given."

"Of course, that still happens, my son. But these are difficult times."

"I think Jesus would have said times were difficult when Pilate was ordering him nailed to the cross."

"You are not being fair, my son. You know as well as I how precarious the situation is in this city."

Octavio was at his wit's end. He was so weary, so exhausted from looking high and low for his wife, from asking friends, strangers, friends of friends, and anyone else he could find for help. But all had told him there was nothing they could do. Now, sitting here in front of him was a priest, a man who had taken an oath to help mankind—a congregation that was his flock to shepherd. How could this *man* now deny him?

Octavio took a deep breath and sat back down in the chair. He placed his fingers over his eyes and massaged his brows to compose himself. "I need to think of this as a challenge, a new acting role," he thought. "I need to use my powers of persuasion. For God's sake, those are what got me involved with Neruda and Allende in the first place! This must be my greatest performance."

So Octavio looked into the priest's eyes, in the same way he had coached Allende to stare into the camera three years earlier. He widened his eyes, cocked his chin high, and held his gaze steadfast.

"Father," he said solemnly. "I can tell from your accent that you're not from Chile, so you never would have heard of me. I am—or I should say, I used to be—an actor. A pretty famous one too. You'll notice I didn't say I was a pretty good one, just famous. I see that now . . . I played the same types of roles over and over. The soulful hero who always managed to save the day—and save the girl—with a few bold gestures in a story line that always ensured a happy ending."

Octavio paused and stared again into the eyes of the priest, who now gazed back upon him mesmerized. A captive audience of one.

"I know now that my life—the lives of my wife and my children are not at the mercy of scriptwriters. I know there is the possibility that this story might not end happily—though I'm trying desperately not to think of that at this moment. If I believed this love story between my wife and me was meant to end in tragedy, I don't think I'd be able to make it through the night.

"I don't sleep anymore. I exist in a nightmare that doesn't seem to end. I have a son and two young daughters who ask me every night when their mother is coming home. I have a father-in-law who looks at me with disgust and a mother-in-law who looks at me with fear. But I am feeling completely powerless. No one has been able to help me. No one—not even people I considered close friends—wants to return my phone calls. I have become a pariah in a world that once christened me their golden child.

"So what am I to do, Father? I played a hero on-screen, but I failed to be one in real life. I've failed to rescue the one person I love most in the world, my wife and the mother of my three children.

"I can sit here and tell you honestly, with God as my witness, that she has done nothing wrong. That she has never committed any crime except perhaps loving and trusting a fool like me."

The priest shook his head.

"She has been wrongly imprisoned. She has never uttered a single word against the regime. I admit that I can't say that about myself—I will be forthright in telling you that now—but my wife, Salomé, has been taken without cause." Octavio's voice remained unwavering, his eyes still gazing into the eyes of the priest. "Please, please help me find her. You are my and my children's last and only hope. Having heard your sermon just now, I know that you're the only man I can come to in times such as these, when my faith is tested. Please do not deny me or my children when I come begging to you for help."

Octavio took a breath. "Please look at me and see a man who is humbled. A man who realizes he was never a hero and doesn't look to be one now." Then, quietly he finished, "All I ask is for your help to save the one thing I love so desperately."

The priest sat there completely transfixed by what the impassioned Octavio had just told him. He paused and took a deep breath, readjusting himself in the high, leather chair. "You've made a strong argument and I can tell that you have spoken honestly with your heart open and your faith in God. You are right to quote my sermon and to show me my hypocrisy."

The priest took a moment more to reflect. He could not disguise that he felt personally challenged. How could he blindly sit back and do nothing if what this man said was true—that a Christian woman, a mother of three and a devoted wife and daughter, was being wrongly imprisoned?

He thought about the others who had passed through his door in search of their missing loved ones. On the other occasions, it had been a woman beseeching him to help find her lost husband, son, or brother. But never before had he heard of a woman being abducted. Those other times—he could at least rationalize that they were strong men who could survive if placed in a difficult situation, or that those men had been aware of the risks they took in challenging the military. But, if what this man was telling him was true, that a young mother had wrongfully been taken, how could he live with himself and refuse to at least investigate the circumstances of her abduction?

He had lost his own mother at the age of three and was raised by his father for ten years before entering the seminary. In his first years in the priesthood, he had always tried to balance his desire to help others and his aspirations to one day have a high-ranking position within the Church. Hearing this man pleading for his help and hearing his own initial callous and certainly cowardly response, he couldn't help but feel ashamed. After all, he had grown up as a motherless son. If he had the opportunity to keep another child from avoiding a similar fate, shouldn't he do everything in his power to do so?

That he had taken the easy way out with the other families now weighed heavily on his conscience. How could he ask something of his congregation that he was unwilling to do himself? Was his own life so valuable that he could not risk it to save hers? Had not Christ sacrificed his own life for those of his flock?

This time, he should gather all his spiritual strength and do the right thing. That which he had sworn to do when he first took his vows. So, he resolved to help this man, these children, regardless of the risks to himself.

After contemplating his decision, the priest lifted his chin from his chest, pushed himself forward in his chair, and gazed back at Octavio with an intensity that matched the young actor's. "Although I am probably risking my own safety, jeopardizing my own career, I promise you I will do all in my power to help. I myself know what it is like to grow up in a family where the mother is absent. My own mother died when I was three. So if I can help your children have their mother returned to them, I will do everything I can."

"Thank you, Father," Octavio said breathlessly. He had been clutching his chest, waiting for the priest to give him the news he so desperately wanted to hear. Finally Octavio had found someone to help him.

"Do you have any idea where they have taken your wife?" the priest asked.

"I suspect to the Villa Grimaldi."

"You suspect?"

"Those were my wife's last words before she was taken."

"I see."

"I have driven there and it is swarming with military police."

The priest frowned and rubbed his brow with his forefinger. "I think you should come back tomorrow. The two of us will go to this Villa Grimaldi and see if it is a prison like you say."

"But what about the police?"

"What about them?" The priest folded his hands on his desk. "I am a United Nations priest, a visiting cleric from Bogotá. I will wear my robes reserved for international meetings. Hopefully, if we are in any danger, this will remind the soldiers that I am protected by international law."

"Yes," Octavio agreed.

"You will dress up as my assistant. I'll lend you a white collar and black shirt, but you must promise not to speak when we go there. Let me do all the talking."

"Yes, of course. But, what do you intend to say?"

"I will ask these policemen if they have a woman, a wife and mother of three, within the premises. And, if so, in the name of God, I will demand her immediate release."

The priest stood up and walked to the coatrack, retrieving his outer robe from the hook. "But we must do this tomorrow, I'm already late for my confessional duties."

"Of course."

"Meet me here tomorrow after midday mass."

"Yes, I will be here!" Octavio was heaving from the rush of his body's adrenaline. "Thank you, Father."

Octavio exited the church that afternoon with his body trembling. His speech to the priest had been his most passionate performance ever. And as he passed the now empty pews, he felt more satisfaction than if he had performed for an adoring audience of ten thousand. For now, he finally had an ally, someone who believed in him and who had sworn to help Salomé. No cameras were rolling, but Octavio, prone to dramatic gestures, kissed his shaking fingers and blew a kiss to the Madonna as he pushed open the heavy door.

Forty-One

◄※►

Santiago, Chile
February 1974

$\mathcal{T}$he next day, Octavio returned to the church. After changing into the robes of a cleric, he ushered the priest to his car and the two of them drove off to Peñalolen, in search of the Villa Grimaldi and Salomé.

Octavio and the priest sped along the same roads that Octavio had driven over time and time again. The sun glowed ahead of them with great intensity, bathing the snow-covered tops of the Andes with a soft, pink light.

"We're almost there," Octavio relayed to the priest, who looked quietly outside his window at a field of migrant farmers working the land.

"Yes? So close to Santiago? We've only been driving for forty minutes!"

"I know. But this is where I suspect she's been taken."

In the distance, Octavio saw the burgeoning tip of a tower. "I think that's it, straight ahead!" He pointed his finger to the horizon, showing the priest what he believed was the infamous Villa Grimaldi.

"Pull over and park here," Father Cisneros said. "We'll walk the rest of the way."

Octavio complied. He parked the car on the side of the road and turned off the car's engine.

"Since you're supposed to be my assistant, you should probably walk behind me," the priest suggested as he got out of the car. "And remember, I will be the one making the inquiry."

"Yes, of course."

Octavio had felt sick all day. He knew it was his nerves and the strain of worrying about his wife, but he tried to appear at ease.

They walked up the long gravel path that began the villa's driveway. Small pebbles kicked under the soles of their feet as Father Cisneros's robe billowed behind him like a large, black sail.

"Can we help you, Father?" one of the military asked as they approached the heavily guarded gate.

"Yes," the priest answered. "Can you tell me what this place actually is?"

"Sure, Father," the guard answered willingly. "It's a recreation center for soldiers. We come here for our retreats."

"I see. So it's not open to the public, I assume."

"No. Sorry, Father," the guard said with a shrug, his rifle butting against his shoulder.

Large black vans and green army jeeps continued to pass through the gates as the two men spoke. Another guard waved them in.

"That's quite all right," the priest said, a tinge of relief in his voice. "Come, Brother Antonio," he said, holding on to Octavio's arm, "we should be returning to our duties."

The two men turned away from the gate and began walking slowly to their car.

"You see, Don Octavio, this is not a prison or a torture center. It's a recreation center!"

"No, it's not! I'm sure of it." Octavio was incredulous at the priest's naïveté. "Father, how can you blindly believe what that soldier just said to you! You haven't been inside! Don't you think it's odd that all these black vans keep pulling past the gate if it's just a recreation center?"

"No, not really."

Octavio had to fight back his urge to hit the priest. He barely had enough strength to talk anymore, and yet his anger and frustration were rising within him.

"Father, how can I convince you? Something very evil is going on in there!"

The priest's glance was firm, his eyes slightly narrow. "Let us go back to the church and speak about this there."

"My wife is inside there!"

The priest shook his head. Behind the two men, a black van was parked on the side. The driver's door was open, revealing that the owner had left the vehicle temporarily unwatched.

"I believe what the guard told us. Why would he lie?"

In a mad, last-ditch attempt to convince the reluctant priest, Octavio ran to the black van. He jumped onto the bumper, his sandals slipping over the waxy, rubber edge, his fingers lacing into the metal handles.

"Look!" he cried, even before he had seen what lay inside.

As the doors opened, both Octavio and the priest recoiled in horror. Inside, there were three bodies badly beaten, their appendages covered in blood.

Neither Octavio nor Father Cisneros spoke to each other for several seconds. They stood there transfixed, nauseated, and shocked by the sight before them. Each of the faces on the three corpses had been smashed, their skin burned and broken. One could see the terror they had endured during their final moments frozen in their bloodstained eyes.

"O Lord in heaven," Father Cisneros whispered as he made the sign of the cross and quickly whispered the last rites for the dead men.

"Jesus Christ!" gasped Octavio as he covered his nose and mouth to stifle both the stench and his own revulsion.

The priest stood there with wide eyes, the blood emptying from his cheeks.

"We must get out of here," the priest urged. Within seconds, he was behind Octavio, who was walking briskly to the car.

As they sped back along the rough roads to Santiago, Octavio turned to the priest. "Now do you believe me?"

Father Cisneros did not answer him, for he could not speak. As they drove through the hills and into the heart of the city, the priest's answer was clearly revealed.

One only had to look at his face.

Forty-Two

Santiago, Chile
February 1974

$\mathcal{A}$s Octavio drove down the dusty roads, his eyes focused on the horizon.

"You see, I was telling the truth!" he said with wild exasperation. "My wife is in there! Who knows what they've done to her!"

"We must keep calm, Octavio," the priest said, his voice breaking midsentence. "You must allow me a few minutes to think. I must figure out how we should proceed with this."

The air inside the car was stifling, and Octavio rolled down the window to let a warm breeze wash over them.

"How many days has your wife been gone now?"

"Twenty-four."

"So it does not appear that they will be setting her free on their own."

"No, it does not." Octavio's reply was curt.

"Let us not lose ourselves," the priest said gently. "It's essential that we maintain our composure."

The priest readjusted himself in the cramped car seat. Underneath his clerical robes he was soaked with perspiration. He had wanted to hide his alarm from Octavio. He wanted to seem that he was in control of the situation and had a plan that could save this man's wife. But his mind was spinning now, his stomach still sickened by the sight of the three disfigured corpses. Never could he have imagined that such terror was happening in this country he was sent to only a few months before. He couldn't believe he had allowed himself to be so blind, so complacent in his moral responsibilities to people who clearly needed his help.

Several minutes of silence passed between the two men as each chastised himself for his shortcomings. Octavio continued to drive while silently berating himself for choosing his beliefs over his wife's safety, and the priest continued to criticize himself for his lack of moral conscience.

Finally, in an effort to initiate conversation and distract himself from his self-criticism, the priest turned to the young man beside him and tried to change the subject temporarily.

"You're no longer acting, my son?"

"No. They don't want me and I don't want to be a part of their obsequious, self-serving faction. A group of mindless idiots, that's what I think of my former colleagues."

"I see."

"Not one of them would help me when I asked. And, believe me, more than a handful of them know a general or two that could pull some strings."

"A general? You think that might be the answer to getting your wife released?"

"Of course, everyone knows that the generals have the power. If they ask for someone to be released, that person will be found—if they're not already dead —and let go the next day! That's how this military state works, for God's sakes!"

"I see."

"Why do you ask?"

"Well, as a clerical representative of the U.N., I might be able to arrange a meeting with one of the generals."

Octavio took his eyes off the road for a second and stared at the cleric beside him.

In profile, Father Cisneros reminded Octavio of one of the clerics in an El Greco painting. His angular features and long, attenuated fingers seemed unearthly. His pale white skin seemed to have rarely seen the light of day and was now reddening from exposure to the afternoon sun. It struck Octavio there, as he drove down the mountainside, that perhaps God had sent him a gift.

"Finally!" he bellowed, as if moved by the musings of his mind. He pounded his fist against the steering wheel, and a broad smile flashed over his bronzed face. "Finally I've received an answer to my prayers!"

Forty-Three

❧

Santiago, Chile
February 1974

*I*n the austere, white-walled government office building, only steps away from the nearly restored presidential palace, an anxious Octavio and a meditative priest waited for a General Martinez to arrive.

Father Cisneros had been petrified all morning. He had barely been able to perform his perfunctory duties at the church. He had mumbled his way through mass, nearly dropping the ceremonial wine over his vestments and tripping over the stairs that lead to the pulpit. He realized that he was placing his own life in danger by getting involved, but the moral ramifications of doing nothing would be far more torturous than any ill fate he might endure at the hands of the regime.

So he now composed himself. He tried to clear his mind as he changed into the official robes of a designated cleric and ambassador of faith from the United Nations. The purple sash with gold wreath that symbolized his association with that organization had strengthened his faith and conviction, though he needed little reassurance now after seeing those battered men at the Villa Grimaldi. He only hoped that Octavio's wife was alive, and that he could in fact gain her release. If he was successful, he would not only be saving a life, but also an entire family. Never could he have anticipated being faced with such responsibility when he'd accepted his position as visiting cleric from Bogotá six months before. Now, he only hoped he could succeed.

Octavio had picked him up in his orange car, and the two of them sped to Independencia Avenue without speaking a word to each other. Father Cisneros could tell by Octavio's expression how tense he was. His lips were bitten and cracked, his fingers white as they wrapped around the steering wheel.

"Do you know this general personally?" Octavio finally asked.

"No, I don't."

"How did you arrange this meeting, then?"

"I wrote a letter on the official stationery of the United Nation's Church and received a reply within three days."

"Unbelievable." Octavio slowed down the car. "What's the name of the man who we are seeing?"

"Martinez. According to some of my colleagues who read the newspaper more religiously than their Bibles, he was appointed to his position less than a month ago."

"I see."

"Just let me do the talking. I have what I am going to say all planned out."

"As you wish, but please stress that we want my wife released immediately. You understand how dire her situation is, Father, don't you?"

"Yes, yes, of course, I do," the priest muttered. "I understand all too well."

"What can I do for you gentlemen . . . for you, *Father?*" Martinez corrected himself.

"I come here on official duties, General. As a priest associated with the United Nations," Cisneros said firmly, looking the general squarely in the eye.

"Is that so? Could you please elaborate, as your letter is a bit vague." Then, strangely, Martinez added in a quiet voice, "I apologize. Perhaps I have just been ill-informed. It is no reflection on you, of course, Father."

The priest smiled as even he saw that he appeared to have the upper hand with the general.

Martinez's politeness surprised Octavio. He had expected a

more brutish man, with a sterner voice and a more intimidating presence. Martinez, perhaps because he only had been a general for less than four weeks, seemed almost apologetic.

"Well," Father Cisneros elaborated, "it has come to my attention that a woman—a wife and mother of three small children—has been abducted by the military police and has remained wrongfully imprisoned for over a month without a trial, without contact with her family, and with no other recourse than to remain incarcerated indefinitely." The priest cleared his throat. "This is clearly an outrage, a human rights violation."

"And why was this woman arrested, Father?"

"For no reason at all."

"And whose opinion is that?"

"Do you need any other opinion than mine—a man of God, one who is affiliated with the United Nations, in case you have forgotten?"

The general once again seemed embarrassed and apologized for his tone. "I am sorry. I just find this very hard to believe that this woman would be taken without evidence of her wrongdoing."

"It is the truth," Octavio said firmly, but without raising his voice. "She has done nothing except be my wife and the mother of my children."

"And your name?"

"Octavio Ribeiro."

"Ah, the actor." The general nodded his head and penciled some notes on his pad. "Of course! I thought I recognized you, though now you're sporting a beard." He smiled. "I used to be a big fan of your movies."

"Is that so?" Octavio replied nervously. Small beads of perspiration were forming just above his temples, but he fought the urge to wipe them away, fearing that the general might see his trembling hands. He slowly turned toward the priest, beseeching him with wide eyes to recover control over the conversation.

"You know, General, next week I am attending a conference in Lima for all of the priests who are assigned as temporary clergy in Latin America. There will be many government officials there from all over the world—from the United States to Great Britain. There is even a rumor that the pope is planning to attend as well."

"Yes"—Martinez nodded—"and . . . ?"

"And at this meeting, I will be asked—as I have been in the past when I attended such meetings—'How are things in Santiago, Father Cisneros? Tell us, how is the situation there?'

"And, General Martinez, I beg of you, what am I to tell them? I will have to tell them that things are not well in Santiago. That women are being abducted from their very homes, right before the eyes of their children. To be imprisoned for no wrongdoing and held without a trial, without evidence of their crime!"

"I can't believe that such a thing could happen." The general shook his head.

"But that is what *has* happened," the priest said firmly. "I have seen this with my own eyes. And what are we to do about my suspicion, General Martinez?"

"I suppose I should investigate your complaint." The general motioned for one of his aides to come closer and whispered something in his ear. Moments later, the young soldier left the room, leaving the general alone with Octavio and the priest.

"I can give you my word," Martinez assured the two men, "if Señor Ribeiro's wife is being held with no evidence, without clear-cut proof that she committed a crime against the state, I will have her released immediately."

"That is what I hoped you would say." The priest smiled.

The general extended his hand in a gesture of goodwill to the priest.

"But remember," Father Cisneros added over their handshake, "next week is the conference, and I expect either Salomé de Ribeiro to be returned by then or for you to have news of her trial."

"Absolutely, I intend to look into it immediately."

"We believe she is being held at the Villa Grimaldi in Peñalolen."

"Ah, the recreation center?"

"Is that what you call it, General?"

"I believe that is how it is described in our reports."

"Well, perhaps you should pay a visit when you need some 'recreation' and see for yourself," the priest said, his voice betraying his disgust.

The general stood there in his unflattering brown uniform with its burnished badges. His eyes were beginning to show the first stages of fatigue. His skin was a pale shade of bronze.

"Please write down the exact spelling of your wife's name and the date she was taken into custody," the general requested before the two men departed, and Octavio quickly complied.

And as Octavio and Father Cisneros exited, each man's eyes met those of the other. Silently, they were each thinking the same thing: their only hope now was that the priest's threats were enough to make the general a man of his word.

"Do you really have a conference next week, Father?" Octavio asked the priest when they'd returned to the car. The accomplished actor was astounded when the priest admitted that he had been bluffing the entire time.

"So you blackmailed him into believing that he had no other choice than to protect the integrity of the state?" Octavio laughed out loud. "That was brilliant! I only hope he believed you."

They did not have to wait long to see that the priest's bluff had indeed worked. Four days later, Salomé was released in a park. A blindfolded, bruised shadow, tumbling from a van.

Part III

Forty-Four

⚜

Santiago, Chile
February 1974

*T*hat first morning after Salomé returned to her home and awakened in a freshly made bed, the smells of verbena permeating her room, she thought perhaps the past two months had been just a terrible nightmare. But her reflection in the standing mirror betrayed her. She had not laid eyes upon herself in weeks. The image of her bruised face, swollen upper lip, and sunken eyes shocked her. Never in her life had she seen such a horrific sight.

She did not recognize herself at all. It was as though a stranger were gazing back at her in the glass. A frail, frightened woman who seemed incongruous and ill-fitting, as if she had never belonged in her marital carved-rosewood bed.

Octavio arrived, interrupting Salomé's thoughts. "I've brought some chamomile tea and warm biscuits for my precious Fayum," he said delicately. His voice was soft and low, as one would use with the sick or the infirm.

He sat down on the bed and looked at her. His eyes were wet and his expression pained with compassion. "I'm so sorry, Salomé. I never wanted any of this to happen."

"Of course you didn't, Octavio," she whispered. Over the past two months, she had become an expert in masking her emotions. Each of her words now resonated with a hollow stoicism.

"But you're home now, darling. I . . . ," he stuttered. "The children and I, your parents," he corrected himself, "we're so thankful that you've been returned to us."

Salomé nodded, her head turning slightly to see the tip of the avocado tree bending in the wind.

"I love you," he said as he extended his arm and reached for her hand under the covers. His fingers searched to grasp those of his wife.

However, Salomé did not respond as he had anticipated. For as soon as his flesh grazed hers, she shuddered. It was as if any human contact was enough to make her recoil.

Salomé was also surprised by the intensity of her response. It seemed that even her own husband's touch triggered memories of how she had been violated at the prison. She didn't want him even to brush against her. Instead, she wanted to be left completely alone. To sleep in her own space, with nothing against her skin except her nightgown and the cotton sheets.

In an ideal world, Salomé wished she could wrap her arms around her husband, embrace him, and let out one giant sob into his strong shoulders. But instead, she felt paralyzed. She couldn't even cry. She had returned, but not as the woman she had once been. Not as the wife Octavio had once known. She felt like a living corpse: devoid of emotion, incapable of human contact. It was as though her blood had frozen in her veins.

"Darling . . . ," he said in the voice he had always used with her, but now she found it weak and cloying. "We must leave this place. You, me, and the children. I am already making arrangements so that we can go where it's safe."

"But where will we go, Octavio?" she sighed. "Chile is our home."

"Not anymore. Not after what they did to you. More importantly, they could take you again. We will have to leave as soon as possible. I've already sent applications for political asylum in the U.S., Canada, Sweden, and New Zealand. Whoever makes us an offer first, we'll go there."

"And my parents too?"

There was silence. Octavio lowered his eyes. "They cannot come with us, my darling. Their lives have not been directly threatened, so their request would be denied."

"I see." Octavio could tell by his wife's voice that she was concentrating hard to appear strong.

"We will start over, Salomé. We will make a new life, and things will be good again."

Salomé feigned a smile.

"Things will work out for us," he said as he brought her hand close to his chest. "I promise they will."

Salomé would have preferred that Octavio had said nothing that first day. If only he had let her have some time to readjust. She wanted to be able to do simple things around the house. Little things, like savoring the air that wafted in from the garden. She had taken it for granted before. Now its fragrance of wildflowers and herbs seemed so exotic to her. She wanted to cup her hands and inhale it like perfume.

But, no, right from the beginning, he told her that she should not get too comfortable. That they would soon have to leave their beloved Casa Rosa and start again, go somewhere foreign and strange.

Her body would barely have time to heal before she would have to start packing up the house and selecting the few things they would be able to take.

There were things that she had not anticipated bringing with her from the prison—memories she hoped she had left behind. But her terror could not be forgotten so easily; it could not be packed away in a box with folded tissue and rolls of bubble wrap. It amazed her that Octavio was so certain that all would return to normal. She too wanted to believe that it could be that simple.

To that end, she had promised herself never to speak of her torture. There was no reason to burden either Octavio or the children with her pain. She would never wish upon anyone—let alone her family—the terrible nightmares that had plagued her since her release. No, she would keep them to herself and hope that, eventually, after things had settled down—after the move was over and their new life had begun—maybe then she would feel better.

Her love for her family would triumph over all she had endured, she told herself. After all, during those nights when she'd slept in a dank cell with no light, the sound of wailing mingling with the sounds of opera, the barking of the guards, and the dragging of the bodies through the channels, she had thought of her family with her eyes shut and her fists packed to her side. She had called for them in hysterical moans, and she had imagined her children as they had been when she had held each of them to her breast, their tiny faces looking up at her in their first gazes of life.

But if she were honest with herself, she would have to admit that while incarcerated, she had thought of her husband with far less frequency than she had her children. Octavio, the man whom she had loved since she was seventeen; the only man she had ever loved.

She had thought of him occasionally while she was in prison, remembering how he had first kissed her or how they had danced in the moonlight with the tall pampas grasses grazing their knees. But she had been afraid to think of him as he was now. Perhaps, she had thought, if she let her mind wander to the months before she was taken, she might start to blame him and she would have hated to do that. Because, in her heart, she wanted to still love him. To forgive him. Because she knew, had their situation been reversed, she would have prayed every night that he be returned to her. And that she too would probably have pleaded to God that the government should have taken her instead of him. Because that's what lovers do, isn't it? But if Salomé allowed herself to think like that, she feared she might go mad.

In his heart, Octavio believed that love could never die. He thought it grew stronger when tested. So while he never doubted for a second that Salomé and his marriage might face difficulties when she was returned, he also felt certain that they would mend things once their lives were resettled. Once they had moved far away from the country that had betrayed them.

Of course, he realized how awful the past months had been for her. He did not want to imagine how she had become so spotted with bruises and how her once voluptuous body had seemed to vanish. He knew that, with the proper nursing, her physical self would return to what it had once been. Her emotional scars . . . well, time could only tell with those. He only hoped that, one day, she would feel comfortable enough to open up and speak to him about what had happened to her. He thought, perhaps naively, that it would actually bring them closer.

He had tried to broach the subject with her on more than one occasion. He had sat on the bed and held her hand, bringing it close to his face and pressing his lips into her delicate, olive skin. But she rejected his advances of tenderness. And when he tried to suggest that they should probably discuss certain things—to get them out into the open—she insisted that she wanted to keep the past behind her in order to move forward. She had closed that door, insisting that it be forever shut.

He too kept secrets from her. He never divulged the lengths he had gone to secure her freedom, thinking it best to concentrate solely on that she had been returned. He never told her how he had convinced Father Cisneros to assist him, or how they had persuaded the general through veiled blackmail to release her. Octavio didn't want to play the role of hero. After all, he knew that his actions had put her in harm's way in the first place.

As a result, Salomé never learned the truth and wrongly believed that her rapport with the young prison guard Miguel had led to her freedom. Octavio never took credit for the one thing that might have proven to his wife how he had changed.

Sometimes at night he heard his wife whimpering in her sleep. From underneath the delicate cotton sheets, he could hear her soft moans, somewhat stifled by her hand that rested underneath her cheek. He would move over to her side of the bed and wrap his arms around her, whispering into her fragrant neck that everything was all right, she shouldn't worry; they were now safe. But Salomé would awaken, stare up at him with her dark, marble eyes and appear startled. As if she did not remember where she was or why her husband was whispering to her in the darkest hours of the night.

Forty-Five

❧

Santiago, Chile
February 1974

*T*he Swedish embassy was the first to respond to Octavio's application for political asylum, and he received a letter in the mail instructing him to come to the office at half past four, that Thursday, for an extensive interview.

He knew he had to be grateful that one of the four countries had responded so swiftly to his request, but he had secretly hoped that he would have received a similar letter from the U.S or Canadian embassy. At least there, there were extensive immigrant communities and ample opportunities for people in the arts. He knew nothing about Sweden except that it was going to be cold.

He changed into his best linen suit and tried to fix his hair. Standing in front of the mirror, however, he could do nothing to mask his fatigue. The past three months had taken such a toll on him that most of his black curls had turned a soft gray, and his eyes no longer looked like those of a prized actor, but rather of a man who was completely and utterly exhausted.

The funny thing was, Octavio could care less. A year ago, had he wanted to emigrate to the United States, he would have been incensed that they had not yet responded to his letter. A year ago, he would have been mortified to see deep lines around his mouth and eyes, his hair the color of pewter. Now all of that seemed superfluous. All he wanted now was to make sure his family was safe, and that was the only thing he had energy for. If Sweden would take them—and take them quickly—he would go. He had learned his lesson—life did not imitate the movies, life was not always beautiful and poetic—one often had to make great sacrifices for those one loved.

As he walked down the hallway, Octavio could see through the open door that Salomé was asleep in the guest bedroom. Her head was to the side and he could see, even through the half-opened door, how swollen her face still was.

Every time he gazed upon his wife now he was overwhelmed not only with regret but also anger. How many times had he replayed in his mind that conversation where she had warned him that they might harm him or the family? She had never dared say, "They might take me, Octavio," and even after they did abduct her that first time, she had never said to him, "They might take me again, Octavio!"

He knew why she had never said those things. She wanted him to come to that decision himself. She wanted him to take the initiative to say, "Enough, I will retract my criticisms of Pinochet. I will place my family above everything else." And not only had he failed her by refusing to take that position, he had also failed to protect her. How many times—how many goddamn times—had he replayed in his mind that afternoon he was asleep in the garden when they had come and taken her. He had been sleeping with a newspaper over his head when his wife was kidnapped! He felt pathetic and ashamed. He felt as though all of his former confidence and loyalty toward his so-called principles had been decimated. All that he felt now was regret and self-loathing. And although Octavio prayed that Salomé would someday forgive him, he was confident he would never forgive himself.

Doña Olivia was reading in the parlor, her book splayed out over her lap when Octavio passed by in his suit.

"Thank you for watching over her, Olivia," he said reverently to his mother-in-law.

"You know you don't have to thank me, Octavio. She's my child. It's already breaking my heart that I won't be able to always watch over her."

Octavio knelt down. "Olivia, you know, I wish that you and Don Fernando could come with us. I know it would be that much easier for the whole family if you two could join us, but they would never allow you to come. Your lives are not threatened if you remain here."

Doña Olivia's eyes welled with tears. "I know, Octavio, I know . . ."

"I don't even know if Sweden will take us. That's why it's so important that I make a good impression on this interview." He stood up and smoothed out the creases in his trousers.

"I wish you luck," she whispered, and it was obvious to Octavio that she was finding it difficult to speak. "She's my only child. All I want is for her to be safe."

Forty-Six

❧

Santiago, Chile
February 1974

When he arrived at the Swedish embassy, he was told—much to his surprise—that the ambassador himself would interview him.

The blond receptionist gave him no other details. She just motioned him to wait in the hallway until he was called.

Octavio's heart was racing, and he tried desperately to remember all the tricks he used to do to get over his stage fright. "Breathe, breathe," he reminded himself. "Think of yourself in a warm bath with the water soothing you . . ."

"Señor Octavio Ribeiro?" another blond woman called from the doorway.

"Yes." He stood up.

She gave him a small, clipped smile and motioned for him to follow her.

As they walked down the corridor, she turned to him and said without any inflection in her voice, "The ambassador will be with you in a few moments. Please sit in this office until he arrives."

He entered a small, white office and sat down. She closed the door.

Octavio was visibly uncomfortable. There was nothing for him to look at while he waited except for a small painting of a child in front of a garden shed. It was one of those unremarkable pictures that one often sees in a hotel room or at a doctor's office. Something that is chosen because it can't possibly offend anyone. Tasteful in the sense that it was positively generic: a child, a flower, and a garden shed. But somehow it disturbed Octavio.

The painting seemed to foreshadow what life in Sweden was supposed to be like. But how would his family—who didn't have blond hair or know anything about Scandinavian culture, let alone speak the language—fit into that lifestyle? Octavio placed his head on the white Formica desk.

"Remember how much is at stake here," he reminded himself. "This is reality for you now. You and your family have no other choice. You cannot stay in Chile. The sooner the better, but regardless, you have to go somewhere."

Octavio was surprised at how buoyant the ambassador was when he entered the room. He was a tall, thin man with a large, broad smile.

"Señor Ribeiro," he said, sounding out the name in a series of perfect, fluid notes.

"It's such a pleasure to meet you."

"The pleasure is completely mine," Octavio responded politely.

"No, no," the ambassador said as he took a seat at the temporary desk that was obviously used as an interviewing station. He placed the manila folder he was carrying down and opened it. "You see, one of my colleagues brought your application to my attention because he knew what a big fan I am of your films."

"My films?" Octavio nearly choked. It had been a few years now since his last performance, and he couldn't believe that anyone but a Chilean would have been familiar with his work.

"Yes, your films. My wife and I have seen every one of them . . . from *Buenos Dias Soledad* to *Siempre Carmen*. My all-time favorite movie moment is when you find that the villainous Cristobal has slain Angelina and . . ."

After Octavio had just spent two months living a reality far more horrific and agonizing than anything he had ever seen scripted in a film, hearing the ambassador relaying something that was obviously just fantasy made Octavio cringe. But to be polite, he indulged the ambassador.

"You mean when I clasp my heart like this"—Octavio pulled a

fist to his chest and made a pained expression—"and I fall to the ground crying, 'Angelina, Angelina, the angels have you now and thus I have no reason to cry' "—his voice became audibly louder—" 'but I have only salt and water in my heart since you left'?"

"Yes, yes!" the ambassador cried. "I used to mimic that at parties, and everyone said I did the best Ribeiro imitation."

Octavio winced. The thought of a bunch of Scandinavians living in Chile eating gravlax on toast and doing imitations of him only strengthened his feelings of self-loathing.

"Really?" he managed to reply. "That must have been quite amusing."

The ambassador stiffened and suddenly became more serious. "Well, getting back to your application, Señor Ribeiro . . . I see you've applied to us for political asylum."

"Yes."

The ambassador looked down at the papers he had just removed from the manila folder. "I've read about all the terrible things that happened to your wife."

"Yes . . . sir," Octavio added quickly.

"I hate to make you feel uncomfortable in any way, Señor Ribeiro, but I have to for the sake of protocol. Did your wife do anything that would have warranted her arrest?"

"Absolutely not," Octavio replied firmly. "She was taken because I refused to retract my criticisms of Pinochet."

The ambassador scribbled some notes on a pad of paper.

"Again this question is for the sake of our protocol, so please do not be offended by my questions."

Octavio nodded.

"Could you please tell me why you believe it necessary to seek political asylum in Sweden?"

Octavio could feel the perspiration dripping down his forehead, and he reached inside his jacket for a handkerchief. He excused himself temporarily while he blotted his brow.

"Ambassador, I have always loved my country. Had Pinochet never come to power under such brutal methods, I would not be sitting across from you today. But because of my beliefs, because of my outspoken criticisms of the new regime, the lives of my wife and family are currently at stake. The DINA already kidnapped my wife twice. The second time they took her, they held her captive for nearly two months and terrorized her in ways that only the worst parts of my imagination can conceive."

Octavio's voice started to waver as he spoke about Salomé. Even now, as he heard himself articulate what was done to her, he had to fight back with every ounce of his strength the urge to cry. "Right now, my wife is sleeping in a bed with bruises all over her body, lacerations on her skin, and huge red scars where once there was only smooth brown skin. What she has suffered internally can only be a million times worse . . . if you can possibly imagine that."

The ambassador shook his head. "This is terrible. Terrible."

"We cannot stay here. We'll take the first country that grants us asylum. We are desperate to go where we can be safe, and if Sweden would take us today, we would go."

"Sweden *will* take you, Señor Ribeiro," the ambassador said with great seriousness. "I will personally make sure of that."

He extended his hand to Octavio, assuring him that in a week's time the papers would be processed and he and his family would be on a plane to Stockholm.

Forty-Seven

❧

Santiago, Chile
March 1974

$\mathcal{A}$s the few boxes from the Ribeiro-Herrera household were
loaded into Octavio's small car, Rafael watched his mother from the
corner of his eye. He had studied her diligently over that week, noticing everything from the fading bruises on her cheeks to the whisper
of her voice. It was as though she had barely enough strength in her
diaphragm to utter more than a string of words. She preferred to
just point with her finger and nod her tiny head.

Had she been well, he would have asked her what political asylum meant, for he did not understand it at his young age. His father
had tried to explain it to him and his sisters as much as he could in
the few days that preceded the family's departure, but it still was
confusing to him. He didn't understand if it meant that he could
never return to Chile, or whether it meant that he would live the rest
of his life like a nomad wandering the world with only the clothes
on his back and his belongings scattered around and abandoned.
What Rafael did know, however, was that he was leaving the Casa
Rosa, the house of his childhood, the summers at the hacienda, and
the temperate life he had always known, all for Sweden, a country
famous for its snowfall and arctic waters.

His grandmother and he had looked at picture books of Sweden
before he left, ones that showed photographs of tiny red houses
with pitched roofs whose shutters were lined with icicles that hung

like white icing on a Christmas cake. He saw pictures of women dressed in the national costume, with sterling buttons and cobalt blue skirts, nearly all of them fair and blond.

Until then, the only woman he had known with blond hair was his grandmother, who insisted the color was her natural shade. And now it was nearly white, the yellow fading from each wisp, like wheat bleached over the long months of summer.

He hated to think how different he would appear to the other children. His dark black hair, his large brown eyes. In Chile, he resembled almost all the other boys and girls. Certainly, each of their features differed, but none were so drastic that one appeared strange to the others.

His grandmother had tried to assuage his doubts. Stoically, she had tried to hide her own sadness and convince Rafael and his sisters that they would soon be surrounded by such exotic animals as reindeer and polar bears. She opened up all the secret drawers of her furniture with the keys that hung within her blouse and let all the children eat all of her beloved marzipan, her cans of Chantilly cream and squares of fine chocolate. She had hoped that it would make them feel better—make her feel better—to see them rejoice in her coveted confectioneries. She had even tried to capture their attention by telling them that, once in Sweden, they would be able to ride their sleighs six months out of the year and store their ice cream out on the terrace! But they were each a conspirator in a charade, each child and each adult trying to pretend to the others that everything would be all right. Each trying to mask his or her feelings of fear and uncertainty of what lay ahead.

Rafael had not wanted to cry when his father informed him that they would have to leave Chile in only a few days. He accepted it without protest, for only weeks before he had promised God that if he returned his mother, he would never complain again.

The first day his mother rose from her bed, he had watched her wander through the house wrapped in a silk robe printed with pale blue irises, and from behind, her spine resembled one of the flower's bending stems.

"Won't you help your mother pack?" she had said to him in a voice that was far fainter than even a whisper. "Won't you bring me your clothes and your most treasured things?" she whispered as she knelt down on the floor and fanned out the unfolded boxes and paper.

He nodded to her, bringing to her after moments of careful pondering his clothes and a few of his sisters' most cherished toys. But he brought no such keepsakes of his own. She did not ask him why he had brought her nothing but his own clothes to pack. She was lost to him in these moments between them. Her mind was elsewhere. She did not utter a word as she laid each of her daughters' toys into the deep, brown boxes. So, in silence, Rafael watched what seemed like a ghost of his mother. Watched as she wrapped each item. Her still pale, delicate fingers wrapping each object in chiffon paper. Her bruised wrists packing a child's treasures with care.

The only thing that Rafael wanted to bring with him to Sweden was a bear that now, tragically, remained on a shelf untouched.

Rafael had spent every night in Chile with a small, beloved bear. He had called him Umberto and loved him dearly; a wondrous bear with soft, chocolate-brown fur, velvet paws, a black stitched nose, and brown, painted-glass eyes.

Umberto had comforted him on all of those nights when he'd lain in bed while his father was out roaming the streets questioning anyone who might have information about Salomé. Rafael had held the bear in his arms, his tears soaking the brown fur until it was dark and salty. He whispered into its gray felt ears all the things he was instructed never to say in public. And only to Umberto, not to his sisters or grandmother, did Rafael ever reveal his fears. Rafael felt that they were already too overwrought from their own pain and anguish to bear his as well.

So, his bear was his only confidant. Silent and stoic, the two of them braving this journey alone until his mother was returned.

And when his mother did arrive home, her delicate olive skin bruised with a garden of plum patches and lilac stains, Rafael silently rejoiced with his velvet-pawed friend. He held the stuffed animal to him, his tiny arm encasing the bear's soft, downy limbs.

Yet when it came time to pack his dearest friend, he left his beloved bear behind. Eventually, Octavio asked Rafael why he had not put Umberto into one of the boxes to be shipped abroad.

"I know I said we'll have limited room in Sweden, Rafael, but I assure you, we'll have enough room for Umberto."

"I don't want to bring him, Papa," Rafael said quietly. "I'll have no need for him over there."

But that was a lie. Rafael had left his bear behind not because he had no need for him. Indeed, Umberto was the object he loved most in the world. But because God had answered his prayers and returned his mother, he would try to convince himself that he needed nothing else now. And thus he had decided days before, when his father had informed him that they could bring only the barest essentials, that he would only bring his toothbrush and his clothes.

When he held his bear on that last night before they were to leave, he justified his reasoning in a child's whisper: "You will watch over the house until we return." He kissed the bear's felt ear. "And I will watch over Mama." With that, he held the bear tightly, as if his hug could convince his friend that his action was not one of betrayal but rather a noble sacrifice.

Now the car was packed and his grandparents stood stoically on the porch trying to manage a heart-wrenching good-bye.

Rafael watched as his mother moved slowly from the front porch of the Casa Rosa, her tiny feet treading carefully over the tile where they had found her collapsed upon only a few weeks before. She seemed to hesitate for a second before accepting Octavio's hand as he ushered her to the front seat of the car.

Doña Olivia and Don Fernando looked like two white statues, their features tight and drawn, shrunken in a desperate attempt to conceal their grief. And their daughter's face mirrored that of her parents' as she turned her head to the clouded glass of the automobile, her fingers bending in a gesture of farewell.

Rafael slid next to his mother in the car and could not help but notice the tears pooling in her eyes. She seemed perhaps more child-like at that moment than either he or his sisters did. He watched her intently—wanting to hold her and protect her—as the car navigated its way through Santiago's winding streets. His father drove carefully through the city, his knuckles white around the steering wheel and his forehead beaded in sweat.

The seven miles to the Swedish embassy felt like an eternity. But once Octavio had successfully driven within the walls of the Swedish compound, where his request for political asylum had been processed only days before, the family's safety was ensured.

They arrived in Stockholm to a gray day, with wet snow falling from the sky. A relocation volunteer met the family at the airport and escorted them to the temporary housing unit that had been reserved for them.

Rafael held each of his sisters' hands when they passed through immigration, his father handing over their passports and responding quietly, "Yes, this is all their belongings: these three valises, five cardboard boxes, and a sack of toys."

His mother looked as if she were in a trance. Her limbs dangled at her side like two limp dandelion stems. Her flowered dress hung on her like a wrinkled cotton bag.

She had hardly spoken to any of them during the entire journey. From the moment they had driven to the Swedish embassy in Santiago to the landing of the plane in Stockholm three days later, Salomé had spoken only a few words.

"Wave bye-bye to Grandmama," she had whispered to the children as the car drove away from the faded pink house. "Help your sisters with their food," she had urged Rafael on the flight over. Otherwise, she remained silent, her hands folded quietly in her lap. The entire time, she did not speak to Octavio.

And it occurred to the young but precocious Rafael, as he followed his family through their first hours in this new and foreign country, that this was the first time in his childhood memory that he'd noticed that his parents didn't hold hands.

Forty-Eight

୧ൕ৸

Salomé's session with Samuel finished later than usual that evening. She walked through the narrow streets of Vesterås until she arrived home to her family's government-appointed apartment on the other side of town. On this night, she was particularly nostalgic for her Casa Rosa. For, unlike most of the quaint houses and thatched cottages that dotted the narrow streets of Vesterås, her own building was erected in the late sixties—created with poured concrete and filled with perfectly rectangular windows and thin plywood doors.

The architect, who had built similar structures throughout Sweden to accommodate its burgeoning immigrant community, had declared the building a "Platonic ideal"—an egalitarian house built for those less fortunate, yet equipped with all the necessities of modern life. There was the standard linoleum tile, pale yellow with faux brown grout. The lighting fixtures were small fluorescent domes that looked like little flying saucers suspended on the ceiling. There was a bathtub with an optional shower nozzle and, down the hallway, a communal washer and dryer.

When Salomé had first arrived in Sweden, she was initially pleasantly surprised at how large their apartment was. When the agency had informed her and Octavio that the family would receive subsidized living quarters until they were able to afford to live on their own, she had imagined a cramped, squalid place—a dark and dirty, crowded tenement reminiscent of one of the Santiago barrios. But in fact, the apartment was spacious and filled with light. Each of the children would have his or her own room, and at the end of the hallway was a large master bedroom with a private bath.

Yet the architect's generous and flowing floor plan that, at first, seemed a blessing to her would later be a curse. Each of the four rooms had a door that could be closed; each had its own four walls that could be employed as a personal fortress. And that is what Salomé and Octavio ultimately used the rooms for—they shut each other out.

During the early evenings when Salomé returned home from her eight-o'clock walk, she would usually find her husband sound asleep on the couch and the children studying alone in their rooms.

So even though over a year had passed since her abduction, and even though she had traveled thousands of miles from Chile, she still felt like that imprisoned woman. The bruised and fragile ghost who slept coiled in a corner in a neatly starched bed.

Salomé wore her misery silently and cryptically. It was as if the two months she had endured in the Villa Grimaldi had taught her how to be a master of disguise, an artist of deception. It wasn't that her ability to deceive was rooted in actual deceit but, rather, in survival. For, just as she had once pretended that she was a lady of great wealth and power to gain the favor of one of her guards, she now pretended to her family that all was well with her. That the tragic past was behind her, and that her life with her children and Octavio would be just as it had been before the coup.

Since their arrival in Sweden, she had learned how to smile even when her spirit felt destroyed. She had mastered the ability to awaken silently from her nightmares without disturbing her slumbering husband, who slept next to her, his body curled like a kitten's, his face smiling, and his fingers nestled against her side.

One thing, however, she could not disguise: her inability to be intimate with Octavio.

She knew that he had been as patient as he could. He had been respectful of her and hadn't initiated any overtures of lovemaking while they still remained in Chile. In a gesture of genuine sensitivity, he had slept in the guest room so she could recuperate more comfortably.

She could see that he was still hungry for her; he still looked at her with the same tenderness and same sense of passion that he had had for her since they'd first met so many years before. But she no longer felt like that young, naive girl in the field of oranges. The men at the Villa Grimaldi had made sure of that.

Octavio waited nearly two months before he got up the courage to kiss his wife passionately on the mouth. By that time, they had already moved into their new apartment in Vesterås.

"I've missed you," he said tenderly as he placed his hand gently on her breast. "I want to take this slowly with you." He was looking at her with deep affection.

"I'm not ready," she told him.

He could feel how her entire body tensed when he went to touch her. How it seemed as though the slightest gesture upon her body was received as an invasion.

He retracted his hand and pulled his mouth away from hers. A great sadness was in his eyes, as if he were helpless to soothe her and remind her that he was gentle, he was kind, and he was her husband. But his voice faltered and he was too full of self-loathing and insecurity now to say anything. He didn't try to be intimate with her again for at least another week.

"Salomé." He tried this time to be even softer with his voice. "I've nearly forgotten what it's like to hold you."

He was turned on his side, the white pillow contrasting with his salt-and-pepper hair.

"I'm not ready, Octavio," she told him. She could tell he wanted her to talk to him—to tell him what she was thinking. But how could she?

How could she tell him how they had raped her. That they had forced themselves on her as sometimes more than one of them looked on as the other one did with her what he wanted.

How could she explain that they had placed wires on her—in those places he used to kiss her most, the ones he had always reminded her playfully were *his*.

Now, the truth was they were no longer *his*. They had made sure of that. And they were no longer *hers* either. The truth was, what wasn't empty in her was filled over by a large, ugly scar. She had become a fortress of tissue and bone, and the mere thought of anything entering her was enough to make her scream.

Salomé, however, never articulated any of this to Octavio. She thought he could interpret her without further explanation. After all, he had always prided himself on his sensitivity. Couldn't he see she didn't know how to tell him that they had taken what was so pure and tainted it? That she was no longer that girl stepping out of the convent school, that she was no longer a woman who had only been with her husband? She didn't even know how he could want her. She wondered when he might realize that they may have returned her to him and the children, but the person whom they'd sent back was not the woman he had once known. That person was dead.

Octavio, however, failed to give up so easily on his wife. He thought if he persisted that eventually she would open up to him. He still tried to be tender to her and to solicit some affection from his obviously still suffering wife. Salomé, however, always seemed to have an excuse to shut him out. "I'm exhausted physically and emotionally from this move," she said during their first few months in Sweden. After another three months had passed, she told him, "I still need time to heal." And now, her response, when he slid next to her and placed his hand on her waist—something that she had always loved before her abduction—was far more direct. She just flatly told him, "No."

She had nearly killed him that evening he'd returned home to their apartment with an armload of oranges and scattered them on their bed.

He had wanted to surprise her, to re-create the scene in which they'd first fallen in love. It was such a desperate gesture. He was floundering—almost to the point that it was embarrassing—but he was at the end of his rope and he could feel the only thing he had ever loved—besides his children—floating away from him.

He wanted to lasso her back. Force her to yell at him, scream at him, tell him how horrible he was to have let this be done to her. But at least, let her tell him! Because this silence between them, this distance that was increasing between them with every passing month, and every night feeling lonelier and lonelier for him, was breaking him into a thousand pieces.

He felt as though he had come to Sweden with nothing but his love for his family, and now he felt as though that which he loved most in the world was abandoning him.

He couldn't be angry with the children. They were facing their own challenges with a new school, a new language, but Salomé seemed to be withdrawing from him completely.

He didn't want to complain to her. He knew how much she had suffered because of his actions. He also realized that the family wouldn't even be in Sweden if it weren't for his stubborn refusal to support the Pinochet regime, but a part of him couldn't help but feel hurt and dejected.

He was now in a country where no one even knew his name. *Octavio Ribeiro* meant nothing to anyone except perhaps the career counselor who was trying to match him with a suitable profession or the social worker who knew his needs only as a newly arrived immigrant who needed time to adjust.

He despised having to wait on unemployment lines and to meet with a counselor every week. After all, in the past, people like the great Allende and Neruda had come to him for his talent; it had never been the other way around.

Forty-Nine

❦

Vesterås, Sweden
March 1975

*S*alomé hadn't wanted to admit that her need for therapy wasn't just about her inability to listen to music, but also about her inability to be intimate with a man she had always loved. The only reason she even went to her first session with Samuel Rudin was because she had grown weary of living without any sense of joy in her life. She had always loved music, she had always considered herself passionate and one who enjoyed the sensual things in life. Now she only knew pain.

She had never expected her therapy to change her as much as it had. Initially, she thought that she would visit Samuel for a few sessions, discuss her inability to disassociate her love of music with the memory of being tortured by its sound, and gradually be healed of her terror. What she hadn't anticipated was how interwoven her experiences in the Villa Grimaldi were with the way she now felt toward Octavio.

She had not wanted to be angry with him. She had struggled to repress her resentment toward him. But therapy was making her unearth all of these emotions, and suddenly, Salomé realized how different she was from that person Octavio had proposed to so many years before. No longer was she that naive seventeen-year-old girl who could so easily be seduced. Now, she was a mature woman decimated by emotional and physical scars. And she was angry.

Octavio had sacrificed her. She had been raped and beaten because of his actions, not hers. And although she still loved Octavio, she had not yet forgiven him.

She sometimes had dreams where she fell upon him and shook him with all her might. "Don't you see? Don't you see?" she envisioned herself screaming at him, his eyes staring at her blankly. In her dream, her linen nightgown opens at the breast, revealing her scars from where the electrical wires were attached. "Don't you see, Octavio, what they have done to me?"

But he refuses to see what she speaks of. He insists that he sees nothing. "What darling?" he murmurs to her, his tone sugar-sweet and slightly confused. "I don't see anything at all." He reaches to caress the long, brown stretch of her thighs, ignoring the areas of her body that still have ladders of scars.

She would awaken at night in a sweat, the scene in her dream obviously revealing what was in her heart. "Is it so difficult," she would wonder to herself, "for him to acknowledge that he wronged me in Chile? Is it too much of a struggle for him to say that he's sorry?" If only he could accept that she was not the same as before. If only he could love and care for her wholly, as a woman who had endured something terrible because of *his* actions. To acknowledge that she had been kidnapped and beaten, to understand that she was forced, in less than two weeks' time, to abandon her home and parents. To recognize that, as a family, their situation had clearly and terribly changed.

And consequently, Salomé found herself withdrawing from the man she had once loved so dearly. The man she suddenly found herself feeling intimately about was the man she talked to every week about her most private thoughts. She soon began to long for her sessions with Samuel. He was the only person who knew her completely, and that intimacy contributed to her burgeoning attraction to him. Samuel Rudin soon began to find his way into her thoughts even after she had left his office. Sometimes she felt he was like smoke, gathering at the base of her neck, traveling underneath her clothes, and clinging to her skin.

At night, it was as though his whisper of a voice followed her home. She could anticipate his answers to the things she envisioned herself revealing to him. She could imagine his gaze as she fidgeted on the low leather couch, her fingers rearranging her skirt. How sometimes his eyes fell upon a stretch of her leg. How he seemed visibly unnerved when she ran her fingers through her hair.

For many weeks, she had tried to deny her attraction to him. She tried to convince herself that the reason she grew despondent between her sessions was that she was making so much progress in her therapy that she wanted immediate continuity. Finally, she told herself, she had been able to find a safe space in which she could air out her feelings (in Spanish no less) and discuss what she had stuffed down deep inside her and willed herself to forget. And finally she had located a person—a willing listener and sympathizer—to whom she could relate all the difficulties she'd encountered as she'd tried to resume a relationship with her husband.

She was discovering that, yes, she could feel like an attractive and viable woman again. But somehow, she always felt most attractive when she was with Samuel, not Octavio. Perhaps it was because only with her doctor did she feel she was being honest with herself.

As her mind began to stray, and her thoughts lingered over Samuel, Salomé's detachment from her husband intensified. She no longer made excuses for why she didn't want to make love with him. She no longer felt guilty that she couldn't perform her "wifely duties" for him. He didn't know what kind of woman was sleeping in his bed! But Samuel—he knew she had been raped—that her body was riddled with razor-thin, red scars, and she could not help but wonder if, knowing all that, he could still find her beautiful.

Fifty

⋖❀⋗

Vesterås, Sweden
March 1975

Octavio never anticipated what befell him when he arrived in Sweden. All he had thought about was getting his family out of Chile. In Sweden, he wanted Salomé and the children to be safe, to be free from the evil that he had seen for the first time.

He believed Sweden would afford them a new life. A clean slate, the chance to start over.

Clearly the suffering Salomé had endured in the Villa Grimaldi had affected and transformed her from the young, idealistic girl she had been when he'd first met her. But Octavio too had endured a life-altering experience, although on the surface it was less obvious than Salomé's.

He had nearly lost what was most precious to him in the world: his one, all-consuming love. He had spent countless nights lying in bed wondering if his wife was dead or alive. Wondering if she was undergoing horrific beatings and brutal interrogations due to his actions. He had been humiliated in front of his in-laws by his inability to protect their daughter; he had shamed himself by not realizing that he had placed both their lives and his wife's and children's in grave danger.

He had rescued her and did not want to reveal the dramatic lengths he had undergone to get her back. But once in Sweden, Octavio felt as though Salomé had completely left him. She might have shared an apartment with him physically, but emotionally she had disappeared. Without Salomé's companionship, without his career, he no longer had an identity. No one recognized his face. No one was impressed by his name or the movies he had made in a country on the other side of the world. He could not speak the language, and his dark, South American coloring only exacerbated his foreignness.

Months passed. The children began school, Octavio remained unemployed, and Salomé strove to reconcile what had happened to her back in Chile months before.

He had foolishly thought that her therapy would bring them closer, that she would have an outlet to discuss her trauma and that she would eventually confide in him. But the reverse seemed to occur. Salomé appeared to become even more withdrawn from both him and the children.

Often, when Octavio returned home from meeting with his counselor at the employment agency, he would discover that Rafael, far wiser than and sensitive beyond his years, had tidied the house, made his sisters' beds, and begun preparing dinner. Octavio would try to tell his son how grateful he was for the assistance, but he too struggled to communicate his feelings.

Indeed, he felt terribly guilty toward his children. Not only had his actions harmed his wife, but his son and two daughters had also been forced to come to this cold, strange country where they would have to learn a new language and make new friends.

So there was more than one night when Octavio lay sleepless in bed, his eyes staring wide at the ceiling, his body restless, drowning in his feelings of failure.

Fifty-One

Vesterås, Sweden
March 1975

"Last week, you indicated that you were thinking of leaving your husband," Samuel said as he began his session with Salomé. The tape recorder hummed in the background as he fingered through his writing pad.

"Yes, and I'm pretty sure I am going to do it this week."

"Have you really thought this through, Salomé?"

"Yes, of course I have! I can't stand it anymore—this constant charade."

"A charade?"

"Yes, didn't I just say that?" She bit one of her nails and slid herself lower into the leather couch.

"Salomé, you know it's important to be absolutely clear with these things . . ."

Salomé exhaled deeply, her chest deflating as she sighed. "Every day I'm pretending that I've adjusted to this new life. That I've put my children in a safe, secure environment where they're better off than they were with their old friends and grandparents in Chile."

Samuel nodded.

"I feel I must keep my spirits high for everyone else, because they're all relying on me to hold the family together. My husband still hasn't found a job he's happy with. The employment agency has suggested various options for him, but none of them ever seem to satisfy him . . . the great actor. . . . Now, he's saying that he wants to be a housepainter because all the identical, little red houses here are driving him mad!"

"It sounds as though he's having problems adjusting here as well."

"But it was his idea that we come here in the first place! And even worse . . . it was his stubbornness that got us in such danger in Chile."

Samuel nodded.

"For God's sake, I thought Allende was a good man, and it was devastating what happened in the coup. But I've always believed in placing my family first. Even now I do! That's why I remain silent about what happened to me. That's why every day I suffer alone."

"And you think that not telling your family how you feel is the best solution?"

"You know I do! No one but I should have to endure these nightmares. I will never speak of them to anyone—except you."

Samuel continued to stare at his patient, almost transfixed. He noticed that her face was flushed from frustration. Tiny patches of pink were spreading across her cheekbones. The blush made her look even more alluring.

Her striking features were even more beautiful in profile: her full lips, her thick mane of hair, her obsidian eyes. Even when she lay upon the couch, her tiny frame encapsulated in a simple green sheath, she had an irresistible ripeness.

During Salomé's past few sessions, Samuel had struggled to sustain his objectivity. He had to remind himself that, as a psychiatrist, he maintained a sacred position. Not only was it his responsibility to listen to Salomé, but also to guide her. He realized it would be wrong of him not to point out that she needed to confront Octavio about her feelings. It would be even more wrong of him to encourage her to dissolve her marriage.

"So you will never share these nightmares with Octavio?" he asked, trying to be fair.

"Not even to Octavio."

"You just plan on leaving him . . ."

"Yes."

"And you don't think he'll demand an explanation, after all you've been through together?"

"He has to realize that something has stopped working between us. After all, we haven't had physical relations since I was abducted."

"These things can take time, Salomé. It is understandable that you haven't been able to make love to your husband."

"But what if I want to be able to make love . . .just *not* with him."

Samuel raised his eyebrows. Something that Salomé had just said struck him as out of character for her. He knew that her feelings were far from unfounded, considering all she had endured. And considering that it was her husband's actions, not her own, that had led to her abduction, her anger was only normal. But why did he feel as if Salomé was trying to tell him something more?

He began to feel uneasy, and to doubt his own professionalism toward his patient. Had he been too aggressive in trying to get Salomé to admit her anger toward her husband? And where did this zeal on his part come from? Was it his own selfish desires?

He couldn't deny that he no longer saw her as just another patient, but also as a woman whom he was strongly attracted to. He wrestled to regain control of his emotions. This was forbidden territory. Not only because he was married, but because he was Salomé's doctor. To harbor feelings toward one's patient was unethical and could bring serious harm as well. But was she now suggesting that she found him attractive as well? His mind began to ache from the tension he sensed mounting between them.

"I don't know." She shook her head and pressed her palms over her eyes. "I want to start over. I still love my husband, I just can't live with him anymore. Is it really that odd that I would now desire to be with someone who is able to acknowledge that I've changed? Someone who has the capacity to understand what I'm going through?"

"No, your feelings are not strange, Salomé," Samuel replied as he tried to regain his concentration. "I think we all sometimes feel that—in any marriage."

"Do you?"

"It would be wrong for me to talk about myself in your session, Salomé."

"Well, I've made up my mind. I'm leaving him."

"I think you should take some more time to think about this."

"What's the point?"

"Your mind should be clear for such an important decision."

Salomé remained quiet.

"What about your children? After all, they are also suffering from the stress of relocating to a new country and having to make new friends . . . learn a new language. Now their entire family structure will be changing."

Salomé was quiet for a moment. "Rafael will be able to handle it. He's strong and resilient. But, you're right, explaining it to the two girls will be difficult."

Samuel nodded.

"Look, I don't think I'll ever love anyone as much as my husband. I doubt there's a more poetic, idealistic soul on earth. But I just can't continue living with him." She paused and readjusted herself on the sofa, crossing her feet at the ankles.

"May I ask you something, Dr. Rudin?"

"Yes, of course." He looked up from his notes.

"Do you think I'm attractive?"

"Attractive?" Samuel blurted. It was though he had been hit with a stone between his eyes.

"Yes, attractive," she repeated.

"I'm your doctor, Salomé. It would be inappropriate for me to answer that question," he said, obviously flustered. "But," he mumbled underneath his breath, "I do think any man would find you beautiful."

She found herself blushing at his answer. A moment of silence lingered between them and increased the tension in the air.

"I'm sorry, I should never have put you on the spot like that," she said. "It was a stupid question. Let's just forget I even mentioned it."

Samuel adjusted himself in his chair, relieved that the subject of physical attraction between them had terminated.

He took a few seconds to gather himself. He glanced over his notes and fiddled with the tape recorder to make sure it was still working. He switched his pen, replacing it with another from his leather blotter, then finally looked up.

"Salomé, are you feeling stronger than when you first came to me five weeks ago?"

"Yes, immensely."

"Good. Have you listened to any music? Have you tried to test your response to it, as we discussed?"

"A little. I'm improving, I think. Sometimes, I allow the children to play the radio when I'm in the apartment." She paused. "I never used to, before our sessions. It was too painful. Even if it was music other than opera, I couldn't stand it. Just as I couldn't stand the sound of dripping water because it reminded me of the electric shocks.

"Still, I am beginning to feel stronger. My nightmares are lessening since our conversations here." She paused, touching her fingers to her throat. "I suppose I've just needed someone with whom I could be completely honest."

"Of course. That's why I'm here."

"And since my sessions with you, I've realized that, ultimately, I need to start over. I need to live on my own for a while.

"Of course I'd take the children with me," she continued. "But I need to have space from Octavio. I need to have time to sort out my feelings."

"Well, perhaps some time apart would benefit the both of you."

"It will devastate him to hear that I'm leaving."

"Life cannot always be beautiful and poetic, Salomé."

She nodded, her eyes finally fixing on the brown-beamed ceiling. "Yes, I know. If only Octavio knew that too."

Samuel tried to regain his objectivity. "Still, I urge you to think carefully before you do anything. Remember, even if you believe your eldest, Rafael, is strong, he is still a child."

"I know."

Samuel pressed the off button of the tape recorder. "Unfortunately, our time today seems to have expired." He glanced at the clock. "Will I see you next week?"

Salomé nodded, and her lips formed a small smile.

He watched as his patient stood up from the couch in her lime green dress and slowly left his office. He admitted to himself what his professional ethics had prevented him from telling her. He was wholly and undeniably attracted to her.

Fifty-Two

⋯❦⋯

Vesterås, Sweden
March 1975

$\mathcal{T}$rying to calm himself after the tension from earlier that afternoon, Samuel remained in his office for nearly three hours before preparing to leave for home. In an overly deliberate manner, he finished going through his notes, filed them in his patients' folders, and inserted the cassettes into the appropriate stapled paper pockets. Finally, after he could think of no further excuse for not leaving, he capped his pens and replaced them in the drawer, stood up, and pushed in his chair.

He had been looking forward to the spring for several months, and now, although the temperature had become somewhat warm and balmy, he had heard that rain was in the forecast. Peering through one of the venetian blinds, he noticed a light drizzle was already dancing off the steps of his building.

The patter of rain soothed him. Samuel walked over to his coat-rack and slipped into his mackintosh, pulling each of his arms through the satin-lined sleeves. "I mustn't forget my umbrella," he reminded himself, smiling as he looked over and saw the red umbrella propped against the corner. His wife had bought it for him several months earlier, before she had grown listless and withdrawn. She told him that she had chosen the color because she knew he would never be able to forget it anywhere. She was always thinking of other people—never herself, even when she was at her most despondent. Sometimes he wished she'd be more selfish and put herself first. He made a mental note to himself to have a talk with her about it soon.

He checked over his desk one last time. The tapes of his afternoon patients had already been filed away. His tea mug had been washed and dried, his notepads stacked high to the left of his phone. Everything was where it should be. He buttoned his coat, smoothed out the pockets, and finally opened the latch of the door.

As he opened up the crimson hood of his umbrella, his black-loafered foot stepping to the first-floor landing, he noticed that the rain was soft and misting. In the gray light of twilight, the fog was lifting off the pavement.

At first, he had thought it was his imagination. He had seen the patch of lime green material and believed he was seeing things. But, as he lifted his umbrella to rest against his shoulder, he saw that, indeed, he had seen correctly. Salomé Herrera was sitting by herself on a bench directly across from his office, her black curls soaking against her shoulders, her face glistening from the onset of rain.

He rushed across the street and stood over her. He held the umbrella over her to shield her from the water, though she was already soaked and shivering. Her teeth were chattering, and the lines of her body could clearly be seen underneath her dress.

"What's the matter, Salomé?" Samuel asked with great concern.

She looked up at him, her eyes not wet from the rain but rather from something deep inside. She was shaking.

"Are you all right?"

"I'm not sure." She stood up to face him. She looked at him for less than a second before wrapping him in her wet, slippery arms.

He surprised himself by kissing her back as strongly as he did. He dropped his umbrella to grasp her more firmly. He moved one hand up her back slowly and felt the weight of her long, black hair, all the while kissing her. She tasted like almonds to him, as if her body were laced with the delectable, intoxicating perfume of marzipan.

She bit him sweetly on his bottom lip and he fell on her bosom, kissing her. He cupped his hands around each breast, caressing them with a wandering thumb.

But then, she stopped.

"We shouldn't do this here, outside. What if people see?" Salomé whispered.

They were staring at each other now, both their faces streaked with water. Their skins felt suddenly cold in places that, only seconds before, had been warm from each other's breath.

"We shouldn't be doing this at all, Salomé." Suddenly Samuel was overcome by great embarrassment. How could he have unleashed himself on this woman who was not only not his wife, but his patient? How could he have shown such a lack of control?

"You're the only person who understands me now," she said, tears now streaming down her face.

"You shouldn't think like that, Salomé."

"You were right to make me see my husband in his true light."

"I never said that, Salomé." He was now trying to peel himself from her arms.

"You didn't have to . . ."

She was shaking and Samuel took off his coat and placed it around her shoulders. "Come," he said softly. "Let's go inside."

In the few minutes it had taken him to run up and open the door to his office and usher Salomé inside, he had told himself that he had to apologize to his patient. What he had done was wrong, a cardinal sin in his profession and to his marriage. But somehow, as he brought Salomé in from the rain, the sensation of her kisses still lingering on his lips and the traces of her fingerprints on his bones, all of his ethics seemed to vanish.

"We shouldn't be doing this," he tried to mumble. But, Salomé had already come close to him again.

"Salomé," he whispered, and at the sound of her name she placed a trembling finger over his lips.

"You never speak this much in our sessions," she said, her mouth curling slightly.

"Salomé," he said once again. But this time, his voice was even fainter, his eyes locked on hers.

He believed he took her by the shoulders to speak some reason into what they were about to do. But he only ended up faltering. He slid the straps of her dress over her arms, the material falling to the ground like tissue paper.

She was so beautiful standing there in the moonlight, the beads of rain having moistened her olive skin. Her breasts were round and high. The small nipples like crushed raspberries, pink and textured.

He wanted to cover her in her nakedness, keep hidden to himself that which was so beautiful and fragile. Yet, he ended up bringing her closer to him, allowing her to unbutton his shirt, his trousers, until he too stood there naked against her, his pelvis nestling into hers.

"You are the first man to touch me since this happened to me." She placed her small, delicate hand on her left rib and touched where the skin was red and raised.

He looked down at her and was overcome by just how beautiful and brave she seemed to be by standing there completely revealed to him.

"You're beautiful, Salomé." He lifted her chin so that her mouth nestled into his.

He felt her pushing herself closer to him. He felt her breath on his neck and her hair light against his skin. He could no longer think clearly, his mind made dizzy by her perfume. He did not utter a sound as he lifted Salomé's tiny form and brought her over to his armchair. He sat down, his damp chest heaving, and held each of her hands as she mounted him, coiled her legs around him within the chair's winged sides, pulling him so close to her that, in the moonlight, he could see the faint traces of her feather-light scars.

Fifty-Three

ぐ֍ぐ

Salomé couldn't shake from her mind something in the way he made love to her. He had tenderly kissed her in all those red, raised places, where the skin had stitched itself up in a feeble attempt to camouflage where there had once been a wound. He had traced his fingers all over her body, like a navigator reading a map. She knew that he knew the story behind every scar he lingered over. He was aware of who had put it there, and how it had felt for her to be branded. Yet still he caressed every corner of her, for there wasn't a part of Salomé that was not beautiful to him.

She had not felt that way—felt attractive—for some time. A year had passed since the Villa Grimaldi, and this was the first time she had ever revealed her body fully to anyone. Now, being embraced by a man, and disrobing completely, she was being seen and revealed in her entirety. Someone could see her scars and accept them as being part of her.

Yes, somehow, Samuel had restored her. She suddenly felt different. She suddenly felt alive and whole again.

Her heart did not love him the way it had loved Octavio in the past, but she craved him nonetheless. It was strange. Samuel knew so much about her, but she knew almost nothing of him.

Salomé knew that her doctor had spent a portion of his childhood in Latin America because she had questioned him once during one of their sessions about the origin of his accent. He had told her that his family had fled France and settled in Peru, thus explaining his soft, melodic way of speaking Spanish, which was so different from a Spaniard's or a Chilean's, but beautiful nonetheless. She had loved the gentle, lulling way he slipped into the language. Having a doctor with whom she could communicate in her native tongue had made her feel instantly comfortable with Samuel.

She also knew that he was married and that he had a young daughter. She had seen their photograph on his desk. The little girl had been dressed in her Midsummer's costume—all in white with a wreath in her hair—and Salomé couldn't help but think of her own daughters, who would back in Chile pick flowers from the garden and place them through the straps of their dresses and slip the larger blooms behind their ears.

Walking down Föreningsgatan, Salomé's fingers still ached from the intensity with which he had grasped her hands. She could still recall the taste of his mouth and the movement of his shoulders pressing into hers. She could not possibly wait until the following Thursday when her next appointment was scheduled. She wanted to see him before then. But by the time she returned home to her apartment, to find Octavio asleep and the children in their rooms, she realized she had other things to attend to first. So, for the moment, the matter of Samuel would unfortunately have to wait.

Fifty-Four

❦

Vesterås, Sweden
March 1975

Samuel walked home that evening, discoving Kaija awake and playing with Sabine.

"You worked late tonight, darling," she said softly. "I'm afraid your dinner got cold."

He immediately felt so guilty seeing her crouched on the floor with their child on her knee. The little girl was fingering the tiny wisps of her mother's blond hair and pulling it toward her own.

"I think she realizes how much we look alike," Kaija said as she stood up and held her daughter close to her hip.

"Yes, it's remarkable," Samuel agreed quietly. Just looking at the two of them together, the traces of Salomé's taste still lingering on his tongue, intensified his already horrible guilt.

"Shall I warm up your dinner?"

"No," he stammered. "No thank you, I mean." He tried to smile. "It's just that I'm really not hungry."

"But you look exhausted, sweetheart." She smiled, her green eyes tranquil and full of affection for him.

"Don't go to any trouble. You should save your strength."

"No, really, Samuel, I am feeling much better today," she insisted. "Let me reheat it for you."

He couldn't believe that, on this day, with all that had just happened with Salomé, he would return home to find his wife in such improved spirits. The irony of the situation overwhelmed him.

Kaija walked over to Samuel and placed Sabine in his arms. The little girl smelled like baby powder. He touched her softly rounded limbs and buried his nose in her freshly washed hair.

The whole familial scene made him feel sick with self-loathing. He couldn't believe that Kaija had suddenly rebounded with so much energy. It was as if the woman he had courted years earlier had returned. Her face was full of color and her voice cheerful. She hadn't been this way for several months.

He did not realize that Kaija had had an epiphany that afternoon. That she had picked herself up from her incessant moping and stared at herself hard in the mirror. "You have a beautiful daughter," she told herself, "so consider yourself blessed. Not having another child isn't the end of the world." She tried to tidy up the house and to make herself look attractive by changing into a freshly starched dress and applying rouge to her otherwise pale cheeks. Above all, she tried to remain positive about her husband's reaction to the news. Tonight, she promised herself, she would tell him of her condition.

That evening, as he sat at the kitchen table, pushing his food around the plate in a desperate attempt to mask his lack of appetite, Samuel's anger at himself intensified.

How could he have betrayed his wife? And let alone with a patient! He shook his head in disgust.

"What's the matter, Samuel?" Kaija asked him from behind. "You look just awful. Wasn't your dinner all right?"

"Yes, yes. Of course it was, darling," he said apologetically. He swung around the chair to face her, but could not look her straight in the eyes. In a strained voice he blurted out, "It was just a difficult day at the office, and the rain delayed me from coming home."

She nodded and went to the sink, tying the apron strings around her waist. The water from the faucet hissed.

"I think I'm going to get to bed early," Samuel suggested. "Has Sabine already been put to bed?"

"Yes, I did that while you were eating."

"I'll kiss her good night after I take my shower," he murmured in a barely audible voice.

"Why not before?" Kaija asked, befuddled by her husband's odd behavior and clearly disappointed that he had ruined the atmosphere she had tried to create for when she would inform him of her situation.

"I'm just a bit clammy from the rain, that's all." He stood up abruptly, slightly kicking the leg of the chair as he made his way upstairs. Kaija remained downstairs.

Samuel had hoped the shower would cleanse him. Erase the traces of his infidelity. Yet standing there naked in the shower, he could still smell the scent of marzipan rising off his body and fading into a thick cloud of steam. The same steam would permeate the terry towels and his cotton robe, so that even after his bathing, Salomé's scent clung heavily to the cloth and navigated its way back again into his skin.

Fifty-Five

Vesterås, Sweden
March 1975

*W*hen Salomé returned home that same evening, she had tried to smooth out her dress and dry her hair with one of her linen handkerchiefs, but she realized soon after walking through the apartment's corridor that no one was around to even notice that she was arriving home slightly disheveled.

The apartment seemed so crowded now. Her collections lined the bookshelves and handfuls of potpourri spilled out of dried papaya skins. But those were familiar and comforting things. It was the children's toys and Octavio's shoes that contributed to the clutter. However, now was not the time to say anything to them about it. She wanted time to herself, a few more moments to savor what had just transpired and to relish the memory of how Samuel had traveled through her. Even now, as she looked at the goose bumps on her arms, she wondered if it was his perspiration and not the rain that had caused it to glimmer as it now did.

She stood in front of her full-length mirror, hearing her husband snoring in the background. From the side of the glass, she could see he had once again gone another day without shaving, the thick black stubble spreading over his brown cheeks. She had learned from Samuel that all of this was a sign of Octavio's depression—his incessant sleeping, his unwillingness to go to job interviews, his lack of grooming. All that opposite to what he had once prided himself on long ago.

Nevertheless, she refused to feel sorry for him. It did not occur to her that perhaps *she* was the reason that he had tumbled into a downward spiral of depression. That all he craved was her forgiveness and her affection. She had chosen not to think that way. She now had little sympathy for the man she had once sworn to be her eternal love.

Instead, as she slid her dress around her bare shoulders and over her hips, trying to simulate what Samuel's fingers had just done to her, she was lost in the sensation of his kisses that had covered her breasts, her hipbones, her neck.

In the mirror, she stared at her naked image. She imagined she was Samuel gazing upon her body for the first time. She cupped her breasts and stood in profile to see if her abdomen seemed flat and firm. She placed her fingers around her waist and tried to see if her two thumbs could still meet in the small of her back.

Then she stepped closer to see her scars where the electric wires and nodules had been placed over her areolae, in the faint creases of her navel, and in the folds of her inner thighs.

In the faint light of her bedroom, she could see them clearly. She traced one of the lines on her breast with her forefinger. She felt none of the pain she had endured thirteen months before. That gripping, terrifying sensation of electricity going through her body, entering through her thinnest and most delicate pieces of skin. Now, all that was left of that experience were her memories and those thin, pink scars. They blended in with the breast itself, just as the ones by her navel and genitalia did, but still she could not deny the obvious: those men who had tortured her had left their hideous mark on her forever.

They had branded her in her most intimate places. Left her with these faint tattoos that basically told the world, "Yes, we have been here. We have touched this and destroyed this. And we will never be punished for any of it."

She thought of how the two men who had truly ever made love to her did so in such different manners. While Samuel seemed to embrace every inch of her body, never shying away from a trace of something uncomely, Octavio had only ever gravitated to those features on her that he found the most beautiful. And perhaps that was part of the problem—perhaps that was just another reason why

Salomé felt she couldn't undress in front of her husband anymore. She didn't think he could get over that she was no longer unblemished. That her most beautiful features—her breasts, her waist, even her insides—they all now had scars.

But, should a man make love differently to a woman after she has been abused? Should he hold her differently—more gently—to keep her from breaking? Should he address these remnants of her attacker and kiss them as if his lips had the power to heal? Salomé didn't know the answer, for Samuel had never known her before her torture. He was seeing her for the first time the way she was now. Octavio had known her both before and after her scars.

That was irrelevant now. After all, Octavio no longer tried to seduce her. He had given up. He no longer slept against her, nestled into her prominent hipbones, his fingers reaching to clasp hers.

Now, he slept with his back toward her, his face stuffed into his pounded pillow, one of his legs half out of the blanket.

She wondered if he would even show a shred of emotion when she packed up his things and asked him to leave. She wondered if he would beg her to take him back and let him try to make things anew.

But she didn't care, one way or the other. For once in her life, she was ready to put herself first. However, she had to admit, she was curious. She wondered if he would see the irony in her decision.

Fifty-Six

⟡

Vesterås, Sweden
March 1975

$\mathcal{S}$amuel awakened the next morning and got dressed in a hurry. His mind was racing, and his stomach was full of knots. All he could think about was getting to the office. He was desperate to meditate over the events of the previous evening—he needed a few hours before his first patient arrived and his day was spent listening to problems that were not his own. He took one quick glance in the mirror and noticed that, in his haste, he had buttoned his shirt incorrectly. "I'm a mess," he thought to himself. "I have to get ahold of myself." As he went to readjust his shirttails, he noticed that his fingers were still shaking.

"Just get yourself to the office as quickly as you can," he told himself firmly. He slipped on his tweed blazer, threaded and straightened his tie, and bounded down the stairs. But the last person he wanted to see was already waiting for him at the base of the banister.

Kaija stood there, wrapped in her cotton robe with her eyelet nightgown peeking through, smiling up at him with coffee in hand.

"I've made you a cup of your favorite blend," she said sweetly. Little Sabine was tugging at the hem of her mother's robe.

"I'm sorry, darling," he responded with great delicacy. "That's really kind of you, but I've got a day full of appointments and some files I need to look over first. I just don't have time." He was already placing one of his arms in the sleeve of his coat.

"Will you be home for dinner on time?"

"I hope so, darling," he murmured as, in one continuous motion, he mindlessly wrapped his scarf around his neck and bent down to retrieve his satchel. "I hope to be home by seven."

"I'd like to talk to you about something," she tried to tell him as he turned to say good-bye to her and Sabine. "It's rather important, Samuel . . ." But she stopped midsentence. He was already halfway out the door.

She shook her head and picked up her daughter.

"Can you believe it, *älskling?*" she whispered as she kissed the child's soft cheek. "I think we need to make an appointment with your daddy at the office. Otherwise he doesn't have time to listen to us!" The little girl giggled. Kaija went back into the kitchen and poured the still warm mug of coffee down the drain.

Samuel hesitated as he reached deep into his pants pocket to retrieve the keys to his office. The events of yesterday evening still weighed heavily on his mind.

The room seemed strangely warm to him. He had left without straightening it, and as he scanned the furniture and the top of his desk, he could immediately see how things were displaced. His tall leather chair was not pushed neatly under the desktop, but rather was slightly off-angled in the direction of his bookshelves. His papers were amiss and his penholder had tipped to the side. And then there was the picture of his wife and daughter. That too had fallen over. It now lay flat, portrait side down, each of their delicate faces pressed against the mahogany wood.

Everything seemed strange to him now. Samuel could still not believe that, only a few hours before, he had sat in this very chair and passionately made love to a woman who was not his wife. Even worse, a patient of his. Someone who clearly needed his help, not his affection.

But making love to her had been a powerful experience for him. She was such a passionate woman, and if he closed his eyes again, he could imagine her calves locking around his knees, her bottom sealed against his thighs. He was afraid even to reflect on the memory, for he feared that, if he recalled the events of yesterday evening, it would unleash his desire to do it again.

Samuel had been with only a handful of other women before Kaija, and none of them had brought out this hungry and lustful side of him. He would never have believed before last night's incident that he was capable of such a thing. Clearly he was, but with Kaija he often felt that she was so fragile that his attraction to her was tempered by his yearning to protect her. With Salomé, it was different. It was as if she had refused to let herself be coddled or merit sympathy; she just wanted to feel like a beautiful and sensual woman again.

Samuel tried self-diagnosis. "You need to stop seeing your wife as your mother. You need to work on your marriage and make sure that you can communicate with your wife. You don't want to lose what you have with Kaija just because Salomé has awakened something inside you that you didn't before know existed."

Samuel wanted to make things better between Kaija and himself. He wanted to be able to love her in every way he was capable of. Tenderly, passionately, and completely. He did not want to sneak around cheating on his wife, fulfilling fantasies to satiate his libido at the expense of his family.

He wanted to be good. He wanted to be devoted. He had spent his entire life trying to be a trustworthy, compassionate husband and a loving father. He had always aspired to be the type of man that his own mother had never had. He wanted to take care of those who were in pain.

But now, he realized he had another side to him. He had almost been wolfish when he'd made love to Salomé. He had been so hungry to have her. To make love to her and grasp her tightly, slipping himself in so that he was completely enveloped by her. And he knew, if he was truly honest with himself, that he wished he could have both Kaija and Salomé.

He withdrew one of his pens from the canister and nervously tapped it on his desk. His eyes met those of Kaija and Sabine, framed within a matted border of paper and lacquered wood.

He placed the pen down on his desk and reached for the photograph, bringing it closer to view. He smiled as he thought about the day it was taken, on Midsummer's eve last year when he and Kaija had taken Sabine to see the city's maypole. Kaija had made matching white dresses for her and Sabine and woven garlands from wild daisies for their hair. Samuel took the photograph just as his two girls had finished dancing. They had rushed toward him, their cheeks flushed and rosy, their eyes sparkling in the crisp, summer light.

Until yesterday evening, Kaija had seemed so unlike that bundle of joy and energy that the photograph had captured.

He would not let himself indulge in the obvious excuse and blame her for pushing him away over the past few months. For making him feel vulnerable and empty, for craving someone who could satisfy his need to be appreciated and loved. He was too honest with himself to take the easy way out. He realized that no one was to blame for his infidelity except himself. Even Salomé could not be judged as harshly as he deserved to be. After all, she was a patient with traumas he would never personally experience. A wounded woman, trapped in a strained marriage, in need of his guidance and expertise.

She was in a fragile state of mind, but he had allowed himself to believe she was his equal. How selfishly he had acted! Salomé was obviously aching for someone to see and embrace her as a complete woman. Samuel should have been focusing on her treatment, so that she realized that she had to embrace herself before anyone else—her husband or any other man—could make her feel whole again.

But he knew how tempting such a situation could be. All he had to do was close his eyes and think of Salomé mounting him as she had done only hours before, and all reason and ethics seemed to vanish from his head.

Samuel stood up and fumbled for the small radio he kept in a drawer for moments like these when he was under stress. He plugged it in and readjusted the antenna, and the sound of classical music floated through the air. It was already 9 A.M., and in nearly an hour, his first patient would arrive. Samuel placed his head between his palms and balanced his elbows on the table. He had to get a grip on himself. He had to put things in perspective. He cared about Salomé. She was his patient and he wanted her to heal. He was also deeply attracted to her, but not enough to leave his wife and child.

The result was obvious then. He would inform Salomé when she came to her appointment on Thursday that they had each made a terrible mistake. He would apologize as her doctor for his poor judgment and suggest that she find another therapist who was more objective. He would never tell his wife of his indiscretion, as it would only hurt her, possibly even destroy her, and he would rededicate himself to his marriage and his family.

If it were only that easy. Even if Kaija were never to discover his betrayal, he would have to live with it. And he knew no one would judge him harder than Samuel Rudin himself.

Fifty-Seven

❧

Vesterås, Sweden
March 1975

Samuel returned home later that evening, exhausted. The emotional intensity of the past day and a half was wearing him down. He wanted to lock himself in his office forever and never face any of the women he had wronged. He especially dreaded facing the warm, soft eyes of his wife.

The low, golden lights of his doorstep finally beckoned him. He slowly trudged down the pathway and rummaged for his house keys.

He walked through the door and discovered Kaija standing patiently in front of the banister, just as he had found her that morning. Obviously, by the look on her face, she had been waiting for him for some time.

"It's half past eight, Samuel. I've been waiting for you since seven o'clock."

He tried to muster an apology, but his fatigue betrayed him. He unbuttoned his coat and hung it on the hook by the door.

"I've made your favorite, lamb and new potatoes." This time she spoke a bit louder than her usual voice, to ensure that he was listening.

"That sounds delicious. Hard day at the office." He stretched his back. "Would you mind if I took it upstairs? I still have some work to do."

"Actually, I would, Samuel." Her tone was unusually firm for her. "I told you this morning that I had something important to tell you."

"Oh, I'm sorry, sweetheart," he said, trying to be as agreeable as he could. He was already silently chiding himself for being so remiss about Kaija's simple request, given his pledge from this morning to be a better husband.

"What do you need to talk to me about? Is it important? Shall I sit down?" He was now overcompensating by lavishing his attention on her.

"Let's talk over our supper. I've already put Sabine to bed."

Samuel nodded. He went into the bathroom, washed his hands, then walked into the dining room, where he found the table set with their best dishes and sterling, two candles burning midtaper. "She must have lit them over an hour ago," he thought, once again feeling bad that he had failed to be home on time.

He ate his dinner and remarked how the meat had been cooked to perfection, and how the asparagus was a wonderful reminder of spring.

"I wanted to tell you that I'm sorry I've been a bit beside myself lately," she said over the meal. "I know that you noticed that I was not myself, but I didn't feel strong enough to tell you why." She paused for a second and took a sip of water, then carefully blotted her lips with the linen napkin.

He looked up at his wife and felt himself getting choked up. She was so delicate sitting there, across from him. Her skin so translucent that he felt he could see right through her. "How," he thought, "could I have done anything to hurt this wonderful woman? How could I have been such a selfish beast, that I could have forgotten who it is that I love?"

"What is it, Kaija?" He was beginning to grow alarmed.

She paused again. As he stared at his wife across the table, he could see the tension and the fear in her finely boned face. Her small, white hands nervously fingered the border of the tablecloth.

She took one final exhale, then said quietly, "Samuel, I'm afraid we won't be able to have any other children besides Sabine." She was trying hard not to cry, but her voice was already wavering. Tears were beginning to well in her eyes. "Samuel"—Kaija's voice was now barely audible—"I'm so very, very sorry."

He sat there for several seconds, stunned, before he could respond. "Kaija, what do you mean? What's happened?"

"I went to the doctor nearly eight weeks ago. I was feeling fine. Really. Actually I was feeling better than fine . . . I thought I was pregnant." She was crying a bit louder now, and Samuel had to concentrate to hear her words through her sobs.

"Anyway, they did some tests, which revealed that I wasn't pregnant at all. But that I'm actually going through early menopause."

"An early menopause?" Samuel was in shock. He couldn't believe what his wife was saying. "But, darling, you're so young! How can that be?"

"I know. I know." Her face was now red and streaked with lines where her tears had fallen.

From across the table, Samuel could see that his wife was shaking. How stupid he had been not to realize that something was deeply troubling his wife these past couple of months. When she needed him most, he had abandoned her for another! His mind suddenly flashed to the memory of Salomé and him embracing in the rain, and Samuel felt himself overcome with remorse.

He tried to compose himself. He took a deep breath and tried to refocus his thoughts on the immediate needs of his wife. "It doesn't matter, Kaija. None of this matters at all. I love you more than anything." She was not listening to him, however. He looked up and saw that her head was shaking from side to side, her face pressed into her palms.

"Kaija," he started once again. This time, he was leaning toward her, his tie draping perilously close to the candles. "You mustn't cry. We are blessed already. We have Sabine."

But Kaija began to cry even harder, her face crumpling like the napkin in her hand.

Samuel, sensing that no words could bring his wife comfort, rose from his chair and went over to her. He crouched beside her and brought her into his arms.

"I love you and our daughter. We have everything to be thankful for, and nothing for you to cry over. You've given me everything a man could want, and I'm sorry if I've never shown my appreciation enough." He too was crying now.

"Samuel," Kaija said as she placed her palms over his head, "I was just so afraid that you wouldn't want me anymore. I know how much you wanted a big family."

"No. No. Never. Don't even say such a thing! Kaija, I'm just so sorry."

"You have nothing to be sorry about." She dabbed her eyes. "You haven't done anything wrong. It's me who's suffering from this crazy thing . . . this early menopause . . ." She looked up at him and tried to smile. "God, Samuel, I have such rotten luck!"

He tried to smile at her. But inside, he felt tormented by just how awful he had been. "Well, you did get me as a husband," he joked. "I guess you're right, others wouldn't consider you so lucky. . . ."

She giggled, and he felt a little better hearing her laugh for the first time in weeks.

"But, Kaija, I feel terrible. I should have sensed that you were in such deep pain." Samuel's voice was becoming more calm and doctorlike now. "I should have been more sympathetic. I should have been spending more time with you and Sabine!"

"Don't be ridiculous, Samuel. You know you tried to get me to talk about what was bothering me. I just wasn't ready to discuss it. I needed more time to adjust."

Samuel shook his head and reached for his wife's hand. He brought it close to his chest. He wanted to appear composed and attentive to his wife's needs, but his insides were churning.

"I don't want to feel pushed away. It makes me crazy. It makes me do things I regret."

"I'm sorry, Samuel," she apologized once more.

"No. Don't say that. You have no reason to apologize. I'm just so sorry that you felt you couldn't tell me."

"I didn't want you to be angry."

"I could never be angry at you, Kaija," he said tenderly, and inside he felt himself drowning in guilt.

Minutes passed.

"I think I need a cup of tea," he finally said as he slowly got to his feet. "Can I get you anything, darling?"

Kaija looked up at him. "Samuel, you look a bit peaked. Come over here." She stood up and placed a cool palm on his forehead, completely forgetting about her own suffering. "You look worse than I do. Are you coming down with a fever?"

"I just think I'm a bit under the weather, that's all—the rain, the cold . . ."

"Forget your tea. Let me draw you a bath and get you off to bed."

He nodded and braced himself on the back of the chair. "That sounds good, Kaija," he said quietly. She motioned him to follow her and took his sweaty hand in hers.

As he followed his wife wearily upstairs, the irony of the situation was clear to Samuel. Even in her darkest hour of need, Kaija was still nurturing him. And that only made him feel worse.

Fifty-Eight

❦

Vesterås, Sweden
March 1975

*H*e had half-expected her not to show up for her appointment the following Thursday, yet she did. Salomé arrived like clockwork at his office on Skolgatan at her usual time, closed the door quietly behind her, and headed straight for the leather couch in which she always reclined.

"I didn't think you'd come," Samuel said quietly.

"I need to come. I need to get better." She paused and looked straight at him. "What I mean is, Samuel, I need to see you."

He had unrealistically hoped that she would avoid bringing up what had transpired between them a week before. He had, however, prepared a speech just in case. He had been practicing it in his head for days now. Yet, suddenly, those gentle but firm words, those rehearsed, perfected sentences that he had constructed to put an end to any future physical relationship with Salomé, evaded him.

"What we did was wrong, Salomé." He cleared his throat and scratched his knee. Clearly, the situation was awkward for him. "Salomé, I am your doctor. We should have known better." He corrected himself, "I should have known better."

"All of this sounded so much better in my head," he thought to himself. Inside, he was chastising himself for stumbling over words that were obviously so important.

"You can't deny that there is something between us," Salomé

interrupted. She paused. "I haven't felt that way for so long . . ."

Samuel shook his head. Seeing her sitting there before him was difficult for him now. He had made love to this woman only a week before, in this very room, and his physical attraction to her was overwhelming. But he would be stronger-willed this time. For the sake of his marriage to Kaija and for the love he had for Sabine, he would concentrate only on Salomé's immediate therapy.

"You have helped me so much, Samuel."

"I only wanted to help you heal and to come to terms with your memories," he said gently. "That is what I do for all my patients."

"You have. I am sleeping better. I am beginning to listen to music."

He laughed, obviously uncomfortable with the conversation. "So you can listen to music now without fear? You mean I've finally cured you, not with my words, but with my embrace?"

"You know it was much more than a mere embrace, Samuel. And as for music? I'm hearing the most wonderful music in my head!" She tossed back her head and laughed heartily. "For the first time in months, beautiful music, not that awful 'Queen of the Night Aria,' but lovely, ethereal music. The kind that fills one's veins and makes one feel as giddy as a schoolgirl."

"I see." He fidgeted again.

"Last week, I felt as though I carried you home with me. I heard your sweet voice in my head, your breaths deep in my ears. I felt your body shuddering over mine, your kisses on my skin." She paused and looked straight at him. "You know everything about me and yet you still accept me for who I am. I don't have that kind of relationship now with anyone else in the world."

For several seconds, Samuel just stared at her. Her pale lemon blouse was a surprisingly sheer choice for such a cold day in March, and he had to consciously try to avoid looking at her full breasts peeking through. He forced himself not to think about the way they had been with each other the last time. How she had threaded her arms around his waist. How he had slipped the straps of her dress around her shoulders only to reveal her naked, splendid form. He did not want to allow himself—to indulge himself with—the memory of the sensation of penetrating her, her ankles wrapped around him like two twisting vines.

She stood there in front of him and he tried not to look at her. He knew if he lifted his gaze, he'd see her all over again as she had been with him days before.

"Samuel," she said, and he lifted his eyes. "This isn't about sex."

She began to unbutton her blouse slowly, not looking down at the buttons, but rather staring directly ahead, her eyes locked firmly on him.

"This is about me feeling comfortable enough to show you everything . . ."

Her pale yellow shirt was now completely open. Her left hand entered her blouse and she touched her right breast. He could see her forefinger tracing over the outline of her nipple, and he remembered how he had kissed her there—that very place where that thick, red scar began, running all the way down to her first rib, where it ended.

He still said nothing to her except her name. "Salomé . . ." He stopped midsentence. She had taken off her blouse.

Something about her standing there exposed—vulnerable—moved him. It wasn't the reaction that he knew most men would have. He knew they would see the scars and lament the shame that something so beautiful could be marred so brutally. But when he saw Salomé now, he felt that he had never been more intimate with a woman before. In her nakedness, he knew she was trying to eliminate all the secrets between them, reaffirming that she was withholding absolutely nothing from him.

He continued to stare at her transfixed. His eyes traced the delicate lines of her shoulders, the tiny scar over her left nipple.

He thought she might try to cover herself while he stood there, his feet locked to the ground. But she didn't. She simply stood there waiting for him to come to her.

"I could never have done this four months ago, Samuel," she said softly. The cold air in the office made her breasts seem even higher and more round, and he wanted desperately to get up from his chair and walk over to her and cover her with himself. But instead he sat in his chair immobilized, his eyes transfixed.

In his eyes, she read that he was confused, that he was most probably thinking about his wife and children, but Salomé couldn't have felt further away from Octavio. She was doing this for herself, and she knew that she could never be completely whole until she had proven to herself that she was still beautiful, still sensual. So she unbuttoned her skirt and slid down the zipper. She pushed her stockings down over her hips, rolling them over her thighs and calves until she could step out of them freely.

She walked over to him, still in her thin, black underwear, and knelt by his feet.

He wanted to tell himself, "Don't do this, don't let yourself fall away and be swept into this love affair that obviously has no future." But instead, he said nothing except her name.

"Salomé . . ." He reached out and placed his hands on the crown of her head. She was curled around his knees like a kitten. Her long, black hair swept down to the small of her back, but through the thick curls, he could see the high, round peaks of her shoulders, the thin ladder of her spine. He felt her hands reach into his lap and unbutton his belt and slide his pants down around his knees.

He could hear a gentle sighing coming from her body as she rose and slipped off her underpants.

She extended her hands to him as one might do when about to dance, and he stood up and let her place her hands around his back.

He took one breath and inhaled her. He wanted to lick the taste of almonds, lift it right off her brown skin. He wanted to hold her up against the light and unabashedly tell her how magnificent she was.

She sensed him relaxing into her, and she soon found her placing her hands on his shoulders and then moving her fingers over the buttons of his shirt, peeling it away from his skin.

"I don't want you to feel as though you have to leave your wife and child for this. But there is something between us and you shouldn't deny it's not there."

She brought his head into her palms and kissed him on the lips.

He wanted to cry when she said this. Because he didn't want to love two women, he wanted only to love Kaija. These things were far more complicated than just acknowledging one's desire for another person.

But there he was not listening to his conscience, or his practical sense. He couldn't help himself. He kissed Salomé back.

Her head rolled back and her neck stretched out from underneath his lips like a swan's. She arched her back and let him look at her completely—that stretch of skin from her throat all the way down to her hipbones. He took his finger and began to trace her, beginning with the curve underneath her chin, through the rivers of small channels that belied her collarbone and the basin between her two breasts. Again, he kissed every scar, every red marking that his lips came across, as if the gentle anointment of his tongue might just have the capacity to heal her that much more.

He followed her as she knelt on the ground. He loosened his embrace as she stretched out on the floor, the patterned carpet making her look like a sultana set against her natural, vibrant palette.

"Tell me again that I'm beautiful," she whispered as he entered her.

He wanted to tell her he hoped he wasn't hurting her, that he was being as gentle as he could. But he answered her truthfully, all the same: "You're so very beautiful, Salomé."

When he said those simple words, she seemed to shudder as if she were releasing her last ounces of pain.

Fifty-Nine

❦

Vesterås, Sweden
March 1975

Salomé's taste was still deep on his tongue, on his skin. He could still feel the sensation from where her fingernails had pressed gently into his back, where her thighs had sealed against his waist. He could not believe that he had betrayed Kaija not only once, but now a second time.

He had to end their affair before they became even more involved than they already were. A lot was at stake here: his marriage, his professional reputation, even Salomé's healing.

He reminded himself to be reasonable. He told himself to focus.

When Salomé arrived at his office the following Thursday, he noticed that she was wearing a little bit of makeup and that her hair was arranged over her shoulders.

"I don't think I should remain your therapist, Salomé," he told her gently.

She looked up at him, her heart sinking all the while she tried to conceal her surprise.

"It would be unethical at this point." He was trying to sound as rational as he could with her. "You must understand, Salomé, I'm no longer objective in my counseling. That isn't fair to you."

"You are helping me, Samuel." Her voice faltered. "I'm better."

He inched his chair up to his desk and stretched his arms over his leather blotter before straightening his back. "Salomé, I fear that you are confusing our therapy with intimacy."

"I know the difference, Samuel." She looked away from him, hurt by his words. "The truth is, Samuel, I think I need to be with someone who didn't know me as I once was. You're the only person who understands me or my history. I would die without having you in my life right now."

He shook his head. "Salomé," he told her gently, but with an undertone of firmness, "you know you wouldn't die without me."

Her face reddened. "I would be miserable, though."

"I have to recommend another therapist for you. It's important that you continue to see someone."

She was silent for several minutes. The room was spinning around her and she tried to maintain her focus. The brown wooden walls that had felt like a protective armor to her for so many months were now suffocating. The low ceiling that she had once found so intimate now felt as though it were crushing down upon her. She wanted to flee . . . to get up and race out the door. She didn't want to hear Samuel speaking to her as if she were a child. She had understood he was married from the outset. He didn't need to explain his obligations to her.

"I won't see anyone else. You've already helped me enough," she said, wanting to appear strong. She crossed her legs and placed one of her hands over her knee. "When I came to you, I couldn't listen to music, I couldn't imagine myself kissing even my own husband. Because of you, I've been able to share what happened to me back there. This is progress, isn't it, Samuel?"

"Yes, but these things can take years to fully understand."

"I don't want to start over with another therapist. I don't want to have to tell my story again, to another stranger, and open myself up again."

"I can understand what you're saying, Salomé, but it is not another stranger to whom you must open up to. It is your husband. It concerns me that you are still avoiding telling Octavio what you endured and how you feel about it."

"That I cannot do. I told you that right from the beginning." Her voice betrayed her irritation. One of her hands wrapped around the side of her neck, and Samuel could see faint pink marks appearing from where she was pulling nervously at her skin.

"I know, but someday you will have to. Even if you leave him, you'll never be completely healed until you reveal your true emotions to him."

Salomé looked down at her fingernails. She fidgeted on the edge of the couch before speaking again. Then, nervously she said, "If you can't see me as my therapist, can you still see me again?" She paused. "Perhaps outside the office for coffee or something . . . as friends?"

Samuel tried to smile before placing his fingers over his eyes. He had not anticipated how difficult this would be for him. He wished he could tell Salomé that they could maintain a friendship outside the office, but he knew such a relationship would be impossible. After all, he still couldn't keep his eyes off her. The way she spoke, the delicate movements of her hands. He still found her beguiling.

"I don't think a friendship would be a good idea, Salomé. For either of us. We both have spouses and have children. . . ."

"I am not asking you to leave your wife and child, Samuel," she blurted out. "I would never ask that of you!"

"I know that, Salomé," Samuel said gently. "But I still cannot see you again. Not because I don't want to but because if I let our meetings continue, I can see myself falling in love with you, and I don't want to complicate what is already good in my life."

With the back of her palm she tried to wipe her tears away.

"I'm telling you the truth, Salomé."

For several moments they said nothing. They sat still and looked in different directions. They could hear the clock ticking, the occasional sound of a car motor passing by.

"Thank you, Samuel," she finally said as she stood up.

He could see she was embarrassed and longed to embrace her one last time.

"You deserve happiness, Salomé."

She tried to manage a small smile for him as she made her way to the door.

And as she left his office for the final time, Samuel inhaled deeply. The scent of marzipan lingered and left him dizzy.

Sixty

❦

Salomé Herrera's affair with Samuel was another secret she never shared with Octavio. But unlike the other secrets she had struggled to forget, this one she kept close to her. It was a precious jewel she could re-create inside her mind's eye whenever she longed for something beautiful.

Salomé found it hard to pinpoint the exact time her marriage fell apart. It wasn't like the shattering of a glass, when a thousand fragments come crashing to the floor. It was more a series of subtle explosions that occurred inside Salomé's head. At those moments, even when she tried to stifle her words, Octavio could read his wife's face and body language as though she were a pantomime miming out her dissatisfaction.

He had hoped things would improve between them once she started therapy. But instead things worsened. Salomé was unwilling to share what she discussed in her sessions, and when Octavio tried to ignite a dialogue between them, he was continually rebuffed.

Octavio grew frustrated with the silence. He longed for the fiery and carefree bride he had taken years before. It was as if the woman he had carried out of Chile was not the same one he had married. The person he now shared a bed with resembled the physical form of his wife, but her spirit had vanished completely.

Ultimately, it was not she who asked him to leave, as she had long imagined. When he finally did say he was leaving, she thought it was another of his performances, a futile attempt to ignite a reaction from her. But she did nothing and instead watched with eyes unblinking as he grabbed his once fashionable suits from the closets, threw his shoes into the canvas bag, and snatched their wedding portrait from the nightstand. She knew the children could hear his tantrum from their rooms next door, but she did nothing to quiet him. It was as though she were a voyeur watching her husband physically exorcise himself from her life. When he finally walked out the door, after looking back at her three times, she still did nothing. He was down the stairs before Salomé finally walked to the apartment's threshold and closed the door.

She was anxious about explaining her separation from Octavio to the children. Already, there had been so many new and difficult transitions for them since they had arrived in Sweden. She knew it would be easiest on Rafael, though. The boy had always sensed his mother's anguish and fragility ever since that day she was released in the park.

She had given birth to him when she was so young, almost a child herself. So, in a way, she felt closer to him than to her daughters. Whenever she was feeling especially low, he would somehow find her and offer her a hug. He never became stubborn or willful. He was her shield, in a way she had always hoped her husband would be, but never was.

"Your papa will be living in a different apartment now," she told Rafael. The girls were still in their room. She could still hear them playing.

"We need some time away from each other because we're making each other sad right now. You understand, Rafael, don't you?" She took him under her left arm and squeezed him.

She had anticipated he would have questions. Any child would ask certain things like "Will Papa come back?" or "Why did he leave?" But Rafael had none. He simply nestled close to his mother and reached for her right hand.

She thought it strange the way he held her fingers so gently. As if they were so fragile, they might break if he squeezed too hard.

"It's all right, Mama," he whispered. "Don't be afraid."

"Afraid?" she asked, surprised that her son would think such a thing.

"I will protect you. You don't have to worry."

She let out a nervous laugh and tightened her arm that still wrapped around his small shoulder. "You don't have to," she reassured him. "I'm stronger now than I was back in Chile." She knocked him playfully with a small fist. "See how tough your mother is!"

The girls, however, reacted to the news with greater difficulty, as Salomé expected. She sat them by her feet in their bedroom and told them that Octavio would no longer be sleeping at home.

"Your daddy is going to live nearby, but not with us," she told them. "It isn't because he doesn't love us, but because he doesn't want you to see him unhappy."

"But why isn't Papa happy?" Isabelle asked.

Salomé sighed. The girls were always full of questions. The difference between her daughters' and her son's reactions suddenly struck her. She took Rafael's lack of questioning as a sign he understood her situation, but the same trait frustrated her in Octavio.

She wrinkled her forehead. Isabelle was waiting for an answer.

"Girls, your papa and I just need some space now. Just like you two sometimes like spending a little time by yourselves, we need to do that now. Papa and I will become happy again, you'll see."

Blanca extended her doll to Salomé. "Sometimes I don't want to play with my dolly, but then I miss her!"

"Well, your papa won't be far away, so none of us will get a chance to miss him."

The girls nodded. Salomé reached down and gave them each a kiss. "Everything is going to be fine," she reassured them again. They looked up at her, watching for a moment as she rose from the bed.

"I'll make *machas* for dinner," she told them sweetly, knowing it was their favorite meal.

Before she made it to the door, they had already scampered back to the corner of their bedroom and resumed playing with their dolls.

When Salomé entered the den, she found Rafael sitting alone on the sofa. His legs were crossed underneath him, and he was staring at one of Octavio's old movie posters. Salomé approached and sat quietly beside him.

He looked up at her, his right hand resting softly underneath his chin. His face seemed a thousand years old. A lineless face that had an etched expression of a grown man who had worried his entire life. As she looked upon Rafael, she could not help but think that, just as she had secrets she kept to herself, so did her children. Even Octavio might be withholding something from her, all in the name of love.

Part IV

Sixty-One

✣

Vesterås, Sweden
March 1985

$\mathcal{N}$early ten years had passed since Samuel had ended his relationship with Salomé. Yet sometimes when he entered a pastry shop and smelled the scent of marzipan, he could not help but think of her. Occasionally when he'd be eating alone at one of the local restaurants or having a coffee at a café near the square, he would think he saw a glimpse of her—the thick mane of black hair, the small curves of her petite frame—but within seconds she'd be gone. Silently he was thankful because he knew that his life remained far less complicated because of it.

Over the years his practice had thrived. The influx of South American immigrants seeking asylum in Sweden continued. Many of them sought treatment with Samuel, often upon the recommendations of former patients. Men and women fleeing the Soviet bloc countries, as well as the occasional refugee from Iran or the Middle East, appeared in his waiting room too.

At first, it did not occur to Samuel how his work with these patients over the years helped to heal his own childhood wounds. But little by little, through hearing the stories of patients who had fled their native lands because of political persecution, he came to realize the overall humanity linking each person's testimony. The themes were universal: patients who had lost loved ones, patients who had survivor guilt, and patients angry that they had been abandoned by their homelands.

The painful memories of fleeing France and being powerless to prevent his mother's deterioration slowly lessened. He now had tremendous satisfaction in helping his patients come to terms with their past, and he hoped that their transition into Swedish life was made just a bit easier by having him as a therapist.

He also felt similar satisfaction with his family life. Kaija continued to dote on both him and their daughter. Sabine continued to work hard at school, and although the girl looked almost identical to his wife, both he and Kaija acknowledged that her personality more resembled his. She was intellectually curious and always sought out his advice, whether she was studying the fall of the Roman Empire or simply needed help with her study of the Romance languages. Like him, she loved all things with a story attached to them; she loved all things with a past.

Recently, however, Samuel had begun to feel physically unwell. He did not tell Kaija when the symptoms first began to appear. The sharp stomach pains, the loss of appetite, he kept all of that to himself for several weeks. "There's no use worrying her," he thought. "Maybe I have an ulcer. I just need to cut down on my number of patients."

The yellowing in his skin intensified. First, he noticed it in his fingertips, and then a deep sallow patch spread alongside his collarbone.

"You're looking rather worn down," Kaija commented one afternoon. "Even a bit yellow . . . are you feeling all right?"

He insisted he was. "It's nothing to fret about. I might have a small ulcer. I'll visit the hospital sometime next week and have an X-ray."

He went to a clinic near his office, where he was examined by an internist, a colleague of his whose opinion he trusted. The doctor, his face serious and his eyes focused on his notes, had listened to Samuel's complaints. "We'll take some X rays and do some blood work and see if there is anything there, Samuel. I'll call you next week with the results."

The doctor called two days later, his voice painstakingly

monotone. "Samuel, your pancreas looks suspicious. We saw some calcifications." He paused. "I think you'd better come in for a biopsy."

Samuel didn't reply.

"Samuel? I know we usually say these things in person. But, as a fellow doctor, I thought you'd want to know as soon as possible." The doctor was trying in vain to sound encouraging. "Let's get this biopsy done right away and see what's there. Strictly an outpatient type of thing. Just make sure you bring your wife along. You won't be able to drive yourself home."

Samuel ignored the doctor's last instruction. He had no intention of bringing Kaija with him. There was no need to get her all upset until he knew exactly what was wrong with him. "When should I come?" he asked.

"Come tomorrow. I've already scheduled it with the radiologist. One o'clock."

Samuel hung up the phone. He could feel his hands trembling, and had he not the slight tinge of yellow, he knew his color would be more like his wife's. The color of snow.

He did not relay to his family the details of his diagnosis. Instead, the following afternoon, he returned to the hospital alone. As if in a trance, he quietly obeyed the nurses who, with gloved hands, neatly arranged him on the table. The crackling of white paper underneath his back increased his anxiety. He felt them apply the cool blue gel to his abdomen, felt the gentle rolling of the ultrasound.

He awakened to see the radiologist and his doctor talking to each other. Their hushed voices clearly unnerved him.

"That's it for now," his doctor told him after the nurse came to help him onto his feet. "I'll call you in three days when I get the pathology report."

The doctor then offered to have the receptionist call his patient's wife.

"Oh, no," Samuel said quickly. "She couldn't come. Something came up with our daughter at school. If she can just call me a taxi, I'll be on my way."

"Are you sure, Samuel?" The doctor's face seemed to reveal his suspicions.

"Yes, I'm positive. Please . . . just a taxi."

Samuel got dressed and decided to wait for the cab outside. The cold air on his cheeks felt surprisingly refreshing to him. His mind was racing. The last three days were a blur for him. Everything had happened so quickly. He had not anticipated that things would become serious so soon.

All his life, he had preached honesty. He had urged Salomé to tell her husband what had happened to her at the Villa Grimaldi. He had become frustrated with Kaija when he'd learned how she'd withheld the news she could no longer bear children. And now, here he was, doing the very same thing. But he wanted to know all the facts before he upset his family with the difficult reality. The doctor had told him he would know in three days' time. So, for three torturous days, Samuel Rudin waited.

"Your pathology report came back, Samuel. It revealed a primary pancreatic cancer."

Samuel remained silent for a moment. He was all too aware of what such a diagnosis meant.

"How much time do I have?"

"I'm afraid that the ultrasound test revealed that the disease has already metastasized to the liver."

Samuel remained quiet. He knew this meant he had only a few months at best. He felt weak, as though his knees were about to give way. He placed one hand on his desk; the other held the telephone receiver tightly.

"As I'm sure you know, once the disease has metastasized, you are no longer a candidate for curative procedure." The doctor paused. "Should the need arrive, we can offer you palliative surgery, however."

Samuel nodded. He had no words left. There was nothing optimistic about his diagnosis. He would have known that even as a first-year medical student.

Thinking aloud, Samuel said, "I'm not going to live to see next year."

The doctor hesitated. "Samuel, I'm so sorry." His voice was thick with compassion.

"Me too," Samuel whispered. "Me too."

* * *

Samuel decided to walk home that evening. The three-kilometer distance from the hospital was exhausting, but he needed the time to reflect.

He had initially thought he would tell Kaija and Sabine about his condition after dinner. But he reconsidered as soon as he walked into their beautiful, tranquil home and saw their two shining faces.

He didn't want to see his wife or daughter cry for him. He didn't want them to twist and sicken themselves over his illness. Instead, he wished they could just accept that everyone must die, only his death would come sooner than they had all expected.

All his life, Samuel had prided himself on being the person who comforted the sick, brought people to terms with their past, and helped them address their future. He had always savored being that person. So the thought that, soon, he would be relegated to the one who needed comforting unnerved him. He knew what would be next for him. He would grow thin, his complexion would turn sallow, and the whites of his eyes would turn yellow, the color of custard. Already he felt an incessant gnawing in his stomach that would only grow worse with time.

How, he wondered, could he convey to his family that he didn't want to spend his last months being coddled and told to "take it easy"? How could he make it clear that he didn't want to undergo the painful, extensive treatments that were incapable of curing him, that would only lengthen his soon-to-be-pathetic existence by at most a few weeks?

For another three days, he said nothing of his diagnosis. He sat at the table rearranging the food on his plate to make it appear as though he had eaten. He went to his study and spent a few hours reading over his monthly journals to the sound of classical music to maintain the appearance of regularity. He checked the locks and the window latches, to make sure they were tightly secured as usual. Finally, after taking the morphine tablets that the doctor had prescribed only days before, he lay down and embraced his beloved wife.

She slept gently in his arms. Her blond hair was beginning to show the first traces of gray at the crown. Only a month before, she had commented on the thin lines around her eyes and the featherlight creases by the corners of her smile. He had told her not to worry. What he wanted to say now, what he should have said then, was that she had never been more beautiful. That he wished he could see how she would be in thirty years' time, when her hair was all white, her skin like rice paper. He would still love her.

There is something about the noble sick. They never want to disturb anyone. But after about a week had passed, Samuel realized he would not be able to keep his illness a secret any longer and that it wouldn't be a quiet ending for him.

Already, his jaundice had intensified, and Kaija still prodded him to go to the doctor. She feared he had hepatitis or a malfunctioning of the liver. He began wearing pajamas to mask his protruding ribs and a stomach that seemed to cave in like a balloon that had lost all its air.

He had no choice but to tell them. So he canceled his appointments for the afternoon and spent the day sitting in his office trying to think of the best way to break the news.

That evening, he arrived home early. His black hair was wet with perspiration around his temples, and his eyelids seemed tired and weighed heavily over his warm, brown eyes.

"Come in from the cold, darling!" Kaija beckoned. "You know you haven't been well lately. What are you doing walking home instead of taking the bus!"

She took off his coat and hung it on the hook by the door. "Dinner will be ready in a few minutes. Why don't you go upstairs and help Sabine with her Spanish homework? She's been bothering me all day to quiz her on the verbs."

"All right, but later, I need to talk to you both," he said.

"How about after dinner, sweetheart?" she called. She was already back in the kitchen with her head buried in the stove.

"Okay," he sighed. He felt as though he were in a trance. All his movements seemed to be in slow motion. He picked up his satchel and slowly made his way upstairs.

"Daddy? Is that you?" Sabine called. "Can you help me with

these verbs before dinner? Mommy said you would do a better job."

Samuel had barely made his way up the stairs before he saw the bright-eyed face of his thirteen-year-old daughter peeking through the crack of her bedroom door.

"Of course, *älskling*. Let me just unpack my things."

He walked down the hallway to his study and turned on the light. His office was his retreat. There he could play his music, savor a cup of tea, and write in his journals without being disturbed. The crimson walls were studded with his diplomas, his certificate of residency, and a few of his treasured maps.

It smelled of books. He had always loved that aroma, for it had the capacity to calm him. Until now, when everything that had previously given him so much pleasure suddenly seemed rather pointless. He only wanted to be with his wife and child.

He went to his daughter's room and, for the first time, saw many things that had previously escaped his notice. He looked out from her bed and saw her small, childlike collections of painted ceramics, her dolls, and the sticker albums and souvenirs that lined her shelves.

As he helped with her Spanish homework, he yearned to savor these priceless, few remaining moments between them. He would suggest a verb and she would conjugate it. He knew his daughter had spent all day trying to memorize the different tenses, but it was difficult for him to remain focused. He had to concentrate to avoid breaking down and crying.

The same feelings of wanting to grow old with his wife were matched by his desire to see his daughter grow up to be a woman, married with her own children. He would be denied sharing those things, never witnessing these milestones in his family's lives. That alone made him crumple like wet tissue when he was again by himself in his office.

His stomach was on fire and needles were floating in his lower intestines. He aimlessly cut at his food. His throat tensed. He didn't know how he would be able to get out the words that needed to be said.

"I have cancer." His eyes remained focused on his plate.

The words fell out.

"What?" Kaija's fork dropped from her hand. The sound of chipped porcelain rang in the air.

"I met with the doctor as I promised, and . . . it's not an ulcer."

Both Kaija and Sabine were staring at him. He felt the weight of their eyes. When he raised his head, he saw that both their faces were white as eggshells.

"Daddy!" Sabine cried. "What are you saying? Are you going to be all right?"

"Yes, Samuel . . . what are you saying?" Kaija's voice cracked before she could utter anything more.

"It seems I have cancer of the pancreas."

The room fell silent.

"I didn't want to have to tell you this way . . ." His voice was weak, his head felt dizzy.

"Cancer of the pancreas?" Kaija whispered. Again, her words seemed to choke in her throat. She covered her mouth with her fingers. "Oh my God, Samuel. Oh my God."

Later that evening, as she lay sobbing in his arms, Samuel tried to explain to Kaija the desperateness of his illness and the futility of any treatment.

"No, no," she insisted. "We must have hope. There are treatments, I'm sure of it! You—we—must fight this!"

"No, Kaija," he told her firmly. "There is nothing. The treatments available will only be painful. They'll only weaken me. I want . . ." He hesitated. "I need to live the next months as close to the way I have lived my whole life."

She shook her head. "I don't understand, Samuel! I don't. Wouldn't you rather live a few more weeks and spend that time with Sabine and me? Wouldn't you choose life at any cost?"

"No, I wouldn't. I honestly wouldn't."

"I don't understand you! After all we've been through, how can you give up without a fight?" she cried as she pushed her face into her pillow and ran her small fingers deep into the mattress. "You're being selfish, Samuel. You're not thinking about how your wife and child might feel about this!"

"Kaija," he said softly, retrieving her from the cocoon of twisted sheets and mounds of pillows. "I need to live, truly live, not just delay my death. I want to remember everything, not just spend my last days in a morphine haze. I need . . . to know the difference between your face and a cloud of steam." She could feel his tears beginning as he pressed himself against the veil of her nightgown, and she thought that night they would both drown in the sadness that flooded the room.

Sixty-Two

❧

Vesterås, Sweden
May 1985

Samuel pressed Kaija to go with him to Mikkeli, the town in Finland that bordered the forest where she was born. For years, he had wanted them to return to his wife's birthplace. "We'll visit the grave of your mother," he told her as he lay wrapped in her arms. "Before I go, I want to see the pale blue and saffron-yellow buildings of Helsinki. I want to walk in the Karelian forest and bathe in the cold, deep lakes."

In the past, Kaija had always resisted. Her mother was dead and her father and brothers were but strangers to her. After her Swedish father had retrieved her, she had sworn that she would never return to the country she believed had abandoned her.

But with only a few months left to his life, Samuel found himself growing more persistent. "We'll take Sabine. She's a teenager now and should see it, " he told Kaija. Only three years before, they had gone as a family to Paris, where his family had come from, and now he was insistent that they do the same with Kaija's homeland. "Children should know where their roots are," he told his wife. "And for you," he told her firmly, "it's important that you return."

"None of this should be about me, Samuel," she said.

He smiled at her, his lips cracked like old parchment. "It's not, Kaija. This is about *us.*"

She cried in his slender arms. He smelled strange to her now. He had only recently begun using cologne. It was his futile attempt to mask the feral smell of the illness leaking from his pores.

Kaija noticed his eyes were now rimmed in pink, like a newborn baby's, and remembered how Sabine had looked when she'd first held her in her arms. Her small head covered in soft, downy fuzz, her lids swollen and finely veined. How odd, Kaija thought, that sickness could reduce a grown man to the image of a child. When she looked at her husband now, swaddled in layers of cotton, with his shrunken, yellow head and swollen eyes, she felt, in a way, that she was seeing him as her baby.

In other moments, he reminded his wife that he was still very much a man. He did not want to be coddled. He did not want to be pitied. "There are things that I want to do," he had insisted. "I want to eat oysters from Brittany. The big blue-gray ones that I ate as a little boy in Paris. I want to taste the salt water as I suck them from the shell."

"We can do that, darling," Kaija promised through her tears.

"And I want to go to Finland with you," he said again. "I want to dance in the midsummer sun when it's midnight and the sky is white with light."

"Of course." She squeezed his fingers tightly.

"And I want to go to your childhood home and see where you were born. I want to go to the church where your mother is buried. Most of all, I want *you* to make peace with her memory. It's important, Kaija."

She looked at him in bewilderment. "Samuel, I made my peace a long time ago when you and I started our own family."

"That's not making peace, Kaija. That's starting over."

"You and Sabine are my family. Anybody still there is a stranger to me."

"We will go together. The three of us. I know that if I don't insist now, you'll never go."

"I will, Samuel. I promise you." Her green eyes were now clouded with tears.

"No, I want to be there. I want to be the one who supports you as you finally visit your parents' graves." He paused. "Also, I don't want you to go to a cemetery and think of me. Not yet."

"Oh, Samuel," she cried as she slid lower in his arms. "Why is this happening to us? Why? Why? Why is God doing this to us?"

He smoothed her blond hair with his palm. She had always seemed so fragile to him. Even with his sickness, he imagined himself far stronger than she.

"We will always be there for each other, my love. I promise." He paused. "For now, we should just concentrate on living the months ahead."

In June, they traveled by train to Stockholm, then ferried by boat to Finland. Samuel was frail from his loss of appetite. His spartan limbs were wrapped in two layers of sweaters, despite the summer heat. A loden-green muffler enshrouded his head.

"I don't even remember the way to my home," she told him.

"Don't worry, Kaija," he told her, as his thin fingers stretched out and found their way into hers. "We'll figure it out when we get there."

The three of them spent two days sight-seeing in Helsinki before boarding a train to Karelia. "I wonder if the station in Mikkeli will be as I remember it," Kaija mused aloud. "Pale green with white trim, the old iron clock by the ticket window. I can see it so vividly . . ."

Stepping off the platform, Kaija felt as though she were again that young Finnish war child. She remembered the pale blue coat she had worn when she was greeted by a woman from the Red Cross and ushered to her family.

The skeletons of the city's wartime past remained. The proud statue of General Mannerheim. The memorial to the lost soldiers. The freight trains that had ferried ammunition to the front to fight the Russians, were those originals or replicas? Kaija wondered of the brown trains that still crowded the rail yard.

"My family lived farther out," she recalled as she turned to Sabine and smiled at Samuel.

"Should we ask at the town hall for an exact address, or a map, maybe?" Sabine asked her mother.

"There wouldn't be a street address." Kaija laughed. "We lived in the forest, sweetheart. I don't remember exactly where. But, if we follow the tracks, I know it will lead us there, eventually."

"Daddy will be too weak," Sabine whispered to her mother as Samuel looked on.

"Yes, I know."

"We could rent bicycles, though, and follow them that way. Perhaps the store has two-seaters, and Daddy could sit while I pedal."

Sabine went into the station and inquired where they might find some bikes.

The two women pedaled alongside the tracks, Samuel seated behind his daughter, who was carrying him as if he were a bushel of bruised fruit. His feet rested on his pedals as they rode past Lake Saimaa, the river, and into the leaf-studded forest. Nearly two hours later, Kaija took her feet off the pedals and stared, almost transfixed, at an expanse of trees. "It was in there! That's it! I remember it! Our house was over there!"

They parked their bicycles and walked over the soft earth, the summer bees flying in the bushes of wild lavender and lupine.

Kaija could see the house in the distance. A long, symmetrical cabin with timber walls and a mud roof covered with straw. There was nothing distinctive about the outside facade save for three long windows with pale beige frames accented with tiny crosses.

She stood there, separated from it by several meters, for what seemed like hours. Throughout the entire journey from Vesterås, Kaija had convinced herself that she would not remember a thing, that she had been too small when she'd left.

But the memories of that seven-year-old girl returning for the first time from a life of privilege in Sweden came flooding back to her. And, to her surprise, this mature woman of forty-five was now thinking the same thing she had as a small girl stepping out from her father's wagon. That this was a place of deep, heart-wrenching poverty, where the forest merged with the end of the world. Where the tall leafy junipers and pine, and the slender white birches, sheltered a strong, proud people who had little but each other, the lakes, and the snow.

Both Kaija's frail husband and her daughter were beside her now. And like reverent pilgrims, they followed Kaija as she made her way to the dilapidated house.

The summer sun struck the modest shelter with warm, canary light that illuminated the overgrown wild poppies, tarflower, and pink clover in a halo of gold.

"Can you smell the flowers, Kaija?" Samuel asked, his voice pained, as he fumbled through his breast pocket to find his flask of liquid morphine. "They smell so wonderful."

Kaija turned back to face Samuel and saw his jaundiced, jawlined face tightening in a smile. She went over to him and slid her arm into his, noticing how much more slender his limb was than hers.

She patted his brown-spotted hand with her own and agreed with him. "Yes, Samuel, they smell sublime."

Inside, the house was far from idyllic. Years of neglect had left it with holes between the rafters and rain-soaked floorboards. One could still see the traces of its former occupants' lives in the ruin of abandonment. One or two chipped ceramic bowls, a birchwood basket, a few spatulas, and scattered empty tins lined the rough cabinetry.

The windowpanes were broken. The lace curtains—probably forty years old—were now tattered shreds, fragile strips covered in ash.

"They must have abandoned it years ago," Kaija said. She didn't want to think that her father must be dead and buried alongside the grave of her mother. As for her brothers, she knew Viktor had died, but she hadn't heard from Olavi or Arvo once she'd returned to Sweden for good.

"My brothers and father slept in this room, near the fireplace," she said as a few rusty nails and broken twigs crushed underneath her feet. She pointed to the large wooden bed and the image of the boys sleeping together, with each of their backs curling into the other's, came flooding back to her. "I slept in the room behind, alone."

Kaija walked slowly through the space, and more memories returned to her.

"I suppose that it was kind of them to let me have my own room. I never appreciated it then. I only felt lonely."

"But it was so hard for you, Mother."

"And it was hard for them. Here, I was this little chubby girl returning from a life that had known no hardship during the war." Kaija paused. "My poor brothers. No wonder they were so cruel to me."

Samuel placed his hand on one of the doorposts to steady himself and readjusted his scarf. In the midsummer sunlight that streamed through the broken glass, he looked like an ascetic who had just walked in from a long pilgrimage.

"I see where your love of the forest and lakes comes from," he said to Kaija before turning to gaze at the view outside the window. Hundreds of square meters of blooming flowers and tall, lush trees surrounded the tiny house. He wondered what it might look like in the snow.

Samuel grew slightly melancholy realizing he would never see this landscape in another season. He wanted once more to be the father who rode through the streets of Vesterås with his little girl strapped to the backseat of his bicycle, not the other way around. He wanted to again be able to love Kaija as he had that first year in Göteborg, with that same virility, and the same mad recklessness that had led them to the balcony of his tiny apartment with hungry passion. But he also realized that he needed to accept that there was still so much beauty around him. He did not want to spend his last days regretting what he would never have.

"You look tired, Daddy," Sabine said, her voice interrupting him from his thoughts. "We should head back to the inn."

"Yes," he whispered. "But only if your mother is ready."

They did not want to rush Kaija, who now stood in the center of the tiny, two-room house where she believed she had been born. Kaija imagined her mother giving birth in the sparse, wooden bed and holding her for the first time.

She had no idea that she had been born on the very lake that made her heart still soar. She had no idea that her mother had cried nearly every night after Kaija was first taken, or that her mother's young life had ended at the very place where her own had begun.

Sixty-Three

❧

Mikkeli, Finland
June 1985

*T*he old church's copper cupola looked like a green cabochon, cut against the blue Finnish sky. Kaija did not want to go to the cemetery, but she did it anyway for Samuel's sake. By this point, if Samuel wanted to trek across the Arctic, she would have agreed, no matter how implausible it seemed for a man in his condition. She wanted no regrets for him or her; she finally understood what her husband had tried to convey to her. He had a few more things left to do on this earth, including making sure that she was taken care of, both physically and emotionally, after he was gone. If he believed visiting her mother's grave would begin her healing, she would follow.

The cemetery was fastidiously maintained, which surprised Kaija at first because she wondered where all the people lived now. She thought of these proud people who had fought for their independence on skis, clad in white uniforms that blended in with the snow.

The small wooden church with the domed peak recalled the architecture of a Russian church. She knew her parents were Russian Orthodox because she remembered the tiny relic by her brothers' bed. And she knew this was the church where they had held her mother's funeral because her father had pointed it out to her the first day she was returned in the winter of 1948.

The cemetery was completely full. Rows of iron crosses lined the grassy hill. Red flowers marked the graves of lost soldiers. Kaija began to walk through the cemetery. She leaned down over each plot to read the names on the graves, wondering if she would eventually stumble on one that read *Sirka Laasko* and, if she did, whether there would be an adjoining one inscribed with the name *Toivo Laasko*.

It was Samuel who finally found the names for her. He had walked only a few meters before discovering both of their iron crosses, rusted over from the years of rain and snow. But what he had not expected to find were the two other names beside the graves of Kaija's mother and father, Viktor and Olavi Laakso, Kaija's two brothers.

"Have you found them?" Kaija called out to him, the hem of her red dress billowing in the wind.

Samuel remained silent for a few seconds, his mind racing to think of a way to tell her. His reflexes were slower now, and before he could speak, she was already at his side.

"Oh, my God," she said as her trembling fingers covered her lips. "I knew about Viktor. He died before I returned home, and I have no memory of him. But Olavi too?" Her eyes started to well up with tears.

"Olavi and Arvo found me by the train tracks that winter I was returned," she said, her voice quivering. "When did he die?"

She gazed at the dates and tried to do the simple arithmetic in her head. "Nineteen fifty-three . . . that would make him only nineteen!" She looked around to see if there was a grave for Arvo, but she found none.

Samuel reached out to take his wife into his arms. The fragility of her husband's embrace only intensified her pain. "Samuel, I can't take this." She wriggled out from underneath his arm. "Look at all this." She pointed to the expanse of graves.

"I know, Kaija." He too looked over the field of iron crosses and blooming flowers. "I know."

"I feel numb, Samuel. These are the graves of my parents, my brothers, and I have little to no memories of any of them."

Samuel reached for his wife's hand and he could see her eyes welling with tears.

"For years I was angry. I believed my parents gave me up because I was a burden to them during the war." She took out a handkerchief and dabbed her eyes. "When I had Sabine and I held her in my arms, I had so much love in my heart at that moment. But as the weeks passed and I became even more attached to our daughter—anticipating her every cry, marveling at every gesture—I secretly raged at my own mother."

Her cheeks were now flooded with tears and she was holding on to Samuel's trembling hand with all her strength.

"I felt as though I was never loved." She was trembling. "Because, how could my mother have possibly loved me if she gave birth to me, held me to her breast, and wrapped me in her arms and still . . . still sent me away?" She paused and took a deep breath. "I know that I could never have done that with our daughter, Samuel."

"I know. I know," he said, trying to comfort his wife. "But there was a war going on, Kaija. And, in war, things are not black-and-white." He took a deep breath. "They saved you."

Samuel looked up at Kaija and saw how her eyes were now rimmed in carmine, her delicate nostrils flaring slightly like the curved edges of a conch shell. He wanted to kiss her, he wanted to hold her and fall to the ground, the two of them floating off into the watery lakes.

She nodded. "I know, Samuel. I know." She looked around at the sea of graves again. "Finally, I see the sacrifice that they made for me. I could have been buried under one of these iron crosses. A victim of starvation or a stray bullet."

She was crying into the hollow of his chest, gripping the cotton fabric of his shirt and fingering the buttons with trembling hands.

He pulled her close and stroked her hair.

"You've been the most wonderful mother to our daughter. The most loving wife . . ." His lips were close to her ear and she could feel his warm breath on her neck. "Your parents acted as we would have, Kaija. We both know, no matter the great heartache it would have caused us, we would have done anything to spare our daughter pain." He pushed her back and gazed into her green eyes. "Your parents sacrificed a great deal when they gave you up, but they did it because they loved you."

She turned her face up to Samuel's, her lips trembling as they managed a slight curl. "Finally," she whispered, "I can see that."

Sixty-Four

Vesterås, Sweden
July 1985

Sabine could barely look at her father. It was as if she were staring at the premonition of his death. After school, she would go to her parents' room and find him lying in the bed surrounded by his books, a tray of barely eaten food resting beside him. Amidst the starched white linen, his head propped up by the pillows her mother had fluffed only a few hours before, his eyelids swollen and his face sunken. The dehydrated flesh hanging from a protrusion of bone.

She held his hand in the beginning of his bed rest. Those long fingers, the knuckles veiled in a web of a few downy, black hairs. But the coldness of his hands made it almost unbearable for her now. She wanted to rub them, hold them between her palms, and massage the life back into them. But it was no use.

Sabine wasn't with him the night he died. Kaija stayed at the hospital, never leaving her husband's side, holding the hand that had caressed her, loved her, swept back her tears for so long. She held his palms against hers, his eye veiled in sleep and hazed by the painkillers. And she too closed her eyes, fighting back her tears to remember him as he would have wished. That first day in Göteborg, when she drew him in profile, marveling at his dark skin and thick black curls. He was the man beside her, not the skeletal impostor who slept in a hospital bed, the smell of ammonia clinging to his skin.

She was not aware of the exact moment he left her. She could not remember the last time his hand had felt warm to her. But when the nurse came in and placed her hand on Kaija's shoulder, whispering that her husband had passed on, she felt herself go numb. The thought that he would never physically return, that she would have to live her life drawing upon her memories, was too painful.

"Samuel, Samuel," she whispered over and over, until she no longer had the energy to speak.

She had stopped wearing her crucifix nearly a month before because she felt betrayed.

In one of his last lucid moments, Samuel had noticed its absence, as she hung over him like a perched seagull.

"Where's your necklace?" he asked her, his white hospital gown accentuating his monklike face.

"I've taken it off, Samuel."

"Why would you do such a thing?" he asked as his saffron-colored fingers reached for the gap in her blouse.

"Well, it certainly hasn't brought me . . ." She paused to correct herself. "It certainly hasn't brought us any luck, has it?"

"There's no such thing as luck. There's no credibility to superstition." She saw that even though his lips were parched and cracked, he was still trying to smile.

Kaija gave him some ice chips, carefully placing them in his mouth.

His eyes were shining now, and he didn't seem to notice the morphine dripping into his yellow forearm, now so tender and patched in blue it looked like a bruised banana.

"But faith is important, Kaija." His fingers reached toward hers.

He closed his eyes for a moment as his wife reached out and took his hand, squeezing his fingers tightly in her own.

"I too have lost my parents, Kaija. I've also lost an entire family—cousins, aunts, uncles . . . all of them perished in the war." He paused and tried to wet his cracked lips with his tongue. "And, yes, I will die soon. But still, I have faith."

"What faith, Samuel?" she said, shaking her head, tears streaming down her cheeks. "What faith? We never kept a Christian or a Jewish home. Maybe we're being punished for that!"

"Punished? I don't think so, my love. I have faith that you and I will always be together. That even in death, you will not be able to get rid of me." He was straining to laugh, his brown eyes crinkling as he squeezed her hand. "I have faith that my daughter will grow up and be a woman with great strength and character . . . like her mother. . . . I have faith that she will know right from wrong. That the lessons that we taught her over the years will guide her and that she will make us proud."

However, one of the last things he wanted to say, he could not say aloud. So he said it silently. In a quiet, precious moment of a dying man, he acknowledged the only other woman who had been in his life, however briefly, besides his wife and daughter. Without uttering a sound, said only between him and his God, Samuel asked for forgiveness. He prayed that Salomé was happy, that she had made peace with herself and her family.

Kaija had to decide whether to bury Samuel in the Jewish cemetery in Stockholm or in the one at the Vesterås church. He had never expressed his wishes to her, so she was left alone with the final decision—to bury him in the traditions of his forefathers or to bury him in a Christian cemetery close to his wife and daughter.

She knew that the Jewish cemetery would forbid her and Sabine from ever being buried alongside Samuel. Neither of them had ever converted to Judaism. She would have, had Samuel asked her to. But burying Samuel in a pasture full of iron crosses and carved angels seemed wrong as well.

In the end, she chose the church cemetery. For even though the crosses were incongruous with Samuel's faith, she believed that he too would not want to be separated from her in death. That, like man and wife who slept beside each other in life, they would rest next to each other in death.

So, on a rainy day, Kaija and Sabine buried Samuel on a grassy knoll against a dark, Nordic sky.

The funeral was attended by over fifty people, many of whom Kaija and Sabine had never seen before and whose faces melted in with the rain. Mother and child placed red flowers on the mound of fresh earth before slowly making their way to the car.

In the distance, they did not see the dark-haired woman, cloaked in a black coat and a lime green scarf, who waited until they had departed. Who kissed the lilies she carried before placing them carefully on Samuel's grave.

Sixty-Five

Vesterås, Sweden
September 1994

$\mathcal{E}$very photograph, every gift she had ever given him that had made it to Sweden, he put in boxes and placed in storage. Even the old silk pouch she had embroidered for him years before, he packed far from sight. He signed the divorce papers that arrived in the mail and never tried to arrange a meeting with her to discuss the dissolution of their marriage. He felt so empty, so emasculated, that for the first time in his life, he no longer had any words.

Octavio had accepted the job of movie projectionist because he thought it was the most appropriate one offered to him. He could admit to himself that he enjoyed sitting behind the winding reels of film and watching another man play out the roles of lover, hero, and artist. At this point in his life, it was easier to sit there and watch someone else do all the acting. Octavio knew that he had already played his most important role nearly twenty-five years before, and never again would anything be as meaningful to him. He didn't even have a script back then, but he had played his part with all his heart, convincing Father Cisneros to help him rescue Salomé.

Now as he touched the American film with his finger, the film delicate and translucent, Octavio smiled. Loading reel after reel for a theater filled with restless Swedish teenagers brought him a strange sense of comfort. He was spending his middle-aged years as a voyeur of sorts. An observer of everything around him and a partaker of almost nothing.

A few times after Salomé and he had divorced, he'd contemplated telling her how he had convinced the priest to help him, and how together they had persuaded General Martinez to gain her release. But in the end, he chose not to. So now he was back where he was when he'd first discovered Salomé, loving and admiring her from afar.

Still he was different from that young man who had gazed upon that beautiful, seventeen-year-old girl from his balcony so many years before. Then he had only seen the world as a good place, where the pure of heart could live and love. But he had since seen things that had changed him forever. Those men in the black van—bloodied and beaten—were enough to ensure that he had recurring nightmares. He could only imagine what they had done to Salomé.

He had eventually exhausted himself by trying to pretend that all could return to the way it once was; that with a few sugarcoated words to Salomé and a flurry of kisses, he could erase the things that had gone terribly wrong.

Now he saw things more clearly. Perhaps it was the reflection brought upon by old age. Perhaps it was living alone for all these years, for he now saw all the mistakes he had made. He had been cowardly in not letting the pieces fall between him and Salomé. He wondered if he had allowed them to completely break, without constantly trying to mend them before they were allowed to shatter, would the two of them be together now in their golden years?

Since the divorce, they had maintained their friendship not only for the sake of their children, but also for themselves. Salomé could never abandon Octavio completely. They were bonded by something stronger than marriage. So although they had failed to find a way to work through their troubles, Salomé was still the great love of his life.

At one time he had tried with all his heart to forget her. He couldn't believe that she had allowed him to walk out of the house without even calling him back. He had thought she would follow him, rush out after him, throw her arms around him and say she was sorry for isolating him. He thought she would never let him just walk away.

But those were the days when he'd believed that his life would mimic a script. Where a happy ending was promised to him, because he naively believed that love would conquer all.

When she failed to follow him, he had been so hurt that he'd vowed never to return. He tried to rid his mind of her. So he took all the mementos he had of Salomé and packed them away.

At one point, he even tried to date other women. But as much as he wanted to forget her, he couldn't maintain the facade of being interested in a woman who clearly couldn't measure up to Salomé. So gradually, as the years passed, he accepted his ex-wife's overtures of friendship. He realized that it was foolish of him to pretend that he could erase her from his heart. She was the mother of his three beautiful children. She was his first and only love.

So he would wait for her, as he had done so many times when they'd tangoed in their living room. When he would release her so she could twirl around, and he would remain—waiting for her with an extended hand.

Sixty-Six

Vesterås, Sweden
November 1998

Over the years, Salomé often replayed in her mind the day Octavio had walked out. She knew that he had yearned for her to stop him and tell him that she too wanted their marriage to work. That they could not let what had happened in Chile separate them and destroy their love.

But she hadn't been able to do that then, as their lives had diverged too much since their arrival in Sweden. And Salomé had also felt a burning desire to start the next stage of her life alone. As Samuel had suggested, she needed to find herself again, and she thought the best way to achieve that was on her own.

She spent her first years as a single mother rededicating herself to the things that were most meaningful to her: her children, her books, and her collecting.

She realized she had been less of a mother to Rafael and the girls since coming to Sweden. So one of the first things she did when she and Octavio separated was to try to reacquaint herself with them. She put more time aside to do creative projects with them and helped them as they did their homework. And she told them she was always there if they ever wanted to talk about their difficulties adjusting to their new life in Sweden.

The girls told her that they missed their favorite foods from back home, so Salomé started cooking again, filling the house with the odors that had been a familiar perfume in their kitchen back in Chile. She journeyed outside her neighborhood and found markets that sold the ingredients she longed for—ropes of garlic, red and green chilies, coriander, and mint.

She bought flowers, even in the winter, and placed them in odd places where the children least expected them. A shelf in the bathroom might have three sprays of freesia, or the top tier of a bookshelf might have a bud vase full of red and blue anemones.

She also began collecting again, just as she had in the Casa Rosa. She mended broken things that others had discarded and placed them in small groupings. Her "little families," she called them. As she set them around the apartment, she would always remind the children that even broken things needed a home.

In a gesture of her newfound independence, and to further her academic pursuits, Salomé accepted the government's invitation to learn Swedish and enrolled in a nearby school. There she met other refugees and befriended a few other South Americans whose stories were not so different from her own.

At night, after she tucked her children tightly in their beds, she would study by lamplight and learn the mechanics of the language of the country she finally came to accept as her home.

She loved those moments she had to herself, when her books were opened in front of her and her sharpened pencils placed nearby, just as they were on her old convent desk. After she completed the intensive yearlong language class, she enrolled in a local college and began studying the classics, fulfilling a lifelong dream of hers. She resumed her study of Latin, Greek, and classical poetry, and even took up art history.

During her studies, a few men at the college asked her out on dates. And occasionally, she accepted. She even took one or two lovers over the years in the hope that she would find the fulfillment she was seeking. But in the end, her need for physical acceptance could never overcome her emotional detachment from these men. Gradually, she realized she was seeking companionship from them, not another great love.

Through the years, Salomé came to realize that no other man could rival the kindness and gentleness of her ex-husband, and she soon came to miss what she and Octavio once had. She missed their conversations, their closeness, and the history that they had once shared. She knew the children longed for their father as well. So little by little, she made overtures of friendship toward him. He resisted at first, but eventually his pride and his stubbornness began to melt.

Over time, as her brief affairs abated and Salomé began to settle comfortably into her role as single mother and part-time student, she found herself thinking about Octavio with increasing frequency. She even wondered whether she had made a mistake in divorcing him. She had never regretted her affair with Samuel, or even letting Octavio leave so she could come to terms with what had happened, to her. But sometimes she did wonder if, had they only separated for a short time, things could ultimately have been salvaged, and they wouldn't have needed to divorce.

Yet despite the divorce, they were all a family still. Indeed, she ended up relying on her former husband more than she would have liked to admit. Octavio was always there when she needed him, either a a sympathetic voice on the other end of the phone or a helpful hand when she needed some assistance with something in her apartment. Salomé had come to see that their love, with its many fractures and fissures, had endured.

Now, as she was finally finishing her graduate classes and had achieved her goal of being able to translate the poems of Catullus, she thought about the promise she had made to him on the night of their wedding, when after he had given her a book on the Fayums, she had vowed to learn the poems in their original form. That memory washed over her, and she was overcome with nostalgia. It seemed like only yesterday to her, and yet a lifetime ago. She went over to her bookshelf and found the book. She opened it to the first page, running her palm over the inscription.

"To my precious Fayum," it said in a deliberate hand. "May I be able to gaze upon you always."

Overcome with emotion, Salomé brushed away her tears. The steadfastness of Octavio's words struck her deeply. Her delicate fingers, almost instinctively, moved over her breast bone, tracing the outline of her heart.

Sixty-Seven

Vesterås, Sweden
November 1998

*S*he had sounded so urgent on the telephone, so he rushed over to her as soon as he could. The streetlights of Vesterås illuminated the gray evening with their warm, golden globes. He buried his chin into his scarf and quickly walked over the cobblestones, the sound of his feet on the wet pavement softened by the occasional puddle of damp leaves.

She welcomed him with a warm embrace, her hair floating softly around his neck as she pulled him close. The smell of her apartment immediately brought him back to Chile: the scent of eucalyptus and wild mint mingled with that of the dish of marzipan that she had half-nibbled on in the kitchen.

"Thank you for coming so quickly," she said as she motioned for him to sit down.

"Of course," he said.

She brought him a cup of tea and unfolded the letter as he settled into the sofa. "I want you to read this," she said, handing it to him.

He looked surprised as he took it from her. He said nothing as he squinted over each word. He read it carefully.

After several minutes, he placed the letter down on the coffee table.

"What are you going to do, Salomé?" he asked gently.

"I'm not sure yet," she said, shaking her head.

Octavio remained silent. He reached for his tea and warmed his fingers around the ceramic mug.

"It's been such a long time, and although I feel strong enough to testify, I worry about unearthing something that might upset the children."

She hesitated for a moment. "I wouldn't want it to upset you either."

He was touched that she would consider his feelings. "Salomé, you needn't worry about me. If you want to testify, I would wholly support it. God knows how I'd like to see the bastard held responsible for his crimes."

She smiled and looked down at her fingers, folded in her lap.

"As far as the children are concerned," he said softly, "I would explain to them about the letter and ask them. But they're grown-up now and I'm confident they'd want you to go, if you're up to it."

"Yes, I know, Octavio." She curled her legs underneath. "But, do *I* really want to recall these old memories? I've spent a lifetime trying to put them to rest. To move on with my life and forget the misery of the past."

When she used the word *misery*, Octavio could not help but wince. "Whatever you decide to do, know that the children and I will support you unconditionally."

She smiled and pushed back the black curls that were falling over her face, revealing her still ax-cut cheekbones and sparkling brown eyes that had grown even more intense with age.

"I know I *should* do it," she said quietly. "But it's so hard to reopen that part of my life now after so many years."

Octavio nodded, his face softening over a cloud of steam.

"Yet, I also realize that there are thousands of others who are no longer alive to testify. So not to vindicate my own experience, but more to honor those who can't speak now for themselves, the right thing, the courageous thing, would be to do it."

She looked at Octavio's face and wondered how he felt about her being so frank with him. Salomé had always avoided speaking about what had happened back in Chile, but now with both the passing of time and the years she had spent living alone, she had realized that one couldn't avoid certain pain. And she needed to discuss the letter's arrival with someone. She was happy Octavio could be a sounding board for her. He hadn't flinched when she'd showed him the letter, and now, as she spoke to him about her feelings, she could see that he was listening to her every word.

"But I'm afraid, Octavio. I don't know what will happen if I have to relive my torture and go through all the details of what happened. I think I've come a long way, but could my progress evaporate if I have to re-create the terror?"

"I can't say, Salomé. I don't know." His face was now relaxed, softer, as if he had waited nearly twenty years for his wife to be this candid with him. "I do know, however, that you have a tremendous amount of strength, and if this is important to you, you should go."

"I think you're right, but I need to speak about it with the children before I reply." She reached for the letter on her coffee table, tapping it gently with her fingertips.

"I think that's a good idea."

"I've invited them all over for dinner this Friday." Her eyes looked out the rattling window. "You should come too."

Octavio stiffened again. "Yes. Yes. Of course, I'll come. If that's what you really want."

"Absolutely it is." As she spoke, her face seemed younger to him, as if she no longer needed to put on that veil of strength and stoicism he had seen all to often over the years.

"Come around eight o'clock, if that's all right. I'll make *humitas* and *machas.*"

He smiled, recalling how the Casa Rosa was once filled with the delicious smells of his ex-wife's cooking.

"I'm looking forward to it." He stood up to return his cup to the kitchen sink, retrieving his coat along the way. "I'd better be going, it's getting late." He gave a quick glance at his watch. Already two hours had passed, and it was nearly eleven o'clock.

"I'll see you Friday then?" she asked, calling out to him from her curled position on the couch.

"Friday, yes, of course. I'll bring the wine."

As he opened the door to the crowded apartment and noticed one of his old movie posters taped to the wall, it occurred to him that, while his wife struggled to forget the past, he had spent too many years trying to regain it. It had been over twenty-three years since he'd walked out of that very apartment, and almost every day thereafter he had silently cursed himself. He knew there hadn't been a single day that he hadn't regretted it.

Sixty-Eight

❧

$\mathcal{F}$riday, Salomé told her children about the letter requesting her testimony and asked if they thought she should go. "I think it's the right thing to do . . . the courts need evidence, and my testimony could help if he is ultimately brought to trial. But I don't want it to upset any of you."

"You must go, Mother," Blanca insisted. "It's your duty."

Isabelle agreed with her sister. "Absolutely, Mama. Absolutely you should go. We would be very proud of you."

The two girls, in their twenties now, looked nearly identical to Salomé as a young girl.

But Rafael said nothing. Salomé watched him from the corner of her eye as he sat crouched in his chair, his expression tense, his eyes squinting, as if he were severely pained.

She went quietly over to him, running her fingers loosely through his hair. "What is it?" she asked with great concern. "Is something wrong?"

He wanted to tell his mother, "They don't remember. They don't remember what you looked like when you returned. Just battered flesh. An open wound with purple skin."

But, instead, he said, "I'm just worried for you, Mother. I don't want you to open up all that hurt again."

She smiled at Rafael. Even after all these years, he was still trying to protect her.

"I'll think a little more over the weekend before making my final decision," she said. "Now, I just want to enjoy myself, enjoy having my family around me." She squeezed his shoulder and stood up.

"Let's open some more wine!" she called out to Octavio. "Blanca, put some Piazzolla on the Victrola!"

Her daughter placed the needle on the old vinyl record, and music filled the room.

Salomé accepted a dance from Octavio, and the two of them tangoed through the room as if each of their feet were connected. "Four legs, one body," she said, laughing as her red dress wrapped between her knees. Her brown arms extended and coiled back into herself, as Octavio led her across the room.

Sixty-Nine

❧

Vesterås, Sweden
November 1998

$\mathcal{T}$he apartment was still disordered from the party. Salomé had yet to wash the dishes or the wineglasses, as the party had lasted too late into the night.

She stood in her narrow kitchen and filled the kettle with some water to make tea.

She looked out the window and noticed the soft, gray light misting over the rooftops. The days were becoming shorter, and she longed for the spring. The cold Nordic winters had never agreed with her, and sometimes when she felt like being particularly melancholy, she would think of how, on the other side of the world in Chile, it was nearly summer.

Salomé realized now that, no matter what happened, whether Pinochet was held accountable for his actions or not, she could never return to her native country. Her children had all found partners in Sweden and would be building families of their own here. Both her parents had died, and so, other than memories, there was nothing there for her anymore. After all these years, Salomé had finally reconciled herself to the likelihood that she would remain in Sweden for the rest of her life.

She had also become accustomed to living alone. She had grown used to the sound of her own breathing, and the gesture of her hands as they swept across her shelves and touched the objects she had collected. Nonetheless, she had missed Octavio more and more over the past few years, although she wasn't exactly sure why. Perhaps it was the onset of old age and seeing her children grown-up and discovering their own loves. But he had remained a good friend to her over the years, someone who—Salomé gratefully realized—refused to just slip away. And sometimes now she found herself surprised by her rekindled feelings for him. Sometimes, even, late at night, she thought of him with the same ardor that she had had when she was a young girl of seventeen.

She emptied a jar of beach shells into the bathwater so that she could pretend she was bathing in the sea and put an old Calandrelli record on the Victrola.

The water smelled like a mixture of salt and sand. She wound her hair on top of her head and sunk her body in the water, careful not to cut herself on any of the edges of the shells. She closed her eyes and thought of Chile. She thought about the endless beaches of the Viña del Mar. She thought of her garden at the Casa Rosa and the time when she and Octavio had made love under the avocado tree when the maid was out and the children were at school.

It had been years since she had allowed herself to relive the good times. But many memories locked inside her brought her joy. She just had to retrieve them now and recall.

At a quarter to eight, she stepped out of her bath. The long soak had inspired her sensual side, and she unexpectedly found herself hovering over her vanity table. She sprayed herself with water steeped in gardenia petals. She lined her eyes with an old kohl pencil and rubbed her cheeks and lips with rouge. It was as if she were that nervous, giddy schoolgirl again, preparing to meet her admirer under the stars. Though she was truly only expecting to spend the night alone.

She was surprised to hear the doorbell ring. She quickly wrapped herself in a robe and went to see who was at the door.

"Who is it?" she asked as she went to undo the latch.

"It's me, Salomé."

When she opened the door, she found Octavio standing in the hallway holding a bushel of field flowers.

"I want to come with you, Salomé!" he blurted out.

"What?" Salomé asked, perplexed. She shook her head. "Come inside." She motioned him into her vestibule. She took the flowers from him and ushered him to the couch.

After she placed the flowers in a pitcher of cold water, she went into her bedroom and changed into a sweater and some slacks. She fluffed her hair and checked her makeup in the mirror.

"So, now, are you going to tell me what you're talking about?" she asked as she reappeared in the living room.

Octavio was sitting on the edge of the sofa, his hands firmly planted on his knees.

"I have thought about it, Salomé. I want to come with you to England." He stammered a bit. "I want to be by your side. I want to hear you tell your story."

She looked at him with surprise. "Octavio, that's really not necessary," she said, instinctively resisting his offer. "You know me, I'll be fine."

"Necessity has nothing to do with it," he said, looking into her eyes. Only seconds before, he had gazed at the objects scattered around her apartment. The broken pieces of glass and the porcelain figures with hairline fissures that marred their otherwise perfect, delicate features. It struck him then that there was little difference between Salomé and her collections. That she had been broken and mended, and because her own tendril-like scars would never go away, she surrounded herself with things that, like her, were damaged but still retained their beauty. He felt he loved her more than ever now. For she had triumphed over her scars. She had made peace with her past.

He wished there were a poem he could recite to tell her simply and succinctly how he felt. But he also realized that they were at a place in their lives that was now beyond poetry, beyond art and beauty.

So he said to her what had been in his heart for years, but what he had never been able to vocalize.

"Fayum." His voice trembled. "Please let me take care of you now like I should have twenty-five years ago."

Kindness and relief filled Salomé's eyes, for she had waited a lifetime to hear those words from him.

He had not the voice to even whisper now, so he simply mouthed the words *I love you.*

Salomé Herrera gazed upon her ex-husband with the same wet eyes she had bestowed upon him that evening when he had scattered oranges at her feet and kissed her underneath a star-studded sky. He felt her trembling fingers reaching out toward his, traveling over the cuff of his cotton sleeve.

And she did what he had been dreaming of for so many years. She took his hand in hers.

Acknowledgments

This book would not have been possible without the help and guidance of many people. Foremost, I wish to thank my Swedish family for their inspiration and unwavering support of this novel.

To my husband, who is always my first and most critical reader—I thank you for all your support and your strength. With every novel, you are there beside me, cheering me on. I could not have finished this without you.

To my readers—Antony Currie, Louisa Ermelino, Nikki Koklanaris, Shana Lory, Sara Shaoul, and my family—I thank you for your invaluable feedback and diligent efforts on my behalf. A special thank-you should be given to Rosalyn Shaoul and Ulrike Ostermeyer, who edited my first drafts and worked on perfecting the novel with me.

To my agent, Sally Wofford-Girand—thank you for your dedication and your tireless efforts on my behalf. Finally, to my editor, Malaika Adero—I thank you for your sensitive eye, your love of language, and your passion and support.

Swedish Tango

Alyson Richman

A Reader's Club Guide

ABOUT THIS GUIDE

The suggested questions are intended to help your reading group find new and interesting angles and topics for discussion for Alyson Richman's *Swedish Tango*. We hope that these ideas will enrich your conversation and increase your enjoyment of the book.

Many fine books from Washington Square Press feature Readers Club Guides. For a complete listing, or to read the guides online, visit www.BookClubReader.com.

A Conversation with
Alyson Richman

❧

1. **How has your writing career been affected by the critical acclaim you received from your first novel, *The Mask Carver's Son*?**

   I think for most novelists, the publication of your first novel is the most agonizing. You want to believe that you deserved being published, that your editor didn't make a grave mistake by taking a risk on publishing you. Having received mostly good notices on *The Mask Carver's Son*, I was able to breathe a sigh of relief. It validated an insecurity that I'm sure I share with most young novelists—am I worthy enough?

2. **Both *The Mask Carver's Son* and *Swedish Tango* are set in countries other than your own. What prompted you to write about Japan in the nineteenth century in *The Mask Carver's Son*, and the bloody coup executed by the Pinochet regime in Chile, the mounting threat to French Jews in the period leading up to the Nazi occupation, and the mass transport of Finnish children during the Winter War with Russia in *Swedish Tango*? How did you research the historical details?**

   Both novels take place against backdrops of national conflict. In *The Mask Carver's Son*, Meiji Japan is wrestling with the influx of

Westernization and that instigates a rift between the old and new generations—those who wanted to retain old traditions and those who wanted to thoroughly modernize the country. In the novel, the main character is a young boy who is born into a traditional Japanese family that had dedicated itself to the ancient theatre of Noh. By having the young boy reject his familial destiny and pursue his dream to become a Western-style painter, I am using the conflict between the father and son as a metaphor of what was happening between the two generations in Japan at that time.

In *Swedish Tango*, all my characters are victims of political upheavals in their respective countries. They are all political exiles—even young Kaija. Sweden offers these characters a chance for a new life, but all of them suffer great internal conflict because they find themselves in a foreign country due to circumstances that were beyond their control.

As far as my method of research is concerned, I try to do my historical research by visiting each country, collecting oral histories of people who share similar background to my characters, and doing library/archival research. Photo archives are particularly helpful; I use the faces and images for inspiration.

3. **One of the central themes that you explore in *Swedish Tango* is the often unanticipated and sometimes tragic consequences the choices we make have on our own lives and the lives of those we love. Just about everyone in the novel expresses the view that Octavio's support of Allende and his refusal to support Pinochet is the direct cause of the kidnapping and torture of his wife and the family's forced exile to Sweden. Even Octavio himself comes to believe they are right—that he was wrong to put his family in danger because he had a primary obligation to protect them. Is this the view you want the reader to come away with? Should we expect people to compromise their principles in order to protect their loved ones? And if so, does this mean stands of conscience can only be taken by unattached individuals?**

No. I do not want the reader to come away with that idea. That is the obvious answer but not the correct one. The dialogue I wanted to initiate by having Octavio's actions result in Salomé's kidnapping, is that every choice—even heroic ones—can have terrible consequences. I think Octavio's actions to stand up to the Pinochet regime were heroic and admirable, but that doesn't make the pain suffered by his wife go away either. Still, if you turn that around and ask had Octavio not chosen to stick to his principles and not stood up in the face of evil, would he have been the man that Salomé had fallen in love with? Probably not. It is true that everyone in the novel- including Octavio- believes his actions caused his family to be at risk and his wife to suffer greatly, but his greatest crime was naïvité, not selfishness. He refused to be hypocritical and he was courageous for not backing down during a time of great political darkness for Chile. Heroism cannot take place without risk. This is one of the questions the reader must decide: should one remain silent in order to maintain their own and their family's safety? We should think about those individuals who risked their lives and those of their families to hide Jews in Nazi Germany or those few who raised their voices in protest to the recent genocides in Bosnia, Kosovo, and Somalia. They are few and far between. Stands of conscience might be easier for unattached individuals, but this does not excuse the rest of us who turn a blind eye when there are injustices being committed around us.

4. **Another key theme is the secrets that people keep even from those nearest and dearest to them—and how those secrets reverberate in our lives despite our unwavering efforts to keep them buried. Many authors have explored the theme of the secrets people keep and the different reasons they keep them. Why do you think the subject rivets our attention and invites such intense and repeated investigation?**

I think as human beings we are programmed to try and spare our loved ones pain. Unfortunately, personal anguish is one of those things that can rarely be contained. Authors like to explore this particular facet of human nature because the impulse is universal, but the effects of maintaining the secret are incredibly varied. The messiness of it all is great fodder for fiction! Although all of the characters in *Swedish Tango* keep secrets in an effort to spare their loved one's anguish, I chose to have some of the characters continue to maintain their secrets even until the end. Salomé and Samuel never reveal their affair, and Octavio does not tell Salomé the efforts he went to secure her release. While other authors might have chosen to have all four characters reveal the secrets they carried for so many years, I felt it was more complex and more accurate to portray it otherwise.

5. **How do you expect the reader to react to Samuel when he violates the bond of trust between doctor and patient by going to bed with Salomé? Although he has done something reprehensible, you don't portray him as a reprehensible human being. Why did you decide to cast him in a sympathetic light?**

For Salomé, the affair with Samuel was a healing process. She is so emotionally and physically decimated from her incarceration in Chile, she no longer believes she is physically desirable. She has an acute desire to feel that someone can still find her attractive even after knowing and seeing what her torturers did to her. Samuel is the one person who knows both her physical and emotional scars, and his attraction to her gives her a strength that she could not have found otherwise. In some ways, I feel their first love scene is one of the most dramatic places in the novel. It is not so much about sex as it is about Salomé's liberation from a body she believes is ugly and scarred.

Samuel is not a reprehensible character because his chief motivation in life is healing others. This is both his weakness and his strength. Had he not had ended the affair and admitted that he had committed a transgression on both a professional and marital level, I think the reader would not find him as sympathetic. But all the character in *Swedish Tango* are fallible. They make mistakes but this is human nature.

6. **Who are some of your favorite authors? What writers and what books have had the greatest influence on your own work?**

My favorite authors are Gregor Von Rezzori and Gabriel García Márquez. Von Rezzori's book *The Snows of Yesteryear: Portraits for an Autobiography* is one of my favorites, as is García Márquez's *One Hundred Years of Solitude*. Although the writing styles of these two authors are different, they both use language so beautifully it's humbling to read them over and over again. For me, writing a novel is as much about plot as it is about the poetry of the words. I also am a big fan of Cynthia Ozick. *The Messiah of Stockholm* left me breathless. Her novels read like a haiku.

7. **Often a writer sets out to write a work of fiction only to discover the completed novel has taken on a life of its own. How did *Swedish Tango* and its characters evolve as you worked on the book? In what ways did any of the characters surprise you and become different people than you had originally envisioned? Do you have a favorite character in the novel?**

Swedish Tango began with the question, "How does someone heal after they suffered something horrific?" I had the image of Salomé unwrapping her Victrola for the first time and the image of Kaija arriving in Sweden with nothing but a red suitcase and her teddy bear. From those two images, the novel began. In the first draft of the novel, Octavio's character was not as complex as it is in the final draft. Because I think we admire and also admonish him, he is my favorite character. In some way, there is a bit of myself in him. I always want to do the right thing, but I'm often naïve about how much I'm actually undertaking.

8. **Tell us something about the process of writing that you follow. Do you write every day? Do you set aside a particular period of time for writing? Or is your creative process more**

spontaneous and unplanned? Do you struggle to perfect a paragraph or a page as you go along? Or do you write in a burst and revise later? What are you working on now?

Before I had my son, I wrote every day. Now as I only have a babysitter two days a week, I must be extra efficient and try and get the same amount of work done but in a sixteen hour time frame. I usually write from nine A.M. to five P.M. and eat my lunch at my desk. I'm the sort of writer that can't get to the next paragraph until I'm satisfied with what I just wrote. I am constantly reworking. Like the authors I admire, the sound of the language is as important to me as the storyline. I try and spend a lot of time cultivating the right images, the cadence of the words and the texture of the landscapes I'm portraying.

Currently, I'm working on a novel about the last seventy days of Vincent Van Gogh's life, seen through the eyes of the young Marguerite Gachet, the daughter of Dr. Gachet, the last doctor who treated him before his suicide.

9. **If there is one message you would like the reader to come away with after reading *Swedish Tango*, what would it be? If a movie were to be made of the novel, who would you like to see as a director? What actors would you like to see play the parts of Octavio, Salomé, Samuel, and Kaija?**

The message of *Swedish Tango* is that as human beings we are emotional and fallible. We love, we make mistakes, and most of us strive to be good. Many readers have told me they think the novel would make an excellent movie. Although there are many competent and talented directors who could translate the novel onto the screen, I think István Szabó, Anthony Minghella, Lasse Hallström, or Milos Forman could still preserve the unusual structure of the novel while maintaining the story's momentum. Antonio Banderas or Javier Bardem would both make excellent Octavios, Salma Hayek or Mia Maestro for Salomé, Ralph Fiennes for Samuel, and Emily Watson for Kaija.

Questions and Topics
for Discussion

1. "Salomé had always believed that God had made women with wombs so that, after they had children, they had a place to store their secrets . . ." Ostensibly to spare her children, but also for her own self-preservation, Salomé decides never to reveal to her family what was done to her during her kidnapping. Do you think it would have made it easier, or more difficult, for her or for them, had she decided to share her experience with them? Under what circumstances do you think a person should try to shield loved ones from knowing the truth? What kinds of secrets do you think you might keep from your family?

2. What role does tango music play in the novel? Talk about the symbolism and symmetry of Salomé's inability to play her antique Victrola and collection of tango records following her kidnapping, and her choice to put the music on, nearly twenty-five years later, as she prepares to share with Octavio and their children her desire to testify about Pinochet's crimes against humanity at an international tribunal.

3. One of the main themes of the novel is the sometimes unintentional, yet often irrevocable and tragic consequences the choices we make have on our own lives and the lives of others. Discuss the ways that this theme plays out in *Swedish Tango*.

4. It is clear that Salomé blames Octavio for her kidnapping and torture at the hands of the Pinochet regime, a view that is shared by many of his friends and which he himself eventually comes to accept. Do you agree or disagree with this judgment? Why or why not?

5. Do you think a man has a right to stand up for his convictions even if it puts his family at risk? Or do you believe it is one thing to act on principle if you are putting your own life on the line, and quite another if you are endangering others? Under what circumstances, if any, does a moral person have an obligation to stand up and be counted regardless of the possible consequences? How different do you think the reader's reaction would be if Octavio had been a German public figure taking a stand against Hitler, or an American Southerner openly defying the KKK? Talk about the dilemma that faces parents who want both to protect their children from physical danger and to teach them by example to live their lives with courage and principle.

6. When she was just two years old, Kaija became a casualty of war—one of the more than 70,000 Finnish children ripped from their families and sent abroad to safety and the prospect of a better childhood during the bitter winter battles with Russia during World War II. What do you imagine it would be like to be forced to send away your child as Sirka was? Why do you think Astrid keeps herself at such a distance from the sad little girl she and her husband take into their Swedish home?

7. What drives Astrid to destroy the letters Sirka keeps writing her daughter? What are the inevitable, and devastating, consequences of that act? Do you think the bitterness that seems to fill Astrid's heart can be explained simply by her inability to bear children? Talk about the intentional acts of cruelty people commit. Do you think some individuals are just naturally mean-spirited, or are they impelled by the hurts and disappointments they experience in life?

8. Talk about Samuel Rudin's experience as the son of French Jewish parents who fled to Peru with their children but could not persuade other family members to also escape from the Nazi threat while they still could. Do you think the memories that have driven him all his life—of his mother's sorrow and his childhood helplessness to ease her survivor's guilt—have made him more or less equipped to provide psychiatric counsel for survivors of torture and war? What role, if any, do you think his own painful childhood memories play in his losing his objectivity as a therapist when Salomé becomes his patient?

9. How does Kaija's intense delight in her newborn infant affect the ache she has long carried for the mother she cannot remember?

10. At one point, when Samuel finds himself thinking about Salomé, he concludes the vulnerable woman who first walked into his office is steadily gaining strength; she doesn't need intensive psychoanalysis; she only needs to be gently guided by someone who will listen to her and ask the right questions. But can he trust himself to ask the right questions once he recognizes his growing attraction to her? Do you think by encouraging her to explore her anger at her husband, he is guiding her, perhaps subconsciously, to distance herself from her marriage? Do you think another therapist, or even Samuel, had he controlled his desire for her, could have helped to heal her while keeping her marriage intact?

11. Samuel recognizes that for a therapist to take advantage of a patient's emotional vulnerability and have sex with her is profoundly morally wrong—not only a violation of the ethical code of his profession but also a terrible abuse of the power imbalance that exists in the therapist/patient relationship. Yet the author never portrays him as morally corrupt. Alyson Richman makes a point of having Salomé tell us that she never for a moment regretted the physical intimacy with Samuel. How does her acceptance of their brief affair affect your own reaction to this betrayal of trust between doctor and patient? What do you

think the author intends to communicate about the complexity of human behavior by painting a nuanced, even sympathetic portrait of Samuel?

12. Upon learning that he is dying of pancreatic cancer, why does Samuel insist that Kaija return with him and the children to Mikkeli, the town in Finland that bordered the forest where she was born? How does he help her to come to terms at last with the unanswered questions that have long plagued her about her past?

13. Praising Alyson Richman's acclaimed first novel, *The Mask Carver's Son*, novelist Jonathan Burnham Schwartz calls the book "a tender novel about different kinds of human masks . . . Alyson Richman deftly explores the various forms of exile, both cultural and familial, in the life of . . . a sensitive soul whose true country is the country of longing." In what sense could this appraisal also apply to *Swedish Tango*? Talk about the cultural and familial exile experienced by the two couples at the center of the story, Kaija and Samuel, and Salomé and Octavio, expatriates who have found refuge in Sweden from political turmoil in their native lands, and whose lives intersect in a poignant dance with destiny.